D0802228

SURRENDERING APPOMATTOX

Jacob M. Appel

C&R Press
Conscious & Responsible

Printed in the United States of America

First Edition
1 2 3 4 5 6 7 8 9

This book is a work of fiction. Any references to historical events, real people, or real places are used fictitiously. Other names, characters, places, and events are products of the author's imagination, and any resemblance to actual events or places or persons, living or dead, is entirely coincidental.

Interior design by Olivia Pritzker
Cover design by Rachel Kelli

Library of Congress Cataloging-in-Publication Data

ISBN: 978-1-936196-87-6
Library of Congress Control Number: 2018932464

C&R Press
Conscious & Responsible
www.crpress.org
Winston-Salem, North Carolina

For special discounted bulk purchases, please contact:
C&R Press sales@crpress.org
Contact info@crpress.org to book events, readings and author signings.

"All warfare is a hoax perpetrated upon the common man…."
-- Congressman Abraham Lincoln, April 28, 1847

"The ghosts of battle make dissemblers of us all."
-- General Robert E. Lee, letter to President Jefferson Davis, October 3, 1864.

SURRENDERING APPOMATTOX

Table of Contents

FIRST SALVO
SEPTEMBER

CHAPTER ONE

"Are you going to teach us the other side?"

For Horace Edgecomb, these proved words that would forever separate the before from the after—although in the moment, the question, which arose from the lips of a sharp-featured girl named Sally Royster, seemed more like a hollow provocation. Edgecomb hadn't anticipated any questions at all. Not final period on a Friday afternoon with the minute hand closing in upon three o'clock. This was only the second week of the school year, far too early to be thinking about quarterly exams, so even those rare students who might harbor a passing interest in what their textbook hailed as "the colossal maelstrom of the American past" likely had their minds focused on pizza or football or sex. Except Sally. As her classmates folded shut their notebooks, Sally honed her large onyx eyes on him—eyes so dark they reminded Edgecomb of a parrot's—and waited for him to tackle a subject that had been settled with the blood of countless New England farm boys, and then re-fought by historians for another century.

"Not today," replied Edgecomb. "I've got a headache."

That drew a laugh—and Edgecomb was a teacher who valued laughs, who cared that his students called him by his first name, and appreciated his jokes, and returned from college over Christmas break to update him on their intellectual adventures. He prided himself on grading generously, and never giving anyone a hard time, and the day he officially received tenure would be the last day that he ever showed up for work at Laurendale wearing anything other than blue jeans. Of all the students in his twelfth grade American history class, only Sally didn't appear to appreciate his laidback style.

"So you *are* going to teach us the other side," she pressed.

"I didn't say *that*." Egdecomb wasn't one to relish confrontation, certainly not with a girl ten years his junior, but he also wasn't about to let her browbeat him into presenting the Union and Confederate causes as moral equivalencies. He glanced at the class's sole African-American student—the overweight daughter of the school nurse—as though seeking her approval. The last thing he desired was anyone walking away with the notion that he might be a Southern apologist. "Most historians today agree that the Civil War was fought over the expansion of slavery," he explained. "And I'm hoping none of us wants to stand on the side of the slaveholders."

To Edgecomb, that seemed a sensible reply. He looked again toward the African-American girl, Louise, hoping she might show her approval—but she was struggling to stuff her textbook into her knapsack. Sally, who still trained her sharp features on him like weapons, now pointed her pencil at him as well.

"That's not what I'm talking about," she rejoined, an angry furrow puckering above her nose. "I don't mean *that* other side."

"What then?" demanded Edgecomb.

"Are you going to teach the conflict as a *theory*, rather than as some sort of incontestable fact? Are you going to teach us that lots of people—very smart, well-informed people—don't think it happened at all?"

He wasn't sure that he'd understood her. "Don't think *what* happened?"

"The Civil War," she answered, but in a tone that might as well have said, '*The Civil War, you idiot.*' "Are you going to admit that numerous people think it's a hoax?"

Edgecomb was still digesting this challenge when the bell rang. To his amazement, not a single student stood up.

"No, I'm *not* going to teach that," said Edgecomb. And he should have stopped there, but she'd riled him to indignation. "I'm also not going to teach that the earth is flat, or that the moon is made of green cheese, or that babies are deposited on doorsteps by happy-go-lucky storks. The Civil War is a hoax? Are you *insane*?"

Every eye in the room now focused upon him. Several of the students looked genuinely frightened. Nobody dared moved.

"Okay, see you on Monday," he said to break the tension. "Class dismissed."

On the way out of the classroom, Sally Royster walked fully erect with her head facing straight forward; Edgecomb called after her at the last instant—and he was positive she'd heard—but she didn't acknowledge him as she strode out the door.

~

The next morning, at brunch with his sister, Edgecomb still had Sally Royster weighing on his mood. They'd chosen a corner booth at Mackenzie's Dinette, near the kitchen, because Jillian preferred not to sit with her back facing the entrance—in case a lunatic showed up brandishing an assault rifle. She'd brought along wet wipes to sanitize the cutlery, and her own variety of toxin-free tea. As much as he adored her, it genuinely amazed Edgecomb that the state of New Jersey allowed his older sister inside a middle school classroom.

"I'm one hundred percent sure she wasn't joking," he explained. "*Any* other student, I'd be thinking this was some sort of prank—it even has the potential to be funny. But I'm telling you, this girl wouldn't know funny if it bit her on the ass."

"So you lost your temper," said Jillian.

"Let's just say that, in hindsight, I wish I'd handled things differently."

He'd replayed the moment in his head countless times over the intervening eighteen hours, even though he recognized that the wiser course would have been to block the episode from his thoughts entirely, preventing his brain from consolidating unpleasant memories, a prophylactic technique he'd learned from public radio. Yet he sensed that Sally Royster was precisely the sort of girl to file a complaint and he wanted to stand prepared for the worst.

"You don't think they can terminate me for this?" he asked.

Jillian shook her head. "Probably not. You didn't threaten her, did you?"

"I'm not *that* clueless. All I did was say that you'd have to be insane to believe the Civil War was a hoax."

"The School Board's not going to like the word 'insane'—if it ever gets that far." Jillian squeezed two drops of organic vanilla extract into her tea. "Let's just hope this kid doesn't carry a diagnosis of depression or ADHD or something."

"I don't see her as that type. Unless self-righteousness counts as a psychiatric disorder these days."

Edgecomb stopped speaking while the server, a flat-chested girl flaunting fuchsia hair and a nose ring, set down their meals: for him, an omelet with bacon and home fries; for his sister, a scoop of cottage cheese and a banana. "Cottage cheese *without* a bed of lettuce," announced the waitress.

"Without a bed of fertilizer and pesticide," muttered Jillian as soon as the girl was beyond earshot. She eyed her banana warily, as though deciding whether to peel from the top or the bottom. "Horace, can you make me a promise?"

"Something tells me I'm not going to like this."

"It shouldn't be a big deal," said his sister. "Just please don't create any trouble."

"*I'm* not the one creating trouble."

"You know what I mean." Jillian's voice assumed a pleading tone and she looked as though she might sob. "All I'm asking is that you don't do anything that gets in the newspapers or on television....Anything that might reflect badly *on me*." She paused and locked her eyes on his. "If I don't get this baby, I don't know what I'll do."

At thirty-seven, single and with few romantic prospects, Jillian had decided to adopt an African orphan. She carried around a canvas bag full of computer printouts describing various parentless offspring in Ethiopia and The Congo. Her plan was to complete the application process during the school year, then visit the home country over the summer to retrieve the lucky youngster.

"Do you really think they're going to care what *I* do?" asked Edgecomb. "*You're* the one adopting the child."

"How should I know? They require a thorough background check," said Jillian. "Why *wouldn't* they want to know what my brother does? It seems only reasonable."

"It doesn't seem at all reasonable to me."

"Please, Horace. You can cause all the trouble you want—you can chain yourself to the Lincoln Memorial, for all I care. Just do it *next year*. Okay?"

Edgecomb glanced up from his omelet. "Look, I'm not causing any trouble. I'm sure this will all blow over…."

"And if it doesn't?"

"It will."

They ate in silence for several minutes—or Edgecomb ate, while his sister inspected her meal like a lab technician. On the far side of the dining room, a party of nine celebrated a fortieth wedding anniversary at a circular table, the kettle-bellied husband regaling his mousy beloved—and every other diner within earshot—with a gravelly rendition of "Embraceable You." In the booth behind Edgecomb's sister, a teenage couple kissed and groped vigorously. Edgecomb's silverware clanked against his plate as he struggled for something more to say.

"Why can't you just pay lip service to her," asked Jillian, "like I do with the creationists? I have one or two of them each year, you know—everything from intelligent design nuts to a fundamentalist kid from Brazil who sincerely believed the earth was six thousand years old. I used to try to change their minds. At some point, I realized it's easier to tell them they're entitled to believe whatever the hell they want, as long as they fill in the correct bubbles on the state exams."

"This isn't like creationism. It's more like Holocaust denial."

Jillian nibbled at her banana, reflecting on Edgecomb's words. "No, it's not. Holocaust deniers are dangerous because, left unchecked, they might actually convince ignorant people that they're right. But this girl is a lone wolf. She could be the only Civil War denier on the entire goddam planet. Seriously, Horace. There are states in this crazy country where half the population owns a Confederate flag. Do you really think we need to worry about people believing that the whole thing was a hoax?"

"It only takes one bad apple," said Edgecomb.

"Whatever. You're starting to sound as crazy as she does."

~

When Edgecomb returned home—to the chaotic Hager Heights bachelor pad which never shook the scent of his housemate's marijuana—he discovered that Sally Royster was far from a "lone wolf." A cursory Internet search revealed thousands of hits for an organization called "Surrender Appomattox" whose website advanced "evidence" against "the greatest deception in the history of humanity." Its homepage included endorsements from several professors at universities that Edgecomb had never heard of—one in Venezuela, one in Equatorial Guinea—and a list of Frequency Asked Questions: *Did Abraham Lincoln exist? Were African-Americans ever slaves, and if so, who freed them? How can the Civil War be a hoax when people occasionally unearth shell casing and cannonballs while excavating in their backyards? Who benefits from perpetuating the Civil War myth?* Edgecomb did not bother to scroll through the answers. He did look up the IP address and discovered that the site belonged to Roland G. Royster of Gettysburg, Pennsylvania. Twenty more minutes on the computer told Edgecomb all he'd wanted to know: Royster was the father of Sally (as well as two younger children); he'd recently purchased a luxury property in Laurendale, New Jersey.

Edgecomb decided to share his research with his housemate, although that meant enduring the hallucinogenic haze that swathed Sebastian's bedroom. It wasn't that he sought the man's opinion. He didn't. In fact, Sebastian Borrelli possessed some of the worst judgment of any human being Edgecomb had ever encountered. Rather, the discovery of a community of Civil War deniers living in one's midst was simply a phenomenon that demanded to be shared, and rapidly, like the death of a relative or the arrival of extraterrestrial life. By telling, one rendered the event real. As he stood outside his housemate's bedroom, bracing his lungs for the cloud of noxious smoke, Sebastian burst into the foyer, nearly hitting Edgecomb with the door.

"Dude. That's a crazy place to stand," said Sebastian.

Sebastian Borrelli towered a head taller than Edgecomb, his coarse, dark hair bound in a ponytail. Although it was already mid-afternoon, he sported a silk dressing gown and appeared only minutes removed from slumber—but since he worked from home, developing and distributing novelty items via computer, he might easily have been fresh from a long-distance business meeting.

When Edgecomb had first met his housemate two years earlier, on the heels of being jilted and ejected by his live-in girlfriend, and after days spent scouring apartment listings for an immediate opening, he'd taken the rental as a stop-gap measure, planning to decamp as soon as it was feasible. Yet Borrelli's easygoing ways had grown on him—a carefree oasis in a desert of anxiety and angst—and while he cursed his housemate for forgetting to pay the utility bills, and occasionally allowing a street-dwelling schizophrenic man named Albion to sleep on their living room sofa, he could no longer imagine sharing a home with anyone else.

"I was about to knock," explained Edgecomb, pushing shut Sebastian's door to trap the cannabis fumes. "I've got the strangest thing to tell you. Even *you* aren't going to believe this."

"Awesome," said Sebastian. "Because I've got something to tell you too. Something totally brilliant."

"Another business idea?"

"*The* business idea," Sebastian shot back. "You're perfectly entitled to your cynicism—but once you hear this, Teach, you're going to have to admit that I'm onto something." He hugged his lanky arm around Edgecomb's shoulders, like a triumphant soccer player. "I've even got a prototype to show you."

Edgecomb followed his housemate into their kitchen. He'd become all-too-familiar with the wacky curios and souvenirs that Sebastian hatched up: sunglasses armed with tiny windshield wipers, ice skates for dogs, condoms containing built-in timers to clock performance. What amazed Edgecomb most was that people actually bought these items—lots of people. Sebastian's "remote control golf balls," which surreptitiously walked themselves across the putting green, had become so popular that several local courses now banned them. If his companion had possessed the slightest financial acumen, Edgecomb suspected he'd be worth millions. But he didn't—not a shred. In fact, the guy was better at hemorrhaging money than he was at earning it, so instead of savoring cognac on the Riviera, he smoked dope in suburban New Jersey.

Afternoon sunlight bathed the kitchen in a warm autumn glow. On the countertop, propped against the cabinets, rested a canvas artist's portfolio. While Sebastian removed a pad of sketches, Edgecomb poked his head into the refrigerator.

"For Christ's sake. Where's all the food?"

Sebastian said nothing. Edgecomb slammed the door.

"You cannot be serious," he objected. "I bought six bags of groceries yesterday—enough food to last a week. Don't tell me you ate it all?"

"Not exactly. I gave it away."

"You *what*?"

Sebastian looked up from the sketchpad. "All they had at Church on the Hill this morning was freeze-dried broccoli," he said, referencing their local soup kitchen. "Something went haywire with their supplier."

"So you decided to fill the void?"

"What was I supposed to do?" asked Sebastian. "I know those guys. I couldn't just let them go hungry…"

This wasn't the first time Edgecomb's housemate had fed their hard-earned food to the downtrodden of Hager Heights, a small but determined band of alcoholics and brain-addled ne'er-do-wells, but it was the first time he'd emptied out their entire refrigerator. The most infuriating part, of course, was that the guy didn't have a clue that he'd done anything wrong.

"It's not a big deal. I'll pay you back," said Sebastian. He reached into his wallet and counted out a roll of twenty dollar bills. "Here's two hundred. That should be more than enough to cover it."

"That's not the goddam point. This isn't a supermarket."

But what was the point, really? Nothing he said was going to make Sebastian Borrelli any more sensible, or less altruistic. If anything, Horace felt a twinge of shame for resenting his housemate's generosity.

He pocketed the cash; it was *far* more than enough.

"Anyway, what's your brilliant business plan?" he asked.

Sebastian held up a line drawing depicting a handsome young man in a turban; then he flipped to the same man in conversation with a second figure. The second individual wore a hoop crown and wielded what looked like a magic wand. "Well? What do you think?"

"I'm sure it's obvious, but I have no idea who that is."

Sebastian grinned. "Dude. I thought you taught history," he said. "That's Mohammed. And that's him with the angel, Gabriel, receiving his first revelation."

"Mohammed? And how exactly is *this* a brilliant business plan?"

Edgecomb's housemate slid the sketch back into the portfolio. "Mohammed coloring books. Isn't it genius?"

"Mohammed *coloring books*?"

"I'm obviously going to hire a professional for the drawings," explained Sebastian, as though the images were of innocuous mermaids or farm animals. "But it's the concept that's going to sell this, not the artwork. Impressed?"

Edgecomb had learned his lesson from his encounter with Sally, so he focused on deep breaths and counted backwards from ten before speaking.

"You do realize that drawing the prophet Mohammed is the Islamic equivalent of flag burning," he finally said. "Even if Muslims were in the market for personalized coloring books, none of them are going to buy one of these."

"Of course they're not, dude," replied Sebastian. "But right-wingers *are*. Every shotgun wielding kid in the Bible Belt is going to want one of these babies—or, at least, their parents will want one for them. I can envision a whole collection of 'Color the Prophet' books…"

"You're going to get killed," cried Edgecomb. "You're going to get *us* killed."

"Nobody's going to kill me over a coloring book. Do you realize how ridiculous that would look?"

"Of course, they'd kill you over a coloring book. And even if they didn't—do you really want to offend two billion people?"

Sebastian shrugged. "Whatever. There's nothing offensive here—just a narrative history of the Quran in pictures. It proves how silly the whole controversy is." Edgecomb's housemate punched his shoulder lightly. "Don't be such a pessimist, Teach. Anyway, what's *your* earth-shattering news?"

Edgecomb knew better than to protest any further. He'd lost whatever marketing credibility he might have had when he'd warned Sebastian against producing a collection of figurines called "Feminists in Bikinis," which featured Susan B. Anthony and Eleanor Roosevelt, among others, in revealing swimwear. He'd anticipated a torrent of bra burnings and invective—and secretly feared that he'd never go on another date. Yet rather than protesting, local women's organizations had embraced the project as "ingeniously subversive" and purchased the toys in bulk quantities. Somehow, Edgecomb suspected that Islamic groups would prove less understanding. But what could he possibly do? Of course, now that his housemate had decided to insult a quarter of the world's population gratuitously, his own encounter with Sally Royster and his research into Civil War deniers struck him as comparatively trivial.

"It's not earth shattering. Just strange," he said. "In class on Friday, one of my students claimed the American Civil War never took place. That it was a hoax. And then I went online this morning—and it turns out there's a whole contingent of nutcases who believe this."

"Yeah. Surrender Appomattox."

"You've heard of them?"

"Sure. Their leader was on the radio this morning," replied Sebastian. "He makes a persuasive argument."

"Good god, Sebastian. He's a lunatic."

"Maybe. All I'm saying is that he's a convincing lunatic. That doesn't mean I believe him—but I understand how someone who didn't know any better might be swayed..."

"Someone who lives under a rock."

Edgecomb opened the refrigerator again, even though he knew it was empty, as though a snack might have generated spontaneously. It had not. "If you'll excuse me," he said, "I'm going to go shopping. *Again.*"

"Can you pick me up some beer?" asked Sebastian. "Oh, and I almost forgot. Your boss called."

"My boss?"

"Your principal. The gal in charge. She's got a hot voice."

"Jesus Christ. She's sixty with grandkids."

"I'm just saying, dude. Hot voice."

"What did she want?" demanded Edgecomb.

Dr. Foxwell had never before called him at home. Not once.

"She wants to meet with you, dude. Seven o'clock Monday morning," said Sebastian. "Sounds like Teach is in the dog house."

~

Even after teaching nearly three years at Laurendale, the prospect of a visit to Dr. Foxwell's office kept Edgecomb tossing and turning with anxiety dreams until the first sounds of morning drifted through his bedroom window. Some of the blame lay in his own experiences as a teenager. He'd never followed authority easily, especially when he perceived injustice. In tenth grade, after his town's school district had banned students from wearing black armbands to protest the Iraq War, he'd been suspended for plastering cars in the faculty parking lot with bumper-stickers that read ROLLESTON HIGH: BRAINWASHING CHILDREN SINCE 1917. Most of the blame for his anxiety, however, fell squarely on Sandra Foxwell, who'd learned the art of school administration from Iago. She smiled and pressed flesh as well as any small-time politician—and local parents adored her as a result—but everyone who worked for her realized quickly that her equine grin carried duplicity in every tooth. During his first week on the job, Edgecomb had been warned by a senior colleague, Lucky Pozner, to duck into the nearest open doorway when he saw 'The Sly Sandy Fox' approaching.

Edgecomb arrived for his appointment at six forty-five, and at seven fifteen, Foxwell emerged from her sanctum and beckoned him inside. The principal bore a striking resemblance, he reflected, to an over-the-hill racehorse—her wavy, frosted mane curled around the sides of her long, bony jaw. Surrounded by terracotta masks and wooden carvings of gazelle, acquired on her frequent trips to Namibia where she'd once served in the Peace Corps and now consulted for the Ministry of Education, Foxwell's features suggested an extinct grassland equid of the variety depicted in the dioramas at the Museum of Natural History. But thanks to Sebastian, Edgecomb found himself assessing the woman's voice for sex appeal. Fortunately, he didn't hear any. Eyeing his surroundings warily, he settled onto a black leather sofa that reminded him of a psychiatrist's couch.

"I'm glad you could join me, Horace," said Foxwell—welcoming and disarming, like a carnivorous plant. "I've been meaning to check in on you for some time. How is the year going?"

Edgecomb had no patience for pleasantries. "It can't be going all that well," he replied, "or I wouldn't be sitting here."

"Oh, I don't know about that." Foxwell flashed her teeth. Behind her—covering every inch of plaster—hung professional certificates and commendations designed to impress, possibly even to intimidate: *Fellow, New Jersey Principals Institute*; *Lifetime Member, Leadership for Progress*. Edgecomb recognized many of these honors as available to any high school administrator willing to fork over the registration fees. "From what I've heard, you're having a rather good year. Word on the street is that students connect with you—and that's more than half the battle…."

"Is *that* the word on the street?"

"More or less, Horace. You're precisely the sort of enthusiastic, innovative teacher that this district needs so dearly."

"Thank you," answered Edgecomb. What else could he say?

"I've heard about those murder games—what do you call them?"

"Simulation mysteries."

The previous spring, Edgecomb had guided his Advance Placement course in American history through a series of interactive simulations focused upon forensic questions from the past: *Was President Zachary Taylor fed poisonous cherries? Had Booth been hired to shoot Lincoln? Did Grover Cleveland really father an illegitimate son?* He had no doubt that his boss knew exactly what these exercises were called—that her feigned ignorance was part of a larger ploy to keep him off balance.

"That's right. Simulation mysteries," echoed Foxwell. "As I said, yours is the innovative voice that progressive education craves."

Edgecomb wasn't thanking her a second time. He sat stoically, hands folded over his knee, waiting for her attack. Outside, visible through the partially open blinds, the first of the morning's busses dropped off the special needs students.

Foxwell toyed with an ornate letter opener—drawing attention to the heavy, gem-studded rings on her fingers—and the preposterous notion entered Edgecomb's mind that his employer might go berserk and stab him. Instead, she set the letter opener carefully at the top of her blotter, like a dessert fork above a place setting, and said, seemingly offhand, "Of course, then there is this Sally Royster business..."

She opened a manila folder on her desk and pretended to scan the contents.

"I'm not sure what you mean," said Edgecomb.

"Isn't Sally Royster one of your students?" asked the principal.

"One of many."

"That's right. One of many...One of ninety-eight, to be precise. But the only one, as far as I'm aware," said Foxwell, "whose father has filed a formal complaint against you."

"That's totally unfounded," objected Edgecomb.

Foxwell held up her hand. "Since you aren't sure what I mean, Horace, I think it's best that I enlighten you regarding all the facts. According to Mr. Royster, you raised your voice at his daughter when she inquired—inquired *innocently*, intending no offense—whether you were aware that some people doubt the conventional history of the American Civil War—and then you ridiculed her mercilessly in front of your entire class. In fact, you compared his daughter to 'Flat Earthers,' and even questioned whether she knew the biology underlying childbirth—"

"—That's not what I—"

"Please, Horace. I realize that there are two sides to every story. I just wanted you to be clear about what you're facing." Foxwell looked up. "So as I was saying, Mr. Royster claims you mocked his daughter with a reference to frolicking storks, and then accused her of suffering from a mental illness."

On the surface, nothing Foxwell related sounded unreasonable. She hadn't taken any sides; as she said, she'd merely outlined the complaint against him. And yet, she'd somehow managed to make him feel as though he'd been in the wrong—that he'd been self-serving, or even abusive, when he'd been motivated only by his passion for truth.

"Sally Royster's father is a Civil War denier, for Christ's sake," he exclaimed, struggling to keep his emotions in check. "I don't think there's much more to say on the subject. You can't expect me to teach the Civil War as a theory..."

"Why not?" asked Foxwell.

"*Why not?* Do you really want me to answer that?"

Foxwell retrieved her letter opener again, running her thumb along the blade.

"Look, Horace, I'll level with you. This is coming from upstairs." Foxwell lowered her voice to a whisper, although he had no doubt her every action was carefully choreographed. "It's not public knowledge yet, but there's an effort underway to nominate Archie Steinhoff—*our* Archie Steinhoff—for lieutenant governor."

Archibald Steinhoff was Chairman of the Laurendale Board of Education and a white shoe law partner in Trenton.

"So?"

"So," replied Foxwell, "the last thing Archie needs at the moment is controversy. And your friend, Roland Royster, has a knack for stirring up trouble. He nearly bankrupted the city of Gettysburg, Pennsylvania, last year with frivolous litigation...Royster is threatening to protest at tomorrow's Board meeting. Can you imagine how that's going to look for Archie?"

"Let me get this straight. You're telling me to teach the Civil War as a theory so that Archibald Steinhoff can get elected lieutenant governor?"

"Of course, not," answered Foxwell. "I would never think of curtailing the intellectual freedom of one of my teachers. All I'm saying is that having Archie Steinhoff in the statehouse would do wonders for school funding—for arts education, for after-hours programs, for *this* community. You may choose to do as you wish with that information, Horace." She closed the manila folder decisively. "That being said, if you'd like me to phone Roland Royster and inform him that you've reached an accommodation with his daughter, I'd be more than glad to oblige."

"I'd sooner rot in hell."

Foxwell shook her head and sighed—like a disappointed parent. "In that case, Horace, I'll have no alternative but to forward Royster's complaint to the district's grievance board." The principal rose abruptly and opened her office door. "As your colleague, I can't help adding that I strongly urge you to reconsider. Having a good friend in the statehouse would do wonders for our children—and your intransigence isn't helping them any."

"I'll take that under advisement," said Edgecomb.

He left Foxwell's office, drained to the brink of exhaustion. His body felt as though he'd worked an entire school day, although the colossal analog clock in the student commons read only twenty minutes before eight.

~

Thanks to the vagaries of block scheduling, Edgecomb didn't teach his twelfth grade history class again until the following afternoon. That afforded him ample time to anticipate his next confrontation with Sally Royster. In one of his fantasies, he forced the girl into his Honda at gunpoint and drove her on an improvised tour of Civil War battlefields, parading his captive through the oak thickets of Shiloh, across the bloody wheat field at Antietam, and on a merciless hike up Gettysburg's Seminary Ridge through the torrid heat of Indian summer until she cried uncle. Only, he didn't own a gun. And even if he somehow acquired a firearm, he had no inkling of how to handle one. In another version of his daydream, he accidentally shot himself in the groin and had to have his penis surgically reconstructed. The bottom line, of course, was that even if he managed to abduct Sally, and to drum the madness from her thick skull, he'd still have faced certain termination from Laurendale, and an equally definite end to his teaching career—and at twenty-eight, with $6,000 in the bank and a credit score so low that the agent who'd financed his car had initially assumed the figure to be a typographical error, Edgecomb wasn't in a position to embark on a second career. Besides which, he just wasn't the kidnapping type. Even watching a shootout in a Tom Mix western unsettled him. So there'd be no abduction, no made-for-television-movie-style jaunt across the Mason-Dixon Line, nothing to land him and Sally a spot on the morning talk shows. Yet that didn't mean he'd be standing down either. Far from it. When Tuesday afternoon rolled around, Edgecomb entered his classroom braced for a lethal struggle.

Sally sashayed to her desk seconds before the bell sounded. Her pale skin flushed a gentle purple under the fluorescent overhead bulbs—and Edgecomb registered that the girl had entered the classroom alone, that she existed outside the cloud of banter and carousing and flirtation that enveloped her peers. It almost seemed as though she inhabited a personal force field, repelling these juvenile antics, and under any other circumstances, Edgecomb would have felt sincerely awful for this isolated young woman. He'd likely have drawn aside a few of the more popular girls and urged them to befriend her—as he'd previously done for a Belgian exchange student. His dedication to historical reality, however, trumped his sympathy for her suffering. Moreover, nothing suggested that Sally was indeed suffering. In fact, he assured himself, the teen appeared perfectly content in her holier-than-thou self-quarantine.

Edgecomb came armed with a battle plan. The day's lesson featured a review of the political crises leading up to the Confederate firing upon Fort Sumter—material covered during the spring of eleventh grade and forgotten over the ensuing summer—and as he reviewed each of these seminal events, the Missouri Compromise of 1820, the Wilmot Proviso, the Kansas-Nebraska Act, he emphasized the historical evidence for it. "Can I prove the Missouri Compromise occurred?" he asked. "For that matter, can I prove that the state of Missouri exists? I've been there, by the way. They call it the Show-Me State. And they sure did show me. Showed me the Cardinals trouncing the Mets 10-0 and 16-1 in a double header." His remark drew snickers from the boys. "That was my way of figuring out which of you are Yankees fans, by the way," added Edgecomb. "So I can take points off your exams." More laughter. "But does Missouri exist? And was it ever compromised? Who can really say? All I can tell you is that I've seen photographs of Congressman Henry Clay, and I've been to his estate in Kentucky, and I've read original newspaper accounts of the congressman's role in brokering the Compromise, and his personal letters on the subject—and there are hundreds of thousands of other documents about the Missouri Compromise that I've never read, and honestly, that I'd never want to." Widespread laughter. "But I suppose they might *all* be forgeries. Part of a giant hoax. In fact, we might all be figments of someone's imagination—maybe characters in a child's dream—or, more likely, the nightmares of a psychiatric patient—so take everything that I say with a sack of salt grains." Edgecomb paced the room while he spoke, painstakingly keeping his eyes away from Sally. "Gravity itself may be an illusion. But until I have good evidence for that, I'm not stepping out of any tenth story windows."

Edgecomb found himself enjoying his own sermon. He did a similar number on the election of Lincoln. "I suppose Douglas might have won," he said. "For those of you who think Al Gore actually received more votes in 2000—that Bush stole the election—imagine how much easier it would have been for Lincoln to steal an election in an era when it regularly took three days to tally the votes." Edgecomb hoisted himself onto the edge of his desk, letting his legs dangle over the side. In the front row, Brittany Marcus and Maria Winch, two of his most attractive and least focused students, exchanged clandestine notes. He glanced at them knowingly and Maria giggled. "Okay, I've talked far too much for one day," Edgecomb announced. "Any questions?"

Now he had no choice but to make eye contact with Sally. She sat with her arms folded across her ample chest, her piercing gaze locked on his. And then, as he'd expected, and dreaded, her slender arm shot up. Edgecomb scanned the room for another hand, but his nemesis faced no competition.

"Sally?"

"Mr. Edgecomb," she asked—civil, yet not friendly—"Would you mind if I made an announcement?"

That caught him off guard. He'd been expecting a direct challenge, while he now sensed a sneak-attack lurking behind her announcement. But he'd allowed countless other announcements over the course of the years—for pep rallies and cancer benefits and Spanish club fiestas—so what choice did he have?

"What would you like to announce?" he asked.

The girl stood up. She was tiny—probably under five feet, although her presence made her seem so much larger. "At the Board of Education meeting tonight," she declared, "a group of citizens will present a petition for equal treatment of all historical viewpoints. I know this might not be of interest to many of you, but for those few of you who are concerned that we're only being taught one side of important issues—that we're being *indoctrinated*—this is an opportunity to fight back." She glowered at Edgecomb. "You're welcome too, Mr. Edgecomb."

"Wish I could, Sally," he replied. "But I already have plans. You see, I'm washing my socks tonight."

That drew a few titters, but not the laugher he'd hoped for.

"Too bad," said Sally. "But better your socks than my brain."

A collective gasp—part alarm, part awe—swelled across the classroom.

Edgecomb grinned. "Touché, Sally. Maybe I will come after all."

"I hope you do. I hope you *all* do," she said. "We already have enough signatures to compel a vote, but we can always use more, so please let me know if any of you would like to sign on." And then she held up a small mechanical device; it took a moment before Edgecomb registered that it was an old-fashioned tape recorder, the miniature sort that journalists had used in the pre-cell phone era. "If you do come tonight, you may even get to hear yourself on tape, Mr. Edgecomb. I'm sure the Board of Education will enjoy your thoughts on the Missouri Compromise."

You little bitch, thought Edgecomb—but this time, he held his tongue.

He took a deep breath. "Please give that to me," he ordered. "There's a policy against recording inside the classroom without permission."

"An unconstitutional policy," countered Sally. "You get a court order, Mr. Edgecomb, and it's all yours."

Edgecomb felt his temper rising, the heat brewing in his forehead.

"Give me that," he demanded, stepping toward her. "Right now."

"I don't think so," said Sally.

She slid the device into her cleavage. The gesture was so provocative that it had the paradoxical effect of bringing Edgecomb to his senses. After all, he couldn't reach into the girl's blouse for the recorder. And the machine was probably still running. If he made a snide remark about her breasts, that would cook his goose.

"Very well," he said. "I haven't said anything that isn't true. If you'd like to share my genius with the School Board, who am I to object?"

He glanced at the wall clock; he had only two minutes to redeem himself. Louise, the nurse's daughter, was already packing up her books. Edgecomb turned toward Abe Kendall, a lanky, stoic, Orthodox Jewish kid who always wore a skullcap and also happened to be the star of the school's basketball team. "I have a tidbit about Judaism that I bet even Abe doesn't know," he ventured.

Kendall looked up with interest.

"Abe, did you know that your namesake, Abraham Lincoln, was Jewish?"

An expression of polite bemusement spread across the boy's features.

"Are you sure?" the teen asked.

"Absolutely," replied Edgecomb. "He was shot in the temple."

Kendall grinned. Other students followed. Brittany Marcus didn't get the joke and looked to her neighbor for explanation.

"Good one, Mr. E.," said the basketball star.

"Thanks," Edgecomb replied. "But please don't write that on the state exam."

He glanced sidelong at Sally. She held the eraser end of her pencil against her lower lip, reflective and resentful. The pendulum of power, Edgecomb realized with relief, had swung back in his direction. For the moment, at least. He still held it, albeit tenuously, when the bell sounded several seconds later.

~

The Laurendale Board of Education met in a small theater on the third floor of the high school that also served as a drama classroom during the day. Posters from various senior class musicals lined the walls—revealing a pattern that included productions of *West Side Story* and *Grease* at least once each decade. Puppets from an avant-garde staging of Brecht hung off the rafters. At the front of the room, three adjacent folding tables, each equipped with a pitcher of water, separated the elevated seats of the seven anointed school board members from the masses who had elected them. A microphone stood at the head of each aisle for audience members to ask questions. When Edgecomb arrived—with Sebastian Borrelli in tow for moral support—the followers of Roland Royster had occupied nearly the entire gallery. They carried placards reading "History Is Often Inconvenient," "Grant and Lee were

Actors," and "Test the Cloak"—the last sign, Edgecomb had learned online, was a reference to Surrender Appomattox's efforts to conduct DNA testing on the clothing that Abraham Lincoln had worn to Ford's Theater. Edgecomb spotted Sally in the front row, styling a striking orange sundress. He presumed the red-faced gentleman sitting beside her to be her father. Roland G. Royster appeared younger than Edgecomb had expected—closer to forty than to fifty; he boasted a towering forehead and a mane of long, prematurely silver hair.

Edgecomb and Sebastian maneuvered their way through Royster's army and joined the standing-room-only crowd against the far wall. Edgecomb had been to a School Board meeting once before—to voice opposition to a plan requiring that newly-hired faculty contribute to their own health insurance—and, in the eighteen months since, the entire composition of the Board had changed. As the five men and two women filed to their seats, he noted how ordinary they all looked, more like beleaguered parents or mid-level executives at the end of a long commute than formidable legislators. Even the chairman, Archie Steinhoff, distinguished by rugged features and an aquiline nose fit for a Roman emperor and sporting a three-piece suit whose value likely exceeded the cost of Edgecomb's entire wardrobe, somehow managed to convey an air of mediocrity and ineptitude accentuated by his poorly-disguised toupee.

Sebastian nudged Edgecomb with his elbow and drew his attention toward a girl in the third row. "She's hot, dude," he said. "You know her?"

"Jesus Christ," hissed Edgecomb. "She's like fourteen."

"I bet she's *at least* sixteen," rejoined Sebastian. "Age of consent."

Edgecomb glared at his housemate. He didn't think Borrelli was serious about the girl—ogling underage women was just part of his shtick—but he was never entirely sure. Every jest held a hint of truth slinking inside, didn't it? In any case, he had no desire to be humiliated in front of a roomful of colleagues and parents.

"Her mom's not half-bad either," said Borrelli, his voice a register too loud. "Great body. Almost makes up for her face."

The woman beside Sebastian—a matron of a certain age, exuding an oppressive scent of lavender—appeared as though she might slap him.

"What do you say we invite them home?" continued Borrelli. "One for each of us. You can take your pick."

"What the hell is wrong with you?" Edgecomb demanded in an angry whisper.

"Chill out, dude," answered Borrelli. "You know I'm just fucking with you."

Before Edgecomb had an opportunity to respond, Archie Steinhoff rapped a wooden block on the tabletop and called the meeting to order. "We have a large audience here tonight," he observed. "Welcome to all of you. As a public official, I must tell you that it's reassuring for me to see so many of my friends and neighbors, my fellow citizens, actively participating in the civic process." Edgecomb wondered what percentage of the audience would have described Steinhoff as a friend. "We'll proceed to approval of the minutes and then we'll follow-up with committee reports. New business—and I understand that one or more members of the community would like to address the Board this evening—is generally reserved for the end of the session."

A rumble of displeasure heaved through the audience. Yet Steinhoff persisted with the Board's customary routine: adopting the previous month's minutes without amendment, hearing updates from the Committee on Capital Expenditures, the Committee on Professional Development, and the Ad Hoc Committee on Substance Abuse. The last had been established after much of the previous spring's graduating senior class arrived intoxicated to their prom, which had taken place on a yacht docked at the head of Barnegat Bay. One drunk girl had stumbled into the harbor. Next, the Board's treasurer asked for technical adjustments to the district's accounting practices, which led to a slew of questions, intricate and seemingly trivial. In the end, the modifications were accepted unanimously.

Another board member, an overweight, moon-faced woman pushing seventy, offered a proposal to commence future meetings with a moment of silence for Laurendale graduates killed fighting in Iraq and Afghanistan. A second member then asked if any graduates had in fact died in either war, suggesting that it would belittle the suffering of "our fallen heroes" to honor these local soldiers if they did not actually exist. A third member proposed a broader moment of tribute for all of Laurendale's war dead—dating back to the seven alumni who had perished in World War I and were now memorialized with a heavily-tarnished bronze plaque opposite the cafeteria. After twenty minutes of meandering discussion, the Board tabled the motion until the next sitting, at which time the moon-faced woman promised to provide the names of graduates who'd perished in recent conflicts. "You'd think she would have looked that up *before* the meeting," observed Sebastian—still too loud. "Come on, lady. I mean: do your homework."

"We're now open to new business and community proposals," announced Archie Steinhoff. "I know this is the first meeting for many of you, so I'd like to take this opportunity to remind our newcomers to say and *spell* your full names before you speak—I'll thank you on behalf of Phoebe Woodsmith, our lovely *Clarion* reporter—and to kindly limit your remarks to under five minutes."

Roland Royster rose from his seat as soon as Steinhoff opened the floor. Every head in the gallery turned toward him.

When it came to mastering an audience, the protest leader certainly knew what he was about: Royster took his sweet time in ambling toward the microphone, allowing his supporters to cheer his approach, appearing almost inconvenienced by the demands placed upon him—as though he were performing a public service, under duress, and would have preferred to be at home dining with his family. He carried a clipboard of papers, presumably leafs of the petition, under his elbow. Edgecomb considered charging past him and grabbing the mic—not because he particularly desired to address the Board, but because he longed to tarnish the lunatic's moment. Alas, too many other spectators stood between him and the aisle to make such an effort feasible.

"Good evening," said Royster. "My name is Roland G. Royster. If the esteemed Board can spare a few moments, I've come to deliver a request on behalf of seven hundred fifty-eight of my fellow citizens of this great country."

"Please spell your name," interrupted Archie Steinhoff.

Royster appeared nonplussed. "Fine," he conceded grudgingly, clearly displeased at the distraction. "R-O-Y-S-T-E-R."

"First name, too," pressed Steinhoff. "For Phoebe's sake."

"R-O-L-A-N-D," said Royster. "Satisfied?"

The reply came from an elfin, bespectacled young woman perched in an aisle seat of the front row, a spiral-bound pad in her lap. The celebrated Phoebe Woodsmith. "And your middle initial, sir? Was that B as in Brave or G as in Golf?"

"That was G," said Royster, "As in, give me a chance to speak, please."

Guffaws tore through the nutcase's entourage. Steinhoff pounded his wooden block until the gallery returned to order. The chairman issued a strongly-worded warning, threatening to retire the session to a private chamber.

"The floor is yours, Mr. Royster," he said. "You have five minutes."

"Very well. Five minutes is not a long time. Especially when the liberty of mankind is at stake." Royster paused to let his declaration sink in. "As you may be aware, my friends, intellectual freedom has always been the bedrock of a sound educational system. And today, as much as at any time during our nation's history, that intellectual liberty is under assault." During the ensuing speech, Royster did not once mention the American Civil War or Edgecomb's conflict with his daughter. Instead, he spoke in the broadest platitudes, invoking the Magna Carta and the Declaration of the Rights of Man and the legacy of Patrick Henry. By the time Royster removed a handkerchief from his breast pocket to dab down his forehead—a clever touch that Edgecomb recalled from a Henry Fonda movie—several members of the School Board were nodding their heads in accord. "So I present to you this initiative, on behalf of seven hundred fifty-eight of my fellow citizens, defending the sanctity of the marketplace of ideas and proposing that all faculty members be required, upon parental request, to devote equal time to both sides of any historical question."

Royster handed the petition to the Board's secretary and returned to his seat. His followers applauded with abandon. "You'll note that more than two hundred of the signatures belong to Laurendale residents," he added before sitting down. "According to your own bylaws, that requires an up-or-down vote of the Board."

Archie Steinhoff conferred for what felt like a good five minutes with the Board's secretary and with the bald member to his left, holding his palm over his microphone. Several other members passed him written notes. "It appears that you are correct, Mr. Royster. However, in light of the seriousness of this proposal, the chair requests that you allow us to delay a vote until our next meeting, which should give the Board an opportunity to review the matter in greater depth."

The request drew a clamor of jeers. "After you're nominated for Lieutenant Governor," shouted a lantern-jawed man in a denim jacket. More jeers followed. Royster's toadies, it appeared, already knew the scoop on Steinhoff.

"We'd prefer a vote this evening," said Royster in an even tone. "Freedom postponed is freedom denied."

A look of anguish flashed across Archibald Steinhoff's face, as though he were having his tonsils removed without anesthesia. He conferred further with the Board's secretary, with his bald colleague, with the member who'd questioned the need for a moment of silence. The moon-faced woman yawned and glanced at her watch.

"Very well," said the chairman. "It seems we have no alternative but to vote on Mr. Royster's initiative at tonight's meeting."

"Hell, yeah," exclaimed the lantern-jawed man.

Steinhoff again pounded his makeshift gavel. "One more outburst," the chairman warned, "and I'll clear the room. Now if there is no further community business, we'll proceed to a vote on the initiative."

A silence descended upon the theater. Edgecomb surveyed the gallery, hoping that someone might rise to challenge Royster. Nobody did. It wasn't even clear that those spectators not affiliated with Surrender Appomattox—and he recognized a handful of parents he'd met on various open school nights in prior years—had any clue what the lunatic's appeal was really about. Most of the local residents who'd signed his petition probably hadn't known either—or were the sort of knee-jerk liberal populists who believed it their duty to sign every initiative and ballot measure that floated their way. Steinhoff understood what was at stake, of course, as did Sandra Foxwell, roosting in the front row several seats off the aisle, but Royster's hazy speech had given them both claims to plausible deniability. In other words, if Edgecomb didn't stand up now, the hallowed dead of Bull Run and Spotsylvania would soon be reduced to mere theory—open to endless debate, or even relegated to the same intellectual dust heap as alchemy and saltational evolution and the Ptolemaic universe. Sally's father realized this too; Royster sat with his arms folded across his broad chest, relishing his victory, an intoxicated grin of power plastered across his ruddy features.

Edgecomb muscled his way forward. "He's a Civil War denier," he called out—not waiting until he reached the microphone. "This has nothing to do with academic freedom or human dignity or anything of the sort. He wants us to teach students that the American Civil War is a hoax." He finally arrived at the mic. "Did you all hear me? He wants us to teach that the Civil War never happened!"

Edgecomb now had the attention of every last person in the gallery, even ancient Leonard Brackitt—longtime president of the Laurendale Retired Teachers Association—who'd snored through the greater part of the meeting. Sebastian Borrelli had followed Edgecomb down the aisle, like a bodyguard; he stood with his arms akimbo, his face steeled with menace, just close enough to tackle anyone trying to silence his housemate prematurely. In the front row, only yards away from her teacher, Sally Royster wore an expression of unalloyed hatred. Archie Steinhoff did not interrupt him to ask for the spelling of his name.

"Do you really want us teaching the Gettysburg Address as theory?" Edgecomb demanded of the Board. "And what about people who question the moon landing? Or Holocaust deniers?" Then he focused directly on Archie Steinhoff. "Even if you're not interested in the truth, think about the optics. How is the media going to respond when I start presenting Auschwitz and Treblinka as controversial hypotheses? What are you going to say when the Anti-Defamation League shows up here with a bunch of concentration camp survivors in wheelchairs?"

Royster shook his head. "The requirement for teaching both sides only applies when a parent requests it," he interjected. "I don't imagine there are many Holocaust deniers or moon landing skeptics living here in Laurendale."

"But there are Civil War deniers," Edgecomb shot back, pointing at Sally's father. "And he's one of them."

"I reject that characterization," objected Royster. "I don't deny anything. I merely demand evidence."

"You've had your five minutes," retorted Edgecomb. "Now let me speak." He drew a deep breath and gathered his thoughts. "The instant you pass this rule, that man is going to insist that I give equal time to the people who believe Mathew Brady's photos were staged and the Emancipation Proclamation to be a forgery. Look at their placards, for Christ's sake. 'Grant and Lee were Actors.' What more evidence do you need?"

Edgecomb stopped speaking, mostly because he wasn't sure what else to say. He suddenly realized that he'd become the center of attention—and a chill of anxiety sizzled up his spine. Out of the blue, he heard Jillian's voice pleading inside his head, warning him. *Please don't create any trouble.* Fortunately, he'd chosen a good moment to yield the floor; momentum seemed to have shifted against Sally's father.

"Is this true, Mr. Royster?" inquired the oldest member of the board—a wizened gentleman with drowsy eyes who Edgecomb had suspected of catnapping. "Do you believe the Emancipation to be a forgery?"

"My personal views," answered Royster with equanimity, "should have no bearing on the matter. We've delivered a petition and now we're requesting a vote."

"I'm afraid Mr. Royster is correct," said Archie Steinhoff, apparently wishing to bring the controversy to a swift conclusion. "He did present more than enough signatures under the bylaws." The grooves in the chairman's brow had grown only deeper during Edgecomb's debate with Royster, as though each salvo had aged him a year. "I would also urge my colleagues to consider the following," he said. "This proposal *does* have considerable citizen support. *Considerable.* It's not every day that more than two hundred Laurendale residents take a public position on anything. If we choose to approve this measure tonight, and it is subsequently abused, we always have the authority to revisit our decision later this year."

The bald man muttered his agreement. The moon-faced woman nodded. Archibald Steinhoff was a man of extensive influence, after all, and his preferences generally swayed the Board. Only the drowsy-eyed gentleman appeared doubtful.

"I realize that this proposal is now the sole barrier standing between many of you and dinner," observed Steinhoff—shattering the tension in the small theater. "So I move to approve the initiative as presented. Is there a second?"

"I second the motion," muttered the moon-faced woman.

"Point of order," shouted Edgecomb. "I have a point of order."

Steinhoff removed his glasses, his face florid with irritation. "Yes?"

Edgecomb squeezed his fists for courage and asked, "Have the signatures been verified against the municipal voting rolls?"

Steinhoff flashed a puzzled look at his bald colleague.

"Seventeen years ago," continued Edgecomb, "the Board voted on an initiative that turned out to be based entirely upon fraudulent signatures. One citizen had signed four hundred different names copied out of the telephone directory. In response, as you may recall, the town amended its bylaws to require that the clerk of the Board of Elections verify each signature on a citizen's initiative against the voting rolls in order to prevent another such incident." He glimpsed Sally's father out of the corner of his eye; Royster still wore his smug grin. "I trust the Board will follow its own rules and have the signatures verified before proceeding…"

"That could take days," observed Steinhoff. "Even weeks."

"Exactly," said Edgecomb.

Another conference transpired between Steinhoff, his bald ally, and the Board secretary. The drowsy-eyed gentleman also shambled up to the conclave and offered a whispered opinion. Several minutes later, once the legislators had returned to their seats, Steinhoff pounded his wooden knocker for the final hush of the evening. "I understand that this ruling will disappoint many of you," he said. "But bylaws are bylaws. I have instructed the Board secretary to verify these signatures with the clerk of the Board of Elections and to report back to us twelve weeks from tonight." And without further comment, Steinhoff adjourned the meeting and retreated quickly into the corridor.

Now it was Edgecomb, not Roland Royster, who had captured the interest of those members of the crowd not affiliated with Surrender Appomattox. Leonard Brackitt congratulated him on "knowing your facts" and slapped him too hard between the shoulder blades, as though he were a choking infant. A handful of parents gathered around him to express their appreciation. Then he conducted a twenty-minute interview with Phoebe Woodson, downplaying his own significance in the controversy and emphasizing the importance of academic freedom. He noticed Sandra Foxwell skulking at the periphery of their conversation—just close enough to eavesdrop on his comments—but she pretended to be rummaging for something in her purse. It was nearly ten o'clock when he finally escaped all the unwanted attention and piled into Borrelli's jalopy, a disfigured Dodge Dart distinguished by its one remaining tail fin. He'd gotten lucky. He'd caught Royster off guard, and the denier had been too self-assured, it seemed, to have prepared a backup plan. Sally Royster hadn't even found an opportunity to play the cassette tape from his afternoon history class.

"That was totally awesome, dude," said Borrelli as the Dodge peeled out of the gravel parking lot. He'd already lit a cigarette. Edgecomb hoped it contained only tobacco. "You really did a number on them with that Board of Elections shit. How'd you ever find out about all that? That was pretty wild."

Borrelli drummed his thumbs on the steering wheel, playing it like a bongo. Outside, the suburban night flashed by at a dangerous speed.

"Crazier than you think," said Edgecomb. "I made it up."

His housemate stopped thumping. "For real?"

Edgecomb wanted to justify himself by blaming the School Board—by claiming that it was the members' lack of institutional memory that was at fault. If you don't know your own history, after all, you're at the mercy of strangers, and strangers aren't always honest. But deep down, Edgecomb knew, his deception wasn't about history; it was about warfare. He was locked in an armed conflict with Roland G. Royster, and his children, and all of the vast minions of their nefarious organization.

"If Royster wants war," he told his housemate, convincing himself with his own words, "he'll get war. But from now on, I'm using live ammunition."

"Teach is one mad motherfucker," replied his companion.

Then Sebastian Borrelli whistled into the darkness and hit the accelerator.

CHAPTER TWO

The headline on Phoebe Woodsmith's lead story in the *Clarion* the following morning read, "MR. SMITH GOES TO LAURENDALE: History Teacher Educates School Board on Rules." An editorial on page seven also criticized Royster's initiative, going so far as to say that any board members voting for the proposal would effectively disqualify themselves from higher office. Since Edgecomb didn't subscribe to the local newspaper, he only discovered his media triumph during his first period prep, when Lucky Pozner slapped the broadsheet down on his desk. The grizzled chemistry teacher settled onto the radiator; its metal frame creaked under his profuse weight.

"You should have seen 'Sly Sandy' this morning," he said. "Old dame looked like she'd just learned she was being dispatched to the glue factory. Yesterday, she counted herself a shoe-in for State Education Commissioner in a Sanchez-Steinhoff Administration, and today she's in line for another decade counting paperclips on the second floor…I finally understand why they shoot crippled horses." Edgecomb's senior colleague unwrapped a piece of Nicorette gum and popped the morsel into his mouth. "So, old fellow, how does it feel to be a B-list celebrity?"

"This too shall pass," Edgecomb replied, leafing aimlessly through his lesson plan. "By next week, nobody will remember that I exist. Possibly not even me."

As far as Edgecomb was concerned, his fifteen minutes of fame couldn't dissolve quickly enough. His sister had already left him three cell phone messages—her voice taut as a hangman's rope—and he wasn't looking forward to Jillian's inevitable rant about how his antics had doomed her to a solitary old age. He also dreaded his upcoming class with Sally Royster; although he'd won their most recent skirmish, he anticipated that her counterattack would prove ruthless. As a teenager, Edgecomb had fantasized about fame and fortune, even of being elected President—mostly with the aim of impressing his high school crush, Vicky Vann—but now he had reached the point where all that he really sought in life was, to quote one of his childhood heroes, Supreme Court Justice Louis Brandeis, "the right to be let alone." Some people, most significantly his mother, deemed his attitude lazy, even pathetic. He preferred to consider it mature.

"History is full of insignificant people," added Edgecomb. "And I've long since reconciled myself to the fact that I'm going to be one of them."

"Au contraire, old fellow," countered Pozner. "You're no more significant or insignificant than anybody else." What followed was a thirty-minute disquisition that could be summed up in one platitude: *All human beings shape history equally, but only a few of them receive any credit.* Edgecomb had heard every last word of it before, down to Pozner's apocryphal anecdote about the never-identified passerby who'd saved an adolescent Rosa Parks from drowning, but he admired the zeal with which the recovering Sixties dropout preached his peculiar-if-inconsistent gospel of individual significance and benevolent Marxism. Only the clamor of the class shift, drifting in from the hallway, brought Pozner's soliloquy to a premature close. "So the bottom line," he said, shuffling out of the room as a brigade of ninth graders surged in, "is that, at the moment, whether you deserve it or not, you're one of those lucky few getting the credit, so you might as well savor it." With that, Pozner flashed him a salute—a curious gesture from a man who'd spent the final years of the Vietnam Conflict in Vancouver—and Edgecomb once again became an ordinary social studies teacher, lecturing antsy fourteen-year-olds on the Monroe Doctrine.

Only not *that* ordinary. During the course of the school day, as word of his Board of Education performance spread, assorted colleagues poked their heads into his classroom to congratulate—and often to tease—him on his newfound renown. His department chairman, Elgin Rothmeyer, called him a "veritable muckraker" and likened him to Clarence Darrow. Stan and Stu Storrow, the egg-bald twins who jointly ran the school's physical education program, serenaded him over lunch in the faculty dining chamber with a chorus of "We Shall Overcome." Most rewarding of all, Calliope Chaselle—the eye-catching and aloof junior librarian who boasted skin so delicate that one could admire the latticework of tiny blue veins in her flawless cheeks—approached him after the midday staff meeting and praised him for his courage. "I showed my boyfriend your picture in the paper at breakfast," she concluded, probably mentioning her boyfriend so he wouldn't get the wrong idea, "and I said: Thorn, I *work* with that guy." It figured that Calliope shacked up with a man named Thorn. Even the students were aware of Edgecomb's stardom—with several suggesting that his newfound fame merited a break from homework.

Not all of the feedback, of course, proved positive. When he encountered Sandra Foxwell outside his classroom on his return from lunch—probably not a coincidence—the principal no longer appeared shell-shocked. Rather, she'd composed herself into a portrait of icy civility, her features as hard as the gemstones embedded in her earrings; on her jacket lapel, she brandished a mariner's cross brooch like a shield. "I'm so glad we've run into each other, Horace. I've been meaning to check up on you," she said. "Sometimes, in my experience, sudden publicity for an untenured teacher can get in the way of his classroom responsibilities—and I just wanted to make certain you weren't having any trouble."

"No trouble at all," Edgecomb answered. He forced a thin smile and kept his hands locked in the pockets of his slacks. "Thank you for thinking of me."

"That's what I'm here for," said Foxwell. "I'm truly relieved that you're not having any difficulties—at least, not *yet*. Should any challenges arise, it goes without saying, my office door always stands open."

Foxwell flounced away and Edgecomb assumed their conversation had ended, but as he unlocked his classroom door, he discovered his boss again at his elbow. "One more word to the wise, Horace," she said, her tone all too friendly. "I like you. Genuinely. I wanted to emphasize that, because, over the years, I've watched my share of young teachers bite off more than they could chew—and, quite frankly, I'd hate for you to end up being one of them." And then the Sly Sandy Fox tramped up the corridor without affording him an opportunity to respond—not that he actually wanted to—her heels drilling the parquet like artillery.

Edgecomb didn't particularly fear his boss anymore—not after the showdown at the Board meeting. He probably should have: Even with the strong backing of his department chair, Elgin Rothmeyer, concerted opposition from Foxwell could, at a minimum, hold up his tenure. But that afternoon, only two threats unsettled Edgecomb—maybe because they so dwarfed all others. The first was the prospect that Phoebe Woodsmith might phone him from the *Clarion* to demand more information about the former petitioner who'd supposedly copied signatures out of the telephone directory. Edgecomb intended to claim he didn't recollect the details—that he'd read about the incident someplace, while doing personal research for his own book, but no longer remembered where. Hadn't "I Don't Recall" supplied a mantra for multiple Presidential administrations? And what other choice did he have? He'd have to hope that the Board of Education's records dating back nearly two decades proved skimpy, a genuine possibility in an overtaxed bedroom suburb where half the families started planning their exoduses the day their kids graduated from high school. If Woodsmith asked him about his "book"—and why shouldn't a high school history teacher be writing a book?—he'd tell her he was researching conspiracy theories.

Edgecomb's other fear was Sally Royster. As much as he had every reason to dread Sandra Foxwell, and didn't, he had no logical cause to be intimidated by an unpopular teenage girl, especially one who looked rather like a quarrelsome macaw. Yet, as much as he hated to admit it, the young woman had somehow managed to burrow deep under his skin. During Edgecomb's fifth and six period classes, while he struggled to maintain focus on the intricacies of the XYZ Affair and the audacity of the Louisiana Purchase, his thoughts repeatedly detoured to various permutations of his impending encounter with Sally. Would she challenge him directly? Or would she bide her time until she caught him off guard? Edgecomb contemplated ways to forestall her tricks—taping his own lessons, for instance, and posting them on the Internet—but, at the end of the day, there was no way to preempt the unknown. What he feared most, of course, was losing authority, and the goodwill of his pupils, of becoming one of those well-intentioned-but-unloved teachers steeped in his own ineptitude. Even in high school, he'd recognized the qualities that made the best of his teachers stand out—approachability, integrity, humor—and, once he'd given up his fantasies of making out with Vicky Vann in the Oval Office, he'd set his sights on becoming one of them. No drug in Sebastian Borrelli's arsenal could make him higher than the surge of energy he felt inspiring teenagers, the thrill he experienced in bringing history to life, and he was determined not to let one thankless renegade derail him from his calling. Rationally, he recognized that he stood far from that precipice, but anxiety isn't rational, so by the dawn of seventh period, Edgecomb felt himself breaking into a sweat.

The bell rang; classes changed. His twelfth-grade students filtered to their seats. Already, after only three weeks, they'd imprinted themselves indelibly upon his psyche: overweight Louise Buxner, seemingly always on the verge of tears; earnest and diligent Abe Kendall; perpetually befuddled Brittany Marcus, scion of an influential banking family, whose smooth legs kept sophomore boys awake at night, but who had no business inside an honors classroom and knew it. Already, every one of them mattered to him. Yet Sally was different. He told himself he didn't give a rat's rump about the girl—that he'd feel only relief if he never laid eyes upon her again—but, if that were really true, then why couldn't he stop arguing with her in his head? When the class mustered to order, in a spontaneous gust of silence, her seat remained empty.

How dare she? It was one thing to challenge his authority directly, quite another to thumb her nose at him by skipping out on the confrontation entirely. That girl was mocking him—and the other students obviously knew it. Edgecomb muddled his way through John Brown's raid on Harper's Ferry, through the nomination of Lincoln, through the secession of South Carolina. But try as he might, he couldn't keep his gaze away from the unoccupied desk in the second row. Sally's vacant chair seemed to beckon him like an open grave. How the hell was he supposed to convince the girl that the Civil War had happened if she wouldn't to listen to him make his case?

As soon as the class—and the school day—ended, Edgecomb immediately called the main office to report her truancy. To his dismay, the attendance secretary was already aware of Sally's absence: she'd been phoned in sick.

~

Edgecomb arrived home to find Sebastian Borrelli and an unfamiliar visitor ensconced in their living room. His housemate's guest wore a pair of grease-stained cargo pants and a T-shirt emblazoned "Genius by Birth, Slacker by Choice;" his bleached hair recalled a well-worn shag carpet.

"Hey, Superstar," welcomed Borrelli. "I want to introduce you to Sevastopol. He's the new designer on my project. Hired him ten minutes ago. Who'd have thought I could find this much talent on Craig's List—and on my first try, too?"

A moment passed before Edgecomb realized their visitor was the illustrator his housemate had employed to draw the blasphemous coloring books. Multiple sketches of Mohammed in various states of undress, strewn about the coffee table, confirmed his worst suspicions. In several of them, the prophet wore a loincloth and bore an unsettling resemblance to Tarzan. In one, he appeared stark naked—and anatomically correct.

"I know what you're thinking," said Borrelli, following his gaze. "We're obviously not including the risqué sketches in the children's version. We're not *that* stupid. Sevastopol drew them as a joke, at first, but then it struck me that we could also market an R-rated edition as a novelty item to adults at NASCAR races and gun shows. Clever, no?"

"Very clever," conceded Edgecomb. "And I'm glad to meet you, Mr. Sevastopol."

"Just Sevastopol," said Sevastopol. "It's my full name."

"I'm sure it is," replied Edgecomb. "Now if you'll excuse me, I'm not feeling terribly sociable. Today was a very long day."

"And it's about to get longer," said Borrelli.

His housemate handed him a stack of paper scraps, assorted shreds in various shapes and colors. They had a hodge-podge of names and numbers scrawled on them.

"What's this?" he demanded.

"Phone messages, Teach. Forty-two of them."

"Jesus. I don't know forty-two people…"

"I sorted them for you. The media requests are on top: Hager Heights *Sentinel-Times*, Newark *Star-Ledger*, WKNJ. Then you've got your social calls—friends and family. Your Aunt Pauline in Arizona, Oliver Nepersall, that camp buddy of yours with the weird lisp, and some chick named Victoria Vann—asked you to call her back *tonight*, no matter how late. The fourteen on the bottom are all from your sister. And there's also a message from your mom on the answering machine that says : 'No need to get back to me today, but it's unfair of you to ignore your sister's phone calls.' I saved it for you."

"Vicky Vann called? You'd better not be fucking with me."

"Sounds like a porn star name, dude," said Borrelli. "Or a call girl. You're not hanging out with a hooker, Teach, are you?"

"What planet do you live on?" Edgecomb snapped.

"Sensitive, sensitive." Borrelli rolled his eyes. "Chick did sound desperate to talk to you, dude. But you still don't want to screw this up. You get your hook in—okay?—and then you run in the opposite direction."

Edgecomb ignored Borrelli's advice. He delved through the scraps of paper. Sure enough, right after his college pal, Oliver, appeared the name Victoria Vann and an out-of-state phone number. Area code 202. District of Columbia. The last time he'd seen Vicky Vann was the summer following his freshman year at Rutgers, when he'd confessed his love to her at the Crossroads Diner, predecessor to Mackenzie's Dinette, and she'd responded by telling him she was "seriously involved" with one of her Yale professors: a visiting faculty member from Italy, whose wife had stayed behind in Verona. Vicky's confession had inspired Edgecomb to express some thoughts he later regretted—he vaguely recalled using the word "delusional"—before he'd slammed a twenty-dollar bill on the tabletop and stormed out. He'd written her an apology the following week, but he'd never received a reply. That hadn't surprised him. Girls as breathtakingly gorgeous as Vicky had no need to look back. So the last thing Edgecomb ever expected, nine years later, was an urgent phone call.

"Teach?" asked Borrelli. "You okay?"

His housemate's voice startled him. "Fine, I guess. What time did Vicky call?"

Borrelli shrugged. "I don't know. Albion took the message."

That was too much. The girl of his adolescent dreams had reached out to him after nearly a decade of silence and she'd ended up speaking to an unmedicated, sexually-preoccupied schizophrenic. Lord only knew what the homeless guy had said to her. But Edgecomb forced himself to swallow his frustration. "I'm going to make some phone calls from my room. Important calls," he said. "Unless the world comes to an end and Jesus Christ shows up in person to escort us into oblivion, please don't disturb me."

Edgecomb retreated into his bedroom. As he was closing the door, he heard Borrelli's illustrator say, "Your roomie has anger issues." *Fuck you too!* Edgecomb thought. *Wait until al-Qaeda crushes your drawing hand. Let's see who has anger issues then.*

He paced in circles for several minutes, marshaling his courage, telling himself that he would phone Vicky when his clock hit 6:15, then 6:20, then 6:30. Then he sat on the bed until 6:45, stewing himself into panic, reflecting on his teenage yearning. How alone he'd been—an awkward, elephant-eared kid more interested in books than sports—and how easily Vicky could have cured his loneliness. If she'd been willing. Their common tastes, and her offer of easy friendship, had only exacerbated his suffering.

At 7:02, he finally dialed her number.

To his amazement, she answered the phone herself. Not a stranger with an identical name, but the musical and slightly hypomanic voice of his ex-crush.

"Vicky? It's Horace Edgecomb. Did I catch you at a good moment?"

Perfect timing," she replied. "I'm *so* glad you called back."

An uncomfortable silence followed. For years, Edgecomb had rehearsed for this encounter, but now that it had arrived, he couldn't generate a coherent thought.

"I bet you're wondering why I'm calling," said Vicky.

"I guess," he stammered. "I mean, it's good to hear you voice…"

"It's good to hear your voice too," replied Vicky. "But I also have something important to discuss with you. And I was hoping we could talk about it in person." She paused for a moment and added, "I know this is all very sudden."

"Not a problem. When do you want to meet?"

"How about now?"

"*Now?*" echoed Edgecomb.

"I can pick you up in twenty minutes," said Vicky. "Are we on?"

He agreed to meet on instinct—and, the words hardly out of his mouth, the line went dead. Only then did he realize that he hadn't even given her his address. Yet precisely twenty minutes later, an automobile horn honked beneath his bedroom window, and there sat auburn-haired Vicky Vann, stunning as ever, at the wheel of a bright lemon Mustang convertible. Edgecomb grabbed his windbreaker and headed for the stairs.

As he raced from the apartment, he passed Borrelli and Sevastopol—the entrepreneurial pair still camped out around the coffee table, surrounded by countless pencil drawings and crumpled balls of paper. Borrelli has stripped to his boxer shorts and appeared to be modeling for the illustrator.

"Enjoy your booty run, dude," his housemate called out. "Get some extra for us."

~

Edgecomb slid into the passenger seat and Vicky peeled away from the curb. On the radio, the Everly Brothers crooned "Bye, Bye Love," their wistful voices straining against the roar from the convertible's open roof. Vicky sported bangs and a pink knit sweater dappled with white reindeer; her delicate nose and dimpled chin still reminded Edgecomb of the features of a fairytale princess. To his relief, her fingers all appeared ringless.

"Thank you again for meeting me like this," said Vicky, making herself heard over the din. She shut off the radio. "It's great to see you."

"You too."

And it *was* great to see her: Even after all these years, his feelings—not just desire, but a genuine ache for her affection—rose quickly in his chest. At the same time, he sensed that she hadn't come to rekindle a romantic flame. Not that one could even rekindle something that had never been kindled to begin with.

"I'm not used to driving a standard," said Vicky—and, as though on cue, she shifted gears and jolted the transmission. "I should have rented an automatic."

"It's a rental?" asked Edgecomb.

What an idiotic question, he realized. She'd just told him it was a rental.

Yet if Vicky thought him an idiot, she didn't show it. "Let's go someplace where we can talk," she said.

So they drove without speaking. Twenty minutes later, after cruising through downtown Rolleston, past the red-brick post office and Lorimer's discount hardware and the low-slung branch bank where Edgecomb had once opened his first passbook savings account, Vicky veered between the colossal granite pillars onto the dirt lane leading to the Marshfield Seashore Preserve. The state park had once been the estate of a nineteenth century dry goods magnate who'd later served as William McKinley's Ambassador to the Ottoman Empire. During their high school days, its countless pull-offs had functioned as makeshift lovers' lanes for popular couples; Edgecomb had visited there only once—on an eighth-grade field trip to explore estuaries with his biology class. If Vicky were trying to send him a message, visiting Marshfield was certainly the way to do it. She eased the convertible up the rocky path, jouncing through ominous shadows, before parking in the mollusk-paved lot opposite the trailhead. Vicky cut the engine and flipped off the headlights—raising the remote hope that she might seduce him. Instead, she opened her car door and said, "Let's walk down to the water." She retrieved a flashlight from the trunk and tested the beam, then switched it off again. "Backup. In case the moon burns out," she said, laughing.

They strolled side by side along a narrow path that weaved between a waist-high meadow and a stone wall dating from colonial times. Beyond the wall towered stands of oaks and shagbark hickory. A salty breeze nipped Edgecomb's ears; he experienced a sudden longing to hug Vicky Vann for warmth.

"I bet you're wondering what this is all about," she said.

Edgecomb wanted to avoid sounding too eager. "It *has* crossed my mind."

"So the bottom line is that I'm working for the Treasury Department at the moment. In special investigations."

As soon as Vicky said special investigations, everything clicked for Edgecomb.

"And let me guess. You're investigating Surrender Appomattox."

"No, I'm not—not exactly. Or I wasn't until this morning. But the Department is. So when you stood up to Royster last night, the section head for the HDC division did some quick research—and discovered that I knew you. And so now I'm here."

"HDC?"

"Historical Denial Cults," explained Vicky. "The official name is the Division for the Analysis and Assessment of Fraudulent Historical Enterprises, but everybody calls them Historical Denial Cults. Although the actual cults prefer the term 'sects.' Go figure." Vicky slowed her pace. "You'd be shocked how many of them there are. Watergate deniers. Women's Suffrage deniers. There's even a nutcase in Kentucky with a small following who believes the Kennedy Assassination is a fraud—not that it was a conspiracy, but that it never happened at all. That Dallas was a Cold War stunt staged to deceive the Soviets, and that JFK continued running the country from an underground bunker in the West Virginia foothills for another five years. The Civil War deniers are the most pernicious though, because there are a lot more of them."

Edgecomb didn't care about Watergate deniers or whackjobs in Kentucky. What alarmed him was that the government could possess enough information about his background, as an ordinary citizen, to connect him to his high school crush in under twenty-four hours. Although he was thrilled to encounter Vicky again, he also resented the invasion of privacy that had made their reconnection possible. And if the Treasury Department kept tabs on his romantic life, who could fathom the degree of personal data that the espionage bureaus held.

"It's rather a strange coincidence, don't you think?" he asked—feeling more suspicious than he wanted to. "I mean: What are the odds that you'd be working for an agency investigating Roland Royster and I'd get into a fight with him?"

Vicky laughed again—a seductive, high-pitched peal of joy. "I guess it *is* a coincidence," she said. "But I'd rather believe it was fate. Besides, if I hadn't existed, the Department would have found a way to create me..."

Edgecomb wasn't exactly certain what she meant. He suspected this was just one of those enigmatic remarks that women like Vicky serve up to render themselves more mysterious and alluring. And it usually worked, too. Of course, if you ever asked them to explain themselves, they grew even more cryptic. After years of dating several of these women, and pursuing many others, he understood not to take the bait.

He waited for Vicky to reveal more. A whippoorwill swooped across the meadow, piercing the night with its sorrowful chant. They continuing strolling down the steep path toward the shoreline, like two spies conducting a covert rendezvous.

"Royster's a dangerous guy," she eventually said. "We're not sure exactly what he's up to at the moment—but we're certain nothing good will come of it."

"You sound like you know an awful lot about an investigation you weren't part of until this morning," observed Edgecomb.

"Not as much as I should. I've got heaps of bedtime reading to do."

Vicky had an answer for everything. Nothing had changed since high school.

"And what does all of this have to do with me?" he asked. "So I stood up to the lunatic at a Board of Ed meeting. I'm betting the Treasury Department didn't just send you here to congratulate me."

"It's good to see you're still as suspicious as ever," answered Vicky. She reached across the darkness and squeezed his forearm—sending a charge through his flesh. "But you're right. I didn't come to congratulate you. I came to ask you for your assistance." Her body was so near, her voice breathless and disarming. "We're hoping you'll infiltrate Royster's group."

Edgecomb couldn't say what he'd expected her to ask of him—but this certainly hadn't been it.

"How am I supposed to do that? Unless you forgot, I'm their sworn enemy."

"For the moment, you are. But soon you'll have a change of heart—a public conversion. They'll trust you."

"Do you realize how crazy this sounds?"

They're looking for history teachers and professors," insisted Vicky. "Trust me. You're their dream convert. And keep in mind that Royster sincerely believes he has the better half of the argument. He's a nutcase, not a charlatan. So when a prominent critic reconsiders his opposition, Royster's cult isn't going to be at all surprised. They're predisposed to believe you."

"How can you be so sure?"

"It's happened twice before already. Ever heard of Bruce McNabb or Mort Herskovitz?"

"Never."

"Didn't expect you to. McNabb was an Assistant Professor of American Studies at St. Anselm's College and Herskovitz taught U.S. history at Amherst. Not exactly household names, but mainstream historians who delivered lectures and published books and attended conferences—that is, until Royster sunk his talons in them. Now they live on his compound and co-edit his newsletter." Vicky looked pointedly at Edgecomb. "Unfortunately, neither of them is working for the Treasury Department."

They had reached the bottom of the trail. From the far cusp of the slender strip of beach, enchanting under the starscape, rose the sound of the current lapping against the breakwater. Across the inlet, a copse of clouds limned the mansions of Hager's Head.

"Can I think this over?" Edgecomb asked.

"Sure. Take as long as you need. But I do have to warn you that this investigation is time sensitive."

As though by unspoken understanding, they both realized that the moment had come to return home. Side by side, they retreated up the hill. The undergrowth along the incline blocked the moon, so Vicky led them through the shadows by flashlight. When they reached the verge of the meadow, Edgecomb asked, "Can I ask you a question? About something entirely different?"

He interpreted her silence as permission.

"What ever happened…?"

The words died on his lips.

"To me and Professor Quaglia?" she asked to fill the void. "He went back to Italy. You were totally right. I was delusional to believe he'd leave his wife." She laughed again, shrugging off her remote loss. "Any other questions?"

He wanted to inquire whether she was single, but he didn't dare.

"Are you sure you're not FBI?" he asked.

"At least ninety percent sure. Trust me, we're not *that* slow. The FBI is still probably searching for your home address on the Internet."

He thought she was joking, but in the darkness, he couldn't be sure.

"That's reassuring," he said. "I guess."

After that, their conversation shifted to mundane matters: his teaching career, her life in the District of Columbia, what little she could share with him about her work for the government. She asked after his parents, and he told her about his stepfather's fatal boating accident and his mother's relocation to the assisted living facility in Tampa. As he described his mother's decline—how her elegant fingers, once so nimble on the piano keys, now trembled with such severity that she couldn't remove her own medication from the bottle—he found tears infiltrating the corners of his eyes. Vicky had that gift for drawing out emotions, for capturing secrets like a magnet. On the ride back to Hager Heights, he even mentioned that his sister was trying to adopt a child. But as he was describing Jillian's efforts, an unsettling realization struck Edgecomb: Vicky already knew the answers to all of the questions she was asking. She'd probably read a file on him thicker than a Russian novel before she'd phoned. To test her, he casually observed, "She gave up teaching a few years ago. Right now, she's working as a flight attendant."

The speed with which Vicky turned her head—the sudden intensity with which she asked, "Is that so?"—confirmed Edgecomb's instincts.

"Not really," he confessed. "I just wanted to keep you on your toes."

"You haven't changed one bit," said Vicky.

She eased the convertible to the curb in front of his apartment complex. It was well after midnight, but the lights burned tenaciously in Edgecomb's living room. Vicky reached over the gear shift and squeezed his forearm again—this time grazing the exposed flesh of his wrist. "Call me when you decide. You've got my number," she said. "If you say yes, by the way, you'll get to see a lot more of me…In case you need any extra incentive."

At eighteen, he'd have caved on the spot. At twenty-eight, he recognized the importance of holding back—not necessarily running in the opposite direction, but also not letting himself be dragged to parts unknown with a hook through his lip.

"I'll think it over," he promised. "I'll call you."

"You do that," she said. "And in case it's not obvious, what we've talked about is for your ears only. Open mind, closed mouth. Got it?"

"Open mind," he echoed. "Closed mouth."

A moment later, he stood alone on the sidewalk. All that remained of the auburn beauty was the warmth of her fingers on his skin.

~

As much as Borrelli had irked him earlier, Edgecomb was now glad to find his housemate awake: He felt as though he needed a debriefing after his tryst with Vicky, and for all of his shortcomings, the guy had a knack for listening—at least, once you could actually get him to pay attention. As for keeping an open mind and shut lips: well, he didn't plan on blabbing about Vicky's investigation to the media, but he also felt no obligation to haul around a cradleboard of secrets on his back.

"That was a quickie," chimed Borrelli. "I hadn't expected to lay eyes on you again tonight."

His housemate still lounged in the living room, sprawled out on the sofa clad only in his undershorts, eyes glued to a women's figure skating event on the television. The event featured scantily clad performers. Blasphemous drawings remained scattered over the carpet. An assortment of crushed aluminum cans—both soda and beer—littered the coffee table. Sevastopol, fortunately, was nowhere to be seen.

"It wasn't like that," said Edgecomb.

He retrieved the remote control and shut off the TV.

"Come on, dude. I was watching that."

"Whatever. I want to talk." Edgecomb pushed Borrelli's feet off the sofa and squeezed onto the corner cushion. "I just had the strangest interaction of my adult life."

"Keep it to yourself, bro. I'm glad you found a kinky babe, but I don't want to hear about it," said Borrelli. "Unless you have pictures."

"Enough, okay," Edgecomb ordered. "For the last time, nothing sexual happened between me at Vicky. She works for the Treasury Department. She's investigating the Surrender Appomattox people."

Vicky's credentials perked up Borrelli. "Treasury Department, dude. That's serious. Like an ATF agent?"

"ATF?"

"Alcohol, Tobacco, and Firearms."

"Nope. HDC."

Borrelli raised his eyebrows.

"Historical Denial Cults," Edgecomb explained, pleased to know an abbreviation that his housemate apparently did not. "The Civil War deniers are the most dangerous, but there are others. Women's Suffrage deniers. Watergate deniers. Some wacko in Kentucky who thinks the Kennedy Assassination was a hoax."

"I've read about him," interjected Borrelli. "Weird dude."

"Anyway," continued Edgecomb, "they're investigating Royster."

He related the details of his encounter with Vicky Vann, holding nothing in reserve, but offering his housemate a version of the romantic backstory that made him look slightly less pathetic. Borrelli appeared fully focused on his narrative, although he kept twirling an unlit joint between his fingertips while he listened. Edgecomb concluded the story by sharing how he'd duped Vicky with the remark about his sister's job.

"Ballsy move, dude," said Borrelli.

"I guess. Anyway, what do you think?"

"I think that is one strange fucking interaction."

"Yeah. But what should I do about it?"

"That depends on your goal," answered Borrelli. "Are you still looking to hook up with this Vicky chick?"

"No. I mean, I don't know. But what does that have to do with anything?"

"What *doesn't* it have to do with anything, dude?" his housemate asked. "Would you really be considering this if you didn't still have a thing for Miss HDC agent?"

Borrelli had a point. If he hadn't been carrying a torch for Vicky all of these years, he'd likely never have considered infiltrating Royster's operation. Despite his moment of bravado at the Board of Education meeting, and his track record of high school chicanery, he was by nature a rather risk adverse creature. Cloak-and-dagger escapades didn't intrigue him—they intimidated him. But Vicky was the sexiest human being he'd ever come across in his entire life. Maybe not as "hot" by conventional standards as Calliope Chaselle, but inscrutable in a way that made her mesmerizing.

He couldn't help wondering what percentage of life's choices, even of history's momentous decisions, stemmed from lust or romantic longing. For all we knew, Caesar had really crossed the Rubicon to rendezvous with some peasant girl from the Roman Campagna. And maybe a pack of lovelorn Druids had constructed Stonehenge to win back their mistresses. Why not? What else but love or sex or some combination of the two could motivate men to quarry boulders and lug them to the midst of nowhere? So who was to say Lincoln didn't pen the Gettysburg Address to impress a Pennsylvania war widow? Hadn't Helen's face launched one thousand ships? Of course, knowing that you were driven by base motives didn't reduce the power of those motives.

"Here's what I would do if I were you," said Borrelli. "I'd hold off for two days before you answer. The longer you wait, the more power you've got. In that case, if you do decide you want to hook up with the chick, the option is still on the table."

Edgecomb doubted that after nine years, two more days was going to make much of a difference, either way. "I'm not into games," he said.

"Not games. Tactics, dude. *Huge* difference." Borrelli looked wistfully at his joint, but their house rules prohibited toking in the living room. "Now can I get *your* advice on something, Teach?"

"Sure," he agreed, surprised that Borrelli sought his opinion.

"Were you serious when you said you were nervous that someone might try to kill me over the coloring books? Or were you just exaggerating?"

Borrelli's tone lacked its usual nonchalance; he sounded genuinely concerned.

"Dead serious," said Edgecomb. "Why? You reconsidering?"

"Not exactly. Here's the thing. I set up a website this morning, hoping to test the waters of the market, maybe drum up a few advance sales." Borrelli climbed off the couch and vanished into the kitchen as he spoke, returning a moment later with another six pack of Budweiser. "So this dude in Texas, some sort of minister, emails me an hour later offering to buy ten thousand units. You heard that right, Teach. *Ten thousand* goddam 'Color the Prophet' coloring books."

Borrelli offered Edgecomb a beer and flipped open one for himself.

"He must have a lot of children," mused Edgecomb.

"If only. The dude doesn't plan on giving them to children. What the dude wants to do is build a giant bonfire."

"Jesus," said Edgecomb.

"You know what the dude said to me on the phone? He said, 'I ain't interested in coloring no false prophets. I'm interested in *burning* false prophets.' So I took his money, but now I'm thinking that was a mistake."

"Can't you just cancel his order?"

"Too late. I already used the funds to make a down payment on a bankrupt printing workshop in Jersey City. Everything came together much faster than I expected. So basically, I owe this dude eighty grand that I don't have."

"Jesus-fucking-Christ," said Edgecomb. "That was *definitely* a mistake. But I don't see why you need advice. It sounds like you've already made your decisions."

"Okay. Maybe not advice, Teach. I guess all I really want is some reassurance that nobody's going to run my car off the road or firebomb my apartment."

"*Our* apartment."

"Yeah. Our apartment." Borrelli took a swig of beer. "So tell me the truth, Teach. Do I really need to lose sleep over this?"

"I don't know what to tell you," said Edgecomb, rising from the sofa. "Should you be worried? If I were in your shoes, I'd be getting massive plastic surgery and applying to the witness protection program."

"Thanks, Teach. Very reassuring."

"Not a problem," said Edgecomb. "And thank *you* for the advice on Vicky."

But as much as he doubted Borrelli's judgment, he decided to wait forty-eight hours before giving his onetime crush an answer.

~

Sally arrived on time to class the next day, but the girl afforded Edgecomb no opportunity to resist her aggression. On the contrary, Royster's daughter played the model student, taking diligent notes, salting away any objections. About halfway through his comparison of Union and Confederate military strategies, as he drew a chalk map of the Southern coastline to illustrate the scope of the navy's "Anaconda" blockade, Sally raised her hand. He expected her to insist that such a sea cordon would have been impossible to implement, or even to question the very existence of its originator, General Winfield Scott; instead, smiling coyly, she asked for leave to visit the restroom. Although such a request was superficially benign, Edgecomb understood it for what it was, yet another affront to his authority, even if he couldn't have voiced precisely how. "Since when do you need my permission for that?" he demanded.

"Is that a yes?" asked Sally.

"Do what you have to do," he answered, returning to his map. But she'd accomplished her purpose; he'd lost his train of thought. After ransacking his memory, and filling his sketch of the Confederacy with extraneous details, he had to ask the class where he'd been when he'd left off.

"Winfield Scott," prodded Abe Kendall.

"That's right. Winfield Scott," Horace said. But even then, he couldn't conjure up anything else about the stuffy Virginia general that merited sharing. "Winfield Scott. Old Fuss and Feathers..."

Abe rescued him again. "General Lee..."

"Yes. Of course. Scott was too old to lead an army into battle—he suffered from painful gout and he couldn't even mount a horse, so Old Fuss and Feathers offered the command of the Union army to his gifted protégé, Robert E. Lee. Lee—as I imagine you are all aware—said no." He'd intended to share more, but Sally's return diverted his focus. Once again, he found that his next sentence had evaporated.

"Turn to your neighbor," he ultimately ordered, to save face. "Pretend you're Robert E. Lee. Would you accept Scott's offer and remain loyal to the Union or would you resign and fight for your home state? Take fifteen minutes to decide." For the first time in his memory, possibly since the torment of his own salad days in high school physics lab, Edgecomb looked forward to the class bell. Royster's daughter had managed to rattle him again—and he refused to tolerate any further distractions. He intended to put his foot down, he decided, once and for all.

"Sally," he called out as soon as the bell sounded. "Please wait a minute."

She'd heard him. This time, his eyes fixed magnetically upon hers, she couldn't pretend otherwise.

"Yes, Mr. Edgecomb?"

"I'd like to speak with you," he said—stating, not asking.

Edgecomb held off until the last of the other students trickled from the classroom. Only once the door had swung shut behind Maria Winch did the notion strike him that being alone with Sally might open him up to fabricated charges. But for all of her shortcomings, Sally didn't strike him as the type to cry wolf. Not at all. Like her father, she seemed a true believer, not some self-interested fraudster. The girl now stood between him and the exit, her messenger bag slung over her shoulders, waiting.

"You wanted to speak with me?" she prompted.

"Yes, I did. What happened this afternoon *cannot* happen again."

"I'm not sure what you mean."

"I am rather sure you do, Sally," he said. "You should have noticed by now that I treat all of you like mature adults. How old are you, Sally? Seventeen?"

"Eighteen."

"Eighteen. An adult—at least, in the eyes of the law. So as I was saying, you may have observed that your peers have been visiting the restrooms for the past three weeks without seeking my blessing."

"Would you rather I had just walked out?" she asked. "After what happened the other night? I'm sorry, Mr. Edgecomb, but you'd have assumed that I'd stormed off in protest…Honestly, you'd have reported me to Dr. Foxwell's office."

She had a point—he had to admit that. And she'd thrown him off course again by being of legal age, even though that was obviously beyond her control. Could she have interpreted his inquiry as somehow sexual? Suddenly, the realization dawned upon him that he was alone with a teenage girl, talking about bathroom breaks, and the tips of his ears started to singe. He feared he might be blushing.

"Anything else?" asked Sally. "Mr. Edgecomb?"

"One more thing," he said. "I'm an easygoing guy, Sally. But that doesn't mean I'm a pushover. You'll interpret my kindness as weakness at your own peril."

He regretted the words as soon as he said them; it was the kind of warning one might offer to a provocative girlfriend, but not to a student. Sally bit her lower lip, clearly uncertain how to respond to his peculiar admonition.

"I have to go home now," she finally said. Royster's daughter sounded like the schoolgirl that she was—flustered, even a bit nervous. "Bye."

And soon Edgecomb stood alone in the classroom, before his hand-scrawled map of the Confederate seaboard, feeling ridiculous and old. Very, very old.

~

Edgecomb drove straight from school to his sister's. At thirty-five, to commemorate her passage into advanced maternal age, Jillian had purchased a vinyl-sided duplex in an up-and-coming section of Gripley Township, and she'd furnished her new dwelling in anticipation of her prospective family. An unused playpen sagged in the living room, weighed down with plush toys; a crib lay waiting beside Jillian's bed. She'd even placed corner-guards on the end tables to shield her hypothetical future child from injury, and plugged plastic covers into the outlets to prevent electrocutions. On the living room walls hung posters for the various nations that might supply her with a son or daughter: Ethiopia, Liberia, Sierra Leone. Edgecomb suspected the adoption-themed décor scared away whatever romantic prospects that his sister might otherwise have, though he had the good sense not to offer her relationship advice. Jillian was an intelligent, attractive woman, after all, albeit more neurotic that the average asylum inmate, yet the only man she'd dated seriously in recent memory has been a disbarred matrimonial attorney who, at age fifty-eight, claimed he "still wasn't ready" to have children. To further inflame Jillian's fear that life had passed her by, the twenty-something couple next door was raising triplets.

Edgecomb genuinely felt for his sister; he just didn't believe that anything he said or did—at least, anything short of shooting up a daycare center—was likely to damage her prospects on the adoption market. But she was distraught over his School Board performance, so distraught that she'd left him several phone messages consisting only of sobs, and he cared about her too much to leave her in such emotional distress for more than a short time. He had come to her home turf to console her, although on the phone she'd assured him that she was inconsolable.

Jillian greeted him wearing only her threadbare bathrobe. She had a towel wrapped around her hair and carried a mug of hot chocolate. "I called in sick," she explained. "I couldn't handle my students in this condition. My nerves have just been on fire."

"You should see someone," urged Edgecomb—as he always did.

"That's a brilliant idea. Because international adoption agencies love placing kids with mental patients." Jillian pantomimed picking up a telephone receiver and added, in a mock-Senegalese accent, "I believe she would be acceptable, Fatou. Our preference would have been for documented psychosis, augmented with an inpatient admission or two, but she does appear to be sufficiently troubled."

"If you ever change your mind," replied Edgecomb, ignoring her sarcasm, "I can have Oliver find you some names." His college roommate had become a neurologist. "As your brother, I feel I have a duty to keep offering."

He set about the complex ritual involved in entering Jillian's residence: removing his sneakers and securing them inside a plastic bag, then scrubbing his hands at the stainless steel industrial sink in the kitchen, each step under his sister's watchful gaze. She also inspected his clothing—front and back—for bedbugs. All it took was one bedbug, she'd explained, to drive a social worker from the premises in horror. When Edgecomb finally settled onto his sister's sofa, he felt as though he'd passed through the security checkpoint at an Israeli airport.

"Are you still upset at me?" he asked.

Jillian remained standing. "That would be an understatement," she said. "I'm *beyond* upset. Why it is so hard for you to keep your name out of the papers? Don't you want to have nieces and nephews?"

Edgecomb often wondered how she'd have responded had he told her the truth: Nieces and nephews were not his be-all and end-all—not at the moment. He didn't doubt that he'd enjoy throwing around a whiffle ball with Jillian's offspring someday, or quizzing the children on the names of the state capitals, as their own late father had done, but why should he worry whether that occurred in two years' time or in ten? If Jillian hoped to have biological children, he might have understood her urgency—but not when she planned on importing the kids readymade from another continent. Wasn't one of the major selling points for adoption that you could stave off responsibility? All he said was, "I didn't *mean* to get my name in the papers. It just happened."

"Do you understand how hard it is to secure a placement these days?" demanded Jillian. "Vietnam won't consider single women. Guatemala is closed indefinitely. Uganda now requires three years of residency. Three *years*. *I* shouldn't have to move halfway across the planet just because *you* like getting into public arguments."

As though to punctuate Jillian's frustration, an explosion shook the entire building at its foundations. And then another. Glassware rattled in the cabinets; a children's pop-up book tumbled from the coffee table. The chandelier in the dining room swayed violently, as though caught up in a squall at sea. Only once before had Edgecomb been exposed to such clatter and roar at close range: during a reenactment of the Siege of Petersburg, Virginia, that he and his roommate, Oliver Nepersall, had witnessed on a college road trip. The series of detonations lasted a full ten seconds, possibly the longest ten seconds of Edgecomb's adult life.

"What the hell was that?" he cried.

"Blasting," Jillian answered without a hint of concern. She'd seated herself on the couch and drawn her legs into a lotus position, holding her back as straight as a ship's mast. "They're extending the Interstate so it connects with the Parkway. It was irksome at first, but I hardly notice anymore."

"You are too much." Edgecomb braced himself for another blast, but the room remained still. "Jesus Christ, Jillian. Do you really believe a social worker is going to be more afraid of bed bugs than dynamite?"

His sister sighed. "Don't you think I've considered that? I have a letter from the Department of Transportation assuring me they'll be finished by June—which is long before I'll get a placement. In the interim, any case worker worth her salt will be able to understand that some things are simply beyond my control."

And maybe I'm one of them, thought Edgecomb. *Maybe I'm more like a stick of dynamite than a bedbug.*

"Look, Horace. I'm making progress," said Jillian. "Three agencies have approved my initial paperwork. I already have a home visit set up for next month. Gears are turning." She lowered her voice and locked her gaze on his. "I'm going to ask you for only one thing. Please don't get arrested. Okay?"

Edgecomb flashed a smile. "I'm not planning on it."

"Seriously, don't. I'll to have to fill out a criminal history for anyone the child is likely to come into frequent contact with, and that includes you." Another blast rattled the room—this one muffled, as though occurring deep underground. Jillian ignored it. "I've given up on you not getting into any public arguments. If you're going to shout at that Royster person, I've made my peace with that. Just don't hit him."

"When was the last time I hit anyone?"

"You know what I mean. I'm speaking metaphorically."

Edgecomb decided this wasn't a wise occasion to mention Sebastian Borrelli's coloring books. "Do I have a surprise for you!" he announced. "A good surprise. Not only am I *not* going to take a swing at Roland Royster, I am not even going to argue with the man. In fact, I'm going to befriend him."

"I don't need you to mock me, Horace. I can feel crummy without your help."

"Nobody's mocking you. I swear. I'm planning to bury the hatchet with Royster."

And then he revealed the details of his encounter with Vicky, in spite of her warning about secrecy, explaining both her proposal and his intention to accept. "At least, I *think* I'm going to accept. I'm waiting until tomorrow to give her an answer."

He hadn't actually decided to accept Vicky's proposal until that very moment—but sharing the scheme with his sister had convinced him. Why did his motives matter? The bottom line was that he'd be serving a good cause, helping to bring down a pernicious threat to everything that he held dear. "I realize having a Civil War denier for a brother might not look so great either, but it's only temporary," he added, suddenly aware that he had no idea how long his infiltration might last. "This way, at least, I won't be hitting anyone. And even if I do, the Treasury Department will have my back."

Jillian's features turned sour, as though she'd swallowed too much mouthwash.

"Do you want to know what I think?" she asked.

"I don't know. Do I?"

"I think women take advantage of you," said Jillian. "I still remember what Vicky was like in high school. She trampled all over you. And let's face it, little brother, she's not the only one. Honestly, you're too eager to please."

"So what are you saying? That I *shouldn't* bring down Royster?"

"I'm not saying that at all. What I'm saying is that Vicky Vann is going to keep using you as a human doormat until you show her some backbone."

Edgecomb wanted to argue—to defend himself—but he wasn't too sure that his sister was wrong. Yet did it really matter if women like Vicky melted his resolve? So he was 'eager to please'—which he preferred to think of as 'accommodating.' Far better, he assured himself, than being an obstinate prick. Yet Jillian had a point. Some days it felt as though obstinate pricks possessed all the romantic luck.

"Thanks for the advice," he said. "I'll take it under advisement."

"I don't want to be hard on you," answered Jillian. "But women can be mean. Especially pretty women. The sooner you accept that, the happier you'll be."

She was right, of course. But there lay love's tragic paradox: knowing that Vicky was taking advantage of him didn't make him like her any less.

~

He met up with Vicky at the Amberly County Aquarium two days later. She'd offered no explanation for why she'd asked to rendezvous surrounded by whales and walruses, but Edgecomb suspected this choice to be yet another attempt by his ex-crush to cloak-and-dagger herself in the trappings of mystery. Not that he particularly minded. Strolling together alongside the tanks of colorful Amazonian fish, the late afternoon breeze carrying the bark of frisky seals, the squealing of rambunctious children, and the briny musk of low tide on Barnegat Bay, his encounter with Vicky felt almost like a date. Once again, he sensed the urge to reach for her hand, but he didn't dare.

"So I assume you're on board," said Vicky, when they'd meandered to an under-trafficked section of the food plaza beyond the polar bear island. "If you were turning us down, you could have done that over the phone."

"Maybe I wanted to string you along," suggested Edgecomb.

"It's possible. But I don't think that's your style."

"Is that your opinion or the Treasury Department's?" he asked. A perverse urge now made him want to reject her offer—just to prove her wrong.

"Both," she replied with a cheeky smile. "My opinion *is* the Department's"

Edgecomb didn't know if she was telling the truth in this regard—and, if so, whether she formed her opinions to match those of her bosses, or vice versa. Alternatively, Vicky could be just flirting for its own sake. They moseyed toward an empty iron table, the encircling bench painted a tacky shade of azure. Overhead, a phalanx of Canada geese honked its way northward.

Vicky sat down at the table and waited for him to speak. He didn't doubt that she could wait him out for an answer—into the next day if necessary.

"Okay. You got me," he agreed. "I'm in."

"I figured as much," said Vicky, disappointing him with her tenor of presumption and indifference. "Welcome to Operation *Damnatio Memoriae*."

"Operation what?"

"*Damnatio Memoriae*. Condemnation of memory," explained Vicky. "The Romans used to punish traitors by banning their names from history forever. Of course, we're using it ironically."

"You couldn't go with something simpler? Maybe in English?"

Vicky bristled. "The director of HDC was a promising classics scholar before he joined Treasury, just so you know. Nobody else has a problem with the project name. Why is your first reaction always to criticize?"

"Sorry," he apologized, surprised at her sudden ire. "*Damnatio Memoriae* it is."

"Good. We're all on one team," said Vicky. She glanced around to make certain that nobody was eavesdropping, and added, "I realize this may all seem like low stakes to you, Horace, but it's not. Trust me: the government doesn't conduct investigations of this scope and magnitude without its reasons."

"And those are…?"

Vicky shook her head. "I can't say."

"You can't say because you're not at liberty to tell me?" he pushed. "Or because you don't know yourself?"

If he'd hoped to provoke her into divulging her secrets, he appeared to have failed. Vicky merely shrugged. "Your job will be to convince Royster you're on his side and to gather whatever information you can on his intentions," she said. "You'll report back to us as often as you think necessary, based upon your progress. Just phone. Unless I'm travelling, I can be at your doorstep in six hours, tops." Vicky tossed him a wink, and added, "Of course, the more information you have to share, the more frequently you'll get to see me."

"Is that so?" he asked.

He'd intended to come across as flirtatious, but his words actually sounded hostile.

"Unless you'd rather have a different point of contact."

Vicky reached inside her purse and retrieved a laminated card. It read HORACE EDGECOMB, TREASURY DEPT, followed by a long series of digits and letters. "In case you get into trouble," said Vicky. "Just don't lose it."

"You really were confident, weren't you?"

"So confident we were willing to risk wasting three dollars on an ID card." She stood up and glanced at her watch. "Anyway, I should get going," she added. "Now that we're on the same page, I have a plane to catch."

Edgecomb hadn't anticipated a sudden departure. He'd expected her to arrive armed with files on Royster and his group, to show him grainy photographs captured with telescopic cameras, to reveal the details of a sophisticated network of saboteurs and double-agents hell-bent on revising America's history to its core. Vicky hadn't even told him why the authorities cared about Surrender Appomattox. He'd learned more, in fact, from twenty minutes of research on the Internet.

"That's all?" he asked. "Aren't you going to supply some deep background?"

Vicky laughed. "*Deep background?* This isn't the movies, Horace." She started walking toward the exit at a brisk clip. He followed. "It's better if you learn about Royster from Royster," she said. "Any information I give you will just be a burden. The truth is that it will just increase your chances of slipping up."

"But what exactly do you want me to do?" he asked.

Vicky stopped walking and spun to face him. Her auburn bangs glistened in the fading sun, adding an ethereal quality to her beauty.

"I already told you. Infiltrate his group. Learn what you can. Call me. How much more straightforward could this be?"

"But *how* am I supposed to infiltrate his group?"

"I can't tell you that, Horace. You're a smart guy. You'll know what to do."

Vicky's words still hung in the air as she disappeared into the mass of exhausted families swelling toward the parking lot. Edgecomb stepped away from the pedestrian traffic, retreating up the path to the cephalopod pavilion. A chill had settled over the aquarium. Edgecomb slid the government ID card into his wallet and settled onto the edge of a knee-high concrete parapet to think; when he glanced up, he found himself staring into the enormous, dopey eye of a massive squid.

~

The next day was Friday, which forced Edgecomb to make a decision: he could either approach Sally that afternoon—despite his trepidations—or he'd have to wait through the weekend for another opportunity. He still hadn't decided on a course of action when seventh period rolled around and he found himself face to face with Royster's daughter. The girl had taken to wearing provocative t-shirts. Thursday's announced "I think therefore I am dangerous;" today's read "Beautiful & Subversive." As Edgecomb reflected on the phrase, he realized he was staring at her chest, and he looked away quickly. For the next forty-five minutes, while his mouth paid tribute to William Lloyd Garrison and Frederick Douglass, his thoughts never veered far from Sally. His lecture meandered; the class looked bored. Even Abe Kendall glanced at the wall clock. At some point, Edgecomb sensed that he was undermining the students' interest in history altogether, and simultaneously damaging his own reputation. In flagrant defiance of Laurendale policy, he declared, "Do you know what the one good thing about the Fugitive Slave Act is? It will be exactly the same on Monday as it is today. We've all had a long week. It's Friday afternoon. Why don't you go home early and we'll pick up with Abolitionism after the weekend?"

Nobody moved. Louise Buxner's broad face looked up at him quizzically.

"Class is over. Go home," he said. "That means you."

This additional prodding was all that the students required; immediately, knapsacks began to fill and legs hightailed for the exit. Royster's daughter, always systematic, slid her pencils into their leather case and then folded her notebook shut. She'd already passed Edgecomb's desk when he decided to act.

"Sally," he called out.

The girl stopped walking and turned around. A few other students glanced in his direction, then proceeded with their departure. Royster's daughter shifted her weight from one leg to the other. Edgecomb forced his gaze to stay above her neck. He had no genuine interest in looking at her cleavage—she was only a kid, whatever her official age—but a self-destructive instinct kept willing his eyes in the wrong direction.

"I was hoping we could speak for a moment," he said.

Sally's features betrayed no emotions, but her hands toyed nervously with the clasp on her bag. "I really should be going…"

"Can you spare a few minutes?" he asked. "Please? I just want to apologize."

An expression of distinct unease spread across the girl's face; she remained frozen in place, as though mesmerized by his sudden transformation. The sounds of horseplay and catcalling floating in from the courtyard—a reminder that releasing his class early would likely bring down the wrath of the Sly Sandy Fox.

"I was wrong to be so dismissive of your beliefs," Edgecomb continued. "Even if they are very different from my own." He drew a deep breath and added, "Honestly, I wish I hadn't been so closed-minded."

Sally's features tightened again. "Now I see what you're up to," she said, her voice strained with latent anger. "You're in trouble, aren't you? Because of Papa's letter. And you're hoping that if you apologize to me, he'll drop his complaint."

Edgecomb winced inside his head. "You're not making this easy, Sally," he persisted. "I'm being sincere. It takes a big man to admit he's wrong—and I'm only five feet nine inches, but I'm trying to be that man."

His foray into humor must have surprised the girl; an inkling of a smile flickered on her lips. "You're really apologizing?" she asked.

"History is about questioning, not dogma," Edgecomb continued—hoping he sounded marginally credible. "I'm not agreeing with you. As far as I'm concerned, I'm right and you're wrong. At the same time, I should have given you an opportunity to explain your side." He lowered his voice and bit the inside of his lip so hard that he tasted the metallic flavor of blood along his tongue, afraid that his next words might degenerate to an outburst of laughter. "I'm ninety-nine-point nine percent certain that the Civil War wasn't a hoax. But ninety-nine-point nine percent isn't one hundred percent. You deserve a chance to persuade me otherwise."

Sally appeared flustered. The girl looked as though she might speak, but she said nothing. Then her pale cheeks turned a deep shade of crimson—and she glanced away rapidly. Even a man as dense as Horace

Edgecomb could often be, especially when it came to women's emotions, was unable to mistake what he'd witnessed: despite all of her intransigence and insolence, Royster's daughter obviously had a crush on him.

For an instant, Edgecomb felt genuinely bad for the girl, fearful that he might bruise her emotions, but then he remembered her father's pernicious performance at the School Board meeting, and his sympathy vaporized. *If she has a crush on me*, he thought, *so much the better.* Didn't a spy have an obligation to use any means necessary to achieve his goals—even if that meant breaking the heart of a teenage girl? Besides, he reassured himself, it was just a puppy crush. She'd shift her affections soon enough without having suffered any lasting damage.

"I need to catch my bus," said Sally—obviously lying, since he'd let her peers out twenty-five minutes ahead of the bell.

"Why don't I give you a ride?"

Edgecomb recognized he was treading on dangerous ground in his offer, but he did have the backing of the Department of the Treasury, didn't he? He even possessed an ID card with a cryptic serial number on it. Edgecomb promised himself that the federal government would step forward to defend him, although, deep down, his gut warned him that Vicky Vann and her Latin-spouting bosses would abandon him to the wolves at the first hint of negative publicity.

"Is that a good idea?" Sally blushed again. "What I mean is, is that allowed?"

"Maybe not," replied Edgecomb. "But I won't tell if you don't."

How much easier it was to flirt with a teenage girl, he reflected, when one's goals were professional rather than romantic. Being twenty-eight didn't hurt either. Yet as he led Royster's daughter across the teachers' parking lot to his Honda, he worried that one of his colleagues might see him. To his relief, since he'd ended class early, the lot was still packed with cars, but not people. A pair of underclassmen tossed around a football at the edge of the adjacent playing fields. Near the entrance to the lot, inches from the limits of school district property, a gaggle of denim-clad girls smoked cigarettes; fortunately, Edgecomb recognized none of them. He hadn't done anything wrong, of course, not legally, not ethically, yet he wished to avoid even the remotest appearance of wrongdoing. His shoulder muscles didn't relax until they'd pulled onto Blenheim Boulevard and advanced several traffic lights.

"Where to?" he asked.

"I live up in Laurendale Ridge," answered Sally, naming the most exclusive neighborhood of the already tony suburb. "Overlooking the water."

That meant they were traveling in the wrong direction. Trying to appear nonchalant, Edgecomb used their detour as an excuse to fill his fuel tank. He returned to Blenheim Boulevard facing the opposite lane, scanning the wayside for cops as he eased into traffic; as innocent as his relationship with Sally might be, he had no wish to get pulled over with a student in his passenger seat. They cruised through the village center, beyond the quaint, Tudor-style shops and the clapboard police headquarters, both aware that the very act of driving together was unequivocally transgressive. Not exactly a tour of Gettysburg and Antietam at gunpoint, but transgressive nonetheless. Edgecomb offered the girl a smile and, to his delight, she smiled back.

"So if you don't mind my asking," he ventured, "why do you believe the Civil War is a hoax?"

Sally's eyes focused upon him intensely, as always, but now her entire expression had somehow softened, her flicker of a smile lifting the tension from around her orbits, easing the strain of her jawline. "For the same reasons you believe it's not," she explained. "My father taught me one version of history and I imagine your father taught you another."

Edgecomb had wanted to know the *justification* for her beliefs, not the literal cause; he'd thought that had been obvious. But maybe the two were indistinguishable. He could tell that the girl wasn't being coy or evasive— at least, not intentionally. She'd genuinely sought to answer his question. Her sincerity struck Edgecomb as admirable, and this unexpected warmth toward his one-time nemesis surprised him.

"Actually, my father died when I was nine," he said.

"I'm sorry," said Sally. "My mother died when I was four, but I know that's not the same. I barely remember her."

So Royster was a widow, thought Edgecomb. He remembered his

own mother's grief after his father's burst aneurism, and, in spite of himself, he felt a twinge of compassion for the unhinged activist. But only a twinge. "I'm not sure which is worse," he said. "At least, I had nine years with my dad." Whether having such an intimate conversation with a student was appropriate no longer troubled him.

Edgecomb pulled off the boulevard onto Laurendale Ridge Road and Sally instructed him to make several additional turns. The foliage had already started to change colors, shrouding the hamlet's narrow lanes in vibrant hues of orange and amber and burgundy. As they approached the water, the homes grew larger, their distance from the street ever farther. By the time they arrived at the driveway to Royster's shorefront compound, only the chimneys of the residences protruded above the tree line.

Edgecomb pulled the Honda up to the entrance; a wrought-iron gate prevented him from progressing onto the property.

"Here we are," he said. "Door to door service. Almost."

"I suppose you wanted me to explain *how* I can believe that the Civil War is a hoax in spite of all of the so-called evidence," said Sally, clearly having stored up this remark until they arrived at her address. "But that's a discussion you should have with Papa. He's much better at convincing than I am." She smiled at Edgecomb again; it was a friendly smile, all eyes and lips—and, he conceded to himself, rather sweet. "Why don't you stay for dinner? If you don't already have plans, that is…"

"I don't have plans, but I do have a lot of paperwork to catch up on," he lied, striving to sound ambivalent. "Anyway, are you sure that's all right? It's such short notice…"

Sally didn't let him finish. "Papa will be thrilled. There's nothing he enjoys more than a good historical debate—as long as his adversary is open to persuasion." Now she was beaming. "Besides, Professor McNabb and Professor Herskovitz are away for the week—and the company will do him good."

"I guess I could have a quick bite to eat," agreed Edgecomb.

"Great," said Sally. "It's settled then."

And the iron gates parted, like the waters of a miraculous sea, controlled by a force beyond Edgecomb's sight or power.

CHAPTER THREE

Royster's driveway extended roughly a quarter of a mile, a two-lane stretch of rose-tinted pea gravel that looped between manicured boxwoods. They rolled up to a guard booth modeled on an alpine chalet, staffed by the same lantern-jawed protester who'd mocked Archie Steinhoff at the School Board meeting. The young man waved at Sally and raised the security bar, giving no indication that he recognized his boss's adversary. "Who's that?" inquired Edgecomb.

"That's Nigel," said Royster's daughter, as though the fellow's name was the only explanation required, or possibly permitted. Edgecomb didn't know how to learn more without appearing nosey, but he surprised himself with his follow-up question.

"Is he your boyfriend?" he asked.

"Nigel?" Sally sounded genuinely shocked. "He's my cousin."

"Just curious," replied Edgecomb.

They arrived at the head of the drive and he eased the Honda to a halt along the lip of the traffic circle. A replica of New York's Bethesda Fountain churned spray into the bracing dusk. The mansion itself, a sprawling brick structure with ornate columns and a wraparound porch, chilled them with its three-story shadow. Sally led him up the front stairs and through the unlocked double doors.

Edgecomb found himself standing in an oak-paneled foyer, beneath a crystal chandelier fit for an ocean liner. Marble busts lined the alcoves along both walls. The two sculptures closest to the entrance depicted Nicolaus Copernicus and the suffragette Emmeline Pankhurst, each identified by a nameplate stenciled along its base. The patter of Sally's boots echoed across the chamber—rhythmic yet delicate, like a percussion instrument powered by raindrops. Edgecomb wondered at the extent of Royster's resources. He felt acutely conscious of his own credit score.

"Hang out here for a second, Mr. Edgecomb," said Sally. "Let me go tell Papa that you're joining us for dinner."

She'd hardly taken a step when her father appeared at the far end of the gallery, under the massive arch, armed with a ceremonial walking stick. "What an intriguing surprise," Royster declared. "I was just thinking about you." His silver locks appeared ghostly as he advanced toward them.

"He's staying for dinner," said Sally.

"That's fine. The more the merrier," said Royster as he allowed Sally to take hold of his walking stick. Then he stopped in front of Edgecomb, placed his left hand on his guest's shoulder and extended his right hand for a shake. "Welcome, Horace, to my modest abode. You don't mind if I call you Horace?"

Edgecomb let Sally's father press his flesh—a firm, convivial greeting. "*Modest* feels like an understatement," he said.

"You're admiring my sculpture hall, I suppose," observed the host. "I brought these with me from Pennsylvania. All folks who spoke truth to power, if you will—Galileo, Thomas More, John Scopes. That's my favorite over there," added Royster, indicating a bald, bespectacled creature peering at his companions with dour eyes. "Maximilian Kolbe. Are you familiar with my good friend, Max?"

"I can't say that I am," said Edgecomb.

He feared, for an instant, that Royster might be luring him into an intellectual trap—but then he reminded himself that his *goal* was to let the madman entrap him. What better way to infiltrate the lunatic's organization?

"Maximilian Kolbe was a Franciscan friar deported to Auschwitz for hiding Jews during the Nazi occupation of Poland," explained Royster. "In order to deter escapes, the Germans randomly selected ten men to be buried alive in an underground bunker and starved to death. Max was not among the men chosen. But when another prisoner revealed that he had a wife and children at home, Max volunteered to take his place."

Sally's father gazed upon Kolbe's bust with admiration that bordered on awe—as John Brown, in his righteous madness, might have idolized a bust of Nat Turner.

"His offer," added Royster, "was accepted."

The gloom of the distant murder swaddled the chamber. Edgecomb had anticipated a wacky story, not a solemn one. He glanced toward Sally to gauge her reaction, but his student's expression revealed nothing.

"Max Kolbe put his money where his mouth was, as they say," said Royster. "He didn't set himself on fire like Thich Quang Duc or challenge an unjust society on a grand scale like Steve Biko and Nelson Mandela, but his small act of generosity was simultaneously an enormous feat of defiance—of empowerment. Even *you* will have to agree with me there's something admirable in that."

Royster's choice of phrasing—"even *you*"—put Edgecomb on the defensive, as though he might somehow be expected to view Kolbe's sacrifice as anything other than heroic. He suddenly felt that by acknowledging the act as admirable, which he obviously thought it was, he'd be making a reluctant concession.

"He was certainly very courageous," said Edgecomb.

"Indeed. And this wasn't merely courage for its own sake, but courage for a worthy purpose," said Royster, eyes wide, nostrils flared, his left hand still resting on Edgecomb's shoulder. "Can you imagine what sort of world we'd live today in if Thomas Jefferson had never stood up to George the Third? If Darwin had been unwilling to challenge the calculations of Bishop Ussher?"

Royster's voice had risen and his words echoed through the chamber. *So you believe Jefferson and Darwin really existed*, thought Edgecomb—but all he said was, "We're fortunate to have had such brave forebears."

Sally's father released his guest's jacket and pointed toward the far corner of the room. "You'll notice there's one figure missing from my sculpture hall," he said. "Eleven heads on the left, but only ten on the right."

Edgecomb had *not* noticed before—but there certainly was an empty pedestal opposite what looked like Mahatma Gandhi. He suspected the space to be symbolic, that it belonged to Harriet Tubman or Sojourner

Truth or some other hero of the Civil War epoch whose existence Surrender Appomattox disputed.

"That's where *my* bust will go," declared Royster. "Once I earn it."

Sally sidled up beside her father and kissed his cheek. She seemed charmed, rather than repulsed, by his florid narcissism. Royster eyed her affectionately, then flashed his guest a look as sharp as an incision. "Well, Horace? What do you think?"

Edgecomb wasn't sure whether Royster's question referred to the estate, or to the sculpture hall specifically, or even his mad plan to join the row of monuments. "Very impressive," he said, striving to sound vague, yet complimentary.

"You mean the opulence?" demanded Royster. "It's all blood money. Every last goddam dime of it." He glanced at his pocket watch. "Let's have a cigar in the study, and I'll tell you all about how the government butchered my wife."

~

Edgecomb followed Royster and his daughter under the massive Gothic arch and through a portrait-padded gallery into his host's study. This chamber recalled an early twentieth century hunting lodge, a room brimming with the sort of Papuan artifacts and Amazonian treasures that a wealthy adventurer like Theodore Roosevelt might have brought back from his travels. Floor-to-ceiling bookcases lined the walls; the remains of a grizzly bear lay before the hearth and a bull elk smiled benevolently over the mantel. Edgecomb examined the free-standing globe beside the harpsichord: it still divided the African continent between the Great Powers of Europe. What struck Edgecomb was how unremarkable the house appeared, at least for the estate of a wealthy family with poor aesthetic judgment. Nothing he'd yet witnessed screamed out cult or lunatic or even Civil War revisionist. Underscoring the semblance of normality, Royster's Rottweilers jumped from the sofa and nuzzled their master. Sally's father embraced the animals. He introduced them as Orwell and Santayana.

Edgecomb settled onto a loveseat whose upholstering suggested the hide of an ill-fated animal. Sally drew up a wicker rocking chair. Royster reached into the drawer of the end table and held out a humidor stamped *Habanos*.

"Montecristo?" offered Royster. "And perhaps a glass of cognac?"

Edgecomb declined.

"Suit yourself," said his host.

Royster savored the tobacco under his nostrils, then clipped the binder and perched the cigar between his teeth. He retrieved a decanter from the sideboard and poured himself a snifter of cognac. To Edgecomb's surprise, Sally also supplied herself with a cigar and an ample dose of brandy. Aromatic, amethyst-tinged smoke enveloped the study. Edgecomb wondered if he could be terminated for condoning the girl's drinking, even if it occurred in her father's presence. At the same time, something in the ease with which the teenage girl wielded the cigar struck him as downright sexy, in a transgressive, uber-tomboyish way, even as he struggled against this impression.

"As I was saying," said Royster, "blood money." He waved his arm dramatically to encompass the room, spreading smoke in his wake. "Your tax dollars at work."

"I don't understand," said Edgecomb, aware that he was being baited.

"How old are you, Horace? Thirty? Thirty-five."

"Twenty-eight."

"Twenty-eight," repeated Royster, drawing out the number as though it were a remote and exotic location. "At your age, I'd already been a widower for several years."

"I'm sorry," said Edgecomb.

"A widower," emphasized Royster, "with three daughters under age five."

Edgecomb realized he was feeling sympathetic toward his nemesis, toward the man who Vicky had characterized as extremely dangerous. If he was going to be an effective spy, he had to stand on guard against Stockholm syndrome, or even minor symptoms. He reminded himself that Royster's claims about his background, however poignant, might ultimately prove a constellation of lies.

"I met my wife in college," said Royster. "I was a junior at Columbia. She was a sophomore at Vassar. Kissinger was giving a speech at Cooper Union—he'd just released a memoir about the war—and we'd both gone downtown to give him hell. In the end, we couldn't get within a five-block radius of his limo. Luckily, Jackie got her sandal caught in a sewer grating and fractured her ankle, and nothing attracts a man like a gorgeous co-ed in need, so I helped her to a park bench and waited with her for the ambulance, and less than two weeks later, we were already screwing like rabbits."

I looked at Sally. She sipped her liquor, unfazed.

"Screwing like rabbits," Royster said again. "Come now, Horace, we have no secrets here. My daughter knows she wasn't delivered by a stork.

"Four years and three daughters later, we left the girls with my mother-in-law and drove down to Hampton Roads, Virginia, to protest against an ostensible reenactment of the sea battle between the Monitor and the Merrimac. That was long before I had a full understanding of the Civil War hoax, back when I was merely acting on the gut instinct that the official story didn't add up. You'd never imagine how naïve we were back then. Jackie and I both. When we couldn't find a document, or when two documents didn't seem to mesh, we'd actually contact the Library of Congress for help."

"And they weren't helpful?" inquired Edgecomb.

Royster's brow furrowed; he eyed his guest as he might a demented relation.

"We'd just started protesting reenactments, mostly to gain public attention. The authorities had no idea what to do with us—this clean-cut, twenty-something couple who wore World War I regalia to Civil War battlefields and carried placards that declared 'Vicksburg: A Convenient Fiction' and 'Revise and Dissent.' At the Hampton Roads event, we'd applied for a permit to sail our own vessel out on the water with an anti-war banner, secretly planning to storm the undefended ironclads from the rear, but the Park Service rubber-stamped a veto. Instead, they relegated us to a poorly-maintained dock behind the bandstand and the cannons."

Sally's father poured himself a second cognac and topped off his daughter's glass as well.

"You can guess the rest," he said—although, in truth, Horace could not.

"They launched the battle with a twenty-one-gun salute, all vintage ordnance. On salvo number three, the pylons beneath the pier gave way and the entire structure washed into the Chesapeake. Jackie went with it. When I came back from the port-a-john, all that remained was the jetty's skeleton and a handful of replica field pieces projecting from the shoulder-deep channel. I'll never forget the words of the 'artillery commander'—a grizzled old timer whom I later read had actually manned a howitzer during the Bulge. I came running up to the edge, where a handful of brass musicians stood ogling the horizon and relishing their narrow miss, and the commander mistook me for someone in authority and said to me, 'Only one casualty. Some lady went out with the current.' In an instant, my beloved Jackie had become '*some lady.*'" Royster didn't sound shattered, merely fatigued. "That 'some lady' cost Uncle Sam a six-million-dollar settlement—and let's just say I invested wisely."

Royster tamped out his cigar and leaned forward, his palms resting on the knees of his slacks. Edgecomb sensed the man had shared this story hundreds of times before, possibly thousands—and yet, in spite of this, the tragedy hadn't lost its raw pathos. Whatever one thought of Royster's current crusade, it was an awful story.

"I'm not angry. What good would that do? But when the person you care about most in the world pays a visit to Davy Jones' Locker because the Department of the Interior skimps on building inspectors, it changes a man." Royster chuckled as though privy to a secret joke. "It's so serious, it's actually hilarious," he mused. "Can you imagine how you'd react if you saw this story on television? 'Women protesting naval reenactment washed out to sea.' When it happens to someone else, it's funny. When it's your own wife, Horace, I assure you there's nothing funny about it."

Once again, Edgecomb felt challenged, as though Sally's father had accused him of finding humor in his wife's demise. He considered fabricating his own parallel tale of woe, of describing how he'd also had a relative swept into the ocean, but duplicity on such a grand scale simply wasn't in his nature. Besides, Royster struck him as the sort of man who did his homework; his adversary probably knew as much about his past as Vicky and her HDC colleagues did. Maybe more. A smirk cracked his lips when he realized that both of these groups might know more about his history than he did himself—and although he dug his fingernails into his palms to stifle his amusement, he feared that Royster took this as vindication that he'd been entertained by the death of Sally's mother.

He did not have a chance to defend himself, if he even could have done so.

At that moment, the lantern-jawed Nigel knocked on the study door and entered without invitation. "Sorry to interrupt," he said. "It's six o'clock."

"We dine at six o'clock sharp, Horace," said Royster. He turned to his nephew and instructed, "Can you ask Mrs. Keefe to lay out an extra place setting? Next to mine."

Sally's cousin gave Edgecomb a hostile onceover, as though he'd just now recognized his guest and found him wanting. Then he walked out of the study ahead of them, without saying a word, sucking all of Edgecomb's confidence with him.

~

Royster's younger daughters joined them at dinner, as did three other large canines named Voltaire and Carneades and Al-Ghazali. Becky Royster, at fourteen, already shared her sister's dark, seductive eyes and ample bust; Carly, a year younger, maintained the boyish look of a juvenile heron. The dining room itself lacked the formal austerity of the sculpture gallery and the earthy warmth of the study; the benign landscapes adorning the walls, and the bottomless platters of chicken and fish spread out on the sideboard, reminded Edgecomb of the sterile private rooms at upscale restaurants, in which, as a freeloader pretending to be a clinical neurologist, he'd heard his friend Oliver Nepersall delivered supper talks for pharmaceutical companies.

Royster presided over the meal with good cheer. Cousin Nigel, sullen and leery, sat at the foot of the table, alongside the swinging doors to the kitchen. Saul Nalaskowski, a rotund, bespectacled attorney sporting a ginger Van Dyke goatee, whom Royster introduced jokingly as his consiglieri, rounded out the company. "He looks like the devil incarnate, doesn't he?" asked Royster.

Nalaskowski guffawed. "More like the devil after he held up a Cheesecake Factory," the lawyer said, patting his paunch.

"Mr. Edgecomb here," continued Royster, "is curious about our mission. Is that a fair thing to say, Horace?"

"I'm trying to keep an open mind," agreed Edgecomb.

"What you're wondering, of course, is how any sane human being could believe that the most crucial event in our national lore—the cornerstone, if you will, of our historical heritage—is a complete and utter sham."

Edgecomb sensed the entire household focused his way. Nalaskowski's narrow eyes interrogated him as though he were a perjuring witness; the younger daughters inspected him curiously. His host, in no apparent hurry, sipped from a glass of red wine while feeding the Rottweilers Dover sole off the tablecloth. "I spoil them dreadfully," observed Royster, rubbing one cynoid head with each hand. "No matter what else anybody says of me, nobody will ever say that I didn't do right by my pups."

Baby Doc Duvalier and Idi Amin loved dogs, mused Edgecomb. Hitler too. He could easily imagine the Fuhrer saying, *Everything I did, I did for Blondi*, but he doubted Sally's father would have shared his amusement.

"Anyway," said Royster. "Since you want to know how I lost my marbles—how I ended up taking my young wife to protest against the Monitor and the Merrimac, I'll be glad to tell you." He nodded toward his daughters and all three, simultaneously, rose to clear the dinner plates. "You'll have to forgive my family if they're not exactly fascinated by this tale. They've heard it one too many times…"

"Just tell the story, Papa," interjected Sally.

"Very well. You can see who wears the pants around here." Royster divided one last strip of fish between the dogs. "It's a simple story. Anticlimactic, really. I was a senior at Columbia and I was taking an honors seminar in nineteenth century American history—I was actually thinking about applying to graduate school, as crazy as that idea now seems—and I just couldn't get my act together to write the term paper. I'd like to blame my procrastination on a sick parent or a debilitating illness, but it wasn't anything so dramatic. I was just hanging out with Jackie, and protesting against the Reagan Administration, and probably enjoying too much Jim Beam for my own good—and then one day the semester was nearly over, and I needed Professor Dunleavy's class to graduate, and I'd written a grand total of one paragraph for a research paper that had to be, at a minimum, thirty-five pages long. In short, Horace, I had screwed myself over big time."

Edgecomb mustered all of his sympathy, as he always did when one of his own students struggled to justify a late assignment; had he been Professor Dunleavy, he'd have afforded his host an extension. If Royster had truly required the credits to graduate, he'd even have given him a passing grade and asked for him to turn in the paper, on the honor system, at a later date. But Ian Dunleavy, Royster explained, wore his crabbiness like a Croix de Guerre. He saw no reason to temper justice.

"In the end, I panicked. The topic I'd proposed for the term paper had been about relations between ex-slaves and ex-slaveholders in the Piedmont of North Carolina, where I'd grown up—specifically, I'd wanted to find out if there were any slaves who'd remained loyal to their former owners in the post-war period. Unfortunately, I hadn't discovered any such relationships in my admittedly skimpy research." Royster leaned forward, his elbows resting on the tabletop. "So I made one up."

Royster paused and refilled his wine glass, topping off Nalaskowski's as well. The lawyer looked sated as a suckling pig, wanting only the apple in his mouth.

"I made one up," Royster repeated. "Whole cloth."

"In my paper, a private named Elijah Stout, who'd excavated ditches for the Army of the Tennessee, returns to Halifax County, during the height of Radical Reconstruction, and finds his former master facing execution for sabotage. In the final days of the war, Algernon Pickens—that's what I called the slaveholder—had attempted to derail an ammunition-laden train bound from Durham to Richmond. Because he'd done it out of uniform, and more likely because he posed the only formidable threat to the county's newly-installed Republican authorities, he'd been exempted from the general amnesty." As Royster related the story, Edgecomb found himself increasingly invested in its outcome—forgetting, for a moment, that the entire narrative was fictitious. "You should have read my description of the courthouse scene, as depicted in the local broadsheet, when Elijah stepped forward to provide his former owner with an alibi."

"I can only imagine," said Edgecomb.

"What you can't imagine is how anxious I was from the instant I turned in that paper until I received my final transcript. I was positive that Professor Dunleavy would expose me as a fraud—that he'd have me expelled on the very morning of graduation. Alas, in quintessential Columbia University fashion, I received an A-. Even then, I lived in terror that Dunleavy might eventually realize his mistake and have my diploma revoked. That's why I never applied to graduate school in history. I couldn't realistically expect to get admitted without a letter from my senior seminar professor, and I feared that if I asked Dunleavy for a recommendation, he'd take a closer look at the essay..."

"I suspect you're overestimating the conscientiousness of college professors," suggested Edgecomb.

"You don't know the half of it." Royster's face had turned florid in anticipation of his punch line. "Two years later, while I was at business school in Boston, I received the History Department's annual newsletter in the mail, and you're not going to believe the title of Professor Ian Dunleavy's most recent publication: 'Elijah Stout, Algernon Pickens and the Politics of Trans-Racial Forgiveness.' I was dumbfounded."

"Understandably."

"For me, it was far from understandable. Here was Dunleavy, a two-time winner of the Pulitzer Prize, ripping off my fabricated term paper. But that, my friend, is not the mindboggling part." Royster looked around the room, making momentary eye contact with each member of his audience. "I hightailed it to the university library and looked up Dunleavy's paper in the *American Historical Review*, and to my amazement, his work was far more detailed than my own. He cited diaries, cavalry dispatches. The article even contained a sketch of the courtroom drama that it attributed to the *Tarboro Tattler*. October 22, 1865. I'll never forget that date."

"So your professor was a fraud," objected Edgecomb. "That's disappointing. But it doesn't exactly disprove the Civil War."

"You haven't let me finish," replied Royster. "On a whim, I ordered *The Tarboro Tattler* on Microfilm via interlibrary loan—I figured that if Dunleavy ever claimed that I had turned in rubbish, I would possess hard evidence to throw the accusation right back in his duplicitous face...Only, it turned out, I didn't uncover any such evidence at all. On the front page of the October 22, 1865, edition of the *Tarboro Tattler* is a drawing of Elijah Stout testifying in the Halifax County courthouse."

"I don't get it," said Edgecomb. "What exactly are you saying?"

"I invented a story about some obscure Black soldier—made it up from scratch—and two years later, after a Pulitzer Prize winning historian published an article about that same soldier, I discovered that imaginary private had left behind a paper trail as thick as the telephone directory." Royster allowed Carly to slide a dish of strawberry shortcake onto the table in front of him. "I verified each and every one of those footnotes, Horace. Including the ones that I'd originally fabricated. Entire magazines I had conjured up from thin air suddenly had complete—albeit brief—print runs. Each last goddam reference checked out perfectly. You can understand my amazement."

Every inch of Edgecomb's being yearned to challenge his host. There were countless explanations for this strange episode, after all—most likely, Royster had heard the story from someone, possibly even Dunleavy, before "fabricating" his own paper, and had simply forgotten the encounter. But Edgecomb was now a spy, not a historian. His job, he reminded himself, was to be persuaded.

"That's a rather unsettling story," he conceded.

"Slowly, I realized that things didn't add up, historically speaking," Royster elaborated. "I'd read about the Union blockade or Admiral Farragut's capture of New Orleans, and I'd say to myself, that just doesn't ring true. How could a sprawling city of 170,000 surrender to a naval force of twelve vessels? At the time, I didn't yet understand the *how* or the *why*—but I sensed something amiss. Keep in mind, this was in the early 1980s, when we were still recovering from a regime that had deceived the American people about Watergate, and bombing Cambodia, and syphilis in Tuskegee, and just about everything else, or so it often seemed, so why not suspect that same government might lie about Gettysburg and Antietam too? Soon Jackie and I were conducting research of our own, trying to unravel myth from fact by pulling on the loosest strands, only it appeared that every strand—if you yanked hard enough—came loose. When we finally arrived at the conclusion that the entire war narrative was a sham—or at least the bulk of it was—we drove down to Hampton Roads to protest." Royster's voice softened and, for a moment, his gaze seemed to transcend the dining room. "I've already told you how that turned out."

"I'm sorry about your wife," offered Edgecomb. "Truly."

"Not as sorry as I am," rejoined Sally's father. "Jackie was twenty-six years old. So that's how *I* got here, Horace. What's not clear is what *you* are doing here."

"Like I told Sally, history is about questioning, not dogma," Edgecomb answered. "I felt that she—*you*—deserved a chance to make your case."

"I see. And have you been persuaded?"

Edgecomb glanced at Sally. The girl winked at him—a first. Whipped cream from the shortcake glazed her upper lip.

"Let's say I'm open to persuasion."

Royster pounded his fist against the tabletop without warning. Glassware rattled. The Rottweilers yelped. "Bullshit!" cried Sally's father. Nigel charged in from the kitchen, wielding a brass candlestick, obviously prepared to defend his uncle. Sally's cousin appeared genuinely disappointed that their guest hadn't gone on the attack. Edgecomb, for his part, experienced an urge to confess his espionage before Royster unmasked him—the sort of panic that he fancied had been the undoing of countless petty crooks. But then he thought of Vicky Vann; in the name of his yearning for her, he intended to endure whatever tortures Surrender Appomattox might inflict.

"Why are you *really* here, Horace Edgecomb? You don't happen to be in the employ of the HDC, do you?" Royster pronounced these letters with alarm-tinged animosity, like a veteran Cold Warrior deriding the KGB. "Or are you FBI? Because you can't possibly expect me to believe that you uncovered those seventeen-year-old municipal bylaws on your own..."

Edgecomb scoured the room for support, but found none forthcoming. Sally's smile had transformed itself into a scowl. Saul Nalaskowski rubbed his meaty palms together like a butcher preparing to tenderize beefsteak. The jig, it seemed, was up.

"Okay, you figured me out," Edgecomb admitted. He had no resort but to go for broke, to expose himself—and depend upon their pity. "I should have realized that I couldn't get away with it. There aren't any bylaws from seventeen years ago. That whole incident was also made up—fiction, just like Elijah Stout and Algernon Pickens." Edgecomb drew a page from his host's playbook and paused for effect. "I owe you a sincere apology. All of you. I had no right to subvert the democratic process like that. At the same time, if not for that deception, I wouldn't be here tonight at all."

"How so?" inquired Royster.

Edgecomb looked pointedly as Sally. "I told a bald-faced lie last Tuesday night—I made up a piece of history, albeit a tiny one—and everybody believed me. Archie Steinhoff, Phoebe Woodsmith at the Laurendale *Clarion*, even *you*. Nobody bothered to ask for a shred proof." As he spoke, his confidence mounted. "So I started to wonder, if I could make up history on a small scale, and get away with it so easily, what was to stop people far more powerful than you or me from manipulating the past on a much grander scale? I'm not saying that actually occurred. Don't get me wrong. All I'm saying is that what happened on Tuesday made me realize that such deceit was *possible*."

"So you're *not* HDC?" demanded Royster, sounding incredulous.

"What's HDC?"

"You really don't know, do you," said Sally's father. He massaged his chin thoughtfully between his thumb and index finger. "I suppose I'm the one who owes you an apology, Horace, but I can't afford to take risks. I've been burned too many times." He exchanged a knowing glance with his consiglieri. "HDC is a division of the Department of the Treasury run by a deranged bureaucrat who fancies himself a classics scholar. He's like Captain Ahab gone amok—and yours truly is his great while whale."

Royster launched into an account of his decade-long battle with Vicky Vann's supervisor—with Edgecomb's supervisor—which he described as a vendetta. "But the white whale wins in the end," he concluded. "Ahab goes down with this ship. And soon enough, my friend, HDC will go the way of the *Pequod*."

"You sound so confident," observed Edgecomb.

"Because I *am* confident," retorted Royster. "Six months from now, I'm going to have all the evidence I need to turn history—conventional history—on its head."

"Am I allowed to ask how?"

"You may *ask*," said Royster. "But that doesn't mean I'm going to answer. I can't divulge all of my secrets at once—especially not if you're still on the fence regarding so-called conventional history."

Edgecomb didn't remember admitting to being anywhere near any fences. *I'm open to persuasion*, was what he'd said. But if his host interpreted that to mean he was undecided, what right did he have to raise objections? The sooner Sally's father 'converted' him, he reminded himself, the sooner Vicky could foil Royster's cult—and he could return to the mundane pleasures of teaching. "You've given me a lot to think about," said Edgecomb. "What did you say the name of that article was?"

Royster clapped his hands together. "Sally, can you please bring Horace some literature for the road?"

Sally opened the cabinet beneath the sideboard and gathered several pamphlets from neatly stacked piles. Edgecomb sensed this transaction to be a well-worn and carefully-scripted ritual: Professors McNabb and Herskovitz of newsletter fame had likely received identical materials. These included the monograph of 'Elijah Stout, Algernon Pickens and the Politics of Trans-Racial Forgiveness,' photocopied sections from the *Tarboro Tattler* and a leaflet that asked: *What Did Happen If the Civil War Didn't?* Among the follow-up questions were: *Did Abraham Lincoln exist? Were African-Americans ever slaves, and if so, who freed them? How can the Civil War be a hoax when people occasionally unearth shell casing and cannonballs while excavating in their backyards?* A succinct paragraph addressed each puzzle. In spite of himself, Edgecomb felt genuinely curious to explore Royster's answers.

"Some light bedtime reading for you," said Royster. "If you have questions, don't hesitate to ask. Call anytime." He retrieved a business card from his wallet that read ROLAND G. ROYSTER, REVISIONIST and inked his personal phone number beneath his title. "All I ask is that you read through our literature and form your own opinions, free of any preconceived notions and received wisdom. Does that sound reasonable?"

"Very reasonable," Edgecomb agreed.

"If you are ultimately persuaded, and I do hope that you will be, a man like yourself would be of great value to our movement. I cannot emphasize this enough. After that performance last week, your credentials are impeccable. Can you envision what effect it might have if we held a press conference and you recanted? We could probably reeducate half the state at once."

"I doubt I'm that influential."

"Don't sell yourself short, Horace. You have an honest face. That alone will get you further than you'd imagine." Royster appeared as though he intended to say more, but he checked himself and rose from the table. He signaled for Nigel to retrieve his walking stick. "It was a pleasure meeting you," he said, extending his hand. "Sally, why don't you escort Horace to the front gate?"

"That's all right," countered Edgecomb. "I can find my way out."

"I think it's best if Sally accompanies you," insisted Royster, his voice calm yet determined. "We wouldn't want to risk you getting lost."

"Very well. If it's not inconvenient," conceded Edgecomb.

"It's not inconvenient at all," Royster answered for this daughter. "If you got lost, *that* would be inconvenient."

Nalaskowski nodded to Edgecomb and rose to follow his boss. Sally's father had already reached the curtain leading to the foyer when Edgecomb finally mustered the courage to speak. "Can you I ask you a favor?" he ventured.

Royster turned—his eyebrows raised. "Yes?"

"About that lie I told at the Board of Ed meeting—"

"You'd like it to remain our secret," Sally's father suggested.

"It was a terrible thing to do. I know that. But now that it's done, I could get into deep trouble if people knew I'd done it intentionally."

Royster waved off Edgecomb's concerns with a swipe of his hand. "You have nothing to fret over, Horace. Think about it. Why would I divulge your secret? You'd be of much less use to the cause if I did that. When you tell the world that you've reconsidered your beliefs, I want you to have as much credibility as possible."

So Royster was already banking on his conversion. The man's presumption galled Edgecomb, even if it fit his espionage goals to a tee. He waited for Sally to finish bussing the dessert plates, then let her lead him out to the Honda. The night had turned cool and crisp, flavored with the scent of fermenting leaves. Neither the drone of the road below nor the fog sirens from the harbor penetrated to the core of Royster's compound. Cracking this silence with an automobile engine felt like a sacrilege. They'd already passed beyond the sentry booth—now unmanned, with the security bar elevated—when Sally spoke.

"So what did you think?" she asked.

"Honestly, I think I have a lot to think about."

Sally laughed. "I guess you do."

The headlights sliced through the shadows of the boxwoods. Only now, as he departed, did Edgecomb sense the extent of his indiscretion—of the lapses heaped upon lapses: driving home a female student, making her blush, allowing her to wink at him without objection. While he'd done nothing truly unethical, boundaries were an area where appearances counted—sometimes even more than reality.

Sally rolled down the window; her hair fluttered in the draft. "We weren't so awful, were we?"

"I had a good time," replied Edgecomb—unsure himself of whether he was telling the truth. "You've got an interesting setup. I can certainly say that. And for a lawyer, your dad's friend doesn't say much."

"Nalaskowski? He doesn't need to." Sally passed her arm through the window and trailed her fingers on the breeze. "You know he sprang the Bare-Ass Bandit."

Edgecomb now recalled the attorney from the news: Royster's lawyer was famous for taking high profile criminal cases, usually those of defendants who'd undermined the social order in some flagrant way, and of winning by burying his opponents in paperwork. The Bare-Ass Bandit had terrorized New York City by holding up park-goers while naked and stealing their clothing. Nalaskowski, Edgecomb remembered, had filed four hundred motions on the first day of the trial—and threatened hundreds more until the DA hollered uncle at top volume and agreed to a suspended sentence. He'd also secured four consecutive mistrials for a New Jersey cardiologist charged with murdering his wife's lover—and subsequently offing six innocent strangers to mask his crime as a serial killing. Sally's father, it seemed, had found counsel worthy of himself.

They arrived at the gate. Once again, through some hidden mechanism, the iron arms parted. Sally opened her car door.

"Thanks for the lift home, Mr. Edgecomb," she said.

"Horace is fine," he replied on impulse. "I mean, outside of school, at least. It seems foolish for you to call me Mr. Edgecomb after I've just had dinner with your family."

"Okay, Horace," she agreed, testing her newfound power. "Thank you."

"No, thank you, Sally," he said. "Thank you for a lovely evening."

Edgecomb didn't register the nuance of the phrase until his ears heard it—and by then it was too late. He had ended countless dates with these same words over the years, only on those occasions, he'd rarely meant them. He hoped that Sally, who'd likely been fixed up with far fewer random partners, didn't yet know this drill. If she did, she didn't betray herself—didn't reach forward to hug him or peck him on the neck. Nor did the girl flee in panic. She merely smiled and said, "See you on Monday, Horace." An instant later, the car door slammed and he was alone.

On the drive back to Hager Heights, cutting through the stifling tranquility of the suburban night, Edgecomb couldn't resist second-guessing his interactions with both Sally and her father. Should he have confessed to fabricating the tale of seventeen-year-old petition fraud? he wondered, regretting giving his nemesis anything to hold over his head. Did Royster really believe he'd never heard of the HDC? He longed to unburden himself to a fellow human being, anyone not enmeshed in the quagmire of Civil War denial, but when he returned to the apartment, hoping Sebastian might serve as a sounding board, his housemate already had company. The sign on his bedroom door warned "LOVEMAKING IN PROGRESS; INTERRUPTIONS UNWELCOME." Sounds of mewing, feral and female, scratched at the plaster in confirmation.

A sudden loneliness, a yearning for connection, seized Edgecomb. He considered calling Vicky—he even removed his phone from its sheath—but he lacked the courage to dial. Not at two o'clock in the morning with nothing new to report. Instead, he climbed under the covers, flipped on the end table lamp, and started to read: *What Did Happen If the Civil War Didn't? If you are asking this question, you are not alone...*

SECOND SALVO

OCTOBER

CHAPTER FOUR

Edgecomb stumbled into the kitchen the next morning, drowsy and dazed, to find his housemate hosting a breakfast party. At one end of the table sat Borrelli's conquest of the previous evening, a flat-chested girl with fuchsia hair and a nose ring. She sported one of Sebastian's plaid shirts, the top three buttons strategically undone to reveal slivers of white breast surrounded by artificially-tanned flesh. At the other end of the table, hidden behind a Panama hat and reflective sunglasses, as though basking on a tropical veranda and not under incandescent panel lights, grinned the jovial schizophrenic, Albion. Between the pair rested a mountain of flapjacks. Sebastian, decked out in an apron and mittens, crooned "Daydream Believer" while drumming on a plastic colander with a wooden spoon. He broke off his singing long enough to urge Edgecomb to draw up a chair. "This exquisite angel is Esperanza, my new inamorata," he added, making introductions. "And that paragon of neuroses is Horace, my old flatmate."

"Remind me not to hire you as a PR person," replied Edgecomb.

Esperanza examined him suspiciously while he poured his coffee, and he wondered if she would recall their prior meeting. He thought he might stand in the clear, when a flash of recognition lit her ovine face, and she exclaimed, "I know you! 'Cottage cheese without a bed of lettuce.' You're OCD chick's boyfriend." The waitress appeared stunned by this realization—as though she'd never imagined Edgecomb and his sister existed outside the confines of the brunch shift at Mackenzie's

Dinette. Maybe it was her surprise that led her to say, more in curiosity than accusation, "I hope you won't take this the wrong way, but what on earth do you see in that woman?"

Edgecomb didn't know which irked him more—to have his sister mistaken for his romantic partner, or to be told that she was a poor catch. "I'm not sure what the *right* way to take that would be," he answered. "But I *can* tell you what I see in her."

"You seem like such a nice, normal guy," Esperanza interjected. "I don't want to suggest that you could do better—I'm sure she's a good person—but I just wonder how she doesn't drive you crazy. I mean, she drives *me* crazy, and I only see her once or twice a month." She turned toward Sebastian and explained, "Do you remember the nutso woman I was telling you about? The one who checks that the fire exits aren't blocked before she sits down to order..." When you emphasized her idiosyncrasies, Edgecomb had to concede, Jillian sounded far from a catch—and Esperanza didn't even know about the various times she'd insisted on *testing* the fire doors, like on their last trip to visit Aunt Pauline in Tucson, when she'd set off half the alarms in the hotel.

But as loopy as Jillian might be, he wasn't going to let Sebastian's plaything disparage her. "What I see in her," he said, "is that she's my sister."

"Oh," said Esperanza. "Oh, shit. I mean—well, I didn't mean anything..."

Sebastian appeared amused by the misunderstanding. He pried a flapjack off the stack with his fingers and gorged himself. Albion, seemingly indifferent to the exchange, slathered syrup onto his pancakes.

"I'm glad you didn't mean anything," echoed Edgecomb, driving home his point like a railroad spike. "Because my sister is one of the most selfless, compassionate human beings you'll ever meet." He was tempted to add that she'd already adopted a dozen African children with rare immunological disorders—which could explain why she disinfected everything compulsively—but he chose not to press his advantage. Besides, after the Board of Education meeting, he was wary of his own proclivity for deception. "Any man would be lucky to marry her. Even Sebastian."

"Geez, I'm sorry," apologized Esperanza. "I didn't know."

"Not a big deal," said Edgecomb, anxious to shift the discussion to his encounter with Royster. "I'm just very protective of Jillian."

"Jackian and Jillian," chimed in Albion, his eyes agleam. "Jackian and Jillian went up the hillian to fetch a pale of water," he recited. "But Jill forgot to take her pillian and now they have a daughter."

"Good one, dude," said Sebastian. "Have some more flapjacks."

It was beyond Edgecomb's understanding why his housemate encouraged the mentally-ill man's obscene repertoire, which ranged from limericks to knock-knock jokes to what sounded like pornographic Norse sagas. At other times, the schizophrenic blurted out a salad of meaningless phrases or cowered mute and motionless on the sofa for hours. Edgecomb never knew how much, if anything, Borrelli's friend understood; he certainly lacked confidence in the fellow's discretion. Nor, he realized, did he have any reason to trust Esperanza. Wisdom argued against revealing his visit to Royster's compound in front of either of them, but Edgecomb knew himself well enough to understand that he couldn't hold back. "I went undercover last night," he announced. "Got my first taste of whack-job counter-history from the inside. Wait until you hear what Kool-aid those Surrender Appomattox folks are trying to sell."

He had stayed up reading until nearly daybreak, simultaneous engrossed and repulsed by the group's literature. What struck him most about the organization's argument was its relentless consistency, its eerie and uncanny internal logic. To an audience with limited historical knowledge, and especially one already prone to distrust authority, Royster's theories projected an air of plausibility.

"You're going to have to tell me later," said Sebastian. "We're off to check out my new workshop this morning. To conduct some due diligence." He stood behind the waitress, massaging her shoulders. "Unless you want to tag along?"

On any ordinary morning, Edgecomb would have rejected his flatmate's invitation out of hand; he had no desire to spend time with Borrelli's motley band of inept compatriots, and he wished to distance himself as far from the coloring book fiasco as possible. But this was no ordinary morning. He longed to tell someone, anyone, about his foray into espionage, and he knew that if he didn't join the workshop outing, he'd end up on the telephone with Vicky Vann—a recipe for renewed heartbreak—so twenty minutes later, despite his misgivings, he joined Albion in the backseat of Sebastian's Dodge for the half hour drive to Jersey City. He was still deciding how much of his experience to share, when Borrelli assumed control of the conversation.

"Esperanza is studying normative prosopography," boasted Sebastian. "She's extraordinarily talented."

"I should probably know what that is," said Edgecomb. "But I don't have the foggiest idea."

"Studies of faces, dude. Specifically, she can tell when people are lying by examining the tone of their facial muscles."

"Can she really?"

Edgecomb had little patience for pseudoscience. At Laurendale, he'd fought—unsuccessfully—to prevent a local "clairvoyant" from setting up a booth at the annual student-run carnival.

"She's practically a human lie detector," asserted Borrelli. "It's not a foolproof method—not yet, at least—but she's pretty damn good. Want a demonstration?"

"Not now," the girl objected. "I just woke up."

"Please, baby, for me," begged Borrelli, tracing his fingers along the inside of his companion's knee to the hem of her skirt.

"I'm not that good yet," insisted the girl. "It's really as much an art as it is a science…"

"She's brilliant," contended Sebastian. "Here's what you do, Horace. You remember that party game, 'Two truths and a lie?' Well, I want you to tell Esperanza three things, but make them run-of-the-mill facts, like what you had for dinner yesterday. Only, one of them should be totally false."

Esperanza unfastened her seatbelt and shifted around to face him. Despite her protest, Edgecomb sensed she was thirsting to show off.

"Fine," said Edgecomb, rifling his brain for suitable statements of fact. "Here you go. Fact one: I'm left-handed. Fact two: I speak French. Fact three: I kissed Sally Royster last night." He folded his arms across his chest and waited for a verdict. "So? Which one's false?"

Sebastian's girl stared at his mouth with chilling intensity, as though she were about to perform a dental procedure via telepathy. Then she broke her gaze and turned again toward the front of the Dodge. "Your friend is a total jerk, hun," she announced. "So much for two truths and a lie. He's right-handed, doesn't speak a word of French, and whoever Sally Royster is, she's dodged a bullet…"

"You thought you'd catch her, didn't you?" demanded Sebastian.

Edgecomb looked out the window. They'd left the changing leaves of Hager Heights far behind and now plodded through a rundown, treeless quarter of Jersey City's warehouse belt.

"It's all in the facial musculature," explained Esperanza. "When you tell the truth, you primarily use the zygomaticus major and the levator anguli oris; when you're lying, you rely more heavily on the zygomaticus minor. The differences are subtle, but detectable. With practice. Sort of like how Pacific Islanders can train themselves to read ocean waves and see the wake of ships hundreds of miles beyond the horizon."

"It's how we met," added Sebastian. "I was parking downtown, opposite Esperanza's restaurant, and this well-dressed, elderly lady approached me and asked if I could loan her seventy-five cents for the meter. Said she'd forgotten her purse at home and needed to run a quick errand—offered to take my address and pay me back. I already had the coins in my hand when this genius charged up to me and cursed out the old biddy for running a con game. I was doubtful and first—but I asked the woman to show me her car—to unlock it for me to prove it was hers—and she stormed off instead." He patted his lover's knee. "Pretty awesome, no? It takes a lot of balls to accuse a well-dressed old woman of lying through her teeth."

"Balls! Bats and balls. Walls and balls," cried Albion. "There once was a man from Alsace, who had balls made out of brass—"

"Please," interrupted Edgecomb. "Enough."

A look of utter dejection seized the schizophrenic, like a deflated children's toy, and Edgecomb felt a twinge of guilt. But then the fellow grinned, entertained by some unspoken private joke. "Don't mind him," said Sebastian—and, for an instant, Edgecomb believed he was the one being addressed. But his housemate was actually speaking to the schizophrenic. "Old Horace isn't exactly Walt Whitman when it comes to appreciating great poetry."

Edgecomb chose to let the matter drop; what did he care if Sebastian took pleasure in mocking him to a man who'd twice eloped from a state hospital?

"Can I please tell you about last night?" he asked.

"Okay, but tell us inside."

Borrelli piloted the Dodge onto the sidewalk opposite a windowless, stucco-faced structure that might easily have housed a clandestine CIA prison. An aluminum board identified the building as the headquarters of "Show Me a Sign Printing." Ailanthus shrubs in various states of ruby and gold sprouted through cracks in the surrounding asphalt, and on the adjoining lot workmen in Tyvek coveralls milled around hillocks of smoldering tires. The air reeked of burning rubber. "I'm glad you've chosen a health-conscious neighborhood," observed Horace. His companions were too busy cloaking their nostrils with their collars to respond.

The inside of Sebastian's new workshop proved no more promising than the exterior. Its previous occupants, a manufacturer of Christian literature for Korean churches, had carted away every vestige of marketable equipment not spelled out by name in their contract—including the doorknobs on the manager's office and the faucet handles in the restrooms—leaving behind only a colossal printing apparatus and several placards of an oriental Jesus being crucified alongside a heading in hangul script. The previous owners even appeared to have carried off the batteries from the carbon monoxide alarm; every thirty seconds, the device issued a series of implacable beeps. Locusts could not have stripped the place barer.

"You paid money for this shithole?" demanded Esperanza. She rifled through the manager's office, yanking open empty drawers. "How high were you?"

"When is your friend in Texas expecting his books?" asked Horace.

"Sixty days," said Borrelli. "Looks like we've got our work cut out for us."

You've got your *work cut out for* you, thought Edgecomb. *This debacle has absolutely nothing to do with me.* Across the chamber, the schizophrenic also distanced himself from the project—standing only inches from the wall, his back to the room, and leaning forward so his nose nearly touched the plaster, as though holding an imaginary quarter in place as part of a cruel, self-imposed punishment. The girl had returned to the main hangar and draped her head on Sebastian's shoulder.

"So I had the craziest night yesterday," ventured Edgecomb. He described his dinner with the Royster household, omitting his sensitive moments in the car with Sally; he also didn't elaborate on the purpose of his espionage. His companions listened politely, although he could sense their lack of interest. Esperanza appeared more intrigued by the unflappable Albion, who'd started running his nose along the wall as though operating a metal detector through his nostrils. "But the wildest part was what's in the literature that the guy gave me."

"Let me guess. It claims the nineteenth century was Golden Age of peace and tranquility for the American people."

"How did you know?"

"I heard the guy on the radio, remember?"

"That's just the tip of the iceberg," continued Edgecomb. "The gist of Royster's argument is that sometime around 1880, greedy politicians and business leaders hatched the idea of inventing a Great American Civil War in order to build national identity and solidify their control over the populace. They hired dime novelists to rewrite history books and unemployed vaudeville performers to pose for photographs. Lincoln and Davis, Grant and Lee—all theater hacks—although in Grant's case, the powerbrokers ultimately elevated a former light opera veteran to the Presidency on the strengths of a fabricated army record.

"In a decentralized nation of small farmers, many of them poorly educated or illiterate, generating the legacy of the war was a bit like playing a giant game of telephone: as actors appeared in various cities, claiming to have served on the front lines at Malvern Hill and Cold Harbor, bystanders hopped on the bandwagon and boasted of their own military service. Who was going to stand up and challenge the stories of young men who claimed to have risked their lives braving Confederate cannonballs? Or had lost limbs on distant battlefields—even if, deep down, old-timers recalled those limbs having been sacrificed in adolescence to rusty nails and gangrene? Establishing statewide public education systems locked the hoax in place. Suddenly, every last grubby schoolboy in every last Podunk one-horse town from Maine to Florida had been indoctrinated with the heroic exploits of Billy Yank and Johnny Reb." Edgecomb paused for breath—still awed by the sheer audacity of the conspiracy that Sally's father proposed. "Royster genuinely believes all this," he concluded. "The alarming thing is how persuasive his ideas can be, in a perverse way, once you start from his premises."

"So you still aren't sold?" asked Sebastian.

Of course, I'm not sold, Edgecomb wanted to say, but then he glanced at Esperanza and recalled the purpose of his espionage. "I'm going to have to be sold soon enough," he replied instead, a cryptic response that he hoped sounded noncommittal. He concealed his mouth behind his scarf on the remote possibility that the waitress actually could detect his degree of veracity through his muscles.

"Royster's explanation is invincible. Anything you offer as proof, he dismisses as part of the conspiracy. And the stronger the evidence of the war, the stronger the evidence of the financial capital invested in maintaining that conspiracy. The linchpin of his hypothesis is that today's leading American historians and political leaders are still very much in on the plot—and they harness their vast resources to fabricate evidence on a massive scale."

"So let me get this straight," interjected Esperanza. "You're saying Abraham Lincoln was an actor?"

"*I'm* not saying anything. But that *is* what Royster believes. He claims that having Lincoln 'assassinated' by an actor at a play was actually an inside joke—that Lincoln, as an actor, had once starred in *Our American Cousin* on Broadway."

"And what about all those battlefields?" the girl asked—aggressively, as though the conspiracy theory was Edgecomb's own. "My aunt and uncle took me to Shiloh when I visited them in tenth grade. It looked pretty damn real to me."

"All built after the fact. By the same teams that constructed Central Park and Boston's greenbelt," he offered. "Here, let me give you a leaflet."

Edgecomb rummaged through his pocket for one of Royster's pamphlets. Esperanza accepted it with obvious reluctance.

"The best part is the section on slavery," he said. "It turns out that the slaves were all emancipated voluntarily in the early nineteenth century. Jefferson was right: The institution wasn't economically viable and died out of its own accord…"

Sebastian whistled. "Dude! You announce *that* at your next Board of ED meeting, and you see how long it is before we get firebombed. Who's going to care about a few coloring books when you're claiming slavery was a hoax?"

"Not slavery. Just the Emancipation."

"You sound defensive, Teach. I thought this was *Royster's* theory."

"Whole thing is deranged if you want my opinion," said Esperanza. "Can we get out of here, hun? You promised we'd just poke our heads inside…"

"Let me take a few measurements," agreed Borrelli, "and we're done."

His housemate produced a tape measure and calculated various distances around the workshop, churning up dust as he scuttled from corner to corner. Then he insisted on smoking "half a joint" before they hit the road back to Hager Heights. Esperanza and Albion each enjoyed a few tokes. Edgecomb politely declined. He offered to drive, but Sebastian refused to surrender the wheel. "I'm more focused like this," he insisted. "Honestly, my reflexes are faster." Unfortunately, his driving itself also proved faster, and they nearly collided with a telephone company truck on a blind turn.

Albion stared into the back of Borrelli's seat, his tongue now touching his nose, performing complex rituals with his thumbs. Esperanza rested her head in her boyfriend's lap, which certainly wasn't helping his concentration.

"Isn't normative prosopography amazing?" Borrelli asked, returning to their earlier conversation. "I wish I'd studied it in school. Far more useful than all that time I wasted learning algebra and history."

"And at what exalted institution of higher learning does one study normative prosopography?" Edgecomb asked, making no effort to conceal his disdain.

"It's called the Solomon Institute. They have courses at all levels," chimed in Esperanza. "They're always looking for good liars to serve as models, if you'd like me to recommend you."

"I keep telling her she can make a fortune at this," said Borrelli. "She could watch corporate executives discussing their stock prices at shareholders meetings, and she'd know whether to buy or sell...Or she could take up professional poker..."

"Thorn would *never* approve," the girl replied. "NP is a noble tradition. Not a party trick."

"Thorn?" Edgecomb asked.

"He's my professor," she explained. "He's also the Director of the Institute— although, technically, we're supposed to call him our 'recognition mentor.'"

Un-fucking-believable! It had to be the same guy. So Calliope Chaselle, the dazzling junior librarian who wouldn't give him the time of day, was shacking up with a man who operated a facial recognition cult. A surge of jealousy threatened to burn a hole through Edgecomb's gut. Not that he had his sights set on his colleague—not really. The woman he desired was Vicky, not Calliope. But Calliope *was* attractive, and she was *not* his, and this combination reminded him that Vicky Vann also was not his, that Calliope had Thorn, and Sebastian had Esperanza, while he, who didn't escape into a chemical haze, or engage in business deals predicated on blasphemy, or swindle waitresses with cockamamie tales of facial lie detectors, was nonetheless very much alone.

~

He did not phone Vicky to report on his infiltration of Royster's compound; he did spend the weekend thinking about her. At moments, his mind drifted to other women: Calliope Chaselle; Jillian's college roommate, Mariella, whom he'd slept with on cold winter nights at Rutgers; Amelia Quockman, his most recent ex, a blonde girl from Berkeley who'd insisted that she was a direct lineal descendant of Pocahontas. Even after he'd confronted her with a thick volume entitled *A Comprehensive Lineage of Pocahontas and Her Descendants*, ordered from the Pocahontas Society of Virginia, from which the surname Quockman was conspicuously absent, she'd refused to yield. Yet mostly he thought about Vicky, about how he'd sat behind her in their eleventh-grade physics class, and inhaled the honeyed scent of her hair without her noticing. Several times, he nearly broke down and called her to declare his feelings, but rationally, he knew the way to Vicky's heart wasn't through candid confession; rather, he'd have to complete his espionage mission and win her admiration. Waiting wasn't easy with the sound of Esperanza moaning obscenities each night through the walls of Sebastian's bedroom.

When he wasn't undressing Vicky Vann in his imagination, Horace found himself reflecting increasingly on his relationship with Sally Royster. Theirs wasn't a relationship in the romantic sense, of course, but the eighteen-year-old had suddenly become more than merely his student. What exactly they were, he couldn't say. Friends? Adversaries? Both? As much as part of him relished the girl's crush, another side of him recognized he had no choice but to deflect it. He'd have liked to unburden himself to his housemate, but the competition proved insurmountable. When he woke up on Sunday morning, Borrelli was already bivouacked in the living room, reviewing coloring book prototypes with Sevastopol. Seconds after the self-styled designer departed, a full twelve hours later, Esperanza had her thighs around his hips and her pierced tongue down his throat. Soon enough, she'd coaxed Borrelli behind closed doors, leaving Horace alone at the coffee table with Albion.

The schizophrenic flashed a set of decaying teeth. A perfectly curved scar graced his left cheek, as though he'd been carved with a melon scoop. According to Sebastian, the fellow had been a chess prodigy before his first psychotic break—as well as something of a ladies' man at Dartmouth—but both his genius and good looks had been worn away by decades of auditory hallucinations and hard living.

"So it looks like it's just you and me, Dr. A.," said Edgecomb. "What do you know about women?"

Albion's grin remained plastered on his thick lips; he eyes traced an imaginary balloon across the ceiling.

"That's as much as I know too. Maybe more," agreed Edgecomb. "How about the Civil War? You remember any military history?"

Again, the schizophrenic didn't seem to register his question.

"Do you want me to teach you?" Edgecomb persisted. "It's your choice. I can teach you the traditional version or Royster's version. Would you prefer that Abraham Lincoln was a mercenary corporate lawyer or a second-rate performer of Shakespeare?"

Albion looked up, but not on account of Edgecomb's inquiry. They both heard the staccato of Sebastian's headboard pummeling the wall. Somehow, asking about the teenager against this backdrop seemed unseemly. In any case, a pang of yearning for his evasive crush quickly derailed him.

"You're no help," said Edgecomb, standing up. "The bottom line is that either Vicky will fall in love with me or she won't."

"Vicky very tricky," rejoined Albion. "Sticky, sticky, tricky, Vicky."

"Have a good night sleep," said Edgecomb. "And thanks for the advice."

~

His mind still felt unsettled about Sally—not that there was anything to be settled, not that anything needed to be done at all—when he pulled into the faculty parking lot at Laurendale on Monday morning. To his consternation, Sandra Foxwell's husband arrived a moment later and deposited the Sly Sandy Fox between him and the path to the nearest entrance. The principal suffered from intractable epilepsy that prevented her from driving, but also made her an icon for local disability rights advocates—ensuring her survival through multiple school scandals, including the drunken prom episode and another in which a senior-class prankster barricaded himself inside the vice principal's office and read an explicit excerpt from *Lady Chatterley's Lover* over the PA system. She spotted Horace before he had an opportunity to hide.

"Mr. Edgecomb," she said. "What a coincidence!"

He despised the way she called him by his last name—as though they were postal workers or toll collectors compelled to feign respect by administrative rules.

"Good morning, Sandra," he replied, feeling bold.

He tried to glide past her—to ignore her provocation—but she ambled up alongside him. A cold front had passed through the previous night, blanketing the day with an early October chill. Squirrels, cheeks fattened for impending winter, hightailed across the grassy apron adjoining the parking lot as Edgecomb and Foxwell approached.

"Aren't you at all curious to know what the coincidence is?" she asked.

"I'm not a particularly curious person. It kills cats."

He picked up his pace. So did Foxwell. She accompanied him into the long, photo-lined corridor that connected the main wing of the high school to the gymnasium. A faint aroma of dried sweat clung to the linoleum. "I don't see any reason to be overdramatic, Horace," said the principal, as though shifting to his first name made their interaction any more intimate or welcome. "I'm not murdering any cats. But I am going to tell you why running into you this morning was such a coincidence."

"Let me guess. Because you were thinking of repealing the laws of gravity and you wanted me to design the lesson plan."

They'd reached the teacher's elevator. Edgecomb pushed the button and waited for the car to arrive. It was only ten minutes after seven, so they had the musty corridor entirely to themselves. Three weeks earlier, he mused, he'd never have dared to scorn his boss openly—but between his Jimmy Stewart moment at the Board of Ed meeting and his undercover work for HDC, he felt liberated as never before.

"I suppose that was a joke, Mr. Edgecomb," said Foxwell. "But this coincidence is *not* a laughing matter. I was looking for you, because I've had several reports that a female student accompanied you off campus last Friday afternoon in your automobile."

Her accusation set Edgecomb on his heels. He'd nearly forgotten about the trip home with Sally, so preoccupied had he become with their exchange on the brief ride back to the compound's gates. The Sly Sandy Fox positioned herself between Edgecomb and the elevator door, as though daring him to attempt an escape. His only hope, he realized, was to play the episode off as utterly incidental.

"Oh, that's all?" replied Edgecomb. "You had me worried for a moment. I was afraid I'd actually done something wrong."

"So you don't deny absconding with the girl?"

"I didn't *abscond* with her. I gave her a lift home. You're the one who asked me to make buddy-buddy with the Roysters."

Foxwell's glee evaporated. She obviously hadn't known the identity of his alleged victim. "I never asked you to lure any students into your vehicle."

"No luring occurred. I *invited* her. You told me to apologize to Sally Royster and that's precisely what I did." Edgecomb stepped around Foxwell and boarded the elevator; she followed him into the car. "In fact, I drove her home on Friday evening and stayed for supper with her father. Quite a character."

"I see," said Foxwell.

"I thought you'd be more enthusiastic," Edgecomb continued. "The truth of the matter is that I've been thoroughly persuaded by Royster's charms. So from this point forward, I'm going to teach the history of the Civil War his way. As far as I'm concerned, it's a glorious hoax until proven otherwise."

The elevator stopped at the second floor with a lurch. He held the doors so Foxwell might exit ahead of him. She did not thank him.

"Do you really feel the need to make a farce out of everything?" she demanded.

"I thought this was what you wanted. Didn't you specifically ask me to accommodate Royster so your friend Archie Steinhoff could avoid controversy?"

Foxwell appeared thunderstruck. "That was before..." Then she regained her composure and said, "I'm afraid the political calculus has changed, Horace. Ever since your started stirring up trouble, Arch has been inundated with press inquiries regarding his views on evolution, on Holocaust denial, on every controversial and divisive idea under the sun. This is far larger than Roland Royster now—just so you're aware of the damage you've caused. A lieutenant governor nomination isn't even on the table anymore. Not this cycle. At this point, we're trying to preserve his chances for next time around..."

Something in Foxwell's tone—in her abridgement of Steinhoff's first name to Arch and her use of the pronoun 'we'—suddenly clicked for Edgecomb. Sly Sandy's concern rang too intimate for a school administrator aspiring to become State Education Commissioner; his boss sounded like a mistress conducting an illicit affair. He possessed no proof, of course, but he tucked the information away, delighted to have an advantage, however slight, over the woman.

"I'll also have you know, strictly between you and *I*," said Foxwell, her voice lowered to a conspiratorial volume, "that Arch has a heart condition. Nothing too serious, mind you, but your monkey business isn't helping it any."

'*Between you and I*' was one of those overcompensation errors that made Edgecomb cringe; he didn't mind bad grammar, but he couldn't handle pretension.

"I had no idea," he said with a sardonic dash. "So you're telling me you *don't* want me to teach the Civil War as a hoax?"

"Exactly. That's the last thing we want you to do, Horace." She softened her voice again, as though they'd been lifelong friends. "I'm sorry about all this misunderstanding. But the past is prologue, isn't it? You go back to doing the excellent job you've been doing all along—and we'll forget this little dustup ever happened."

Edgecomb dished out his most sympathetic smile and continued to play dumb. "So let me make sure I understand. Between you and *me*. You no longer want me to teach my students that the federal government spent millions of tax dollars casting replica shell casing and burying them in the trenches at Petersburg?"

"Certainly not."

"And you don't want me to explain that the Gettysburg Address was written by a second-string pitch man for a Madison Avenue advertising firm?"

"Nothing like that."

"Nothing? Not even Royster's account of how the bodies of potato famine victims from Ireland were imported to fill caskets at Arlington?"

"That will *not* be necessary."

Edgecomb nodded as though he understood. For an instant, the pair smiled at each other, seemingly sharing a meeting of the minds. Anyone passing in the hallway might have mistaken them for the best of pals. And then Edgecomb laughed. He laughed so hard he feared he might shatter his teeth.

"Are you all right?" asked Foxwell. "You're not going insane, are you?"

"I'm fine. Just dandy." He wiped the tears from his eyes. "And I appreciate your concerns, especially where *Arch's* political career is concerned. But it's too late."

"What is that supposed to mean? Too late for what?"

"You heard me," he replied, keeping his voice matter-of-fact. "It's too late to return to my former ways of teaching, excellent though they might have been. It's too late to put the genie back in the bottle. You asked me to reach an understanding with Royster—and I've done just that. And now I intend to keep my pledge."

As these shocking words registered, Foxwell clutched at her mariner's cross.

"You're mocking me, aren't you? Of course, you are, Horace. I can tell you're not being serious."

"We'll find out soon enough," he replied. "Now won't we?"

And then he stepped around her and strode briskly toward his classroom, still uncertain which version of history he intended to teach.

~

Edgecomb didn't have to confront the issue directly until the mid-afternoon, as his first three classes of the day were all sections of History Survey I. These students, non-honors tenth graders, remained bogged down in the eighteenth century, muddling through the particulars of the Stamp Act and the Gaspee Affair and the Boston Massacre, all events about which the textbook and Roland Royster apparently agreed. At lunchtime, he strolled past the student cafeteria on the way to the faculty dining chamber, and spotted Sally Royster, seated alone, her nose buried in a book. How isolated she looked, although not necessarily unhappy. In fact, she appeared to be quite content. Her long fingers maneuvered a cookie to her mouth while she read. Yet he still felt badly for the girl—so much so that he contemplated seating himself opposite her and striking up a conversation. On paper, there would be nothing inappropriate about that. Elgin Rothmeyer, his department chairman, often had lunch with students, and the Storrow twins made a habit of eating with the football team on Fridays in the fall. Yet somehow Edgecomb sensed that sitting down across from Sally would be different—even risqué. Instead, he ordered a cod sandwich from the blind cashier who served the faculty, on an honor system, and listened to Lucky Pozner's disquisition on the future of democracy. *If we chose our representatives randomly, instead of through elections*, Pozner declared, *the popular will might actually see the light of day.*

After lunch, Edgecomb stopped by the main office to pick up a new bulb for his overhead projector and he arrived several minutes late for his seventh period class. The students quieted rapidly as he deposited his cache of books and folders beside his lectern. Louise Buxner wiped her nose with a ragged tissue; Maria Winch adjusted the hem of her skirt. In the second row, wearing a v-neck shirt that read, *Reality is a Fixed Delusion*, sat Sally, her expression polite and impassive. If the girl felt any residual awkwardness, as Edgecomb did, she betrayed nothing. "So where did we leave off?" he asked the class. "As I recall, I was boring you to tears with a lecture on Abolitionism…" He'd never understood why the textbook's chapter on antebellum race relations followed the political history, as though slavery were an afterthought, and not the horse that pulled the war cart, until Elgin Rothmeyer revealed the disturbing truth: if they didn't include a separate chapter, teachers in some downstate districts wouldn't teach about race at all. Of course, if slavery had died out naturally around 1820, none of this mattered.

Abe Kendall looked up from his notebook. "You'd just told us that *Uncle Tom's Cabin* sold 300,000 copies," offered the boy.

"Did I?" replied Edgecomb, his mental gears churning. "I guess I did."

Kendall did not appear to sense his teacher's uncertainty. He read aloud: "300,000 copies in the United States. More than 1,000,000 in Great Britain. Second best-selling book of the nineteenth century after The Bible."

Edgecomb glanced at Sally; he thought he detected a hint of hope, of expectation, on her face—but he couldn't be sure.

"So I said," he agreed. "Thank you, Abe. But was the book a success?"

Edgecomb scanned the room, letting his students take the lead.

"It sold a lot of copies," offered Brittany Marcus.

"And it started a war," called out chipmunk-cheeked Zinny Watkins.

"That's one theory," said Edgecomb. "I recall that I mentioned the story of Abraham Lincoln greeting Mrs. Stowe and saying to her, 'So this is the little lady who started this great war.' That is *one* theory."

He looked again at Sally and drew a deep breath.

"There is another theory," he continued, "that argues the early Abolitionists were so successful in championing their cause that no war ever proved necessary..."

All of the attention in the room immediately became his, full and undivided. Students who had been texting under their desks now refocused on the lecture, fearing they'd misunderstood a crucial point. Louise Buxner lowered the tissue from her nose, revealing a blank slab of astonishment.

"No war," Edgecomb repeated again, feeling more confident, "ever proved necessary."

He'd intended to offer a balanced account of the conflict, presenting both the traditional approach and Royster's version, but under the combined influence of Sally's presence and his commission from Vicky, he allowed himself to parrot Surrender Appomattox's propaganda nearly verbatim. He described the pastoral Eden of America at the middle of its first full century, how Jefferson had lived to see the last of the African slaves freed voluntarily, how large-scale plantations had given way to small homesteads across the rural South. And then he related the conspiracy of robber barons in New York and Philadelphia—Astors and Vanderbilts and DuPonts—who systematically propagated the myth of a war between the states to serve their own political and economic aspirations. No student dared interrupt. Twice, Abe Kendall raised his hand—and then lowered it rapidly under Edgecomb's withering glare.

"This was an era when men rarely settled more than a twenty-minute horse ride from their hometowns," he declared, "when only one in ten thousand ever visited the national capital during a lifetime. So if the governor announced the need to raise taxes to pay off war bonds, or the President demanded increased revenues for veterans' pensions, what basis did any ordinary citizen have to object? And if the Grand Old Party nominated candidates who'd supposedly fought to preserve the Union, who dared challenge their credentials? Anyone who questioned the official line was either inducted into the conspiracy, if he were an opinion leader, or locked up inside an institution. By 1880, the state psychiatric hospital at Milledgeville in Georgia had 40,000 patients, more than half of them Civil War deniers. Other dissidents were quarantined in leper colonies or jailed on frivolous charges. All the progress that African-Americans had achieved after winning their freedom was reversed—and those who dared to suggest life had ever been otherwise faced torture or lynching. If the textbook version of the Civil War was bloody, the efforts to generate a Civil War legacy proved nearly as brutal. That, at least, is the other version of history."

There. He had done it. Not exactly endorsed Royster's theories, but presented them as a perfectly plausible "parahistory," as Surrender Appomattox termed its reckoning of events. Edgecomb let his gaze dart toward Sally. To his delight, the girl wore a broad smile—maybe a tad smug, but unquestionably approving. His other students appeared genuinely flabbergasted. Abe raised his hand for a third time, tentatively, and Edgecomb acknowledged him.

"I don't mean any disrespect, Mr. E., but did they make you teach us that?"

Edgecomb glanced at Sally again for moral support and turned back to Kendall. "Let me ask you something, Abe. Do I strike you as the kind of guy who anybody can make teach anything?"

"No, sir."

"I didn't think so. In fact, Dr. Foxwell specifically ordered me *not* to teach you the non-traditional history of the war. But I wanted you to hear both sides—to let you form your own opinions."

"And which theory do *you* believe?" asked Abe.

"If I answered that," replied Horace, "then I wouldn't be giving you an opportunity to form your own opinions, now would I?"

Abe frowned, seemingly unsatisfied, but said no more.

"Any other questions?" asked Edgecomb.

He felt as though he'd lectured for hours, even days, but the wall clock read only 2:45—ten more minutes to go. Maria Winch raised her hand, her silver bangles clattering down her forearm along her creamy skin. "Mr. Edgecomb, I know you hate when we ask this type of question, but which theory should we use for the exam?"

A fair inquiry, under the circumstances. He'd forgotten that they were to be tested on these materials.

"I *do* dislike it when you ask about exams, Maria. But I can understand your confusion in this case." He paced up and down the rows between the students' desks, his fingers toying with a rubber band behind his back. "I'll tell you what. You can use either version, as long as you're consistent. But don't switch back and forth between theories. Abraham Lincoln was either an actor or a statesman, but not both."

Edgecomb thought he'd offered a fair compromise, so he was genuinely unnerved when he caught sight of Louise Buxner. Unlike her white classmates, who mostly appeared puzzled, the chubby African-American girl looked as though she might burst into tears at any moment. Her lower lip actually quivered. And then, without warning, she grabbed her knapsack and bolted out of the room, colliding haphazardly with desks and neighboring students along the way. But the worst part was the two-word imprecation that Louise, usually sweet and deferential, muttered en route to the exit—a curse so unexpected and damning that Edgecomb tried to convince himself he'd misheard her, even though deep down he knew that he had not. The girl had cried: "Racist bullshit." Her accusation settled over the room like a cloud of soot.

Edgecomb's instincts urged him to run after her—to beg her forgiveness for pushing an agenda that, in hindsight, did seem easily mistakable for racist bullshit. But what could he possibly say? If he were to infiltrate Royster's movement, he had to play the part, and that meant embracing the man's agenda unapologetically. So the die had been cast. From that moment forward, Edgecomb understood, his own ego would have to take a backseat to the demands of Vicky's agency—even if that meant humiliating himself in front of his friends and family or, as with Louise, leaving his students under the impression that he'd become a dimwitted bigot.

"Was it something I said?" he asked—hoping to leaven the moment with humor, as he usually did to smooth over his missteps, but this time nobody laughed. "I guess it was," he answered himself. "There's a lesson in this. I know I've told you over and over again that history should be fun. But it's also serious business. If you control the past, you also control the future. To put it another way, you can think of American history as a giant omelet, and in this class, as of today, we're going to start breaking some eggs."

He let his eyes pan across the room from bewildered Abe Kendall to indifferent Maria Winch, gnawing her bubble gum, and finally to Sally, whose pale cheeks now glowed as though exposed to the elements. Beyond the plate windows, in the courtyard, a brisk autumn wind churned the dried leaves in eddies.

"Okay, see you tomorrow," Edgecomb announced. "Class dismissed."

His students filed out in a stream of subdued murmurs, a striking contrast to their usually boisterous departure. Abe Kendall hovered around Edgecomb's desk for a moment, as though he might stay to chat, but then the boy seemed to think the better of it. Eventually, only Sally remained with Edgecomb in the classroom.

"Well? Was that evenhanded enough for you?" he asked.

Sally, never without an opinion, now appeared too flustered to speak. She stood halfway between his desk and the door, her fingers fretting with the hem of her blouse. Edgecomb noticed goose flesh on her bare arms. Secretly, he relished his effect on her.

"I'll take that as a yes," he said. "I do feel bad for Louise. It must be hard for her..." All he had intended to say was, *'It must be hard for her, being the only African-American student in our class.'* Yet Sally's presence, and maybe a subconscious desire to treat Royster's daughter as an equal, loosened his tongue. He found himself finishing his sentence with the words, "... not being popular. Or, quite frankly, very pretty. I know I shouldn't say that, because she is such a sweet kid..."

Another rule out the window: discussing Louise's appearance with Sally didn't violate any official procedures or policies, but it did alter the terms of their relationship. What struck Edgecomb was that, unlike during their encounter a few days earlier, he no longer even second-guessed his indiscretions. Sally's entire face had suffused with blood; her throat glowed crimson to the neckline of her blouse.

"I'll have my dad call you," she finally said—each word seeming to cost her precious breath. "I have to go," she added, stammering. "The bus..."

For a split second, Edgecomb anticipated that the girl might run toward him and kiss him on the neck—but she didn't. She just grabbed her satchel and fled. Whether he felt relieved, or disappointed, or possibly both, he couldn't say. Fortunately, Lucky Pozner knocked on the classroom door a moment later, to escort him to the children's hospital, sparing him the solitude of his own thoughts.

~

Every fourth Monday, Edgecomb and Lucky Pozner and a pair of colleagues from the English Department volunteered an evening at the children's hospital in Marston Moor. They'd been recruited by Pozner's wife, Lorinda, the nurse manager on the oncology unit, to deliver one-on-one tutoring to pediatric cancer patients who might otherwise fall behind in school. They also performed a Christmas Eve show for the ward each year, during which Lucky entertained the kids with chemistry tricks, and Mickey Bickerstaff taught them how to juggle. Edgecomb found the experience rewarding—he'd tutored five different boys over thirty months—but he also dreaded the day, all but inevitable, when one of his pupils didn't survive to discharge.

For the past ten weeks, Edgecomb's charge had been a Korean-American twelfth grader named Benji who suffered from a low-grade glioma of his brain's parietal lobe. What that meant, in layman's terms, was that the neurosurgeons had mucked around inside the adolescent's skull for fifteen straight hours, and done enough collateral damage so that the boy no longer registered the left side of his body as his own. Edgecomb hadn't believed such a condition could even exist—despite reassurances from both the physicians and Lucky Pozner—until he'd verified it for himself on Wikipedia. The boy literally shaved only the right half of his mustache; abandoned to his own devices, he'd have wandered the halls wearing only one sneaker. In spite of these challenges, Benji knew more about American history than any of Edgecomb's own students. If the brain tumor didn't kill him—and the verdict still remained out—he had Supreme Court Justice material written all over him. Edgecomb could easily imagine him sitting in the Chief Justice's chair someday, beneath the portrait of John Marshall, a black judicial robe draped over half of his scraggy body.

At first, the nursing staff tried to compensate for Benji's deficits, combing his hair symmetrically, brushing his overlooked teeth. Eventually, they backed off, so that the teen now wore glasses with only one lens. But he greeted Edgecomb with a broad smile that spanned both sides of his face. A chemotherapy line connected a port beneath his gown to a translucent bag atop an IV pole. "I was afraid you might not come," said Benji, "now that you're famous and all."

"Famous? Far from it," replied Edgecomb.

He hadn't imagined that a short speech at a local board meeting would impress a critically-ill teenager in a city forty-five minutes away.

"In *my* world, you're famous. My parents sent me clippings from the *Clarion* and the *Sentinel-Times*. You were awesome. Just like Joseph Welch."

Welch's name rang familiar to Edgecomb, but he couldn't place it. "I know I should remember who that is."

"Hell yeah, you should, Mr. Edgecomb." The teen shook his head in mock disappointment. "Joseph N. Welch. The lawyer who stood up to Senator Joseph McCarthy at the Army-McCarthy hearings in 1954."

Of course, thought Edgecomb. How had that slipped his mind?

"It's hard tutoring someone who knows more than I do." *And you only have half a brain too*, he added to himself. "In any case, it wasn't such a big deal. Roland Royster isn't exactly Joe McCarthy."

"My dad thought it was a big deal," countered Benji. "I was so proud to know you. Honestly, I've been bragging about you all week."

The kid's praise unleashed a pang of guilt in Edgecomb's psyche. Soon enough, this young man, and probably many others, would be roughly disabused of their ill-founded notions regarding his heroism. What would his former students think, he wondered, once they learned of his defection? Edgecomb recalled his own disillusionment when his stepfather, a civil rights attorney and self-styled liberal, had demanded that he register for the Selective Service to qualify for college loans.

"It's dangerous to place anyone on a pedestal," he warned the boy. "Even me. The high and might have a tendency to fall hard. Think about all the Leftists and fellow travelers in the 1930s who idolized Stalin."

Benji laughed, but his laughter soon degenerated into a deep, nasty cough. "I'll take my chances," said the boy, once he'd recovered his breath. "You know how you always say, 'I'll take that under advisement,' Mr. Edgecomb? Well, I'll take that under advisement." The boy hawked a gob of bloody phlegm into a tissue. "Now if you're done with the gratuitous advice, it's time for you to earn your keep and start tutoring. I have an exam next week on the 1920s."

Edgecomb was relieved that Benji's class, at a private school in Gripley, devoted two years to the Advance Placement history curriculum; that meant the twelfth grader was already steeped in the Twentieth Century, the American Civil War long behind him. After a school day defaming Lincoln, Edgecomb took pleasure in deriding Presidents who actually deserved the scorn: philandering Warren G. Harding, taciturn and starchy Calvin Coolidge, the inept Herbert Hoover, who'd hoped for America to volunteer its way collectively out of the Great Depression. Benji spent much of the session speculating about whether modern DNA testing could resolve the mystery of Harding's illegitimate daughter, allegedly fathered with a twenty-something Jazz Age groupie named Nan Britton. "I have my doubts," the teen said confidently. "I've seen her photo. If I were the Leader of the Free World, Nan isn't the girl I'd be doing it with in the White House broom closet." The kid had a point, Edgecomb reflected: Miss Britton, even at her prime, resembled a barn owl. But who could say? Eva Braun looked a bit like a puffin, and entire kingdoms had been sacrificed for women whose faces appealed to only one emperor.

Edgecomb's phone rang at five minutes to eight. He was going to let the call pass to his voice mail, until the name R G ROYSTER appeared on his console. "I've got to take this," he apologized. "A historical emergency." He stepped into the corridor and ducked behind a cart of freshly-laundered sheets. A shiver juddered his spine as he answered the call.

"Horace? Rollie Royster here," said the denier. "You have a moment?"

"I suppose I do," he answered. "I mean, yes...Yes, I have a moment."

"Good. Because my daughter informs me that you've seen the light. Or, at least, that you're groping your way through the darkness..." Sally's father spoke with a brand of affected intimacy that Edgecomb associated with funeral directors and vendors of term life insurance. "So here's what I propose. Why don't I have Nalaskowski set you up for a press conference tomorrow afternoon? Steps of City Hall. Two o'clock."

"To say what?"

"That's your call, Horace," said Royster. "I'm not giving you a script. You say what you'd like. If you're still on the fence about the war, that's fine. Just your saying that both sides deserve equal air time in the classroom is a coup for us. Whether you're ready to embrace our full agenda is entirely up to you." Royster served up another of his dramatic pauses and concluded, "I'll let you surprise me." And somehow, without overtly expressing any firm commitment, Edgecomb nonetheless discovered himself committed to a public announcement the following afternoon. Later, when he wished Benji good luck on his exam, he felt more shame than he ever had in his life.

On the ride back to Laurendale to pick up his own car, Edgecomb listened indifferently as Lucky Pozner and Mickey Bickerstaff debated the merits of democracy.

"The problem, I tell you," insisted Pozner, "is that all the people fit to run the damn country are too busy running espresso machines at Starbucks." He popped a pistachio nut into his mouth and tossed the shell out the window. "Okay, that's not entirely true. Some of them are too busy searching for affordable daycare or waiting in line at the Department of Motor Vehicles."

"Would you rather be ruled by a Committee of Platonic Guardians?" countered Bickerstaff. "Democracy is the worst form of government except all others."

"Thank you, Mr. Churchill. And yes, I'd take the Platonic Guardians over the New Jersey state legislature any day."

During a lull in the debate, as they approached the high school parking lot, Edgecomb posed a question of his own: "On the subject of democratic government," he asked, "I've got a practical question for you would-be Solons. Where's Laurendale city hall?"

Neither man, it turned out, had the slightest idea.

~

The next morning, at Saul Nalaskowski's insistence, Edgecomb called the main office at Laurendale and requested a personal day. This was his first school day away from teaching in over two years—since his ex-girlfriend kicked him out and he'd required time off to go apartment hunting—and it started with Royster's lawyer ringing his doorbell at six a.m. sharp. Nalaskowski poked his nose around the apartment while Edgecomb showered and dressed, inspecting books and even opening cabinets. When Edgecomb stepped out of the bathroom, he encountered the portly attorney on his knees, nonchalantly investigating the space under Edgecomb's bed.

"Did you lose something?" asked Edgecomb.

"Nah. Just looking around," replied Nalaskowski, as though snooping beneath people's furniture was a widely-accepted social convention. "Ready to roll?"

"I don't understand the hurry. It's hardly seven o'clock. I thought this thing was scheduled for two p.m.?"

Nalaskowski looked at him as though he'd sprouted a second head. "My dear young man, do you suppose the municipal elders of the City of Laurendale are going to yield their doorsteps to you without a fight? Why would they issue a permit to a known rabble-rouser at a time when the city, through its School Board, already faces the threat of extensive litigation over its retrograde curriculum?"

"I hadn't thought of that."

"Of course, you hadn't. That's why you require an attorney," said Nalaskowski, a devilish smirk flickering above his ruddy goatee. "We're off to court, my dear young man. Federal court in Newark. If we're going to get a permit for your presser, we're going to have to file an injunction."

"Why not just wait until tomorrow then? That way we won't have to rush…."

Nalaskowski hit his forehead with his palm—a gesture Edgecomb had only ever witnessed in movies. "'Why not just wait until tomorrow?' he wants to know. *This* is why!" The lawyer snapped open his attaché and slapped a stack of papers, a solid ten inches thick, on Edgecomb's bed. "Because you don't actually have a case, I'm afraid—it is *their* city hall. They own the steps. What we *do* have is the advantage of surprise.

It should take their counsel a good twenty-four hours to answer each of these motions. If we wait until tomorrow, my dear boy, we might as well wait until the day after doomsday."

While Edgecomb digested this lesson in civics, Royster's attorney stuffed his tome of paperwork back into his briefcase. Then he settled onto Edgecomb's bed to adjust his socks; the bedsprings squeaked under his weight. "My dear boy," he said, "I expect you're accustomed to thinking for yourself." Nalaskowski shook his head—as though thinking for oneself were the height of all folly. "You have representation now. The point of having counsel is not doing your own thinking. *Capiche?*"

"I guess..."

"Good enough."

~

Nalaskowski could have charged admission for his courtroom performance. All of the court personnel from the judge to the stenographer already knew his antics, which in this case included filing one hundred fifty-two separate requests for injunctions and directives in assorted shapes and sizes. He requested to use each of the fourteen steps of city hall individually, as well as several other sections of the municipal plaza, and even pled for an order to silence a public fountain in the vicinity. "As you may or may not be aware, your honor," Nalaskowski warned the bemused judge, "various municipalities have gone to extraordinary lengths to silence the organization that I represent. In Gettysburg, after Surrender Appomattox won the right to speak in front of borough hall, the city council voted to install a temporary curtain around the structure. So you'll understand if my client wants your directive to be airtight."

"Very well," agreed Judge Pastarnak. "I will grant temporary relief on all one hundred and fifty-two motions, pending a reply from the defendant."

"Thank you, your honor," said Nalaskowski. "Now if you'll bear with me, I also have three ancillary motions..."

And so the drama continued for much of the morning, Royster's attorney requesting, Judge Pastarnak granting, the bailiffs biting their lips to keep from laughing. Many of the spectators who filed in as the proceedings advanced, Edgecomb learned from one of the security guards, had in fact come from other courtrooms and even a local law school specifically to watch Nalaskowski litigate, as word spread that he was "chasing paper" in court that day. By the time they departed for Laurendale, armed with enough motions to sink an aircraft carrier, it was already past one o'clock. "A good lawyer wears both a belt and suspenders," explained Nalaskowski. "A great lawyer wears a second pair of slacks under the first." Edgecomb assumed the attorney was speaking metaphorically, until they paused as a traffic light in Haddondale, and Royster's lawyer peeled down the waistband of his dress pants to reveal the top of a pair of dungarees.

Royster's lawyer drove even faster than Sebastian, but without the drug-induced recklessness. He had them in downtown Laurendale at exactly one fifty-five, parked opposite the Greek Revival city hall at one fifty-eight. To Edgecomb's amazement, a crowd of several hundred already awaited his appearance. Sally's father was warming up the audience. Royster stood before a rollaway lectern, in front of the building's imposing pillars, lambasting "enemies of truth, dastardly conspirators and defenders of the Lincoln-Lee fairytale." Lantern-jawed Cousin Nigel stood behind Royster on the platform, arms folded across his chest like a bouncer's, as did the two turncoat professors, McNabb and Herskovitz, whom Edgecomb recognized from the media coverage. The *Clarion*'s insatiable Phoebe Woodsmith crouched at the foot of the steps, dwarfed by a hooded windbreaker, pad and pen in hand. It was an exquisite afternoon for a public event, practically balmy for mid-October. A flock of starlings foraged in the moribund grass around the plaza.

"I've done my part," said Nalaskowski. "Now it's your turn."

But before Edgecomb had an opportunity to mount the marble steps, Sebastian Borrelli had him by the elbow. His housemate sported fashionably-patched jeans and a denim jacket with an upturned collar—like a hipster James Dean. The flat-chested waitress, Esperanza, hovered at his side, sporting an identical outfit. A stray leaf had settled in the girl's nest of fuchsia hair.

"Jesus. Who invited you?"

"Didn't realize this was invitation-only event, Teach," retorted Borrelli. "I was picking up Esperanza from the café. We drove by and saw the commotion…" He clasped the waitress's hand. "We're actually on our way to meet up with Sevastopol. You remember Sevastopol, don't you? We've got first edition *Color the Prophet* coloring books to show him."

Esperanza retrieved a sample coloring book from her canvas bag. The volume's cover depicted a line drawing of Mohammed, in a lofty turban, surrounded by scantily-clad female bathers. To Edgecomb, the prophet looked more like Aladdin.

"That was quick."

"Turns out the workshop only needed a good dusting, Teach. The presses are still in first-rate shape, so I've been printing twenty-four hours straight. If we stay on schedule, we should have ten thousand copies to dispatch by Wednesday." Borrelli, beaming with pride, seemed to have forgotten the risk involved. "You want one, dude? On the house."

"Not right now."

"Come on, Teach. Don't look a gift prophet in the mouth."

Borrelli shoved the book into Edgecomb's hands. And an instant later, Roland Royster took note of his arrival.

"Here's the man of the hour," declared Sally's father, his baritone reverberating across the plaza. "Step right up here, Horace. Now's not the time to be shy."

The ragtag band of dissenters and bystanders on the plaza cleared a path for Edgecomb and, a moment later, he found himself at the lectern, Roland Royster's arm draped over his shoulder in a masculine hug. Half a dozen microphones competed for his attention; a television camera from CBS-9 recorded his every gesture. "I give you a man who means what he says and says what he means," declared Royster. "A man who stands up for what he believes in, but who is big enough to admit his mistakes. This is the future of American education—if truth is fortunate enough to win the day. So with no further delay, I give you the man of the hour, Horace Halden Edgecomb."

The multitude cheered and applauded. Many of the same activists who'd derided him at the Board of Education meeting in September now waved banners emblazoned with his initials. They chanted his name as they stomped their feet. What unsettled Edgecomb the most was that

Royster had welcomed him with his full name, including a middle portion that appeared on his birth certificate and absolutely nowhere else. Even his social security card read only, HOLDEN H EDGECOMB. Let no one claim that Surrender Appomattox didn't do its research—at least where potential enemies were concerned.

Edgecomb surveyed the crowd. He'd initially intended to remain cautious, to stick to the call for balance that he'd advocated in the classroom. But the enthusiasm of Royster's followers took hold of him—and whether it was his fear of disappointing them, or his desire to win over Sally's father, and ultimately Vicky, he could never truly say, but he found himself embracing their cause whole hog. "I read one of those pamphlets," he declaimed, "and instantly, I realized that I'd been sold a bill of goods—that, all these years, I'd been drinking the Kool-Aid and regurgitating it for my students. Did I really believe that four thousand soldiers had been killed at Sharpsburg in one afternoon with muzzle-loading rifles and Minié balls? Or that Admiral David Farragut captured the entire city of Mobile, Alabama with eighteen gunships, half of them made from wood? I'm sorry, but the pieces just didn't add up." He might have stopped there—but then he caught a glimpse of Sally, perched atop a milk crate at the corner of the esplanade, seemingly glued to his every word. How funny that, only a week ago, he'd have reported her to Laurendale's truancy office for such an absence. Now, her presence inspired him.

"This afternoon, I taught my students that there are two theories about nineteenth century America—and both deserve to be heard. I regret having said that. Presenting the Civil War as a theory does a disservice to the truth. And the truth is that the Civil War isn't a theory, it's an outright hoax, an utter sham, malarkey—no more real than the Loch Ness Monster or the jackalope. And it's a hoax that our political and business elites continue to perpetrate to this day."

Only at the conclusion of his fiery speech, which lasted nearly ten minutes, did his doubts take hold: How would he have the courage to face Lucky Pozner and Elgin Rothmeyer at school the next day? Or Benji at the children's hospital in two weeks? He dared not think of Jillian's reaction—although he already anticipated a relentless barrage of phone calls, supplemented by pleas from his mother in Florida and his Aunt Pauline in Arizona. And his mother had already been through so much: what a selfish ingrate he would be to cause her any distress. So lost was he in his own dread and despair that Royster had to nudge his shoulder before he realized he was being questioned by the media.

"Are you receiving any compensation from Mr. Royster's organization for your remarks today?" asked a journalist who identified himself as in the employ of the Hager Heights *Sentinel-Times*.

Royster didn't afford him an opportunity to answer. "That's defamation," cried the dissenter, taking hold of the microphone. "Neither I nor my organization has ever exchanged a dime with Mr. Edgecomb. Period. End of story."

Sally's father permitted him to field several inquiries on the evolution of his beliefs, and one on what reaction he anticipated to his conversion. Edgecomb muddled through. He was asked by a reporter from WPLK whether he expected to be disciplined by the Laurendale School Board, and in response, he joked that Archie Steinhoff was going to thank him for distracting the public from his own political disintegration. That was bound to ruffle Sandra Foxwell's slick feathers. He'd agreed to accept one final question when Phoebe Woodsmith's brook-no-nonsense voice penetrated the din.

"What's in your hand?" demanded the journalist.

Horace had forgotten Sebastian's first edition. Now, in an act as incriminating as it was instinctive, he slid the coloring book behind his back. An ominous silence had slashed across the plaza, punctuated only by the distant rumble of trucks at the municipal garbage facility across the avenue.

"Are you reciting someone else's speech?" persisted Phoebe. "Did they give you a script to memorize?"

"Show us what you're holding," interjected the *Sentinel-Times* correspondent. "The public has a right to know."

Edgecomb looked to Royster and Nalaskowski for guidance, but neither man knew what lay in his hands, or the danger it entailed, so they didn't seem to recognize his desperation. And he was indeed desperate—

for an instant, he even considered bolting from the podium—vaulting himself over the side of the staircase to freedom, or at least a temporary escape. Meanwhile, the WPLK reporter advanced up the steps, as though she intended to yank the novelty item from his grasp. "It's just a coloring book," Edgecomb stammered. "A gift for my nephew." His imaginary relative rolled easily off his tongue, a cousin to the fabricated petition drive of the previous week.

"What is it *really*?" demanded the reporter. "Show us."

"It *is* a coloring book." The voice belonged to Sebastian. He'd pushed his way to the foot of the stairs and now stood alongside Phoebe Woodsmith. "I should know. I'm the guy who manufactured it."

"And who are you?" asked the radio reporter.

"Sebastian Borrelli. Owner of Borrelli's Publishing. And what my friend, Horace, is holding is a first edition *Color the Prophet* coloring book. Available on line, starting next week, for $9.95 at www.colortheprophet.com." And to Edgecomb's horror, his housemate began distributing free copies to the press pool. "It's part of a series," Borrelli explained. "And you don't have to be a Muslim to enjoy it."

Edgecomb heard Royster shouting, "Who the hell is that?" in the background. And in his next breath, "Get that bastard out of here." But neither Nalaskowski, nor lantern-jawed Cousin Nigel and his security goons, could do much about Sebastian in front a half a dozen journalists. So Borrelli continued to hijack the press conference, transforming it into a free media launch for his merchandise. The spectacle entranced the crowd, many of whom probably believed Borrelli and Surrender Appomattox to be intimately linked.

"And what about you, Horace?" Phoebe asked. "What's your involvement with Mr. Borrelli's firm?"

Edgecomb sensed the panic rising in his throat—a burning that prevented him from forming any sounds. Fortunately, this time Saul Nalaskowski came to his rescue. "My client has nothing to do with this tasteless product," declared the rotund attorney, "and absolutely nothing further to say on the subject." Then Cousin Nigel stepped between Edgecomb and the press corps, his shoulders squared, effectively terminating Edgecomb's participation in the Q&A. A moment later, the lawyer and ex-professor McNabb shepherded him into the foyer of city hall and then through a side exit. Outside the building once again, but shielded from the press, he could still hear Sebastian Borrelli touting the merits of his novelty as a Christmas and Hanukah gift.

"Do you know that guy?" asked Nalaskowski.

"He's my housemate."

"He's an imbecile, that's what he is."

The lawyer said nothing further as they waited for Royster and the rest of his personal entourage to join them. But that afforded Edgecomb plenty of time to reflect on the calamity he'd created. In fact, short of actually dying during the press conference, he couldn't imagine a worse turn of events. On the one hand, he'd alienated Surrender Appomattox by blowing the organization's moment in the spotlight. At the same time, by embracing the group's peculiar ideology, he'd disappointed nearly everyone he knew, from Benji Kim to Calliope Chaselle to the random strangers who'd sent him fan emails over the previous week. And on top of all that, thanks to Sebastian, he was now publically associated with a children's novelty geared at offending a quarter of the world's population. *Intentionally.* Even sudden death, in hindsight, had its merits—at least, when compared with the torture he'd probably face after some underground al-Qaeda affiliate kidnapped him.

He didn't imagine his plight could sink any lower. And then his phone rang. The console read DEPT OF THE TREAS. That meant only one possibility: Vicky Vann was calling to fire him. Edgecomb glanced at his companions. Royster's lawyer wore a none-too-friendly expression.

"It's my mother," he lied. "She's sick. I have to take it."

He retreated around the back of the building for a modicum of privacy. To his relief, McNabb and Nalaskowski did not follow. Vicky's voice, in spite of everything, managed to elevate his mood. "I saw the whole thing on television," she said—without even asking how he was.

"I'm sorry," he said.

"What are you sorry for? That was brilliant."

"Seriously?"

"Yes, seriously. You couldn't see behind you while you were speaking, but I could. Royster bought all of your bullshit. Every last word of it—hook, line and bloody sinker. You're in."

"You really think so?"

"I *know* so. You've infiltrated his organization and you've managed to make his followers look like idiots in the process. You cannot imagine how ridiculous you sounded while that guy was trying to sell his coloring books. *Both of you.* You came across as the two nuttiest halfwits on the planet."

"Thanks."

"Say, is that guy even for real?"

"I'm afraid he is."

"I figured he might be. You always had weird friends, even in high school," replied Vicky. "But it was a brilliant touch. Just don't let anyone kill you before we get the scoop on Royster."

"And after that?"

Vicky didn't answer. "Look, I should let you go. Before anyone gets suspicious. Just keep doing your thing and we'll touch base soon."

She hung up before he said goodbye. But her call had leavened his spirits. Never could he have imagined that being told he'd humiliated himself in front of a television audience would bring him such cheer, yet it had. That was the difference between history and real life. In real life, the past did not predict the future. In real life, the sun might rise in the west, or the Civil War might be exposed as a hoax, or the prettiest girl at Rolleston High might someday fall for the most average of men. Anything was possible. Or so it seemed, for a brief moment, in the afterglow of Vicky's praise.

CHAPTER FIVE

Jillian's phone calls started within the hour. She left pleas on his cell phone, on his home phone, and on the voice mail at his office, as well as enlisting his mother, his aunt, and Oliver to pressure him to respond. He did not understand the urgency; after all, he already anticipated exactly what she was going to say—and the tone of beseeching desperation in which she would say it. But after shaking off Royster's minions with a promise to contact them as soon as he'd addressed his mother's "acute medical concerns," complications existing only in his imagination, and after a long, solitary hike at the Marshfield Seashore Preserve to clear his head, Edgecomb returned to his apartment and dialed her number. His sister sounded shocked to hear his voice.

"Let's not argue, okay?" he said—before she had an opportunity to berate him. "I'm going to call in sick tomorrow. I'm not ready to show my face at school yet. Do you want to take the day off and meet me for brunch?" As soon as she agreed to a plan, he hung up the receiver.

So at ten o'clock the next morning, instead of lecturing his History I Survey on the shortcomings of the Articles of Confederation, he met Jillian in front of Mackenzie's Dinette and found them a corner booth, while she scouted the fire exits. The restaurant proved far less crowded than on weekends, the clientele mostly retirees and troupes of mothers with small children. A chipper, clean-cut young waiter deposited a pair of menus on their table and rolled off the breakfast specials. Edgecomb feigned interest. Meanwhile, his eyes scoured the restaurant, searching for Borrelli's girlfriend. He'd nearly given up, convinced that she was off duty, when he glimpsed a shock of unkempt fuchsia hair reflected in one of the wall mirrors.

Esperanza was busy covering her own tables in the adjoining room, and appeared not to have noticed them. That was fine by Edgecomb. He'd wanted to meet someplace else entirely, but Jillian had insisted, because Mackenzie was the only local restaurateur who'd allowed her to inspect his kitchen. "We have nothing to hide," the high-browed Scotsman had declared. "If you come early one morning, before things get hectic, I'll give you a grand tour." In contrast, Penelope at Penelope's had shown Edgecomb's sister the New Jersey state bird and cursed her out in Greek.

To Edgecomb's surprise, Jillian did not appear to be upset. She ordered her usual scoop of cottage cheese and her banana without so much as one word of recrimination; instead of launching into an attack on his judgment, or denouncing the press conference, she casually rehashed her previous night's conversation with their mother, in which the pair had discussed potential baby names. "I've been thinking I might name the child after its country of origin, depending on how everything works out," she chirped. "Obviously, Kenya or Ethiopia are fine, Central African Republic not so much." Jillian's good cheer seemed so out of character, especially under the circumstances, that it left him uneasy. "I guess we could abbreviate it to C.A.R. and name her Carrie or Carin."

She paused to let the waiter set down their plates, affording Edgecomb a chance to interrupt. "You're scaring me," he said. "We've been here nearly fifteen minutes already, and you haven't once accused me of ruining your life. What have you done with my real sister?"

"It's reassuring to know you think so highly of me," replied Jillian, systematically inspecting her banana. "Can't I just be in a sunny mood?"

"You could be. But the odds favor invasion by Body Snatchers."

His sister sponged down the banana with a baby wipe and then unpeeled it. "Would a Body Snatcher disinfect a banana peel?" she asked. "It's the same old me. I promise. In fact, I was planning on telling you how much I hated you, but on the way out the door, I got a phone call from one of the big placement agencies letting me know they've approved my initial application. Usually that means waiting another couple of months for a home visit, but they had a cancellation, so they're sending out a social worker to see me the day after tomorrow. Isn't that amazing?"

Jillian spoke so quickly that Edgecomb could hardly keep up with her.

"So you're not angry about my television appearance?" he asked.

"Of course, I am. Angry and outraged and distraught. Honestly, Horace, you sounded like a deranged lunatic. Espionage or no espionage, do you really want people believing you've lost your gourd?"

"It's only short term."

"Keep telling yourself that. Think about all those people who are falsely charged with horrific crimes—kiddie porn, terrorism. Everybody remembers the arrests, but nobody pays attention when they're later exonerated. Like that scientist who allegedly mailed out the anthrax, only didn't, or that guy they accused of blowing up the Atlanta Olympics. You're going to end up being the 'Civil War Denying Teacher' long after you've gone on television and revealed your motives. Is Vicky Vann worth all that?"

Jillian explored her cottage cheese, running a fork through it as though straining for foreign objects. The skin on her fingers, red and raw from washing, had started to peel. Edgecomb looked beyond her toward the dessert case, where napoleons and layer cakes revolved slowly, their bright colors speciously seductive. An elderly couple shared a single poached egg at the table opposite them—the old couple reflected through the parallel wall mirrors into infinitely smaller and smaller versions of their better selves. At the counter, a stooped old timer with hangdog jowls sipped soup alone, a warning against long term bachelorhood. It was a warning not lost upon Edgecomb.

"Is Vicky worth all that?" he echoed. "Yes. The short answer is yes, she is. And more."

"Okay, suit yourself, baby brother. Just don't say I didn't warn you..."

Jillian steeled herself, as though braving lions, and sampled a dollop of cottage cheese. Once she appeared confident that she hadn't been poisoned, she chased down the spoonful with a swig of organic tea.

"Women are a dime a dozen," she said. "They're *highly* overrated. Trust me on that. I'm one of them."

"I'll take that under advisement," agreed Edgecomb, self-conscious about this expression ever since Benji had called him out for overusing it. "What's that proverb about women? You can't live with them and they won't live with you."

"Clever," said Jillian. "But just because they won't live with you doesn't mean that they won't walk all over you." She looked at him pointedly. "Anyway, I shouldn't be antagonizing you, because I need to hit you up for a favor."

"Another one? You should be thanking me for not getting thrown into jail."

"This is a real favor," explained Jillian—but before she revealed the details, Sebastian Borrelli's 'inamorata' sidled up to their table. Esperanza sported what looked like a human rib on a pendant around her neck.

"You were totally hilarious yesterday," she said. "I'm so glad we stuck around to hear you speak..."

Edgecomb toyed with the packets of artificial sweetener, stacking and unstacking them. He would have much preferred to endure a string of Greek expletives at Penelope's. "Jillian," he said, "This is Sebastian's friend, Esperanza."

Esperanza ignored the introduction. "I don't think I've laughed so hard at anything since I went to church for my confirmation," she continued. "I'm not a history buff. Don't get me wrong. I can hardly put World War I and World War II in chronological order. But when a grown man starts saying that Abraham Lincoln was a paid stooge who couldn't hack it on Broadway, and a whole crowd of whack-jobs is cheering him on, even I can get a good chuckle at their expense. Wow, did you sound out to lunch..."

"Thanks, I think," said Edgecomb. "At least, *you* knew I was lying." He turned to Jillian and explained, "Esperanza studies normative prosopography. She can detect dishonesty through facial musculature."

Jillian shrugged and shielded her teacup with her forearm.

"That's the thing," said Esperanza. "I don't think you were lying. I watched your mouth closely, following the risorius and the quadratus labii superioris, as well as the two zygomaticus muscles, and the levator angulis, and you didn't look like a man engaged in outright deception. You struck me as ambivalent, at best. Like a man who wasn't sure whether he was lying or not. Just saying…"

That was too much for Edgecomb. If crazy people wanted to believe in face reading, or palm reading, or phrenology, that was all the same to him—but nobody had the right to accuse him of speaking the truth. "Are you done?" he demanded. "Because my sister and I would like to enjoy our meal without interruption."

"You're a prickly one, aren't you?" responded Esperanza, and then she retreated quickly through the kitchen's swinging doors.

Edgecomb's body literally trembled with indignation. Who the hell was she to set herself up as the arbiter of honesty? The girl takes a few lessons at some quack unaccredited college and suddenly she's a human lie detector!

"Talk about audacity," he griped. "Did you hear that…?"

Jillian smiled. "So you really *don't* believe Honest Abe was a hired hack?"

"Not you, too!"

"Jesus, I'm joking, Horace. But that's a good warning for you, a taste of what you're in for," she added. "Anyway, I really do need your help."

Horace glanced over his shoulder at the kitchen doors. They stood motionless, separating him from his pink-mopped accuser. "My mistake was calling in sick," he muttered. "Next time, I'm calling in dead."

Jillian ignored his sarcasm. She took hold of his hand, risking the bacteria, so he knew her favor would be high stakes. "You know how they're blasting for the Interstate near my apartment," she explained. "Well, I have my home evaluation scheduled on Friday, and I'm hoping they'll take a break for a few hours…."

"I thought you said the noise wouldn't matter. Don't you have some paperwork from the state?"

"I do. And they'll be done with construction long before the adoption goes through…But you know how these things are. Home assessments can be very subjective. I want to make a perfect impression."

"And where I do come in?"

"I phoned the Department of Transportation, and they told me the blasting schedule is entirely up to the individual contractor. So I'm hoping you can come down to the construction site with me to ask them to take a short break on Friday afternoon. Only a few hours—just from noon to two o'clock."

"Why me? Or shouldn't I ask?"

"You're a man, Horace. Construction workers respect men."

"I'm hardly *that* kind of man. I'm a high school history teacher, for heaven's sake. And a Judy Garland fan. I'll be lucky if they don't lend me a pair of concrete shoes."

"But you'll come with me?"

Edgecomb understood this effort would be futile: that no federal contractor was going to suspend operations to help a local looney tune adopt a child. On the other hand, he also realized that saying no meant another barrage of phone calls from his mother, his aunt, and any other hapless collateral relatives that Jillian could recruit. And most of all, he loved his sister, and didn't have the heart to turn her down.

"Do I have a choice?" he asked.

A hopeful expression curled across his sister's thin lips.

"No, Horace," she replied. "Of course you don't."

~

Jillian insisted they take her station wagon to the blasting site. She'd purchased a well-worn Plymouth Suburban over the summer and had even installed a child's car seat in anticipation of her long-term needs. A triangular sticker on the rear passenger window read "baby-on-board"—as did decals in each of Jillian's apartment windows, so that firefighters might rescue the future hypothetical child from a future hypothetical blaze. Horace's sister drove in the right-hand lane, with her blinkers on, and never exceeded the posted speed limit. She also refused to risk left turns across oncoming traffic, fearful of being broadsided. Instead, she relied upon a series of consecutive rights, a process which often required considerable detours. But Edgecomb knew enough not to object. The alternative—driving himself, with his sister in the passenger seat, criticizing his technique while intermittently bracing for impact—promised far more aggravation than it was ever worth.

The sluggish trek toward Gripley Township carried them through New Jersey's industrial heartland, past the boarded-up shoe factories and machine tool plants that had clouded the skies above Paterson and Marston Moor with soot a century earlier. Jillian's favorite radio station played nonstop folk hits: Peter, Paul & Mary, John Denver's "Rocky Mountain High," Joan Baez covering Dylan. All wistful and depressing. These were the songs that drove unpopular teenage boys to slash their wrists.

"How's your love life?" asked Edgecomb. "Am I allowed to ask that?"

One never knew what question might send Jillian into a tizzy. The previous spring, he'd inquired about her plans for the Memorial Day weekend, and she'd lambasted him through tears for his insensitivity.

"You can ask. But there's not much to tell," said Jillian. "That guy I was writing to online disappeared when he found out I was thirty-seven. So my ad said that I was twenty-nine? When my profile revealed my actual age, nobody answered…"

"Nobody?"

"Nobody worthwhile," answered Jillian. "At first, I was afraid my lying had scared him off. I actually felt so bad, I wrote him a long apology. And you won't believe the message he sent me in reply. He wrote back that thirty-five is his absolute cutoff. He's fifty-three, goddammit. What the fuck is wrong with men?"

"Isn't that a bit harsh? He's only one guy."

"A representative example," countered Jillian. "No hard feelings, he wrote. Like hell there aren't…"

She paused at a green light and waited for it to turn yellow. The vehicle behind the Plymouth honked, then swerved through the intersection as the signal shifted to red—blasting its horn all the way. Edgecomb's sister did not seem fazed. "So that's my sob story, little brother," she said. "What about you? Any prospects?"

"Not unless you count Vicky Vann," Edgecomb said. "Calliope Chaselle—that new librarian with the flawless skin—is shacking up with a fellow named Thorn who teaches people how to read faces for a living." He considered mentioning Sally, but to what purpose? "I thought I had another prospect," he finally said. "But she's too young."

"I never thought I'd hear a man say that."

"She's eighteen. Even I have my limits," said Edgecomb. To change the subject he added, "But I haven't lost hope. You only have to get it right once."

"You do realize that won't be any easier once you're the public face of the Civil War denial movement," replied Jillian. "Women don't exactly flock to conspiracy theorists and wing nuts."

"I thought notoriety was supposed to be sexy. What about all of those murderers who get sacks of love letters in prison? I read somewhere that Charles Manson got more fan mail one year than President Carter."

"Let me rephrase that," said Jillian. "The sort of women *you're* looking for—or *should be* looking for—don't flock to wackos."

And what sort of women were those, exactly? Horace didn't dare ask. He wondered whether he'd be better off married to Vicky Vann and spying for the HDC, or supplanting Thorn and enjoying a quiet suburban existence wedded to an attractive high school librarian. That was the problem with romance: he could picture a future life with many different women—with Vicky, with Calliope, even, he conceded, with Sally Royster—and yet each one of those futures seemed so obvious, so compelling, and yet so strikingly dissimilar, that it was hard to understand how all of them could co-exist simultaneously in his imagination. Not that any of them, at the moment, looked to be realistic possibilities.

"Can I tell you something?" asked Jillian. "I just want you to know that no matter how much you humiliate yourself in public, I'm still going to love you. One hundred percent. Always."

"Deep down, I know that," said Edgecomb. "But it's still nice to hear."

The ensuing silence left him feeling uncomfortable, and he expected that Jillian felt the same way. They'd never been an emotionally open family; he couldn't remember the last time anyone among his immediate kin had said, "I love you." That didn't mean they cared about each other any less, merely that the Waspy reserve of the Edgecombs, which they'd carried across the Atlantic from Cornwall in the late seventeenth century, remained inexorable after fourteen generations. Edgecomb was tempted to promise to love Jillian too, no matter how much she humiliated herself publicly, yet he feared she might take his gest at face value and burst into tears, so he said nothing.

"Just because I love you doesn't mean I'm not going to castrate you barehanded if you get arrested," said Jillian, breaking the tension. "So if you plan on having children, you'd better keep your ass out of trouble."

"As long as you love me one hundred percent," quipped Edgecomb.

His sister made a series of right turns and parked the Plymouth around the corner from her duplex. The neighborhood in the vicinity of the Parkway deteriorated rapidly: only two blocks from Jillian's condo, abandoned row houses stood in various states of neglect, some boarded with plywood, others crumbling to rubble. Opposite the chain-link and barbed-wire perimeter of the construction site, a crabgrass lot housed an assortment of discarded washing machines, mounds of used tires, and the gutted body of a forlorn backhoe. An olive-skinned girl, probably no more than fifteen, led two younger children across the cluttered lot by hand. The trio eyed Edgecomb and Jillian with suspicion; they looked no less destitute than the orphans in Jillian's photo album, only far less friendly. How ridiculous to argue about the Civil War, Edgecomb thought, when toddlers ran barefoot in forty-degree weather—and yet, knowing this, he'd still return to Laurendale, sooner or later, to quibble over century-old battles.

He slid open a mesh gate that screeched against its brackets. They crossed a dusty yard and approached a low-slung trailer. Signs along the fencing warned them not to trespass or snap photographs. Jillian removed a pair of rubber cleaning gloves from her purse and slid in her arms to the elbows.

"What's that Bette Davis line? '*What a dump*,'" said Jillian.

"You're the one who chose to live out here," answered Edgecomb. "It's hard to believe this place and Royster's compound exist on the same planet. Sometimes I think Sally could use a few months in Gripley Township to chop her down to size."

"You talk about Royster's daughter an awful lot," observed Jillian.

She knocked on the trailer door before Edgecomb could respond. *Why shouldn't he talk about Sally?* he wanted to know. *She was his student, wasn't she?—and also the original source of all of his ongoing distress.* An explosion—much louder and closer than those he'd endured the prior week—shook away his ruminations. Edgecomb clutched Jillian's elbow to steady himself. He'd hardly regained his wherewithal when the trailer door swung open, and they found themselves facing a reedy, bespectacled workman in his forties. The man carried a Styrofoam coffee cup in one hand and wore a cardigan. He looked absolutely nothing like the grizzled, tattoo-cloaked construction chief whom Edgecomb had anticipated.

"Do you want something?" the man asked. "You shouldn't be here."

A voice from inside the trailer demanded to know the source of the interruption, addressing the man as Fritz. "It's nothing," he called back.

"We were hoping to see whoever's in charge," said Jillian.

"I'm the foreman," said Fritz. "And you are…?"

"Jillian," said Jillian. "Jillian Edgecomb. And this is Horace. Horace Edgecomb. We were hoping to have a word with you about the blasting."

"Got all the papers on file," answered Fritz. "Nothing to talk about. We're sorry for the inconvenience, but if you folks want highways, somebody's got to build them."

The foreman started to shut the door.

"Please," pleaded Jillian. "One minute, okay? I know you're just doing your job. But I'm hoping you could suspend it for a few hours on Friday afternoon. Just this once. You see, I'm trying to adopt a baby, and I'm afraid the noise might frighten the social worker who's coming to evaluate my home."

Her appeal managed to keep Fritz in the doorway; he looked genuinely intrigued. "You're adopting a baby. What a fine thing," he said. "Still, we can't halt construction every time somebody in the area expresses a personal need. We're on a schedule, ma'am. You've got to understand that. I'm sure you and your husband will find a way to make do."

"He's not my husband, he's my brother," answered Jillian, her voice starting to sound distraught. "I'm doing this on my own. Do you know how difficult it is to adopt a baby on your own?" And then Edgecomb's sister yielded to outright sobs.

The foreman appeared dumbfounded. He removed his handkerchief from the rear pocket of his jeans, as though to pass it to Jillian, but after examining the cloth, he appeared to think the better of his offer and stuffed the rag back into his pocket with embarrassment. "I'm not sure what to tell you, ma'am," he said.

Jillian continued to cry, her tears ebbing and surging in waves.

Fritz flashed Edgecomb a look of desperation. "You really her brother?"

"That's what my mother told us."

"In that case, Ms. Edgecomb, I'll make you an offer." Fritz opened the door to the trailer fully, exposing waist-high stacks of manila folders. "What do you say I call off our excavation work on Friday afternoon—just this one time—and, in return, you let me take you out to dinner on Friday evening?" The foreman's gaze shifted to the floor. "I hope that wasn't too forward."

Edgecomb's sister slowly composed herself. Meanwhile, a second construction worker appeared at Fritz's side. This fellow, all scars and sunburn, lived up to Edgecomb's preconceived expectations. "What's going on out here?" he demanded.

"I was just making a fool of myself," said Fritz. "I didn't—"

But his colleague cut him off, pointing at Edgecomb. "You're the guy! Fritz, he's the guy I was telling you about. From the TV. The one with the weird ideas and the funny coloring books." The workman extended his beefy hand for Edgecomb to shake. "You got any coloring books with you? I want one for my nephew."

"I'm afraid I don't," replied Edgecomb.

Another explosion—slightly more distant—saw Edgecomb reach again for Jillian's elbow. Neither of the men in the trailer paid any heed to the blasting. "Why don't you both come inside?" suggested Fritz. "Before something falls on you."

And an instant later, the foreman helped Jillian up the steps. Edgecomb followed them into the trailer, and along a narrow channel that snaked between filing cabinets and rows of cardboard tubes and samples of congealed concrete in assorted tins. He heard Fritz informing Jillian that he had an adopted sister of his own; soon, the pair of them were chatting up a storm about the international placement process. They disappeared into the foreman's office, leaving Edgecomb in the break room with his deputy.

The second workman offered Edgecomb a cup of instant coffee. Then he examined him afresh, as he might an excavation site, and asked, "Tell me the truth, man. Do you really think the whole Civil War was a sham?"

Edgecomb paused in the finest Royster style, letting the tiny chamber fill with suspense and the far off staccato of a jackhammer. He took a sip of his coffee, which was tepid and tasted vaguely of copper.

"Yes, I do think it was a sham," he replied. "And you should too."

~

Over the next several weeks, Edgecomb found himself recognized—and dogged by the same two questions—nearly everywhere that he went: *Did he really believe that the Civil War was a hoax?* And: *Where could one buy a Color the Prophet coloring book?* Some folks offered justifications for the second question, blaming their interest on "idle curiosity" or insisting that they wanted to make a statement in favor of free expression, not against Muslims, but others, including his barber, used the novelty item as an excuse to deliver collusive rants about "Arabs and Terrorists," assuming Edgecomb must share their objectionable views. "Damn best idea for a Christmas gift I've heard in a long time, chief," said Maximo, while trimming the tufts above Edgecomb's ears. "And as far as that war business goes, I wouldn't put it past Old Uncle Sam to put one over on us." At the bank, the walleyed teller with the asymmetrical jaw whispered to Edgecomb that she'd always struggled with history in school, so she found it reassuring to learn that a large portion of what they'd taught her wasn't even true.

In all fairness, Edgecomb's auto mechanic made a point of challenging him, crawling out from under the axle of the Honda to inform Edgecomb that his grandfather's grandfather had been "a full colonel" in an Irish regiment who'd lost an arm at Spotsylvania. He also received a deprecating letter from the executive secretary of the local chapter of the Daughters of the American Revolution. Yet on the whole, support for Edgecomb's "evolution" in the community ran roughly two-to-one in favor of the deniers. The warmth of this reception alarmed him. What was the point of teaching history, after all, when nobody actually believed it?

If the man on the street embraced Edgecomb's contrarian ideas, his colleagues at Laurendale proved far less accepting. On his first day back—he couldn't avoid facing the coworkers forever—Calliope Chaselle greeted him in passing with a frosty nod. Elgin Rothmeyer avoided eye contact entirely. In the dining room, he'd hardly settled down opposite Mickey Bickerstaff, who'd always struck him as an outside-the-box thinker, when the blustery English teacher muttered something about returning an overdue library book and hurried off with his lunch tray. Yet the most shattering rejection, one that made him seriously reconsider his entire enterprise, albeit only for a brief instant before he fortified his psyche with images of Vicky Vann, arrived in the person of the usually soft-spoken and affable school nurse, Ida Buxner.

He'd stopped by the main office following lunch to retrieve his mail, which, after three days away, consisted entirely of glossy flyers pitching continuing education credits, and an annual ballot for the Retired Teachers Association elections. Although Edgecomb stood a good four decades away from retirement, some glitch of fate or computing had added his name prematurely to their voting rolls, and no reasonable effort on his part had been able to correct it. Since Leonard Brackitt and his deputy both ran unopposed every year—more a testament to collective indifference than to widespread support—Edgecomb considered taking the time to write in the name of Attila the Hun, as he'd done on past ballots, but such trivial humor seemed pointless now, so he slid the whole trove into the garbage receptacle opposite the photocopier alcove. Ida exited the nearby ladies room as he was returning to the corridor. Her presence reminded Edgecomb of her daughter's flight from his classroom—and he felt genuinely ashamed.

At first, Ida appeared as though she intended to ignore him, shuffling briskly down the passageway with her eyes fixed on an imaginary horizon. She shared her daughter's flat features and hid her girth under a floral-print smock. Edgecomb wondered whether he should take the initiative—maybe apologize for any "misunderstanding"—when Ida confronted him by name. "Horace," she said, "What's this I hear from Louise about you saying slavery never happened?"

So *that* was what she'd heard. It *was* a misunderstanding, of sorts—but he also recognized that the reality wasn't much more excusable.

"That's not what I said," he ventured. "I said *some people* believe that the institution of slavery died out of natural causes. I offered two different theories, so the students could decide for themselves." He glanced over his shoulder, surveying their surroundings. Only yards away, one of the school secretaries labored at replacing the schedules on a bulletin board; down the hall, a gaggle of girls slumped on the floor, gossiping about photographs in a magazine. Edgecomb lowered his voice. "I'm certainly not denying that slavery ever *existed.* I don't think anyone is claiming that…"

His own words made him cringe inside. He sounded like one of those Holocaust apologists who insisted that the Nazis had slaughtered only one or two million Jews, rather than six. But Ida Buxner listened with care, as though she were genuinely weighing the merits of his defense. "I'm sorry if I've offended Louise," he added. "That's the very last thing I'd ever want to do."

Ida shook her head. "Honestly, Horace, I didn't think you were like this."

That was all she said. Louise's mother turned abruptly and walked away, leaving Edgecomb to reflect on her disappointment.

He took a circuitous route to his classroom, avoiding his usual shortcut through the administrative annex in an effort to avoid Sandra Foxwell. The notion entered his mind that Sly Sandy might be lying in wait for him, that she planned to escort him from the building, humiliated, with a security guard at either elbow. Instead, he found a jovial Lucky Pozner perched atop his radiator. The chemistry teacher's beard nested strands of lettuce residue from his half-eaten pastrami hero.

"I figured you might want some company," said Lucky.

He offered Edgecomb a section of his sandwich.

"No, thanks," said Edgecomb. "But I'll confess I'm happy to see you. I was afraid you'd joined the cold shoulder club."

"Because of your nutty views?" Pozner paused to pick between his teeth with the nail of his pinkie. "I don't scare off that easily. Besides, you're not the first teacher at Laurendale to go astray. Years ago, we had a young tyke in our own department who went through a skeptical phase and insisted on teaching Lamarckian evolution as an alternative to Darwin. He'd teach the students that giraffes grew long necks from reaching for leaves, that ducks gained webbed toes from generations of paddling. So I'm used to this. You'll sort yourself out eventually."

"It's true, what they say," said Edgecomb, "about finding out who your friends are when the chips are down." He longed to tell Pozner that he'd *already* sorted himself out—that he didn't genuinely embrace Royster's worldview—but he didn't dare. As it was, he'd already confided in an inflammatory publisher, a sex-obsessed schizophrenic, a waitress who read faces like tea leaves, and a germ-phobic woman perpetually on the brink of stealing a stranger's child—all against Vicky's express warning to tell nobody. Taking a draft-dodging Marxist in his confidence was one step too far. "I know you say that friendship means not having to say thank you, but I *want* to say it anyway. So thank you for being such a loyal friend. It means more than you can imagine."

"You'd do the same for me," said Pozner. "I have many shortcomings—and enough of a gut to carry them around in—but I'm a good judge of character."

"Thank you, just the same. Nobody else seems to feel that way. Bickerstaff fled from me like I was Typhoid Mary. Rothmeyer didn't even say hello."

Pozner glanced at his watch; he wrapped the remnants of his hero in wax paper, stuffing into his mouth those snippets of meat that fell free. "I wouldn't be too hard on them. They're just frightened. Dissent has that effect on most people."

The grizzled chemist shoved off his perch. "Anyway, it's time for me to share my limited wisdom with the lightly-washed masses. But hang in there, okay." Pozner patted him on the back and ambled toward the door.

"I'll do my best," agreed Edgecomb. "Say, what happened to your Lamarckian? Did he ever sort himself out?"

"More or less."

Edgecomb decided to go for broke. "It was you, wasn't it?"

"A good guess," replied Pozner. "But a wrong one. The guy's name was actually something like Robustelli or Rostubelli—sounded like Robitussin. He ended up quitting teaching entirely and joining a seminary in Canada. The rumor was that he eventually became a full-fledged monk—but that's just a rumor..."

Only once Pozner had vanished into the corridor did Edgecomb register that the story actually undermined its own point. Mr. Robitussin hadn't recanted and embraced Darwin; he'd abandoned science entirely. Yet at a moment when the entire world seemed armed against him, Edgecomb gladly accepted his colleague's good intentions, even if he couldn't puzzle his way through the logic of his anecdote.

Not even Lucky Pozner's loyalty, welcome as it was, made up for the tangible loss of admiration Edgecomb sensed in the classroom over the ensuing weeks. He'd never realized how much he'd depended upon his students—how much his own good spirits derived from their approval—until their enthusiasm evaporated. Other than Louise Buxner, who requested to change classes, none of them challenged him directly. They completed their assignments; they scored well on their quizzes. A few of the least engaged, like Brittany Marcus, still asked reductive questions. But gone was the line of curious minds seeking a moment of his time and insight after class, the gusto with which previous students had enveloped themselves in his simulation mysteries. Where his top talents had once been his allies, brimming with intellectual zeal, they now filed to and from their desk like factory hands awaiting a shift change. Only Sally Royster posed thoughtful questions, and volunteered to read aloud from historical texts, and stayed after class to probe the depths of his knowledge—but one student, no matter how dedicated, no matter how loyal, could not carry the weight of ninety-seven others. Yet that's how precisely Edgecomb experienced the classroom from his first day back at Laurendale and onwards. It was him and Sally versus the world.

~

Jillian and Lucky Pozner weren't the only ones to embrace Edgecomb unequivocally; Royster's followers also invited him into their fold.

He received a phone call one Friday evening from Nalaskowski, asking after his mother's health and inviting him to a "strategizing meeting" at Surrender Appomattox's headquarters the following morning. So on Saturday, after sharing a bagel and lox with Albion, while he pretended not to hear Sebastian's early-hour sexual escapades across the apartment, Edgecomb drove out to the deniers' compound on Laurendale Ridge. Lantern-jawed cousin Nigel met him at the gate, tapped on his car window and swung into the passenger seat of the Honda. "Uncle sent me down to meet you," he said—his tone not exactly friendly, but also lacking the overt hostility of their prior encounters. "You've got good timing. They're just settling down to business."

Nigel did not volunteer the subject of that business and Edgecomb did not ask. They drove in silence along the pea gravel, pausing at one point to let a flock of pheasants cross the drive. At the chalet-style guard booth, Sally's cousin instructed him to stop. "I get out here. Security duty," he said. "You'll find Uncle Rollie in the conservatory—cross through the sculpture hall into the main foyer and take the first door on the left." The Royster family's sudden confidence in him astonished Edgecomb, and Sally's cousin must have sensed his surprise, because he added, "Uncle trusts you not to get lost." Edgecomb sensed that Nigel didn't share Royster's change of heart, that beneath his civility lurked a seething animus, but the young man kept his hostility in check. "First door on the left," he repeated. "You'll find the house unlocked."

Edgecomb thanked his reluctant escort. He followed Nigel's directions to the letter, proceeding across the traffic circle, up the stairs into the vestibule, and between the marble busts of the Truth-to-Power brigade. A perverse question tickled his imagination: how, he wondered, would the martyred priest, Maximilian Kolbe, feel about someday sharing this gallery with the likeness of Roland Royster?

Edgecomb heard Royster's voice before he saw him. "Brilliant. Incontrovertibly brilliant. You have outdone yourself, Professor Herskovitz." He considered eavesdropping further, but suspecting that Cousin Nigel had already relayed news of his arrival, he decided not to press his luck. When he entered the conservatory, a sprawling chamber with a pair of grand pianos entrenched in the two far corners and a concert harp stationed halfway between, Royster bellowed out his name with relish. "Horace Edgecomb," he cried, "the very chap we've been waiting for." He rose from his chair and, with a flourish of his arm, insisted that Edgecomb occupy his own seat. "I haven't had an opportunity to congratulate you for your fine speech last month," he said. "I'm sorry we got derailed the way we did, but you still managed to strike a blow for truth. It was quite a coup, if I may say so."

Edgecomb scanned the room. In addition to Nalaskowski, who seemed all the larger when ensconced on an upholstered loveseat, Royster's inner circle consisted only of the two renegade academics, Herskovitz and McNabb, and Sally. Bruce McNabb was a handsome, open-faced young man who didn't look much older than thirty; he sat atop a piano bench, one leg folded over the other, cradling a meerschaum pipe in one hand. Mort Herskovitz, pushing sixty, boasted eyebrows as thick and unkempt as foliage. He shared a leather divan with Sally, who'd curled her slender legs beneath her rump. On the glass table at the center of this disparate caucus lay what appeared to be a heavily-stained cloth. What struck Edgecomb most was how small the spiritual core of Surrender Appomattox actually was—six, all told, if one included Cousin Nigel, seven if one counted himself. While Edgecomb exchanged polite greetings with Royster's entourage, Sally's father retrieved the cloth from the tabletop.

"Do you recognize this, Horace?" Royster asked.

The black cloth resembled the snoods worn by Orthodox Jewish matrons, only soiled with hideous brown patches.

"Is that Lincoln's bloody cloak?" asked Edgecomb—aghast.

The infamous cloak, which Abraham Lincoln had worn to Ford's Theatre on the night of his assassination, had become something of a cause célèbre, maybe even a casus belli, among Royster's followers. According to one of Surrender Appomattox's pamphlets, the organization believed that comparing the DNA on the cloak with that of Lincoln's collateral descendants would prove that the blood stains did not belong to the "alleged President" at all—which made perfect sense if the assassination had never actually occurred. *We don't even know if it's human blood,* the organization argued. *It might be pig blood or goat blood or tomato paste. How can we tell if we can't conduct scientific testing?* But the Gettysburg Historical Society, where the cloak had been on display since the 1950s, refused to yield to Royster's requests for a fabric sample. A year of litigation against the city had proven fruitless. Yet now the cloak appeared to be in the group's possession.

"Indeed. Lincoln's bloody cloak," confirmed Royster. "Although who can say it's blood? Let's not get ahead of ourselves. I'm sure you're aware of my recent efforts to gain access to this artifact. But a few months ago, I realized how foolish I had been: of course, we could never win access to the cloak through legal action. The cards are stacked against us—because the very individuals who run the court system are the same parties behind the conspiracy. Far better, I decided, to help myself."

"You mean it's stolen?" asked Edgecomb.

"Not yet." Royster tossed the stained cloth to Herskovitz. "This is merely a fine replica prepared by Professor Herskovitz. Professor Herskovitz and Professor McNabb paid a visit to Gettysburg several weeks ago to perform reconnaissance." Sally's father delivered another of his legendary pauses, literally drawing Edgecomb like a magnet to the physical edge of his seat. "We're going to pinch the cloak and replace it with a replica. Nobody will even know it's missing until we're ready."

He didn't specify ready for what.

"And when will that be?"

Royster shooed off his question. "The real cloak isn't the one on display anyway," he continued. "That's *also* a replica. The real cloak—or the cloak that's *purported* to be real—lies inside an airtight vault deep in the Historical Society's basement. Fortunately, my genius of a nephew has developed a device that can harness sound waves to crack the combination. I'll have the boy explain the technology to you one day, when we're less pressed for time..."

Edgecomb was itching to return home to phone Vicky. Already, he'd acquired enough juice on Surrender Appomattox to justify a call, but he also didn't wish to appear overanxious to depart—and he suspected the cloak-napping plot might prove merely the tip of the group's nefarious iceberg. "So you're going to break into the vault and replace the cloak?" he prodded.

Royster stepped to the door and whistled. The pack of Rottweilers charged into the room, competing for a chance to lick their master. "I knew you were a sharp fellow, Horace," he said. "Yes, Herskovitz and McNabb will pinch the cloak. But that's only half the battle. We also need DNA for comparison." Sally's father strolled to the mantel piece, the dogs trailing dutifully. If one counted Orwell and Santayana, Voltaire and Carneades and Al-Ghazali, mused Edgecomb, Royster's inner circle expanded to twelve. Sally's father poked at the cold logs in the hearth with a fire iron. "That's where you come in, Horace."

Edgecomb waited for his host to say more. He couldn't help being impressed with how the man commanded the attention of his followers, charismatic yet soft-spoken like a silver-haired Ho Chi Minh. Nobody ever attempted to interject or to complete his sentences. Even Sally, his own daughter, appeared transfixed by his voice. Edgecomb found his eyes drifting toward the girl more than he intended: she looked particularly cute in her V-necked Laurendale sweatshirt and bunny slippers. He shifted his gaze quickly toward Nalaskowski, who scribbled notes in longhand on a yellow legal pad.

"Did you ever wonder why I moved to Laurendale?" asked Royster.

"For the schools?" asked Edgecomb, grinning.

"In a way, yes," replied his host, but without a trace of humor. "But not the public ones. Have you ever heard of the Solomon Institute?"

The name sounded vaguely familiar, but Edgecomb couldn't place it.

"Your pal's girlfriend is a student there," continued Royster. "The one with the pink hair."

Now the name registered. The Solomon Institute was that crackpot academy where Esperanza studied normative prosopography. He felt no need to mention this sudden recollection to his host.

"As I was saying, we relocated to Laurendale because access to the cloak is merely half the battle. We also need access to Mr. Lincoln's descendants." Royster puffed heartily on his cigar. "The actor who played Lincoln sired only two children who survived to adulthood, as you may know, and neither of them produced any living descendants of their own. So the closest male relative to the Grand Impostor is the great-great-grandson of

Abe's purported uncle, Josiah Lincoln, who happens to reside a quarter of a mile from where you stand now. *That* is why I moved here from Pennsylvania. Hunting is easier when you live near the prey."

Royster retrieved a framed snapshot from the mantel and urged it into Edgecomb's hands. Its subject was a comely, fair-haired lad in a tuxedo. "This is decades old now," observed Sally's father. "From a wedding album. You cannot imagine the lengths we went to in order to obtain it. The current Mr. Lincoln, you see, is paranoid about being photographed. He teaches his classes from behind a screen. He's also obsessed with protecting his genetic residue. On the rare occasions when he dines in a restaurant, he pours the leftovers into a paper bag and washes the glassware himself in the men's room. Mr. Lincoln seems determined to prevent us from comparing either his DNA or his image to his supposed forebear—although, as this photo demonstrates, he looks nothing like Old Abe. Even if he isn't part of the conspiracy—and we're honestly not certain whether he's in the know—he has every reason to resist our efforts. Without testing, he's the heir to a United States President. A part of history. With testing, we'll prove he's nobody, and, deep down, his instincts must be telling him this."

Or maybe, reflected Edgecomb, *the man just doesn't want to be harassed by crazies*. But if, to a man with a hammer, every problem looks like a nail, then to Sally's father, widowed at twenty-five, all human behavior resembled conspiracy.

"So, as I said," Royster continued, "that's where you come in. Your job is to persuade Esperanza Arcaya to invite you to one of Thorn's classes and to steal something he's touched."

"Did you say *Thorn*?"

"Indeed, I did. Thorn Lincoln."

"But I work with his girlfriend. Calliope Chaselle. He's bound to know I've joined your team. Besides, what makes you think Esperanza will invite me to her class?"

Royster retrieved the photo and returned it to the mantel. "You'll find a way. I'm confident of that. Miss Arcaya is your friend, isn't she?"

Edgecomb instantly regretted his earlier tiff with Sebastian's girlfriend. It also unnerved him that Royster already knew the woman's last name. "Not exactly a friend," he said. "She's just a chick who's sleeping with my housemate."

"Close enough," said Royster. "She's been studying under Lincoln for years. He trusts her. If she says she's bringing a friend, he won't ask any questions—or let's hope he won't—and then you grab something, a sneaker, a pair of glasses, anything, before he realizes what's hit him. Sound good?"

Sounds crazy, thought Edgecomb. *Crazy and improbable.*

"I'll try my best," he agreed.

That provoked spontaneous clapping from Sally. "I knew you'd try. I just knew it. Didn't I tell you he was on our side?" Her remarks seemed directed at Nalaskowski, who raised his eyebrows in acknowledgement. She jumped up from the seat, threw her arms around Edgecomb without warning, and pecked him on the bare flesh just above his collar. This time, he hadn't anticipated her assault—and she was already back on the sofa before he registered the extent of her lapse. The entire movement, so quick and fleeting, hardly seemed real.

Edgecomb pressed his fingertips to his neck, to the moist spot on his skin.

Sally's father didn't even acknowledge the encounter. "I *know* the DNA doesn't match," he announced to the room, the gleam in his corneas reminding Edgecomb of John Brown at his most maniacal. "Now all I have to do is prove it."

~

As soon as he turned onto Blenheim Boulevard, Edgecomb plugged Vicky Vann's number into his phone. She answered on the first ring.

"So I've got your juice on Royster," he said. "When can we talk?"

"Why don't I meet you at your place?"

That surprised Edgecomb. He'd expected another rendezvous destination culled from an espionage novel: the international terminal at Newark Airport or under the board walk in Atlantic City. "Okay," he agreed. "When?"

"How about now?" asked Vicky.

"*Now?*"

"I'll be at your front door in fifteen minutes."

She hung up without giving him an opportunity to express his astonishment. When he arrived home twenty minutes later, cruising through Rolleston and Hager Heights at speeds well above the posted limit, Vicky Vann's rented lemon convertible already sat in front of their building, one rear tire breaching the curb. Inside the apartment, he found Vicky and the designer, Sevastopol, chatting on the sofa. It took a moment for Edgecomb to recognize Sebastian's accomplice. The artist had trimmed his hair, which no longer revealed a trace of bleach. He still wore the grease-stained cargo pants and a shirt that had once been a janitor's uniform. The name Reggie was emblazoned in Gothic script above the breast pocket. All around the pair stood open cartons of *Color the Prophet* coloring books, bathed in a faint draft of weed. "Your friend let me in," explained Vicky.

Edgecomb bristled at being linked socially to Sebastian's associate.

"I know what you're thinking," said Sevastopol. "He cut his hair, so he's selling out—applying to law school or something. Well, for the record, my douchebag of an ex-boyfriend gave me lice. Like anyone over five years old, not in a prison camp, gets lice."

"I didn't ask," said Edgecomb.

He stared at the visitor, waiting for Sevastopol to explain his presence. After a solid forty-five seconds, the designer said, "Borrelli's picking up the rest of the boxes. Turns out those Korean fuckers didn't own that shithole after all."

"You mean the workshop?"

"City marshal showed up this morning," explained Sevastopol. "He gave us just enough time to carry the current lot onto the sidewalk. We've been taking turns driving it here by U-Haul while Esperanza stands guard."

Edgecomb now registered that cartons lined the side wall, stacked shoulder high and three boxes deep.

"And get this," added Sevastopol, shoving a crumpled paper at Edgecomb. "Some asshole in California is suing us for trademark infringement. Guy claims he's been making Mohammed coloring books since 9/11..."

Vicky flipped through one of the coloring books, wearing a look of mild distaste, while Sevastopol related his travails. Yet the designer broke off when she reached a particular page and, pointing at an image, said, "That's my favorite. Mohammed and his wife, Khadijah, kissing in front of the Grand Mosque in Mecca. You like how I modeled it on a headshot of Bogie and Bacall?"

Edgecomb cleared his throat. "Would you mind if my friend and I had a word alone?" he asked the designer. "You're welcome to wait in Sebastian's bedroom."

"Secrets, secrets," replied Sevastopol. He took his time rising, adjusting the cushions on the sofa, straightening a stack of coloring books atop the end table; finally, as Edgecomb was about to speak again, he departed.

"So," said Edgecomb.

"Quite a character," said Vicky. "I bet he *does* end up in law school eventually. They always do." Now that they'd been left alone, Edgecomb was able to absorb the full extent of his crush's radiance: her low-cut blouse and her hair color matched nearly perfectly, augmented by scarlet tourmaline earrings. She twirled an auburn lock between her fingers, a coquettish, insouciant gesture that recalled their high school days. "You really ought to do something about that marijuana, by the way," she said, waving her hand in front of her face. "I do work for the Treasury Department."

"It's not mine," he said defensively. "Not ours, I mean. Maybe it's coming from the next apartment."

"Chill out, okay?" Vicky laughed, shaking her head. "My nose is off duty." She adjusted the pillow cushion under her thighs. "So what did you want to talk about?"

"I have the goods on Royster," he explained—the speed of his thoughts nearly eclipsing the pace of his tongue. "He's planning on pilfering the bloody cloak that Lincoln wore to Ford's Theater and comparing the DNA to a sample I'm supposed to snatch from a relative of Lincoln's who lives in Laurendale Ridge. The goal is to show that the samples don't match—and somehow, in an indirect way, this also proves the entire Civil War never happened." Edgecomb paused for effect—and suddenly realized that he'd adopted Royster's technique subconsciously.

"That's the gist of it, anyway. I'm charged with befriending my housemate's girlfriend and then she'll get me access to Thorn. The one thing I can confirm with certainty is that Royster's not a huckster. He believes absolutely everything he preaches."

Vicky didn't appear at all shocked, or even particularly intrigued, by his disclosure. She fingered her hair again, her other hand still marking her place in Borrelli's closed coloring book.

"Well?" he asked.

"I'm pleased you managed to infiltrate Royster's group. Operation *Damnatio Memoriae* is shaping up to be a success."

Her calm infuriated him.

"That's all? You don't even sound the slightest bit excited."

And suddenly, the reality struck him. "You already knew everything I just told you, didn't you?" he demanded. "You even knew I was going to phone you this morning to tell you—that's how you got here so quickly."

Vicky flashed a look of feigned innocence. "Could be." She slid the coloring book onto the table. "Anyway, we're not done yet."

"Wait a second," objected Edgecomb—and another notion hit him. He reached into his pocket and fished for his wallet, then slid out the Treasury Department ID badge. "It's a bug of some sort, isn't it?"

Vicky laughed. "You *would* make a good spy. You have the right mindset," she said. "But I have to disappoint you this time around. It's just an identity card."

"Nonsense," snapped Edgecomb. He pried at the card, ran his fingers along the surface—and in desperation, retrieved a scissors from the utility drawer in the kitchen and snipped the plastic into quarters. Nothing.

"You owe the federal government three dollars," said Vicky, clearly amused. "Satisfied? The reason I know what you just told me is that we've been following Royster's crew for months. Did you honestly think you're our only source?"

Edgecomb slid the dissected ID badge into his trousers.

"Sorry I made a mess of this," he apologized, sheepishly. "Anyway, what should I do now?"

"About what?"

"Jesus, Vicky. About Royster. Do you really want me to steal this guy's DNA?"

"Sure. Why not?"

Multiple reasons flooded Edgecomb's mind—foremost among them, the fear that he'd get arrested and earn Jillian's eternal displeasure. "Because it's illegal," he answered. "And because it's totally cuckoo. And because, for all I know, Thorn Lincoln might fillet me with a stiletto."

"At HDC, we prefer to term such authorized initiatives as 'less than legal.' Illegal has a nasty connotation," observed Vicky. "And anyone on the street might fillet you with a stiletto. But you can stock up on life insurance, if you're concerned."

"You're not reassuring me."

"My job isn't to reassure you," replied Vicky. "My job is to manage your fieldwork. If you need reassuring, you might consider talk therapy...or you could always place an ad in the personals." Her quip was obviously meant tongue-in-cheek, but still struck Edgecomb as a stinging rebuke. A woman who wants to sleep with you doesn't suggest searching for romance elsewhere. Here he was, risking his reputation—and his sanity—to impress Vicky Vann; the least she could do would be to *pretend* that she might date him someday.

Vicky opened the coloring book again and displayed for him the photo of Mohammed and Khadijah making out, cinema style, in front of Islam's holiest site. "This is repugnant, just so you know," she said. "You should be ashamed."

CHAPTER SIX

They received their first hate mail within forty-eight hours of the press conference—a missive from Georgia-based fraternal organization called the Commanders of the Stars and Bars—and by the end of the following week, they'd garnered so much correspondence that the letter carrier had to stack the surplus on the package table in the building's lobby. Albion opened the letters and sorted them meticulously into four piles, the contents of which condemned Edgecomb on four distinct grounds: for his Civil War heresy; from Muslims, for offending the Prophet Mohammed; from well-intentioned liberals and non-Muslim religious leaders, for stirring up anti-Islamic prejudice; and from supporters of either Civil War denial or Islamophobia, who bashed him for linking their own cause with the other. Nearly all of these communiqués were addressed to Edgecomb, not Sebastian. In addition, they both receives hundreds of orders for coloring books, containing checks or cash or, in one case, "payment in kind" via a vitriol-filled pamphlet attacking Arabs and Jews; the hate mail settled over the apartment like a dusting of black snow, the envelopes competing for space with the novelty items themselves.

"We did get one fan letter," announced Borrelli, waving an envelope at Edgecomb. He'd brought home takeout for both of them from the new sushi bar in Rolleston. Esperanza was attending her evening prosopography class with Thorn. "Kind of. From a bookstore owner in Belfast, Maine, who happened to be visiting her niece in New Jersey and caught us on TV. You want to hear the good parts?"

"Sure," agreed Edgecomb. He was still brooding over Vicky's quip about placing a personal ad.

"*You may be familiar with the quotation, 'I disapprove of what you say, but I will defend to the death your right to say it,' apocryphally attributed to Voltaire, but actually the words of his biographer, Evelyn B. Hall, better known to you as Tallentyre. Well, let me echo that sentiment and magnify it times ten thousand. I find every last word you said to be utterly repugnant and disgraceful; in my opinion, you may be the most ignorant and bigoted human being on the planet. At the same time, moral vermin of your ilk do push the bounds of freedom of expression, thus preserving a core marketplace where decent people can share ideas and disagreements with impunity. So I thank you for what you have done, although I feel nothing for you exempt utter contempt. Sincerely, Iris Lustgarten, Lobsterman Books.*"

"*That's* a fan letter?"

"Compared to the others," said Borrelli. "Of course, there are a handful written in Arabic—so, in theory, one of those could also be supportive. On a positive note, that minister dude in Texas ordered another five thousand units. What's that Mark Twain said? 'It's better to be rich and despised than poor and despised.'"

"He didn't say that," objected Horace. "You made that up."

"Maybe I did, Teach. But I'm sure he thought it once or twice."

Borrelli slid a tuna maki roll onto his plate and lathered it in ketchup and mustard—a habit that made the dining idiosyncrasies of Edgecomb's sister appear tame. "I've got something I've been meaning to ask you," Sebastian said while chewing, "but you've got to promise not to get mad at me."

"I don't think I can promise that."

"Fine. Can you at least agree to keep an open mind?"

Edgecomb sipped his miso soup, keeping his gaze from housemate's mouth. Every time someone asked him to keep an open mind—Sandra Foxwell, Vicky Vann, Roland Royster—what followed was an attempt to slug his brain.

"I'll take that as an affirmative, Teach," said Borrelli. "So here's my question: Is there any chance that Royster's right?"

Edgecomb nearly spit out his soup. "My mind is never going to be *that* open."

"Hear me out, dude, okay? I'm not saying he *is* right, I'm just asking you if it's *possible*. After all, the United States government has pulled off some pretty implausible stunts. They built an entire army of balloons before the invasion of Normandy that German aerials mistook for real tanks and vessels, right? And they managed to keep to the Manhattan Project so secret that even Vice President Truman didn't know about it."

"Thanks for the historian lesson," said Edgecomb, genuinely surprised that Borrelli has come across these military tidbits. "Where did you learn so much?"

"I haven't killed all my brain cells yet. Try as I might." Sebastian took a swig of sake and lit a cigarette. "Governments are capable of all sorts of crazy things. Didn't the Soviets have entire cities that never appeared on any map?"

"So what's your point? Is it plausible? Sure. But is it true? Of course not."

Borrelli ashed his cigarette onto his sushi tin. "How can you be sure?"

"Are you asking because you really have your doubts? Or are you just trying to give me a hard time?" demanded Edgecomb. "Because I'm not in the mood for an intellectual exercise."

A long pause followed. From the airshaft came the sound of the starter couple in the apartment below arguing about where to spend Thanksgiving.

"Honestly, Teach, I'm feeling skeptical." He held up his hand before Edgecomb could interject. "I heard Royster on the radio again and he didn't just sound persuasive, he sounded *smart*. And honest. And I keep asking myself, why's a dude like him fighting this battle unless he's really onto something?"

"Or *thinks* he's really onto something," said Edgecomb.

Borrelli downed the last of his sake. "So you really have *no* doubts?"

Edgecomb's housemate smiled at him innocently, his chin smeared in condiments. The overflow cartons of coloring books stood behind him, forming pillars on either side of the refrigerator door. "When can you move into your new space?" Edgecomb asked.

"Next week, dude," said his housemate. "Like I already told you. Now answer my question: Do you any doubts at all?"

Edgecomb let the question ricochet through his mind like a stray bullet. He reflected on Royster's story about the fabricated article that turned real, on Admiral Farragut capturing New Orleans with twelve wooden warships. But what unsettled him most was his own undercover work and the efforts of Vicky Vann and the HDC and Operation *Damnatio Memoriae* to silence Surrender Appomattox. If the group were just a half-dozen crackpots harassing a few local officials, why did the federal government of the United States care so much? The very existence of the Treasury Department's investigation lent Royster some credibility.

"Okay, I have my doubts," conceded Edgecomb. "But they're just reservations, nothing more. As far as I'm concerned, the verdict is still out."

"I knew it, Teach. I just knew it. Esperanza is never wrong."

"*She* put you up to this?"

"All she did was confirm what I already suspected." Borrelli stood up and patted him on the shoulder. "That girl is a regular human lie detector, I tell you. My cheating career, it seems, has come to an end."

"Do you think she'd take me to class with her one day?" asked Edgecomb.

"Good luck with that, dude. I've been asking for months," said Borrelli. "Turns out this Thorn guy is rather particular about who he teaches. But you're welcome to take it up with her directly." Edgecomb's housemate retrieved a six pack of beer from the refrigerator and headed toward his own bedroom. "I'll clean up in the morning. But don't be too hard on yourself. After all, certainty is the hobgoblin of little minds."

"That's consistency," Edgecomb called after him. "It's Emerson."

~

Edgecomb was fighting his way through the Barbary Wars with his History I students the next afternoon when the wall phone rang in his classroom. He couldn't remember the last time that had happened, and the sound prickled his nerves; when the secretary in the main office, Mrs. Wentletrap, informed him that she'd be patching through an urgent call, his pulse kicked into overdrive. Taking the call under the curious gaze of twenty-four eleventh graders did nothing to calm him.

"Horace Edgecomb? This is Frederick Fradkin," said the caller. "I'm sorry to disturb you, but I really need you to come down here."

Fradkin's voice sounded familiar—deep and resonant and kindly, despite its edge of alarm—but Edgecomb couldn't place it. "I'm in the middle of teaching," he protested. "You'll forgive me, but do I know you?"

"Frederick Fradkin. I'm the foreman at the Gripley Connector site," explained the caller. "You came by with your sister a few weeks ago."

"Fritz!"

"Yes, Fritz. Anyway, can you come down here ASAP? I need some help with your sister and I don't want to get the police involved...It's hard to explain over the phone..."

"Is everything okay?" demanded Edgecomb. "Can I speak to Jillian?"

Life had taught him hard lessons about unexpected phone calls: a neurosurgeon calling from a hospital in Cleveland, where his father had been at a convention, to inform his mother of the aneurysm; the harbor patrol telephoning during dinner to report his stepfather's boat drifting empty; an early morning ring from Tampa, announcing that his mother has fractured her collarbone. Unless you heard your loved one's voice, Edgecomb understood, the outcome usually proved grim.

"Jillian's not hurt. But she's upset," Fritz explained. "Honestly, she's out of control—but if I call 9-1-1, she's liable to end up in a psych ward..."

"I'll be there as soon as I can," promised Edgecomb. "Where can I find you?"

"Same place you found me last time. You can't miss us. Trust me."

Edgecomb hung up the phone. Two dozen sets of prying adolescent eyes stared up at him, expectant. "We're going to end early today," he announced. And then he taped a paper sign to his classroom door that read: "Personal emergency. Mr. E.'s classes are cancelled for the afternoon." What amazed him was how easy it was to just dismiss his class and walk out; nobody came chasing after him—although he'd probably have to explain himself to the Sly Sandy Fox at some point. Or maybe not. As he crossed through the faculty parking lot, he glanced over his shoulder, wondering if any of the principal's minions might be spying on him; he didn't see anyone, but on a reckless whim, he flashed his middle finger at her invisible spies before climbing into the Honda.

He peeled onto Blenheim Boulevard and merged onto the Parkway three minutes later. *Please let her be all right,* he found himself bargaining—with a God he otherwise didn't believe in. *Please let her be alive. I'll never ask for anything again, not even Vicky Vann, if Jillian's okay.* Within half an hour, he'd parked opposite the construction site at the edge of the crabgrass lot. Since his previous visit, someone had abandoned a ravaged pinball machine and a pair of plush green turtles alongside the charred tires, making the scrapyard appear even more forlorn. From across the street drifted the stench from a row of port-o-johns.

The mesh gate stood open; inside, as Fritz had promised, Edgecomb had no difficulty spotting his sister. Jillian was lying on the dusty yard, about twenty feet from the foreman's trailer, rolling back and forth in the dirt like a wildebeest. She'd tossed away her coat, which lay with her shoes a good distance from her body. Soil caked her dress, her elbows, her knees; chunks of earth clung to her hair. A half dozen laborers in hardhats congregated at the perimeter of the yard, held back by Fritz Fradkin's command. As Edgecomb approached, his sister cried, "Are you satisfied? Poison me, okay! Why do I care?" And then she fell silent again, rolling with somewhat less vigor.

"She's been doing this, on and off, since she got the letter," explained Fritz. "She didn't pass the home evaluation."

"I see," said Edgecomb.

"Last time I ventured out there, she took a chunk out of my hand," he added, showing Edgecomb a track of bloody scratch marks below his wrist. "But I'm afraid to do anything that might end up on her permanent record."

"So you thought *I* could help?"

Fritz's expression turned from stoic to cold. "You're the reason she failed the evaluation," he said. "The letter cited you by name under Background Investigation."

"Me?"

"Yes, *you.* Unless she has another brother who belongs to a 'known hate group.' Apparently, calling slavery a hoax isn't so popular in some circles."

"Jesus Christ," exclaimed Edgecomb.

"Jesus Christ is right," echoed Fritz. "Now I'm hoping you can do something."

But what am I supposed to do? mulled Edgecomb. *Those aren't my views, dammit—not even my undercover views.*

He inched his way toward Jillian. When he stood only a few meters distant, she lurched up and glowered at him. "You! You bastard! Leave me alone." A torrent of sobs ensued. "Just please leave me alone."

"It's going to be okay," he soothed, kneeling down beside her. A harsh wind curled around the abutments of the unfinished highway and lashed Edgecomb's face. "I promise you'll get your baby. *Somehow.*"

Jillian's tears had turned the dirt on her cheeks to mud; when she rubbed her eyes, she left behind ferret-like rings. Edgecomb reached for her shoulder, but she shook him off with a twist of her torso. "I finally have a boyfriend, a boyfriend *who actually likes me*, and I'm at the front of the baby line—and then you get yourself mixed up in some deranged sting operation. It's not fair."

"I know it's not fair," agreed Edgecomb. "We'll find a way to fix this."

"It's too late," cried Jillian. "I've been blacklisted."

Edgecomb again reached for her shoulder; this time, she did not fight him. "I'll talk to them. I promise. We'll get you a baby," he reassured her. "Now let's go home and get you cleaned up."

Jillian looked up at him, hopeful. "You swear I'll get a baby."

"I swear," he pledged. "Even if I have to give you mine and Vicky's."

The pledge sounded absurd as soon as he offered it—he had little prospect of having a child with his crush, and even if he did, no reason to suspect that she'd surrender their infant to his sister. But as ludicrous as his vow was, it had a calming effect on Jillian. With his assistance, she rose and hobbled toward her shoes.

"Oh my god," she groaned. "I must be crawling with carcinogens. Fritz! Do you have a hose?"

"You'll go home and take a warm shower," suggested Edgecomb.

"I don't want to carry this filth into my apartment." Jillian slid her shredded stockings into her pumps. "What was I thinking? Fritz!"

At Jillian's insistence, the foreman hooked up one of the industrial hoses his team used for spraying down equipment, weaving it through the piers of a topless exit ramp and along the concrete wingwall. "I'm going to aim it into the air," he advised. "That's the best I can do for a shower." And while Jillian leaned on Edgecomb for balance, her boyfriend generated a crude, gravity-driven downpour that drenched all three of them.

The icy water peppered Edgecomb's necked and forehead. It soaked through his shirt and eked into his boots.

"Give the lady some privacy," Fritz ordered his construction crew. "Back to work. There's nothing to see here."

"Is this water potable?" demanded Jillian. "Are you sure it's safe?"

"No, I'm not at all sure," replied Fritz, matter-of-fact, as he gently massaged the mud from Jillian's bare arms. "But it's the only water I've got."

Once Jillian decided she was clean enough to shut off the hose, the pair of them accompanied her, soaked and shivering, into the trailer. Her dress cleaved to her flesh, revealing the outline of her undergarments. Edgecomb draped her coat over her shoulders for the sake of modesty. "I'm sorry I screwed things up for you," he said as he steered her toward a ragged couch. "From the bottom of my heart."

"Give me my bag," cried Jillian.

Fritz retrieved her canvas satchel. She snatched it from him and dumped the computer printouts of African orphans onto the cushions. Grinning, cocoa-skinned faces, each more adorable than the next, beamed from the pages. "I was so close," she said—as much to herself as to them. "So close."

"You're going to get a baby," said Edgecomb.

Fritz set a tea kettle to boil on the gas range. "You heard him, darling. You're going to get a baby." He brushed away the photos and sat down beside Jillian, hugging her tiny body to his chest. "We're in this together." The foreman's no-nonsense tenderness impressed Edgecomb—a striking contrast to the disbarred matrimonial lawyer who'd strung Jillian along for years with his histrionic commitments.

Less than three weeks earlier, Fritz and Edgecomb's sister had been total strangers; now, the pair looked to be quite an item. That was how courtship happened after thirty, he understood: Rapid and efficient, complex emotions condensed to adjust for the limited time remaining.

"I'm sorry," murmured Jillian between sniffles. "So, so sorry. I don't know what I was thinking…."

"Nothing to be sorry about. These things happen," replied Fritz, as though fits of madness and hose-baths were a routine part of his work-day. "It's all over now."

Edgecomb watched as his sister snuggled against the foreman's wiry frame; then he tiptoed down the passageway and out into the barren yard.

~

While Edgecomb coaxed his sister back to sanity, Leonard Brackitt, longtime president of the Laurendale Retired Teachers Association, set a tea kettle on his gas range in the modest efficiency apartment that he'd rented three blocks from the high school, and promptly fell asleep; when the kettle burst twenty minutes later, it extinguished the flames on the burner—and two hours after that, while Brackitt still napped, an errant spark, likely caused be the dripping water's interaction with a nearby toaster oven, generated an explosion far greater than any of the blasts at Fritz's construction site. By nightfall, the seventy-eight year old former French instructor's body lay on a cold slab in the basement of Gripley's Methodist Hospital. Edgecomb's inbox filled with invitations to a prayer vigil that soon transmuted into a memorial service.

"Brackitt was quite a character," Edgecomb explained to Sebastian. "He used to spin these hilarious yarns about his fishing trips with William F. Buckley, and of delivering a toast at Henry Kissinger's wedding, and about the time his former college flame, Jeanne Kirkpatrick, introduced him to the Queen of England. There wasn't a word of truth in any of it, but the stories were funny nonetheless—and he'd told them so many times, and with so much enthusiasm, I think he actually believed them."

"Sounds like a great role model for young minds, Teach," said Sebastian.

"At least he didn't claim that the French language is a hoax," Edgecomb replied. "Or that France itself is a convenient fiction and that Germany borders directly on Spain."

"I love how you teachers all circle your wagons to defend each other," observed Borrelli. "Just like doctors and cops. In business, if we see a competitor's shortcomings, we tear him to shreds."

Yet Brackitt had been well-liked, despite his farfetched tales of dinner dances with the wealthy and influential, so while no A-list celebrities or European royals appeared at his funeral, a Who's Who of current and pensioned faculty members stayed after school the following Tuesday to pay their respects. Edgecomb suddenly acquired faces to go with the names of the school's teaching legends of yore: Mrs. Geiff, so dedicated that she once suffered a mild stroke in the classroom and insisted on finished a calculus problem from her knees before the ambulance carted her away; the unfortunately-named Mr. Bumblenit, also a math teacher, so pompous that he referred to himself in the third person; Mr. & Mrs. Yarmouth, who'd taught introductory and advanced Latin for a combined total of eight-seven years, before budget constraints saw the language expunged from the Laurendale curriculum. A glance at the flock of mourners, frail and diminished, was—for better or for worse—a window into Edgecomb's own future.

The service took place at four p.m. As per the deceased's written instructions, it occurred in the same small upstairs theater that also hosted the quarterly Board of Education meetings and countless performances of *West Side Story* and *Grease*. Lucky Pozner delivered a poignant eulogy. "You don't have to weekend at Camp David or dine with the Queen to change the course of history," he declaimed, somehow capturing Brackitt's foibles without mocking them. "The measure of a human being is how he improves the lives of ordinary people, his coworkers, his students, men and women who will never wield scepters or command armies or have their names documented in newsprint. Every day, as an advocate for our elderly and most vulnerable compatriots, Leonard proved himself as influential as any sultan or king or president." Edgecomb's eyes teared up—not specifically for the dead man, but for all the loved ones that he had ever lost.

The service concluded with Brackitt's only surviving relative, a wheelchair-bound niece who appeared as old as any of the attendant retirees, offering the mourners a brief and tearful thank you. Stu and Stan Storrow played a duet of Amazing Grace on the piano as the bereaved filtered across the corridor to a cozier meeting room for a reception. *The students have rehearsals in here at six*, Edgecomb overhead one of the theater teachers relating to explain the relocation. *The Pajama Game.*

Funerals generate solidarity among the living, and Edgecomb discovered himself an unexpected beneficiary of this good will. Fellow teachers who, only days earlier, had snubbed him over his Civil War antics, now proved eager to chat about the comedy of Brackitt's life and the tragedy of his death. Edgecomb congregated in a circle that included Calliope Chaselle and Mickey Bickerstaff, listening to Elgin Rothmeyer recount the time that Brackitt had taken a "personal day" to visit Governor Tom Kean in the hospital after his emergency appendectomy. "But the best part," regaled Rothmeyer, "Was that the governor wasn't even in the hospital. He was on some trade association trip to Ireland."

"I wish I'd known him better. He sounds very complex," observed Calliope. "You have to wonder how his psyche was put together."

Edgecomb contemplated offering his own reflections on Brackitt's psychological makeup in an effort to impress the librarian, based on his two psychology classes at Rutgers, but he feared making a fool of himself. It also struck him that he had a second competitor for Chaselle's affections in Mickey Bickerstaff.

"I have no wisdom to offer on psyches," interjected Bickerstaff. "But Leonard did get a nice turnout. That's the one advantage of dying before your time."

"You aim to strike the right balance," added Rothmeyer. "Nobody wants to keel over at sixty-five. Anything short of seven-five or so and you feel shortchanged. On the other hand, you don't want to be one of those folks who survives to ninety-nine and dies alone and forgotten. It's not that different from retiring. You hope to choose the right age and you don't want to overstay your welcome." The department chairman seemed impressed with the profundity of his own remarks. "Of course, for me, that right age seems to inch upwards every year."

"Nothing sadder than when a person dies so old that nobody comes to the funeral," added Bickerstaff. And he proceeded to share a depressing anecdote about his own late cousin, who'd commanded an armored cavalry division during World War I, but later died forgotten at a veterans' home in Wyoming. Edgecomb was contemplating how to break free from the conversation without offending Bickerstaff when Sandra Foxwell slapped a stack of papers—like a subpoena—against his chest.

"What's this?" he demanded.

"Formal notice of your employment review before the Board of Ed," replied the Sly Sandy Fox. "You'll appreciate the timing. First, they'll vote on the proposal you forced them to table in September and then they'll vote to terminate you."

Edgecomb wasn't sure which unsettled him more—the content of the principal's message or her pleasure in delivering it. The circle surrounding Elgin Rothmeyer broke up quickly, and dispersed, leaving him alone with his boss.

"*Really*, Sandra? At a funeral?"

"I stopped by your classroom yesterday afternoon," retorted Foxwell. "But you weren't there. So you're aware, I had no choice but to pass your 'Gone to Lunch' sign along to the grievance review board as well."

"I had a family emergency," objected Edgecomb. "My sister suffered a breakdown."

Foxwell nodded. "I'm confident you're telling the truth. Unfortunately, there is a procedure to follow in such situations." She adopted a genial tone that, to the uninitiated, might have passed for sympathetic. "Can you imagine the fallout if one of your students went unaccounted for? In any case, had this been a first-time lapse, I'd have suggested you bring in some documentation of your sister's illness, and we might have been able to shelve the matter with a formal warning. Unfortunately, as you know, dereliction of duty is among your less serious infractions."

"I wasn't derelict," insisted Edgecomb—but what was the point, he decided, of protesting? He didn't even possess any paperwork, like a police report or an EMS run sheet, to verify Jillian's crisis. "You really are too much, Sandra. Do you realize how this is going to sound at the

Board meeting? First, you tell me to teach the Civil War as a theory, and then when I do *precisely what I was told to do* and teach the war as a theory, you try to fire me. You can't have it both ways."

Foxwell frowned. "*I'm* not trying to fire you, Horace. I assure you that I have absolutely nothing to do with this. You'll note there are two formal complaints against you: One from Roland Royster for humiliating his daughter and the other from Ida Buxner for condoning racism. To be frank, I tried to dissuade Ida from pursuing her concerns through official channels, but it seems you've traumatized her daughter. I am sorry it has come to this."

"I'm sure you are," replied Edgecomb.

His confrontation with Foxwell had drawn the attention of several colleagues, who no longer tried to conceal their interest. Among them was Calliope Chaselle, leaning against a folding table and sipping a glass of non-alcoholic cider. Maybe it was the junior librarian's presence, and his fear of being discredited in her eyes, that led Edgecomb to call after Foxwell as she departed. "Sandra. Let's just clarify this, for the record. Do you want me to teach the Civil War as a hoax, like Royster's daughter asked, or as the truth, like Ida's girl wants? Because it's either one or the other."

Foxwell turned to face him again, but did not approach, leaving a solid five yards between them. "Your problem, Mr. Edgecomb," she said, her voice loud and carrying, "is that you think too much. You're not paid to think. You're paid to teach. You might still make a decent educator someday—*somewhere*—if you were able to accept that."

The principal smiled politely at the contingent of nearby teachers, remarks clearly intended for them as much as for Edgecomb. She stepped past them and headed toward the far doors without waiting for a response.

"Thanks for the advice," he shouted after her. And then, "I can't imagine what Arch Steinhoff sees in you!"

His arrow hit home. The Sly Sandy Fox stopped walking and her back stiffened—but, adjusting to the blow and, without turning around again, she strode through the double doors and disappeared into the corridor. Edgecomb noticed Calliope Chaselle eying him closely; he glanced down at Foxwell's summons, pretending to be transfixed by its tortuous legal jargon. Insulting his boss had felt good for approximately the length of time it had taken her to leave the room; now he found his mind racing through all of the catastrophes that might result, from a slander suit to Archibald Steinhoff ordering his kneecaps fractured. He shuffled his way toward the nearest door, hoping to avoid further eye contact with Calliope, when her voice stopped him from behind.

"You're a strange one," she said. "I can't figure you out."

It was the perfect opening, in hindsight, to let her figure him out through a friendly conversation. Instead, like the idiotic adolescent he remained at heart, Edgecomb darted from the room and didn't pause for breath until he reached the parking lot.

~

Never had Edgecomb felt as desperate for advice—for sound guidance—as he did on the drive home from Leonard Brackitt's memorial service. With this desperation arose a profound sense of loneliness, a realization that he simply didn't have many people to rely on in a moment of need. His sister, of course, loved him unconditionally, but Jillian was too fragile to depend upon in a pinch and too psychologically damaged to ask for wisdom. Both his mother and his aunt shared an inflated opinion of his merits that undermined their ability to assess his predicament with any accuracy. So that left Oliver Nepersall, who viewed life through clinical and unforgiving eyes of a neurologist, or Lucky Pozner, a friend as cluelessly optimistic as he was loyal. Edgecomb had read in a magazine at his dentist's office that the average person had only one friend with whom he could intimately discuss a personal problem, and to his consternation, he realized that, for him, that friend was none other than Sebastian Borrelli. His housemate might not possess the solidest judgment on matters of business or romance, but he did know how to listen, and he genuinely cared, which placed him well ahead of the vast majority of human beings whom Edgecomb encountered on a daily basis. If anyone could offer him insight into how to handle Sandra Foxwell's latest onslaught, Sebastian was the man.

Edgecomb parked in front of their building, looking forward to a heart-to-heart with his housemate, hoping that Esperanza would be attending class that evening. Yet the instant he stepped off the elevator, he recognized that something was amiss: a sound that could only be described as anguished—like a regiment of toddlers let loose on a collection of orchestral instruments—gusted through their apartment door. Any hopes he had that the noise might be coming from the television were dashed a moment later, when he entered the flat to find his living room infested with derelicts. More than a dozen men and several women in various states of dishevelment mingled around his belongings. They snacked on pizza from boxes stacked high atop the coffee table; some fisted beer bottles in both hands. The "music" was the creation of three elderly gentlemen who'd equipped themselves with a harmonica, a fiddle, and what appeared to be a bassoon wrapped in green ribbons. The fiddler sported a bright orange do-rag that made him resemble a traffic cone, while the elderly bassoonist had removed his shirt, revealing a concave chest flecked with hoary curls. In the midst of all this chaos sat Albion, playing chess against himself.

"Sebastian!" screamed Edgecomb. "What the hell?"

His housemate emerged from the kitchen at the head of a makeshift conga line that included Esperanza, Sevastopol, and a transvestite in six-inch heels.

"We're celebrating, Teach," declared Borrelli. "You've got to join us."

Sebastian reached for his arm, but Edgecomb wanted no part of the chaos.

"I've *got* to do nothing of the sort. Who *are* these people?"

"My friends from Church on the Hill," said Borrelli. "We're having a party."

"I can see that," snapped Edgecomb, grabbing a beer bottle from his housemate's hand. "But the party is over. I live here too, you know."

"Don't be such a stick in the mud, Teach," Sebastian protested. "Don't you want to hear the latest good news? I've been invited onto the Spotty Spitford show."

Edgecomb recognized the radio host's name. Spitford was an African-American minister who hosted a rightwing talk program on which callers voiced racially-tinged opinions that a white moderator could never have tolerated. He branded himself "The Conservative Oprah"—but his followers were largely unreconstructed Southerners and blue-collar bigots who touted Spitford's imprimatur to justify their offensive views. Edgecomb couldn't imagine why appearing on the man's show was a cause for celebration.

"We've also sold another twenty thousand units. Orders are coming in from as far away as Israel and Norway," added Borrelli, swatting his girlfriend's behind playfully with a coloring book. "I've had to hire Esperanza as a fulltime secretary. And it turns out I have the French to thank for all of this! The French Interior Ministry banned our product last night…and somehow Spitford got word of this and announced the ban on his show this morning. There's nothing like good old-fashioned censorship to move merchandise." He turned to his three-piece band. "How about you fellows strike up 'The Marseillaise' in honor of our benefactors?"

The trio of musicians attempted to indulge their host, but the cacophony they generated sounded more like an LP being played at the wrong speed. When their rendition hit its crescendo, Albion pounded his fist triumphantly on the coffee table and shouted, "Checkmate!"

"I really need to talk to you," said Edgecomb. "In private." He lowered his voice and added, "Sandra Foxwell is threatening to have me fired."

"Sandra Foxwell. I remember her. The chick with the hot voice." Borrelli flashed a thumbs up to Albion from across the room. "That's a good lesson for you, Teach. The boss is never your friend, no matter how sexy her voice is."

The notion entered Edgecomb's mind that Sebastian was drunk, but he didn't know whether that would impair or improve his judgment. What mattered, at the moment, was reclaiming his apartment—*and his life.*

"Please, Sebastian. I need your help."

Edgecomb's tone must have revealed his desperation, because his housemate's mood quickly sobered. Borrelli silenced his orchestra with a wave of his hand and commanded a couple dancing on the sofa cushions to step down. "Okay, let's go into my office," he suggested, indicating the kitchen. "We'll sort this out." And as irrational as it was, Edgecomb found the confidence of this dope-fiend-turned-blasphemous-publisher reassuring.

The scene in the kitchen mirrored the living room fiasco on a more modest scale. A woman was seated on the countertop, legs dangling off the side, swatting imaginary insects with a fly swatter. Two emaciated men arm wrestled at the table. Sevastopol stood with his back to the refrigerator, kissing a heavyset man twice his age.

"Everybody out," commanded Sebastian. The arm wrestlers and the swatting woman shuffled off quickly. It required a "You too, loverboys" from Borrelli to drive the designer and his date from their perch. Soon only Esperanza, who'd followed them from the living room, remained.

Edgecomb frowned pointedly at Borrelli's girlfriend. "This is confidential," he explained, adding apologetically, "It's nothing personal."

"Don't sweat it, Teach," said Sebastian. "I'm going to tell her everything later anyway—even if I tell you that I won't. It's like with doctors. You have to figure anything you share with them in confidence is fair game for their wives."

Borrelli reversed a folding chair and seated himself with his elbows resting on the back; reluctantly, Edgecomb sat down across the table from Esperanza. He was about to speak when Albion strolled into the kitchen, chessboard under his arm, and launched into the maneuver in which he vacuumed his nose inches from the plaster.

"So what's eating you, Teach?" asked Sebastian. "Because if it's Foxwell, we can fix that. But if it's chicks, that's more of a challenge."

What if it's both work and *women?* Edgecomb wondered. He glanced at Albion and then at Esperanza. *Fuck it*, he decided. *The more, the merrier.*

"The whole thing is insane," he said. "Do you remember how Royster filed a complaint against me at the beginning of the school year? Well, Foxwell is using it as a pretext to get me canned. And if that doesn't work, she's got a parent who wrote a letter saying I'm teaching that slavery never happened—basically, that I'm a racist."

"That's rough, Teach. Can you get Royster to revoke his complaint? Maybe he can give a speech in your defense of something..."

"And say what? That he's no longer upset with me because now I'm a Civil War denier too?" Edgecomb uncapped a beer, the first alcoholic beverage he'd tasted in months. "Or that his daughter's so happy with me now that she tried to kiss me?"

"That wouldn't go over well," agreed Borrelli.

"Besides which, even if Royster comes to my defense, Ida Buxner won't. I suppose I could ask to speak to the Board in private and explain that I'm working undercover for HDC, but even if they believed me—and the odds are against it—there's no way Archie Steinhoff's going to want to look soft on a slavery denier. So the bottom line is that I'm royally and magnificently screwed."

"That is certainly a Catch-44."

"I don't get it."

"You can't tell the Board you're working for Royster, because that will make you a Civil War denier, and you can't tell the Board you're working for HDC, because that will undermine your work with Royster and he'd have no reason to defend you—so you've got yourself two Catch-22s. You add them up and you've got a Catch-44."

"I've never heard that before."

Sebastian crumpled up a ball of wax paper from the pizza box and fired off a three-point shot at the trash pail; he missed. "It's like when you date two seventeen year olds," he explained, "Instead of one thirty-four-year-old."

Horace wiped his mouth with his sleeve. "You are such a pervert."

"Just kidding, dude. Take a chill pill." Sebastian removed a pouch of loose tobacco from his shirt pocket and rolled himself a cigarette; he drew alternating bites from his slice of pizza and drags from his cigarette. "What do you say to tobacco-flavored pizza as a business idea?" he asked. "I'm toying with the slogan 'If you're going to indulge, you might was well go for broke,' or something along those lines."

"You really do hold nothing sacred, do you?"

Borrelli laughed and extinguished his cigarette butt on his pizza crust. "I'll take that as a compliment, Teach—coming from you. So are you ready to stop casting aspersions and hear what I think about your situation?"

"You think I'm screwed too, don't you?"

"Not exactly. You would be—except we have a secret weapon."

"And that would be?"

"My inamorata," replied Borrelli. "Here's the trick, Teach. Everybody lies. White lies, half-truths, exaggerated stories. Your foxy boss is no exception. So our plan is to get her talking at the next Board of Education meeting, about her credentials, her experiences—and then, once she's sprung a few whoppers, we call her out on them and discredit her. Having a human lie detector on your side never hurts." Sebastian turned to his girlfriend and asked, "What do you say, honey? Are you willing to help Teach here save his pathetic ass?"

Esperanza leaned against the radiator with her arms folded across her chest, chewing gum, looking about as friendly as a Turkish prison warden. Edgecomb now doubly regretted having insulted her in the restaurant. "What's in it for me?" she asked.

"I'll make it worth your while," promised Sebastian.

His girl laughed. "Oh, will you?"

The pair ogled each other without shame. Edgecomb hid his disgust. And then he found himself seized with inspiration of his own.

"I've got a better idea," he proposed. "Why don't you take me to class with you one night so I can learn how to read faces on my own?"

"Not going to happen," retorted Esperanza.

"Why not? I'll pay tuition."

The girl scowled at him with utter derision. "Do you think that Thorn accepts any random person off the street as a student?" she asked.

Edgecomb forced himself to shrug away her insult. "I didn't mean to offend you. I'm genuinely interested."

"Normative prosopography is an art form. A *calling*," said Esperanza. "One of the skills Thorn teaches us is how to identify potential training candidates, so he doesn't squander his time meeting people who lack promise." She laid emphasis on the phrase *lack promise*, as though these shortcomings extended well beyond face reading. "I don't mean to be rude, Horace, but quite honestly, you just don't have what it takes."

"How can you tell?"

"It's hard to explain. I just can."

Before Edgecomb had a chance to protest any further, Albion interjected himself into the conversation. "I once knew a whore named

Booth," he crooned falsetto, "Who had a penchant for hiding the truth…" Then the schizophrenic stopped, mid-limerick, as though the remaining verse had been sucked from his brain. From the living room came the sound of glassware shattering.

"It's not a big deal," said Sebastian—and for an instant, Edgecomb thought his housemate meant the glassware. "You don't need lessons. Esperanza will do the lie detecting for us. She's already called out the President twice this week. I even sent an email to whitehouse.gov demanding an explanation."

"I'm sure the White House was thrilled."

"I'm a concerned citizen," replied Sebastian. "I'm doing my civic duty."

That was the amazing thing about his housemate, Edgecomb reflected: Borrelli could catch an elected official lying as a result of a pseudoscientific evaluation and then write a sincere letter to that official asking for an explanation. Whether he would prove a match for Sandra Foxwell and Archie Steinhoff wasn't so clear—but Edgecomb had to hope that he might. What other options did he have?

THIRD SALVO

NOVEMBER - DECEMBER

CHAPTER SEVEN

Edgecomb received another summons to Royster's headquarters the following Friday. Sally approached him after class—they'd finally moved beyond the Civil War Era to the Gilded Age, for which he was grateful—and asked, "What are you doing tonight?" For an instant, believing she might be asking him on a date, his mind whirred in search of excuses. Fortunately, before he told her that he was meeting a relative at the airport, the only plausible lie he could conjure up, she added, "Because Papa would like to see you." Edgecomb should have felt only relief, he knew. Instead, he felt snubbed. Just because he didn't want to become romantically involved with an eighteen-year-old girl—and he assured himself that he did not—didn't mean that he didn't want *her* to desire to become romantically involved with him. At least, a wee bit. After his experiences with Vicky Vann and Amelia Quockman and so many other women who would have rejected him had he given them the opportunity, a teenager's crush worked wonders on his ego.

"I'm completely free," he said. "I thought I'd have to pick my aunt up at the airport, but she postponed her visit at the last moment."

"Great," said Sally. "Then you can give me a lift home."

She waited while he packed his lesson plans into his briefcase. "What would you have done if I already had plans for tonight?" he asked.

"I'd have told you to cancel them," answered Sally. "Papa doesn't like delays."

"And if I'd refused?"

The girl flashed the most brazen simper. "You wouldn't have."

Edgecomb led them out to the parking lot—first approaching the faculty elevator and then rethinking his plans and taking the stairs. He didn't want to have to explain Sally's presence in the lift to any of his colleagues, even though, he assured himself, he'd crossed no unpardonable boundaries. The girl tossed her book bag onto the backseat of the Honda—as Edgecomb had once done in his own mother's '77 Chrysler LeBarron. "Can we stop for a snack?" she asked.

"I though your father didn't like delays."

"A *quick* snack. Papa won't mind," said the girl. "How about a slice of pizza?"

Horace weighed his options. A slice of pizza was far more like a date than merely offering the girl a ride home, and the fact that he feared other students might see them together, that he was already contemplating a drive to a pizza parlor in an adjacent town, strongly suggested that acceding to the girl's proposal was a mistake. On the other hand, how different was this really from the Storrow twins taking the football team out for dinner during homecoming week? Or Elgin Rothmeyer, a Yale alum, inviting the New Haven-bound seniors to his home for Sunday brunch? Besides, he *was* famished after back-to-back lectures on the Haymarket Riot and the Bay View Massacre, and his body relished the prospect of a hot snack. "Okay," he agreed. "But just this once."

He had the entire ride to Tarantino's in Hager Valley to ruminate on the stupidity of the expression "just this once," with its presumptuous implication that he'd be driving the girl home more often in the future. For her part, Sally said little, preferring to gaze out the window as though they were travelling through exotic locales rather than the backstreets of suburban New Jersey. If she found it strange that he'd driven halfway across the county for their "quick" snack, bypassing both Vinny's and The Pizza King in downtown Laurendale, she didn't object. Had she remarked on his detour, he intended to tell her that he preferred the thinner-crusted pizza at Tarantino's, which wasn't exactly true, yet sounded plausible enough.

At Tarantino's, they ordered at the counter and Sally carried their slices into the crowded dining area in the rear while he settled the tab.

Edgecomb had once been a regular at the pizza joint during his high school summers, when ceiling fans churned overhead and black flies cavorted in the rafters. But on a bleak November afternoon, the fans stood silent and warm air huffed through the vents. Packs of adolescents shouted and laughed at the long, cafeteria-style tables, but none of these faces appeared familiar to Edgecomb. One lanky, long-haired teenager followed Sally hungrily with his eyes, but otherwise, nobody paid much attention to them as they staked out a space near the beer coolers. The teens probably thought he and Sally were brother and sister, he reflected. Or maybe even father and daughter. Not that it mattered. Even if these kids believed they were on a date, that was *still* perfectly harmless, since they weren't, and nobody knew them.

"Thanks for the pizza," said Sally.

"My pleasure." Edgecomb sprinkled crushed red pepper over his slices. "Thank *you* for suggesting this."

Sally cut her slice into segments, as though preparing the meal for a child. He looked at her handiwork and they both burst into laughter. Pink blotches clouded the nape of her neck and rose into her cheeks. "Don't even say it," she warned. "I'm going to tuck the napkin into my blouse too." And she did, covering her cleavage and drawing attention to it simultaneously.

"I'm not saying anything," said Edgecomb. "You eat your way and I'll eat mine."

He took another few bites of his pizza, still wearing a grin. He enjoyed watching the girl's idiosyncratic method of dining, the methodical exertion involved in carving her pizza into small squares. How easy it was to forget that they were in a busy restaurant—that, all around them, eighteen-year-olds were snacking with their peers. Several times, he considered coaxing Sally into conversation, but it was far less demanding, and more pleasurable, just to look at her.

"Can I ask you something?" she finally asked.

"You can *ask*."

She tossed her crumpled straw wrapper at him playfully. "What do you think of us? I'm not asking what you think about the Civil War. I'm asking what you think of *us*—me and Papa and Surrender Appomattox. I mean: Do you think Papa's naïve to take on the whole United States government like this?"

Edgecomb chose his words carefully. "Your father's a very brave man," he said—which wasn't terribly untrue. "I admire his determination."

"I worry about him. A lot," replied Sally. "Honestly, I'm afraid something might *happen* to him." She lowered her voice. "I'm afraid that if he gets too close to the truth, someone will try to silence him."

"I wouldn't worry so much about that," said Edgecomb. "If anybody were going to hurt your father, I imagine they'd have done it already."

"You don't understand these HDC people. They're relentless." Sally took a swig of her Diet Pepsi. "Not that I blame them. If the credibility of my government was on the line, I'd probably be just as aggressive."

"You're genuinely scared of them," observed Edgecomb, surprised.

Sally nodded. "How could I not be? If anything happened to Papa, I don't know what I'd do."

Never had the girl seemed as vulnerable to Edgecomb as she did at that moment—and under different circumstances, he might have offered her a hug. Instead, he stacked their oil-soaked paper plates on the plastic tray and returned it to the counter. "Nothing is going to happen to your father," he declared. "But we'd better get you home, young lady, before he calls out the cavalry." He was pleased with himself for addressing her as young lady, which at first rang appropriately parental. On reflection, however, it struck him as sounding more ironic than authoritative. Edgecomb wondered if Sally Royster spent as much time parsing his sentences for latent meanings and ulterior motives as he did himself. Probably not.

Twilight had already settled by the time they reached the winding roads up to Laurendale Ridge. A low-set star—or possibly a planet—gleamed in the dusky sky above Royster's compound. Sally punched a number into her cell phone and, an instant later, the gates yielded to Edgecomb's Honda. By now, he was accustomed to the uneven ride over gravel, the shadows of the yews and boxwoods, the unmanned guard post with the security bar in the upright position.

"Nobody's on duty," observed Edgecomb.

"Don't be so sure," said Sally. She was reclining with her clogs propped against the glove compartment. "We have more than three hundred motion detectors with cameras attached. Everything here is totally computerized. Papa only sent Nigel down to the guardhouse last time you visited to intimidate you—purely for effect. Usually, he works from the situation room in the basement."

"You have a *situation* room?"

Sally laughed. "That's what Mr. Nalaskowski calls it. It's actually just a concrete bunker with computers and video monitors and a giant oval table."

"Thanks for the heads-up."

Edgecomb parked the Honda behind Nalaskowski's Jaguar, a monstrously long vehicle with suicide doors. They found Royster huddled with his attorney in the study, enjoying a round of cocktails. Cousin Nigel did the serving. When they arrived, Sally's father checked the time on his pocket watch. "I was hoping McNabb and Herskovitz would have returned already, but they've been delayed by traffic," he announced. "Last check, they were just approaching Allentown, Pennsylvania." Royster signaled for Edgecomb and his daughter to seat themselves on the sofa. Nigel offered them each a drink. Sally accepted; Edgecomb declined. "I'll confess I'm anxious," said Royster. "When you've waited so many years for something, the last few hours can be torture."

Sally's father vaulted himself from his armchair. He paced across the study, trailing cigar fumes in his wake. The grizzly bear and the bull elk eyed him mournfully from their permanent perches. "I have become something of a worrywart in my old age, I fear," he lamented. "The truth is that the news from the front lines is only good. Our friends have been successful in their mission."

Edgecomb questioned Royster with his eyes.

"Professors McNabb and Herskovitz have acquired the cloak," explained Royster, punctuating his sentences with his cigar. "Thanks to my brilliant nephew's technological genius, the city elders of

Gettysburg Pennsylvania now possess a blood-soaked linen mantle that belonged to Professor Herskovitz's grandmother. And you should be pleased to know that blood actually did once belong to Abraham Lincoln—or to a laboratory mouse that went by such an illustrious name." Royster paused; even for an audience of three, he couldn't resist elevating the drama. "And *we*, my friends, are in possession of the cloak that their hero allegedly wore to the theater in the year of our lord, 1865."

Sally jumped from the sofa and wrapped her arms around her father. "I'm so proud of you," she chirped. "You've done it."

Nalaskowski cleared his throat, but said nothing.

"Not yet. We're only halfway there," said Royster. "Which leads me to the purpose of this gathering." He focused his gaze on Edgecomb. "*Well?*"

Edgecomb experienced genuine fear. Would they think that he'd intentionally sabotaged his mission with Esperanza? He regretted turning down a cocktail.

"You want to know about Thorn, don't you?" he asked.

"Indeed, I do," replied Sally's father. "So tell me."

Edgecomb glanced at the door, hoping Royster's dogs might rescue him. But all eyes remained honed upon him, awaiting an explanation. Nalaskowski drummed his foot on the carpet ominously. "I've run into some difficulties," Edgecomb apologized. "I asked Esperanza to take me to class with her—more or less begged her to—but she said no. Apparently, I'm not cut out for normative prosopography."

Nalaskowski's foot came to an abrupt halt, mid-thump. Cousin Nigel appeared capable of throwing a brandy snifter at him. Edgecomb didn't dare look at Sally, fearing her judgment.

"That *is* disappointing," said Royster. "And if there's one thing I don't like, it's being disappointed."

"I'm sorry," muttered Edgecomb.

"You're sorry? *I'm* sorry. Bruce McNabb and Mort Herskovitz risk their freedom—risk their very lives—acquiring that so-called bloody cloak—and now I'll have to tell them that it was a wasted effort. Because without a DNA sample for comparison, all we have it a soiled old tatter of fabric. Do you see my point?"

Royster dropped his cigar onto the hardwood floor and ground the embers out beneath the sole of his shoe.

"I tried," said Edgecomb. "I didn't know what else to do."

"Don't you work with Lincoln's girlfriend?" asked Royster. "Why don't you try *that* route? Many roads lead to Rome."

"Calliope Chaselle—," said Edgecomb.

He cut himself short. He'd intended to say, Calliope Chaselle won't give me the time of day, but was ashamed to make this admission in front of Sally.

"That's right," agreed Royster. "Calliope Chaselle."

"I'll see what I can do," said Edgecomb.

Royster nudged the dead cigar with this foot and Cousin Nigel removed the offending object rapidly. "We're counting on you, Horace," he said. "And you don't exactly have to take the fellow to bed with you. All we're asking is a few minutes of his time—steal a sneaker or his dentures or something. Anything with DNA."

"Thorn wears dentures?" asked Edgecomb. He had pictured Calliope's boyfriend as rugged and dashing.

"How the hell should I know?" Royster shot back. "I've never laid eyes on the man."

"Please, Papa," said Sally. "Don't get yourself worked up."

"I'm *not* worked up. I'm appropriately frustrated," said Royster. "Now if you'll please excuse me, I'm going to take a warm bath to steady my nerves." He retrieved his walking stick from his chair. "Nigel, do me a favor and let me know when Herskovitz and McNabb arrive. I don't care what the hour is."

"Absolutely, Uncle," agreed Nigel. "Would you like me to escort Sally's teacher to the front gate?"

Royster pondered the proposal. "Why not? Can't hurt," he said. "And it will give you a chance to edify him on the wonders of your safecracking device. I believe I promised him an explanation on his last visit."

Edgecomb had long forgotten about both the promise and the invention itself, but Royster, he realized, never said anything gratuitously. As he followed Nigel out to the Honda, after a wave from Sally and a severe handshake from Nalaskowski, he wondered to what extent the details of his departure had been previously planned. Outside, the night was still and silent and cold; the evening star had vanished below the tree line.

Nigel had to adjust the passenger seat to accommodate his legs. Once his companion appeared settled, Edgecomb turned over the ignition. As they retreated from the lights of the mansion, he feared—without justification—that Sally's cousin might be planning to kill him.

"So how does it work?" he asked.

Cousin Nigel eyed him strangely, as though he feared a trick question. "You mean the ComboBlaster?"

"Your uncle seems to think it's important that I understand how it functions."

A silence followed. "He's just proud of me," said Nigel. "Do you really want to know the technology behind it? Or are you being polite?"

"Maybe both," replied Edgecomb. "Or maybe neither. But tell me anyway."

So Sally's cousin explained the concept underlying his device, which relied upon bouncing sound-waves off the lock and comparing reverberation times with those tested upon known combinations. If the design were so simple, wondered Edgecomb, why hadn't anyone thought of the concept before? It strained credibility that Nigel Royster had succeeded where celebrated bank robbers like Eddie Chapman and Roy Saunders had failed. But Edgecomb's passenger proffered the explanation himself: the technique required precision measurements not available until the advent of handheld computers. "Saunders could have done it with one of those early IBM machines," explained Nigel. "But it would have taken him several hundred years for each lock."

"Impressive," said Edgecomb. "Are you going to file for a patent?"

He'd been joking, but Nigel took him seriously. "I wish I could. Unfortunately, tools of criminality don't qualify for intellectual property protections." Nigel sighed—his frustration apparently rather genuine. "I didn't believe Nalaskowski, so I did some legal research myself. On the Internet. It turns out you can't copyright, trademark or patent anything 'immoral, deceptive, or scandalous,'—and while I personally believe the ComboBlaster is a device of considerable public merit, the consensus on my chat group is that I don't have a chance in hell with the Patent Bureau."

"I'm sorry," said Edgecomb. What else could he possibly say?

"What right does the government have to tell me what I can and cannot patent?" demanded Nigel. "What business is it of theirs?"

Edgecomb listened sympathetically. The moment seemed poor for a discourse on the nature of positive law and the necessity of government for the existence of intellectual property. That might have truly provoked Sally's cousin to murder. Yet he couldn't resist saying, "The patent system certainly would work a lot better if Uncle Sam stayed out of it."

Nigel cupped his fist in his palm—as though, given the opportunity, he'd sock Uncle Sam in the kisser. "I'm glad we see eye to eye. But I don't want to talk about patents. It makes my ulcer flare up," he said. "So that's the story with the ComboBlaster. Now do *I* get to ask a question?"

"Sure, why not? Everybody seems to have a question for me today."

They passed under the eaves of the guardhouse. Edgecomb kept track of his passenger's hands through the corner of his eye, on the remote chance that Royster had uncovered his espionage and dispatched his nephew to do him in. He didn't actually believe Sally's father capable of violence, but he also hadn't suspected that Vicky Vann was capable of running a spy outfit or, for that matter, that he'd ever denounce the Civil War as a hoax on live television, so experience argued for a smidgeon of caution. He waited for Cousin Nigel's question—or possibly a blow from a crowbar.

"What's your romantic situation?" asked Nigel.

Edgecomb slowed the Honda.

"I didn't see *that* coming," he answered. "Why do you care?"

"Just curious, okay? Humor me. Are you seeing anyone?"

The man's tone brimmed with enmity. It was quite clear that Nigel neither wanted to date Edgecomb himself nor to fix him up with someone else. And suddenly the man's motivation loomed obvious: poor Nigel was in love with Sally! That explained his antagonism far more than any suspicions about Edgecomb's loyalties.

"Not at the moment," replied Edgecomb, testing his theory. "But I do have what you might call a prospect."

"What's that supposed to mean? A prospect?"

The rage in Nigel's voice was raw and toxic. Theory confirmed.

"And it's not who you think it is," Edgecomb continued. Of course, he dared not describe Vicky Vann as his so-called prospect, for fear of exposing his HDC connection. "She's a junior librarian at Laurendale," he continued. "And she's stunning and brilliant and could give a damn that I exist."

"Oh," said Nigel. "The librarian."

"Yes, the librarian. *Not* Sally," said Edgecomb. "In case you were afraid I had eyes for your cousin. In the first place, I'm her teacher and that would be totally inappropriate." He let his words hang in the still air. "And besides that, my affections lie elsewhere."

"I didn't mean anything," stammered Nigel sheepishly.

"Of course, you didn't," agreed Edgecomb, deciding not to embarrass the unfortunate fellow any further. "You were just protecting your cousin," he said. "I'd do the same thing if I were in your shoes."

"Sally is a special girl," said Nigel. "I've known her for her entire life…"

"She's lucky to have you around to look after her," said Edgecomb. "So let's put this behind us, okay? No hard feelings."

"No hard feelings," agreed Cousin Nigel.

They shook hands.

When Sally's cousin said goodbye, Edgecomb felt genuinely good about himself for the first time in weeks—as though he'd bestowed a gift of great value to a stranger. Which he had, in a sense, although the gift wasn't exactly his to offer.

~

Approaching attractive women had never come easily to Edgecomb—he usually required overt bidding to pursue romance, and any sign of reluctance or ambivalence on the part of a potential mate sent him scurrying in the opposite direction—so befriending Calliope Chaselle, even for professional reasons, launched him into panic mode. Three afternoons straight, he spent his prep period in the school library, pretending to be compiling a reading list for an eleventh grade research paper, but secretly scrutinizing the junior librarian through the glass panes of her office. Calliope wore ergonomic braces on her wrists while she typed and paused frequently to rest her arms. During these breaks, she chatted on the phone—even at a distance, Edgecomb sensed these were personal calls—or read from a paperback novel that she stored in the top drawer of her desk. Occasionally, the chief librarian, a superannuated creature who still didn't know how to use a word processor, sought his deputy's assistance; otherwise, the coast stood clear for Edgecomb to knock on Calliope's door and intrude. But the librarian's flawless skin acted both as a magnet and a force field, preventing him from either approaching or escaping. Instead, he merely ogled from afar; what struck him most was that, for all of her beauty, the woman behind the glass appeared profoundly unhappy.

On the third afternoon, to his surprise, Calliope rose from her desk and strode directly to the carrel where Edgecomb was pretending to sort through books.

"I don't mean to be rude," she said, "but can you please stop doing that?"

Edgecomb shoved the volumes in his hands onto the nearest shelf. "Doing what?"

"I don't even know. Staring at my office. Prowling about. Honestly, I have no clue what you're doing, but it's creeping me out."

The temptation crossed Edgecomb's mind to issue a complete denial, to pretend his loitering existed only in Calliope's imagination, but dishonesty hadn't been getting him very far of late. "I'm sorry," he replied. "I'm not sure what else to say."

Chaselle seemed perplexed by his answer, as though she too had expected a full-blown denial. "How about telling me what you're doing here?" she demanded. She retrieved the topmost book from the stack he'd deposited in the carrel. "You're obviously not reading *The Mystery of Nancy Drew and the Shattered Medallion.*"

"I guess I wanted to talk to you," spluttered Edgecomb.

He scanned his surroundings like a hunted animal, hoping that no students had overheard their interaction. Usually, when he crossed through the library, the dearth of teenage researchers disappointed him. Now, encountering the library in its perpetually underutilized state brought him only relief.

"I see," said Calliope, her expression more reserved than icy. "You *guess* you wanted to talk to me. Had you considered knocking on my door?"

"Yes, I considered it." Edgecomb kept his eyes glued to the adjacent carrel. "I guess I should have done that."

"Very well. Why don't we go into my office and talk?"

Calliope turned on her heels and strutted back to her desk, the toned musculature of her calves flashing below her skirt. Now was Edgecomb's chance to flee; instead, he followed her. The cozy size of her office forced him to squeeze past her to reach the room's only empty chair; his hip brushed against her shoulder, causing him to recoil as though electrocuted. Edgecomb seated himself, avoiding eye contact. He noted the books on the shelves: nearly all historical novels.

"So?" asked Calliope.

At first, Edgecomb struggled to find words: not the right words, but any words at all to quell the silence. But then, meeting Calliope's opaque gaze, the realization struck him that she was entertaining herself at his expense, that she genuinely enjoyed watching him twist in the wind. That broke her spell—and he grinned.

"What's so amusing?" she demanded.

"Nothing," he replied. "Just thinking."

His sudden confidence seemed to throw her off guard. "What is with you, Horace?" she asked. "At first, I figured I was intimidating you. Honestly, you wouldn't be the first man—or the first teacher at Laurendale, for that matter—who's been too intimidated to speak to me. But now I'm beginning to think you're just weird. Like you were raised by wolves or something."

"Thanks," said Edgecomb, inexplicably and completely liberated from his earlier fear. "I'm glad my wolf-stock shines through."

He couldn't help cracking a smile; to his utter surprise, Calliope's lips curled slightly in response, before she sobered herself. The periwinkle web of veins around her temples remaining captivating, but no longer a cause for anxiety.

"So what did you want to talk to me about?" she asked.

His make-or-break moment had arrived. Although the stakes remained high, they *felt* lower since the ice had been shattered.

"I know your boyfriend," said Edgecomb. "Or rather, we have a mutual friend in common."

"You mean Thorn?" Calliope's expression froze again. She halted as though selecting every word with painstaking care, and added, emotionless, "Thorn and I are no longer dating."

Now Edgecomb was the one caught by surprise. He'd assumed the relationship between Chaselle and Lincoln's heir to be permanent—that it existed, in essence, primarily to further his own efforts on behalf of Royster's plot. Without his connection though Calliope, he stood little prospect of accomplishing this mission.

"That's terrible," exclaimed Edgecomb. "I mean, I'm sorry."

"Not *so* terrible," replied Calliope. "Better today than ten years from now. The truth, Horace, is that I figured you already knew. I just assumed you were another one of those desperate assholes waiting to pounce the moment you hear about a breakup."

"Thanks again," said Edgecomb. "Actually, I prefer to find my dates through the obituaries. With breakups, you always have exes to deal with—either couples get together again or you end up getting threatened by some dejected loser who wants his girlfriend back—so I make a point of sticking to young widows."

Another dash of amusement flickered across Calliope's features. "You're funny, Horace. I mean that. Weird, but funny."

Edgecomb decided to press his advantage. "Can I ask *why* you two broke up?"

The junior librarian glanced through the glass at the empty library, then slid the door shut with her foot. Edgecomb no longer feared meeting her eye-to-eye; what he'd mistaken for reserve, or even antipathy, he realized, was merely a protective carapace worn to ward off unwanted demands—demands from men just like himself. But he also sensed these demands didn't irk Calliope; rather, they scared her.

"If you know anything about Thorn," said Calliope, "I imagine you're familiar with his research into normative prosopography."

"I've heard it mentioned," answered Edgecomb, trying to sound indifferent.

"He's *obsessed* with it. Honestly, it's his life. So, although I had my doubts, when he insisted on teaching me the basics, I figured I'd humor him and play along. What else was I supposed to do?" She stopped and glared at Edgecomb, as though challenging him to contradict her. "Anyway, I practiced his stupid lessons, and I actually learned out how to read faces pretty rapidly. Faster than the jerk expected. It took me less than a month to figure out that he was having an affair." Calliope wrung her wrists, either for ergonomic reasons or to shake off the pain of her relationship with Thorn. "Three years together and already he's double-dipping."

"I'm sorry, truly," Edgecomb said again.

"I know you are," replied Calliope. "Remember, I can tell. I was all prepared for you to lie to me earlier about skulking around outside my office—candidly, I was ready to file a formal complaint with Sandra Foxwell—but I'm genuinely glad you told the truth." The librarian paused as though she might say more, yet remained silent, creating a pregnant intimacy around them both. A ripple of nerves returned to Edgecomb's chest.

"If you're going to complain to Foxwell about me," he quipped to break the tension, "you'll have to take a number."

Calliope bared a full set of perfect teeth—which he recognized a moment later as a smile. The crazy notion struck him that she might actually be romantically interested in him after all, but he quickly dismissed this as wishful nonsense.

"Are you still in touch with Thorn?" he asked.

"No," she said. "I don't see the point."

The point, Edgecomb thought, *is for you to introduce me to Thorn so I can take his goddam class*. But then an idea struck him. He was reminded of Borrelli's absurd pizza slogan: *If you're going to indulge, you might was well go for broke*. Besides, at this point, what did he have to lose?

"Do you have anything of Thorn's you want help disposing of?" he asked. "I mean anything of low value—like a pair of old sneakers?"

"Excuse me?"

"Or it doesn't have to be sneakers. I was just using that as an example. It could be a couple of old shirts. Or underwear. Or even toiletries. Like if he left all of his extra dental floss and disposable razors in your bathroom and you need help trashing it."

Calliope examined him quizzically. "I don't understand. Am I missing something? Or are you asking me for my ex-boyfriend's used underwear?"

Edgecomb could have kicked himself for mentioning the underwear; he'd wanted his offer to sound generous, not deviant.

"I know. You're thinking I'm weird again," he said defensively. "But I understand what it's like to have an apartment full of one's ex's belongings. I remember what it feels like to sit around all weekend staring at your ex's stuff and moping." None of this was even remotely true: Amelia Quockman had carried off every last shred of her property—not only her boundless assortment of Pocahontas memorabilia, but even the bedding and dishes that they'd shared for eighteen months. Edgecomb held his hand over his mouth as he said this, as though holding back emotion, but also concealing his facial muscles. "I figured I could do you a favor by helping you get rid of Thorn's junk. You name the time and I'll do the carrying."

Calliope shook her head, but she was clearly entertained. "You certainly are one of the oddest ducks I've ever met," she said. "It's a sweet offer, I suppose, but no thanks." Her eyes met Edgecomb's again, and she paused as though considering whether to reveal something more personal, then said, "Honestly, I'm not ready for that."

"Okay, I understand," agreed Edgecomb. "If you ever change your mind..."

He rose from his seat and squeezed past the librarian a second time.

"I'm glad we had a chance to talk," said Calliope. "But next time, please knock on my door like a grown adult, okay?"

A man more debonair might had answered: *What makes you think there will be a next time?* But even in his liberated state, Edgecomb's confidence had its limits. All he managed to muster was a polite, "I'll do my best," delighted as he was that Calliope Chaselle anticipated socializing with him again.

~

That Monday had been Veterans Day, so Edgecomb and Pozner had agreed to visit the children's hospital in Marston Moor on Thursday instead. Mickey Bickerstaff had been scheduled to join them too, but he backed out at the last minute, claiming he had to pick up his wife's sister from Newark Airport. This might have been true, too—high school English teachers all across the nation picked up in-laws from airports every day—but, to Edgecomb, his colleague's timing seemed fishy. How could he avoid the conclusion that Bickerstaff, with whom he'd once played softball on weekends, was now intentionally avoiding him? He expressed his frustration to Pozner on the ride to the hospital, but the chemist assured him it was "all in his head."

"You think *you* have problems," said Pozner. "Bickerstaff has problems. You've probably heard his wife's got leukemia. A bad case. But that's not the worst of it. Between you and me, he's been seeing a woman on the side—for a long time now—and she's been diagnosed with a lymphoma. Can you believe that? Turns out both of their oncologists belong to the same practice."

"You're making that up," said Edgecomb.

Lucky Pozner held up two fingers. "Scout's honor. His sister-in-law's coming to look after Francine while he looks after the mistress."

"Scouts sign and salute with three fingers. Just so you know."

Pozner chuckled. "Do they really?"

Edgecomb considered broaching the subject of his impending disciplinary hearing with his companion—but to what end? So that Pozner could share another entertaining anecdote at his expense. Instead, he switched on the radio. A hockey game had commandeered his usual 24-hour news station, so he surfed. Sebastian Borrelli's voice brought his fingers to a cold halt.

"My crazy roommate," he warned Pozner.

"I'm not a Republican or a Democrat or a Libertarian-Socialist," said Borrelli. "I'm just a humble businessman trying to market a product. I saw a niche, as they say, and I took it. At the same time, I do believe in freedom of speech and if our coloring books can further the cause of liberty, so much the better."

"But you've been threatened, haven't you?" asked Borrelli's interviewer—who Edgecomb recognized as the rabble-rousing minister, Spotty Spitford. "You may think of yourself as a simple, God-fearing businessman, but Mohammedans have threatened to cut off your hands and put out your eyes. Is it safe to say that the future of American democracy depends upon the success of your books?"

"We have been threatened, yes," agreed Borrelli. "Yet I've also been thrilled by the outpouring of support we've found in ordinary consumers. For only $9.95, your listeners can buy a wholesome product that promises hours of fun for the entire family. Again, that URL is www.colortheprophet.com."

"You heard that, my friends," echoed Spitford, his voice rich as caramel and deep as a bottomless pit. "Wholesome fun. Here we have an Administration protecting pornographers and dope-pushers, but they're trying to censor a children's coloring book."

"Nobody's actually tried to censor us—" interjected Sebastian.

"The Mohammedans have," cried Spitford. "The French have! We save their sorry rumps in two world wars and this is how they repay us..."

Pozner shut off the radio. "I can't listen to this," he said. "I feel my neurons committing hara-kiri."

"At least you don't have to live with it," answered Edgecomb. "The problem with Sebastian is that he's either a goddam genius or a complete fool, but nobody's figured out which yet—including him."

"It's a fine line, isn't it," agreed Pozner. "Sometimes, it takes a Presidential election to find out. Other times, you never know. That's why we need to nurture every ditch digger's son like he's the next Einstein..."

Edgecomb sensed a sermon approaching, a Lucky-Pozner-all-hail-the-common-man special. Had he been in brighter spirits, he'd have warded it off with a request for advice or an anecdote of his own. Instead, he listened as his colleague shared a deeply improbable tale of a Delaware waiter who'd performed a life-saving Heimlich maneuver on Supreme Court Justice Earl Warren. "Not that it was called the Heimlich maneuver back then," added Pozner. "But the waiter—ironically, a young black man who'd attended a segregated high school—had studied anatomy on his own in the hope of becoming a surgeon, and he had a gut instinct, if you will, about how to dislodge the chicken bone; ten years later, Warren returned the favor in *Brown v. Board.* The real hero of the school desegregation movement was a quick-thinking twenty-year-old kid from Wilmington with a dream of going to medical school."

Pozner wound up his story as they pulled into the hospital's garage. It was a few minutes past the shift change and the lot teemed with nurses and physician's assistants in various stages of exhaustion. Any one of these women, according to Pozner's theory, might yet transform Western Civilization.

"I doubt Sebastian's going to be saving any lives," said Edgecomb. "I'm just hoping he doesn't get anybody killed."

He locked the Honda and they took the elevator the fourth floor, where a bridge over Ingraham Street led directly to the pediatric cancer ward. A bearded, acne-scarred security officer, familiar from their past visits, greeted them at the entrance. Edgecomb and Pozner provided the names of the patients they'd come to tutor; they handed over their driver's licenses for scanning.

The officer ran the licenses under a red beam of light.

"Here you go, Mr. Pozner," said the jovial guard, returning the chemistry teacher's ID. He turned to Edgecomb. "I'm sorry to say this, Mr. Edgecomb, but your visiting privileges with Mr. Kim have been suspended."

The guard sounded sympathetic rather than judgmental; nonetheless, Edgecomb felt humiliated. "But there must be a mistake," he objected. "I come here every month. Can't you call him and ask him?"

"I'm afraid the patient left clear instructions, Mr. Edgecomb," said the guard. He tilted his computer screen so that Edgecomb could read the monitor. Under Benji Kim's name, the machine warned:

HORACE EDGECOMB NOT TO VISIT. REQUEST BY PATIENT.

"I don't understand," stammered Edgecomb. But, of course, he did understand. How could the boy not be disappointed in him—especially after that press conference? If he'd been in Kim's shoes, he'd probably have done exactly the same thing.

"I'm sorry, Mr. Edgecomb," said the guard. "You're welcome to phone during business hours to discuss the matter further with the unit chief."

Pozner placed his hand on Edgecomb's shoulder. "I'll talk to him for you," he offered. "Why don't you get a cup of coffee? I'll call you."

"That's a good idea, pal," said the guard. "Cafeteria's still open for another half hour. Get a cup of coffee. Clear your head."

So Edgecomb rode the elevators down to the ground floor and followed the arrows to the hospital cafeteria. Only one cashier remained on duty, a buxom, corn-fed girl with braces. Chairs had been stacked upon most of the tables, except for those in an alcove near the exits. Several young surgeons in scrubs dined at one, two elderly women side-by-side at another. Edgecomb purchased a coffee and a croissant, and seated himself at the far end of the table from the doctors. They glanced his way—a few seconds too long, as though trying to place his face—then looked away quickly and conferred in hushed tones; Edgecomb had become accustomed to such interactions. Across the atrium, a janitor ran an industrial vacuum along the carpeting.

Edgecomb nibbled at his croissant; he couldn't decide whether it tasted peculiar, or he had no appetite, or both. At 7:30, a supervisor arrived to shutter the dining hall. So he roamed the public areas of the hospital for another forty-five minutes, glancing at his phone periodically, hoping for good news from Pozner. In the grander scheme of things, of course, it didn't really matter whether he ever saw Benji Kim again. The teen wasn't a family member or a close friend—he was just some random sick adolescent Edgecomb had been tutoring as a good deed. And yet, the teen's rejection felt cataclysmic. As though the entire course of Edgecomb's own future depended on it. As though the boy really were destined for the federal bench, rather than a premature grave, and he would soon be passing judgment on his former tutor.

At 8:15, Edgecomb gave in and called Pozner himself. "Well?" he asked. "Any luck?"

"Sorry, Horace," said his colleague. "For a kid with half a brain, that boy is one stubborn son of a bitch."

~

When Edgecomb unlocked his apartment door that evening, his spirits already at rock bottom, his first reaction to the bedlam before him was that al-Qaeda had revenged itself upon Sebastian. Boxes of coloring books lay strewn haphazardly across the living room, blanketed in strips of shredded drawings that coated every horizontal surface like confetti. The avengers had torn his aunt's framed watercolors from the walls, shattered beer mugs against the bookcases, toppled the stereo system onto the coffee table. In the midst of this maelstrom, like a witness to the apocalypse, the schizophrenic, Albion, played a makeshift game of chess against himself, using shattered chips of glassware as pieces. As Edgecomb was about to shout for help, the fear struck him that the perpetrators might still be lurking inside the building—or worse, that the flat had been booby-trapped with explosives—and he froze at the edge of the carpet. That's where he remained, a full ten seconds later, his mind still racing, when he heard the screams.

"Where the fuck are you hiding?" cried the voice, enraged, and distinctly female. A door slammed deep within the belly of the apartment—and a second time for effect. "Screw you, Sebastian Borrelli. I know you're in here somewhere. Show your face, goddammit, so I can claw your eyes out." Edgecomb was still trying to place the speaker when Esperanza Arcaya, her fuchsia hair a tangled mass, emerged at the head of the corridor. She sported sweat clothes, her midriff expose above the bow of the bottoms. "You!" she shouted at Edgecomb. "Tell your asshole of a friend to get the fuck out here, or I swear to God I'll set the place on fire and smoke him out." To underscore her threat, she heaved an empty carton onto the tattered heap that separated them.

"Please calm down," pleaded Edgecomb. "At least, tell me what happened..."

Albion interjected with his own answer: "A buxom young hooker named Speyer," he recited. "Really liked playing with fire...."

"*That's* what happened!" hollered Esperanza, pointing at the schizophrenic. "The jerk you live with—the jerk I used to be dating, God-only-knows-why!—promised me he was harmless. *Wouldn't hurt a fly*, the bastard said. *Sweet and innocent as a child.* Idiot that I am, I actually believed him." The girl's stamina appeared to be fading; she leaned against the arm of the sofa. "Poor lunatic should be locked up and they should throw the key into the harbor—but it's not his fault. *He* can't help being deranged. But your asshole of a friend should have had the common sense to warn me..."

Edgecomb inched further into the apartment, navigating the graveyard of his housemate's merchandise. Whatever Albion had done, Esperanza's outrage seemed misplaced; one didn't need a Ph. D. in psychology to recognize the poor creature was prone to sow chaos. "Is Sebastian here?" he asked.

"Somewhere. Hiding," replied Esperanza—drained, for the moment, of her destructive energy, if not her wrath. "I chased the bastard up the stairs." She laughed, and added, "I bet he regrets giving me a spare key."

Something in her phrasing drew the schizophrenic's attention. "Spare keys don't please," he declaimed. "Dirty sleaze, get on your knees!" A moment later, apropos of absolutely nothing, he moved a fractured mug handle across his game board and shouted, "Checkmate!"

"See what I mean?" demanded Esperanza. "How could I be so stupid?"

Edgecomb retrieved an empty carton and started stuffing it with minced paper. "You don't mind if I do some tidying up, do you?" he asked. "Or do you have any more destruction planned? You do realize I live here too."

"You should choose your companions more carefully," retorted the girl. "What's that Aesop's fable? The stork and the crows?"

"The stork and the *cranes*," said Edgecomb.

He climbed onto his knees and continued filling the box with crumpled and tattered images of Mohammed. He hadn't realized how salacious Borrelli's volume was until he registered the drawings of the prophet topless, pectoral muscles bulging, arms draped over his protégé, Ali, like an advertisement for a gay fitness club. To his surprise, Esperanza joined him on the carpet in the cleanup effort. For several minutes, they labored side by side in silence.

"So can I ask what happened?" Edgecomb inquired.

The girl sighed. "I took that imbecile to Thorn's class with me. His *advanced* seminar. We were studying the natural variation in facial musculature among different types of people—men versus women, various ethnic groups—and I thought your psycho friend over there might offer an interesting example. Needless to say, interesting was something of an understatement."

"Dr. A didn't like show and tell?"

Esperanza flashed him a hostile leer, as though trying to decide whether he was mocking her. "Thorn prefers to teach from behind a screen. He's rather particular about his privacy and he doesn't like the idea of his students being able to read his own features. You can understand where he's coming from, can't you?"

"Certainly," said Edgecomb.

"Anyway, your schizo pal took it upon himself to poke his sorry nose onto Thorn's side of the curtain and he refused to leave. Eventually, Thorn tried to drag the moron away—and then he grew violent. Knocked out Thorn's front teeth. Probably broke his nose too, although Thorn obviously wouldn't let us call an ambulance."

Edgecomb looked up at the schizophrenic, biting his lip to suppress amusement at the notion of the disturbed fellow socking Calliope Chaselle's ex, who in his mind's eye remained the flax-haired, tuxedoed lad from Royster's snapshot. Maybe Thorn would end up with dentures after all. For a man who'd so recently crushed the face of Abraham Lincoln's only heir, Albion seemed untouched by fame.

"What a dude. Lewd," said the schizophrenic. "Took my food."

"That was the worst of it," explained Esperanza. "He *did* take Thorn's food. When he knocked over the screen, the class discovered that Thorn was eating a sandwich during class—not that there's anything wrong with that—but there's a strict no food policy at the academy, because we practice on each other, and chewing obviously interferes with the facial muscles, so it looked rather awkward—even hypocritical—for Thorn to be eating his dinner during the session."

"I can only imagine," agreed Edgecomb.

"You *cannot* imagine. Thorn's never going to let me invite another guest again," lamented Esperanza. "And I'd promised my sister to take her when she visits…"

Edgecomb's spirits sunk. No more visitors! Now he too wanted to murder his housemate.

"What happened to the sandwich?" he asked.

It was a stretch, but even a Kaiser roll might carry some DNA.

Esperanza glowered. "Excuse me?"

"I was just wondering. Who ended up with the sandwich?"

"For fuck's sake. How the hell should I know?" She pushed aside her carton and stood up. "Why am I straightening up this pigsty anyway? Sebastian can clean up his own shit." She raised her voice and announced, "Did you hear that, Sebastian Borrelli? You can clean up your own shit from now on!"

Edgecomb was hardly listening. His mind remained focused on the sandwich, cursing the schizophrenic for not carrying the meal back to him like a golden retriever. "You didn't bring me anything, Dr. A.?" he asked rhetorically. "Not even a toothpick?"

"You two are *both* nut-jobs, aren't you?" groused Esperanza. "Peas from the same defective pod." A humorous whim apparently struck her, and she added, smirking and glaring at Albion, "All three of you are perfect for each other." Yet an instant later, her fierce expression returned. "What's that?"

The schizophrenic held what appeared to be an improvised slingshot; he held his thumb through the loop and drew the bow back with the other hand. Sebastian's ex-girlfriend stepped toward him, indifferent to the threat.

"Give me that," ordered Esperanza. "That's Thorn's headband."

"Thorn's headband!" exclaimed Edgecomb. "Brilliant!"

The girl grabbed hold of one end of the nylon headband; Albion now clenched the other end between his teeth.

"Let go," she cried. "That's not yours."

She tugged with her full bodyweight—and then, without warning, the schizophrenic opened his mouth and she toppled backwards. The coveted headband fell to the rug between them. Edgecomb pounced upon it.

"Mine!" he cried.

Esperanza sat up, dazed but undaunted. "What do you mean? I need to give that back to Thorn."

"No, you don't," declared Edgecomb. "This is historical evidence."

He held the cusp of the fabric pinched between his thumb and forefinger, afraid of depositing genetic residue of his own. The nylon felt damp from Albion's saliva. Unsure how to proceed, he carried the artefact into the kitchen. Taking pains not to touch any more of his treasure than necessary, Edgecomb slid the object into a zip top bag.

Thank you, Dr. A., he thought, pledging to himself that he'd bankroll a pizza party for Church on the Hill at the first opportunity. He opened the refrigerator door, intending to stash his prize in the battery hatch for safekeeping—and found himself standing face to face with Sebastian Borrelli.

His roommate had slid all of the shelves from their grooves to create room for his hunched and contorted body, consigning their groceries to a heap on the appliance's floor. Cracked eggs floated in a lather of soup and breakfast flakes and crushed peaches that lapped against Sebastian's wet socks. Borrelli wore only a T-shirt and gym shorts; he hugged his arms across his chest, shivering. A gray pallor tinged his cheeks.

Borrelli held up a finger to his lips, his eyes pleading.

Edgecomb shut the refrigerator door and, in a burst of generosity, yanked the plug from the outlet.

CHAPTER EIGHT

The clouds that had settled over Edgecomb's life seemed a little less dense the next morning as he stumbled through the shipwreck of coloring books into the kitchen. He'd slept poorly, kept awake by the erotic symphony that announced a truce between Esperanza and Sebastian, but now the prospect of delivering his genetic loot to Royster lightened his spirits. He wasn't happy, not exactly, but he also didn't feel like a Puritan under a pressing board, which was a step in the right direction. Once he'd retrieved the zip top bag from the fire escape, where he'd stashed it for safekeeping among the previous tenant's earthenware jugs, believing the frosty overnight temperatures might preserve Thorn's sweat more effectively, he found himself immune to the usual stressors of the morning: the yapping of Mrs. Arluck's Pekinese across the courtyard did not irk him, as it usually did, nor was he peeved by the relentless scampering of their upstairs neighbor's Yorkshire terrier along the hardwood. Even finding that the coffee maker had been returned to the shelf unwashed, grounds cemented to the carafe, failed to faze him. On the way out of the apartment, he retrieved a blanket from his own bed and tucked it over Albion, who'd snuggled into a fetal ball on the sofa.

Keeping his spirits up during the school day proved more challenging. Although his Advance Placement history section had progressed beyond the Civil War—and his History I classes had not yet neared it—the doubts that Surrender Appomattox had instilled in him infected his attitude toward other events. Why the Civil War, after all, and not the War of

1812 or the Spanish-American War? Like a man whose wife has cheated on him once, and now scents infidelity in each passing smile, Edgecomb found himself questioning nearly everything he taught, inserting caveats like "alleged" and "supposedly" before uncontested historical phenomenon. When Abe Kendall asked him to repeat what year Jacob Riis had published *How the Other Half Lives*, he answered, "The history books tell us 1890," as though to shift responsibility elsewhere for a fact both utterly innocuous and universally accepted. Low attendance compounded his own lack of enthusiasm for his subject matter: Bittany Marcus's seat in the front row remained unoccupied for six consecutive days, while pudgy Zinny Watkins hadn't appeared in his classroom for nearly three weeks, although he had crossed paths with the girl in the hallway. Officially, this truancy was to be reported. In practice, Edgecomb feared these absences reflected more negatively upon his teaching than upon their learning, so he did nothing.

He'd tucked the zip top bag with the headband inside his pocket and he fingered it surreptitiously like a talisman during his lecture for moral support—then stopped abruptly, fearing the students might suspect him of masturbating. Toward the end of the class, he realized he'd skipped an entire page of notes, and what he'd taught as the economic policy of President Grover Cleveland was actually that of his successor, Benjamin Harrison, who had opposed nearly every last fiscal principle that Cleveland had stood for. Undoubtedly, the top students recognized his error. Abe Kendall wore an expression of polite indulgence; behind him, Tina Serspinksi appeared genuinely bewildered. But nobody challenged him as they would have two months earlier. He'd become a caricature of himself, his lessons as absurd as Leonard Brackitt's tales of dining with European royalty, an intellectual buffoon unworthy of correction. The hour could not have ended soon enough: another twenty minutes and he might have stormed from the classroom in a barrage of profanity.

Sally had taken to staying late after class without his asking. Maybe she sensed that waiting for him to call her name drew undesirable attention to their relationship, or possibly, she just wanted to spend time alone with him. In either case, once her disgruntled classmates bolted from the room, he was grateful for her presence. She wore a T-shirt that read: "Some say yes, some say no. I say maybe." Poor Cousin Nigel, reflected Edgecomb, had his work cut out for him.

"You okay, Horace?" she asked.

"Kind of. Not really," he said. "But I do have good news for you."

Sally's enormous eyes widened with expectation.

"I have a DNA sample from Thorn Lincoln," he revealed. "Can you tell your father I'll bring it over in a couple of hours? As soon as I check in on my sister."

Edgecomb had expected his revelation to delight Royster's daughter, but to his surprise, her expression betrayed no emotion. "I *could* tell him that. But I won't," she replied. "Not unless you tell me what's bothering you."

You sure have gumption, thought Edgecomb, *for an eighteen-year-old kid.*

"It's kind of personal," he said. "You *are* my student."

Sally settled onto the edge of a nearby seat, crossing her legs. "I thought I was also your friend," she replied. "Now what's eating at you? You were all over the place during class—and right now you look like you've seen the Ghost of Christmas Past."

Gone was the girl's earlier timidity, replaced with a confidence that seemed unfettered by his own decline in fortunes. She was reaching out to him, trying to offer her help—entirely unaware that, at least on paper, he served her worst enemy. Whether he actually believed in HDC's cause any longer, or merely viewed his mission as a vehicle to win over Vicky's affections, was a question he refused to contemplate. Thinking too much had rarely earned him what he desired.

"You've ruined me for all of history," he said, forcing a smile. "Seriously. Every time I tell the students that this happened or that happened, I keep asking myself: did it *really*? How can I be so sure? Why Gettysburg and not Little Big Horn?"

"Doubt contagion."

Sally said the words like a physician rendering a fatal diagnosis.

"That's what Papa calls it," she explained. "You're not the first convert to find yourself sliding down a slippery slope. You should talk to Professor Herskovitz. That's why he left Amherst. He wasn't even a Civil

War historian. He studied twentieth century cultural history—Josephine Baker and the Beach Boys and the meanings of pharmaceutical package inserts. But once Papa won him over, he couldn't shake the suspicion that *everything* was a hoax."

"That's exactly what I'm feeling."

"It will pass. You can't live this way for long."

"And if it doesn't?"

"It will," said Sally. "Trust me. In the first place, why would anyone in his right mind make up the Battle of Little Big Horn or Josephine Baker? The powerbrokers and business elites who created the Civil War didn't just stumble upon the idea haphazardly. They had very specific motives." Sally paused in true Royster form. "We're not nihilists, Horace. We're truth seekers. Don't lose sight of that."

What made both Sally and her father so remarkable was how reasonable they sounded when taken on their own terms. One would think their harshest critics weren't mainstream historians, but rather more radical cults that denied all historical truth.

"I'll try not to," agreed Edgecomb. "Now tell your dad I'll be over later."

"Yes, sir," said Sally, delivering a saucy mock-salute.

She turned to depart and he nearly swatted her behind playfully with a manila folder, catching himself at the last instant. Not good. Edgecomb realized he was one public ass-swat away from losing his teaching credentials, from ending up a mug shot on the local news, from destroying Jillian's chances at parenthood. What made the whole situation so absurd was that he didn't really have designs on Sally, neither sexually nor romantically—certainly not in the way he yearned for Vicky or even as he lusted after Calliope Chaselle. He was merely flirting for the sake of flirting. Risking everything, in other words, for nothing. He'd become rather skilled at that.

Edgecomb gave Sally a five-minute head start before exiting the building. He passed Elgin Rothmeyer in the parking lot and waved, drawing only a civil nod, but he cared less than he would have the day before. Gulls circled over the football fields, their cries piecing the late afternoon sky like lances. Runoff from an overnight rainstorm gushed over the storm drains and babbled into a nearby stream. With Thorn Lincoln's sweat-stained headband in his pocket, Edgecomb felt invincible. He no longer knew which side he was on—his heart still lay with Vicky Vann and the HDC, but his soul increasingly belonged to Royster's outfit—yet, at that instant, none of these concerns particularly mattered. It was the espionage itself, and the sense of efficacy, of accomplishment, that he experienced in delivering the goods to Surrender Appomattox, that somehow dwarfed any larger questions of truth and history. Of course, it didn't hurt any that, in proving himself to Royster, he also earned an opportunity to report his success to Vicky.

All that stood in the way of his triumphant moment was a brief visit to Jillian. He'd spoken to her numerous times since the incident at the Gripley Connector site, and Fritz Fradkin had updated him on her condition daily, but on the foreman's recommendation, he'd stayed clear of his sister's apartment while she recovered. Only yesterday had her boyfriend finally issued an all clear. "They've agreed to reconsider her case," Fritz explained over the phone. "She signed an affidavit pledging that she'd keep the child as far away from you as possible, or something like that."

"Why don't I just move to the Congo and trade places with the kid?"

"That would work too," said Fritz. "But don't make any promises you can't keep." His tone had turned grave. "Your sister is very fragile. Please don't do anything to upset her."

"I won't," Edgecomb promised. "Scout's honor."

So when he parked opposite her condo, estimating the distance between his Honda and a fire hydrant, he was determined to give full indulgence to his sister's folly. If she wanted his shoes in plastic bags and his hands scrubbed raw, he could live with that. After all, she had to put up with a Civil War denying blasphemer.

Edgecomb pushed Jillian's lobby buzzer and rode the elevator to the fourth floor with a boy of about twelve who steadied a dirt bike against his lanky body. The kid's hair tapered to a rattail; soil streaked his basketball jersey. Edgecomb sensed that he was being scrutinized—possibly assessed for his potential as a robbery victim—but he dared not make eye contact with his companion. On the third floor, as the steel doors snapped open, the boy turned to him and said, "You was on TV!" And then, grinning, he wheeled his bike into the hallway and disappeared around the corner.

The encounter left Edgecomb nonplussed; more than a month after his press conference, even middle school students in rundown neighborhoods still knew him by sight. Maybe Jillian had been on target: he'd end up being the 'Civil War Denying Teacher' for all time.

His sister met him in the hallway. She'd lost weight—not that she'd ever had much to lose. Her jawline appeared sharper, her cheekbones stark like barbicans on the corners of her face. One of the elbows of her ancient bathrobe had been worn through to the underlying flesh.

"Clothes off!" Jillian ordered. "Straight into the shower with you."

She handed him a robe that matched her own.

"I can't strip in the hallway," he protested, his intention to cosset her shenanigans yielding to his own sense of self-respect.

"Put the robe on first, then undress underneath it," instructed Jillian. "It's not a big deal. Fritz does it all the time."

"Maybe he has a stronger incentive," muttered Edgecomb. But he donned the robe, thankful that they had the hallway to themselves, and slid off his trousers. With considerably more effort, he extricated himself from his shirt.

"Underwear too," ordered Jillian.

She held out a plastic garbage bag. Reluctantly, Edgecomb deposited his clothing. Then he followed his sister into her apartment.

"Use a new bar of soap," she said. "You'll find fresh towels in the hall closet."

Edgecomb did as commanded. Asking Jillian to explain this sudden lurch to a higher level of hygiene was like asking the TSA to explain its security measures. Or like asking Albion to justify the odd rhymes and rhythms of his limericks. Far better to accept the reality on its own terms. So Edgecomb retrieved a bath towel from the closet in the foyer and unwrapped a fresh packet of soap. He even washed behind his ears, as his father had instructed him in kindergarten. Fifteen minutes later, he stepped from the bathroom as sterile as a surgeon entering an operating suite. He found his sister seated in the living room, surrounded by her orphan photographs.

"What did you do with my clothes?" asked Edgecomb.

"They're in the laundry. Should be done long before you go."

The horror struck him with the force of a cannonball and he literally staggered backwards a step. She'd washed Thorn's headband!

"Are you insane?" he shouted. "Get them out!"

"They'll be fine. It's just a soft rinse."

"Where is your washing machine?"

"In back by the nursery," said Jillian. "But it's not a big deal..."

He charged through the apartment—past the nursery, into the alcove that housed his sister's washer and dryer. Not that it was at all clear what he hoped to accomplish: once the headband had been submerged in detergent, retrieving any residual DNA seemed like a farfetched prospect. But he yanked open the lid anyway. Inside, his garments lay snarled in a web of suds. He reached for the pockets of his trousers, hoping the zip top bag might have insulated his evidence, although recognizing such a wish to be highly unrealistic. The pockets were empty. He ran his hands though the frigid water, searching for the lost artefact. No luck.

Jillian approached him from behind. "I wrapped up your wallet and keys for you," she said, handing him a bundled dishcloth. "And I saved this thing for you too—whatever it is," she added, pinching the corner of a zip top bag between her thumb and index finger. He saw that she'd slid his zip top bag into her own larger zip top bag. "Don't take this the wrong way, but it stinks."

Horace grabbed the bag from her hands and hugged it to his chest. "Of course, it stinks. It's *supposed* to stink." He shut the lid of the washing machine and leaned against it as the appliance rumbled back to life. "It's Presidential musk."

"Whatever it is, please keep it wrapped up while you're here," she said. "Now if you want me to stop your laundry, I can do that—but I don't like the idea of you going home in wet clothes."

"It's okay," said Edgecomb. "I've changed my mind."

Jillian rolled her eyes. He followed her back into the living room.

"So they're giving me a second chance," she explained. "I've got another home visit scheduled for three weeks from tomorrow. Fritz promised no blasting."

"He seems like a good guy," said Edgecomb.

"A *great* guy," countered Jillian. She explained how he'd spoken to each of his men personally to make certain that nobody would report her mud-wallowing incident to the authorities. "We're going to try to adopt siblings if we can. Now that I have a partner, two kids doesn't seem so daunting…"

Edgecomb adjusted his robe and seated himself on the couch. All of the children in Jillian's albums appeared so endearing, so loving—so improbable. The reality, he imagined, was a horde of chronically mistreated creatures suffering from cleft palates and rickets and reactive attachment disorder. Despite the advertisements from Bonnie Franklin and Sally Struthers advocating for Save the Children, common sense told Edgecomb that nothing easy and adorable in life came for the price of a cup of coffee.

"Isn't it a bit quick to be adopting *with* Fritz?" he asked. "How long have you been together? Six weeks?"

"Fifty-three days," replied Jillian. "Fifty-three *magical* days."

His sister's tone told Edgecomb to drop the subject of her relationship entirely, but he couldn't resist one small nudge. "I hate to state the obvious," he said. "But now that you have such a magical partner, maybe you can have a baby the old-fashioned way."

"Grrrr," exclaimed Jillian. "What on God's green earth is wrong with you?!'

"I don't understand."

"Why do you have to be so judgmental? Maybe Fritz and I *want* to adopt. Maybe we want to offer a better life to a boy like Eyasu in Ethiopia," she said, thrusting several photographs into Edgecomb's lap, "or Oudry in the Congo." Jillian's eyes flooded. "Have you listened to a single word I've said for the last five years? Clearly you haven't, or you'd realize how offensive you're being."

"I'm sorry. I didn't mean to be," said Edgecomb. "I wasn't saying there was anything *better* about having a biological child. I just thought it might be easier."

"*Easier?* I'm thirty-seven years old. I'm about as likely to have a biological child as I am to be hit by a bus."

"You're exaggerating."

"Not by much."

They'd had this conversation before—so many times, in fact, that Edgecomb had looked up the odds of both conception at thirty-seven and being killed in a traffic accident. The numbers still favored fertility, but by less than he'd anticipated.

"Let's not argue, okay? Please," said Edgecomb. "I came over to cheer you up, not to upset you."

"Do you know what would cheer me up?" she asked.

"What?"

"What would cheer me up is if you would drop this whole Civil War nonsense and tell Vicky Vann to go screw herself. She's *using* you, Horace. She used you in high school and she's using you now."

Maybe so. But what business was that of Jillian's? He'd never once criticized her doomed relationship with the matrimonial lawyer—a man whose only promising attribute was that, in his youth, he boasted a striking resemblance to Burt Lancaster.

"Everybody uses everybody to some degree," he said. "How is this different from you using Fritz to hold up the blasting?"

"How is it different? I'll tell you how. Fritz *loves* me. Vicky Vann wouldn't bat an eye if you dropped dead tomorrow." Jillian put her hand on his knee. "I'm sorry to be so brutal, but if I'm not willing to tell you the truth, nobody will. Vicky Vann cares about one thing only. *Vicky Vann.* And honestly, the same was true with Amelia Quockman. And even Mariella. God knows I love her—I *lived with her* for four years—but at the end of the day, she's probably the most egocentric human being I've ever met. You have a talent for attracting self-absorbed women."

"You sound like a broken record," said Edgecomb.

"I'm trying to be helpful," said Jillian. "Most of the women in the world are not like Vicky Vann or Amelia Quockman."

Just the ones worth dating, thought Edgecomb. But he didn't dare say as much.

~

In Edgecomb's imagination, he'd anticipated showing off Thorn's cloak before the collected leadership of Surrender Appomattox—much like a detective in a whodunit gathering the suspects together in a drawing room to reveal the killer. To his surprise, and disappointment, Royster greeted him alone in the bust-lined foyer and led him through the portrait gallery into the adjoining study. His host motioned for him to seat himself in one of a pair of horsehair chairs by the window; Royster settled onto the other, hooking his walking stick over the arm. Edgecomb realized he'd never been alone with Sally's father before. Either Nalaskowski, or Nigel, or Sally herself had always served as a chaperone, or possibly a bodyguard. He appreciated what he chose to interpret as a vote of confidence in his loyalty; at the same time, he missed Sally's company.

"It's very quiet here tonight," he said.

"Indeed, it is. The calm before the storm, one might say." Royster selected a cigar from his humidor, not bothering to offer one to Edgecomb. "The professors are preparing a special edition of our newsletter. Mr. Nalaskowski is looking over the contracts with the genetics firms. I understand you've brought a sample to make all of those efforts worthwhile."

Edgecomb wasn't ready to yield control of the conversation. "And Sally?"

"My daughters are doing their homework," replied Royster. "You may think my girls spends all of their time crusading for truth, but I also expect them to master the laws of grammar and physics and calculus."

"And history," suggested Edgecomb.

"Possibly. Sometimes I fear they already know too much history for their own good." Royster filled his cognac glass, once again offering Edgecomb nothing. "But that's a conversation for a different day. Now, if you don't mind my getting down to brass tacks, Sally tells me you come bearing genetic gifts?"

"I have some of Thorn Lincoln's sweat, if that's what you mean."

Edgecomb placed the zip top specimen on the end table between them.

"And you're certain that this is his?" demanded Royster.

"I'm not *certain* about anything these days. But I did get this straight from the hands of the man who ripped it from Thorn's head."

At Royster's insistence, Edgecomb related the bizarre tale of how he'd come to possess the headband and the brief trajectory of his ownership. Sally's father interrupted him periodically to ask very precise questions about what he'd done with the artefact at various moments.

"And this Mr. Albion," asked Royster, "you say he's mentally impaired. Any possibility he's faking?"

Edgecomb suppressed a chuckle. "I highly doubt it."

"I'll have Nalaskowski look into the matter. Just to be safe," said Royster. "It is imperative that we establish a chain of control—so we're certain nobody has replaced the article, or tampered with it." He fingered the headband through the plastic. "So except for those few moments at your sister's apartment, the article in question never once left your possession?"

"Never once," echoed Edgecomb. "And for the record, since I imagine you're going to ask, my sister's not an HDC agent or an impostor or anything else."

"*That* we already know," said Royster.

"You do?"

Royster ignored his surprise. "You've done well, Horace. I'll confess I'm highly pleased. Almost giddy. I expect you're wondering what comes next."

Edgecomb nodded and waited for his host to continue. Sally's father seemed far from giddy, and he didn't dare risk betraying his own flame of curiosity.

"Have you ever heard of Levi's Genes?" asked Royster.

"Like the pants?"

"Like the genetic testing firm run by Herbert Levi."

"Clever name," said Edgecomb.

"Behind that clever name stands one of the most scrupulous scientific minds in the United States. He also happens to be, I am delighted to say, one of my dearest friends from my days at Columbia."

Edgecomb instantly formed an image of Levi that involved gorgon-like tangles of white hair and steaming beakers of colorful chemicals. He'd be to the biological sciences what Royster was to history. "And let me guess," he ventured. "You've hired him to see whether the DNA on the headband matches the DNA on the cloak?"

"Not exactly."

Royster swished his snifter. "I've asked Herbert to test only the cloak. I've asked him to identify a competitor to test the Thorn Lincoln sample. That way, nobody can accuse us of rigging the results, and HDC will have that much more difficult a time interfering with them." Sally's father paused long enough for Edgecomb to count backwards from five in his head. "Nobody will know the official results until the press conference where we present the data. Not Herbert. Not his competitor. Not even me. That will add to the drama—and drama means free publicity."

"I see," said Edgecomb. "A surprise."

"Of course, it won't really be a surprise," said Royster. "Because you and I both know that the samples don't match. How could they match if the Lincoln assassination never actually took place?"

The crux of Royster's theory was that the actor hired to play President Lincoln had posed for fake war photos as late as the 1880s; that meant he couldn't possibly have been assassinated in 1865, when he was touring the heartland, playing Iago and Henry V in sod-walled theaters.

"You don't look convinced," said Royster.

"I'm just thinking. Let me play devil's advocate for a moment. Isn't it possible that the war was a hoax—but the actor hired to play Lincoln was actually killed, somehow, and that the same men who orchestrated the mass deception also preserved his bloody cloak for posterity?"

"Are you familiar with Occam's razor?"

"Kind of," lied Edgecomb.

"Occam was a fourteenth century monk," said Royster. "Smart guy. Old fellow wrote dozens of treatises on philosophy, law, theology, even dentistry. But all anybody remembers is one principle: *The simplest explanation is usually the correct one.* So while it's possible that Lincoln was assassinated later, under different circumstances, and the powers-that-be managed to preserve his clothes and weave them into the Civil War story, the odds stand against it. Keep in mind it's also possible that the hoax itself is actually a hoax—that the war *did* occur but the powers-that-be wanted to create the illusion that it was a hoax for some purpose yet unknown, and have fashioned evidence to steer us in that direction—but such a proposition seems farfetched, to say the least. I prefer to deal in the probable, Horace, not the possible."

While Royster had been offering his homily on probability, Sally had entered the room and slung herself on a hassock. "I just came to say hello," she said.

"Hello," said Royster. "Homework done?"

"It will be. I'm taking a break."

Royster turned to Edgecomb. "Incorrigible," he said, but with clear pleasure.

"Now where were we?" Sally's father asked. "Oh, yes, I was about to thank you for your efforts, Horace, and wish you a good night." He rose from his chair and glanced at his pocket watch. "I do not wish to be rude, you understand, but there is much work to be done. Herb Levi tells me he can finish the testing in two weeks—and our press operation has to be up to the task by then."

Edgecomb wasn't prepared to be dismissed so suddenly, especially as he had concerns of his own to discuss.

"Do you need any help?" he asked.

"No, Horace, but thank you for offering. You've done your part."

Royster was in the process of pouring himself a nightcap—"for the long road to the bedroom"—when Edgecomb found the courage to speak.

"What are your plans for the Board of Education meeting next week?" he asked.

Sally's father looked up, one fist wrapped around the brandy bottle. "My plan is not to have a plan. I probably won't even go."

"I don't understand. What about the referendum? The signatures?"

Royster shook his head. "The curriculum in your pitiable little school is small potatoes now. Don't you understand what that cloak means, Horace? We're going to be able to rewrite history across the nation."

That was not the response Edgecomb had expected. And without Royster—both to retract his accusations and defend him against others—Edgecomb sensed that his job was lost. "Please come. I need your help."

"How's that?" asked Royster.

"You wrote a letter about me to the principal. So did another woman—an angry parent. I was hoping, since I'm obviously not forcing the traditional history of the Civil War down students' throats anymore, you might come to my defense. You're the only chance I have of keeping my job."

Royster stepped forward and patted Edgecomb on the shoulder. "I didn't realize my opinion had such an impact," he said. "I feel for you, Horace. Genuinely, I do. But I have only two weeks to prepare for the news of the century. What's one person's job when the history of a nation is at stake?" Sally's father ambled toward the door, snifter in hand. "No one man is more important than truth. You, of all people, as a history teacher, should understand that."

Such was the wisdom of a man who planned to display a marble bust of himself alongside those of Martin Luther and Mahatma Gandhi.

Sally launched herself from the hassock and wrapped her arms around Royster's knees. "Please, Papa," she asked. "Can't you help him? He's my favorite teacher *ever* and I'll be miserable if he gets fired."

Her emotion surprised Edgecomb. For a moment, he thought she was being facetious, or exaggerating for effect—but she appeared genuinely distraught at the notion of him losing his post. What a difference a few months made!

Royster looked down at his daughter and then gently patted her head. "As our guest is so fond of saying, 'I'll take that under advisement.' Now go do your homework, young lady, before you fail out of school and it doesn't matter who does the teaching."

"Yes, Papa," said Sally, standing and straightening her skirt.

She darted from the room before Edgecomb had an opportunity to thank her.

"Looks like you have a fan club," said Royster. And then Sally's father strode from the room too, leaving Edgecomb alone with the bear carcass, and the mounted elk, and the strong sense that Royster viewed him, like these trophy animals, as belonging to a distinct and decidedly inferior species.

~

He telephoned Vicky the moment he returned home, armed with his knowledge of Royster's agenda and hoping for a late-night tryst at the Seashore Preserve. "I can meet you in half an hour," he offered.

"I wish I could," replied Vicky, "but I'm not available tonight. How would Sunday afternoon work for you? Let's say two o'clock. Why don't we meet at the international terminal at Newark Airport?"

"I guess," said Edgecomb.

"Good. See you then."

And the receiver clicked, solidifying their appointment.

That gave Edgecomb three days to anticipate their rendezvous and also to reflect upon how he appeared to have dropped several rungs on Vicky's priority list. Most of that time, when he wasn't teaching, he spent brooding inside the apartment. He was at home when his mother called on Friday evening to warn him not to be so judgmental regarding Jillian's adoption plans, and again on Saturday morning when a female process server knocked on the front door and slapped an injunction against Borrelli's chest.

The process server was an attractive blonde in her twenties, which had caught Sebastian off guard; during the brief interaction with his flatmate, Edgecomb noticed that her opposite hand was prosthetic. "Sorry. It's nothing personal," she said. "And here's a dollar."

She slid a crisp one dollar bill into Sebastian's palm.

"What's this for?"

"So you remember."

"But I don't want your dollar," objected Borrelli.

He tried to force the bill back into her grasp, but it fell to the doormat.

"Relax, chief," she said. "It's the way we do things."

She nudged the offending currency into the apartment with her toe and then departed from the corridor through the fire door and down the emergency stairs.

"That's not how *I* do things!" Borrelli called after her.

He retrieved the one dollar bill from the floor. "This is bullshit, dude," he said, browsing the injunction. "United States District Court for the Central District of California...Cease and desist at once...All books, leaflets, posters, games, toys, and similar items depicting the Prophet Mohammed and other figures from the Islamic Quran and suitable for coloring..." Borrelli kicked the side of the sofa. "They're going to fine me $1,000 a day, starting Monday morning."

"Do you need a lawyer?" suggested Edgecomb.

If anybody could rescue Borrelli's enterprise, Nalaskowski was the man.

"I need a Valium," replied Sebastian.

Edgecomb had taken the remark as sarcasm until his housemate removed a medication bottle from his jacket pocket and spread an assortment of colorful pills on his open palm. He carefully selected a baby blue tablet. "You want anything, Teach? Something to take the edge off?"

"Thanks, but no thanks."

Sebastian slumped onto the couch and lit a joint. "Don't get on my case, okay," he said, preemptively warding off Edgecomb's objection. "I got enough problems right now without having to worry about where I toke."

"Maybe this is a blessing in disguise," offered Edgecomb.

"How do you figure?"

"The way I see it, it's an easy out. Your comrade in Texas can't blame you for following a federal court order."

"Like hell, he can't," said Sebastian. "I still owe him twenty thousand units. This is a man who quit the NRA because it's too liberal and boasts owing the second largest weapons collection west of the Appalachians after the federal arsenal at Rock Island." Borelli rested his eye sockets on the balls of his thumbs. "First Sevastopol and now this! And things were just starting to go so well..."

The past week had indeed witnessed a series of triumphs for Sebastian's venture. First, the United States military had banned the coloring books by name from care packages being sent to troops overseas. Then a prominent liberal congresswoman had waved a copy on the floor of the House of Representatives as a symbol of "everything wrong with America's culture of scapegoating." And finally, a terrorist cell in North Africa had called upon its followers to rise up against the "idolaters of New Jersey" who stood behind the blasphemous product. These condemnations led to an exponential surge in sales. Borrelli's new warehouse, located on the site of a former lawn chair distributorship in Newark, had more floor space that the city's central library. For Edgecomb, that meant their apartment had been liberated from Borrelli's inventory.

Yet the injunction was the second setback of the weekend for Color the Prophet Industries. Earlier that morning, Sevastopol had phoned to announce that he was, in fact, applying to law schools—and wanted no more part of the business. Borrelli's designer feared any association with the coloring books might prevent him from passing the "character and fitness" portion of the state bar application.

"Any brilliant ideas?" asked Borrelli.

"I don't know. Are you selling more than $1,000 worth of books a day?"

Sebastian choked on his joint. "What are you saying, dude? That I should just ignore this and pay the fines?"

"Isn't that what other businesses do?"

Borrelli cupped his fist with his palm. "Works for me, dude. We'll write it off as the cost of doing business." He picked stray grounds of weed from his tie-dyed T-shirt and returned it to his pouch. "Screw the lawyers," he added. "Now I finally understand why people vote for Republicans."

~

Vicky kept him waiting for nearly an hour. She hadn't instructed him where in the crowded international terminal to wait for her, so he bought a cup of coffee and hunkered down on a bench opposite the TSA checkpoint. His hope was to catch her either arriving through customs or entering the airport from the street: in other words, to determine whether she'd chosen their meeting place because she was actually flying that day, or merely for effect. His eyes darted back and forth between the stream of inbound travelers emerging from the screening bay and the concourse of automatic doors that welcomed outbound passengers to the airport. But he wavered for an instant—long enough for his gaze to trail a stunning, almond-eyed flight attendant into a variety shop—and then he glanced up and Vicky Vann was standing in front of him. Her auburn hair had the fresh bounce of a model in a conditioner commercial. She carried no luggage. But whether she'd been deposited curbside by a taxi, or emerged from the VIP lounge, or jetted in on a redeye from Istanbul, he had no sure way of discerning.

"Let's walk," she said.

He did as instructed. She led him from the building and up an escalator into the parking garage. The cars thinned as they distanced themselves from the terminal; when they reached the far end of the structure, where a low wall yielded a third-story view of several traffic islands and a distant runway, she stopped. The nearest vehicle, a Transportation Department cruiser, stood nearly fifty yards distant. A plane roared past overhead and Edgecomb ducked.

"Is this really necessary?" he asked.

He could see the vapor of his breath in the chill.

"Is *what* really necessary?"

"You know what. All of this lurking and evasion and trekking to the corners of the earth. Is there anything you can say over here that you couldn't tell me back inside?"

Vicky shrugged. "I like the fresh air."

Of course she did. Had he really expected a more forthright answer? A deep revelation of HDC strategy? Deep down, he understood that Vicky Vann—like Roland Royster—would reveal precisely what she wanted him to know about herself, and never one iota more. But he couldn't resist one last try.

"How was your flight?" he asked.

"What makes you think I was flying?"

"You asked me to meet you at the airport. I put two and two together."

Vicky laughed. With him? *At* him? It was hard to say. "That's enough mathematics for one day," she said. "The one good thing about graduating from Rolleston is never having to think about math again." Her remark instantly sent Edgecomb's memory back to their year of calculus together, to the hours he spent unsnapping her brassiere in his fantasies while Dr. Wilturp droned on about Euler's Law and differential equations.

"Do you remember Dr. Wilturp?" he asked. "How he used to phone in sick for weeks on end? Someone told me he was picked up on a child porn charge."

"Long time ago," said Vicky without interest. "Now what's your exciting news?"

In his mental blueprint for their meeting, Edgecomb had intended to hold back the details of Royster's plan until he won a concession from his crush. What exactly that concession might be—a hint at the reasons for the government's interest in Surrender Appomattox, or even just clarification toward his own role in their efforts—he couldn't say, but he yearned for some quid pro quo, no matter how tiny. Yet once he was in Vicky's presence, he revealed everything he'd learned about Royster's group in a matter of minutes. "The company really is called Levi's Genes," he added. "It actually exists. I looked it up on the Internet."

Vicky laughed again. "You are too much. Trust me: everything you see on the Internet doesn't actually exist."

Something about her tone—her carefree amusement at his expense—rubbed Edgecomb the wrong way. It didn't help that she removed her phone from her purse and started texting during the middle of their conversation. While he hadn't expected his juice on Royster to leave her swooning, he had hoped to impress her.

"How about the Civil War?" he asked.

She looked up. "What's that?"

"Should I believe what I read on the Internet about the Civil War?"

Vicky's expression turned sober. "Do I detect a hint of animosity?"

"Not animosity. Just healthy skepticism. Here we are working to protect our version of history from the Roland Roysters of the world, and I'm just wondering how you can be so confident that we're right and he's wrong?"

Her indifference suddenly melted. "Do you really need me to answer that?"

"You don't *need* to do anything," said Edgecomb. "I'm just wondering. Because there's this one version of history that the vast majority of people seem to believe—the one that I've believed my entire life. But there's another version—Roland Royster's version—and it's no less internally consistent than our own. You say Abraham Lincoln was shot at Ford's Theatre on April 14, 1865. Royster says he was an actor hired by the Rockefeller family in the 1880s to appear in posed photographs. How is a mere peon like me supposed to decide which version is right?"

The words had rolled off his tongue before he could filter them. But they'd hit home: for the first time in his memory, he sensed that he'd pierced through Vicky Vann's outer armor, that she was genuinely unsettled by his rambling inquiry. But even as he enjoyed this flicker of vulnerability, additional defenses rose to protect her.

"Are you joking?" she asked. "Or should I be worried?"

That was enough to jolt him back to his senses. He'd never win Vicky's heart if she doubted his loyalty—and, in spite of everything, he still wanted her.

"I'm joking," he replied. "But you should still be worried."

His crush clicked her tongue against the roof of her mouth as though expressing displeasure with a wayward child. "I suppose there's always a kernel of truth in every joke, Horace, so I'm going to give you a piece of advice. It's yours to do with as you please, but I'm telling you for your own good." Vicky's voice had regained its confidence. "The world is full of ideas. Plausible ideas. Implausible ideas. Lots of ideas that rest somewhere in between. There's nothing wrong with recognizing, on a theoretical level, that if you start with different premises, you can arrive at different conclusions. Am I making sense so far?"

"More or less."

"But at the end of the day, Horace, no matter how many vantage points have some degree of plausibility, you have to accept some and discard others. Do you hear what I'm saying? You have to believe in something."

Edgecomb couldn't resist a jab. "So you're saying you believe the Civil War happened because it's easier than believing the opposite?"

"Not easier. More functional," objected Vicky. "Let me put it another way, a way you might understand better. Someday, I imagine you're going to get married. And you're going to love your wife very much. At the same time, you'll be able to conceive of countless other women you might have fallen in love with and married under different, hypothetical circumstances—but that won't make you love your actual wife any less."

All of Edgecomb's being yearned to ask: can you be that woman? But he lacked the courage to dare. And, deep down, he already knew the answer, as much as he clung to the thread of possibility that he was mistaken.

"Isn't it possible to love more than one person?" he asked.

Vicky groaned. "Do you know what your problem is, Horace Edgecomb? You're too open-minded for your own good."

"I'll take that as a compliment."

What Edgecomb actually found himself thinking was: why were attractive women always telling him was his problem was?

"And since you asked about my flight," added Vicky, "I'll tell you why I asked you to meet me at the airport. There's nothing I enjoy more in life that visiting the airport when I don't actually have to fly—when I don't have to worry about taking off my shoes, or fitting my belongings into 2700 cubic inches, or how to use my seat cushion as a floatation device when the hydraulic system fails."

"At last," cried Edgecomb. "And honest answer."

"My sister always says: 'I'm not afraid of flying; I'm afraid of crashing,'" observed Vicky. "But these days, the flying itself isn't much better."

She engaged Edgecomb in similar small talk on the stroll back to the terminal. But now he knew in his gut she was lying, that she'd arrived by plane from somewhere, although he also sensed that he'd never learn where, and even if he did, knowing more about Vicky Vann would only make his life more complicated, not more meaningful.

~

In anticipation of an unprecedented turnout, November's Board of Education meeting had been relocated to the high school gymnasium. Two hundred white wooden folding chairs ran in parallel lines from half court to the opposing team's basket—a sight that reminded Edgecomb of the wooden crosses at Ypres and Pas-de-Calais. Additional seating was available in the bleachers, beneath the pennants commemorating Laurendale's occasional victories at various state athletic tournaments dating back to 1906. Under the home team's backboard stood the three rectangular tables and the elevated seats of Archibald Steinhoff's micro-legislature.

Edgecomb arrived an hour early, while the custodial staff was still setting up the final rows of chairs, and volunteers from the PTA were filling the officials' water pitchers. He chose a seat on the aisle in the second row, close to the side exit, in case an escape route proved necessary.

Borrelli and Esperanza, his moral support, filed into the row alongside him. Phoebe Woodsmith had run a front-page story in the *Clarion* about the effort to fire him—as well as an editorial in his defense—so he anticipated his enemies would show up in full force. He stood to be the first teacher terminated for cause mid-year, the *Clarion* reported, since five suspected Communists had been sent packing during the height of the Red Scare in 1949.

"You point out your boss, dude," said Sebastian. "Even the slightest exaggeration and Esperanza will nail her to the wall."

"And what good is that going to do?" asked Edgecomb.

"We'll expose her. The whole world will know she's a liar."

Edgecomb wished he could be more appreciative of his friend's efforts, but he understood that Borrelli's strategy wouldn't pan out. He scanned the influx of concerned citizens for Roland Royster and Saul Nalaskowski. "Everybody already knows she's a liar," said Edgecomb. "But nobody cares. And besides, normative prosopography can't actually *prove* anything. Even lie detectors aren't admissible in court. Do you really expect the School Board to take Esperanza's word over Sandra Foxwell's?"

"We've got to try," insisted Sebastian. "Come on, dude. Have some faith."

But whatever faith Edgecomb still possessed was vested in the silver tongue of Roland Royster—and the patriarch of deniers remained conspicuously absent. Sally did arrive, just at the board members were filtering to their seats, but she'd entered through the main door and found a seat near the three-point line. She waved to Edgecomb, smiling, then flashed him a thumbs-up. Did that mean her father was on his way? Or only that he had the girl's unconditional backing? In either case, Sally's was one of the few friendly faces in the audience. Many in the crowd appeared to be politically vested in Edgecomb's departure: a dozen men in identical Islamic garb, including *ghutras* and *igals*; an elderly gentleman sporting a fez; an entire American Legion post outfitted in full regalia, replete with a Korean War-era color guard; and an obese couple decked out in replica Confederate military uniforms. One man held a sign that read: "Color the False Prophet with Blood." Not exactly the home field advantage that one might desire.

Edgecomb had hoped for a showing of support from his colleagues, although he knew this to be wishful thinking, yet he found himself disappointed none-the-less that Mickey Bickerstaff and Elgin Rothmeyer and so many of his one-time friends had stayed away. To his surprise—and delight—he observed Calliope Chaselle several rows behind Sally. Closer by, Ida Buxner and the Sly Sandy Fox sat front and center, conferring in whispers. "This is sort of like being on *This is Your Life*," Edgecomb muttered to Sebastian. "The suicide-inducing version."

"It'll work out," Borrelli insisted. "Trust me. Esperanza will come through."

Edgecomb felt himself disassociating, looking down upon the scene from above. How ridiculous it all suddenly seemed: why had he jeopardized a job he loved for a woman who treated him like a serf? And, beyond that, why did it matter which version of the Civil War was taught in the public schools? If thousands had died at Gettysburg and Antietam, they were already dead. There was no bringing them back. And if they hadn't, their concocted legacy proved a unifying force for the nation. Was that such a horrible offense? Edgecomb doubted, given a replay of the preceding months, that he would make the same choices again. Unfortunately, life didn't afford do-overs, and the Laurendale Board of Education wasn't likely to offer him one either.

Archie Steinhoff called the meeting to order—cutting short Edgecomb's ruminations. "Let me begin with a word of welcome," he declared. "As a public official, I must tell you that it's comforting for me to see so many of my friends and neighbors, my fellow citizens, actively participating in the civic process—especially when our agenda contains several items of a rather sobering nature. Before we get to the business that has likely drawn you to this evening's meeting, let us proceed with the approval of the minutes."

The committee reports followed. Then the moon-faced woman who'd proposed a moment of silence for the war dead of Laurendale announced the results of her research: precisely one soldier from the community, Lance Corporal Julien K. Deal, had perished in combat during the War in Afghanistan. Whether a single fatality merited a moment of silence in his own right, or whether the moment of tribute should also commemorate the seven alumni who had lost their lives in World War I and another three who'd died during World War II consumed twenty minutes of intense debate—until Steinhoff silenced the controversy by announcing that, at future meetings, they would have a moment of silence for "Lance Corporal Julien K. Deal *and* his fellow servicemen who sacrificed all during the Two World Wars." The chairman flashed a look of satisfaction—he clearly relished playing Solomon—and rapped his gavel twice.

Sebastian asked Esperanza in a whisper loud enough to crack asphalt, "I wonder if that includes guys who fought for the other side? There used to be lots of Nazis in this part of Central Jersey."

Steinhoff pounded his gavel more aggressively. "We now turn to a personnel matter. Usually, these are handled behind closed doors. However, in the opinion of the Board, the charged and highly-publicized nature of this particular case justifies a hearing in public view. I'd like to turn the floor over to our esteemed high school principal, Dr. Sandra Foxwell, who will lay out the district's concerns. I do wish to remind you that the chair will not tolerate any interruptions from the gallery."

Sandra Foxwell rose to the freestanding microphone. The Sly Sandy Fox was decked out in a colorful batik robe and matching headscarf, probably a souvenir of her sojourn in Namibia, which recalled the wives of Cold War-era African dictators. She read her complaint from prepared notes—first outlining Royster's charges, then relating how he'd allegedly told Ida Buxner's "innocent" daughter that African-American chattel slavery was "a useful fiction." To the uninitiated, Foxwell likely sounded genuinely distraught at Edgecomb's conduct. "A year ago, this young girl loved the study of history," declaimed Foxwell. "Today, she can hardly stand to open a history textbook without feeling traumatized. *Violated.* Whatever Horace Edgecomb's intentions—and I do not presume to explore his motives—the outcome has proven tragic."

When Foxwell finished her oration, the crowd cheered. The row of men wearing traditional Islamic attire stomped their feet in a show of enthusiasm.

"Do you have anything on her?" Sebastian asked Esperanza. "It sounded to me like the dame was lying through her teeth."

"I can't tell," she answered. "She's had too much plastic surgery. None of the muscles in her face are in the right place anymore…"

Archie Steinhoff made no effort to silence the jeers of Edgecomb's detractors. He waited for their zeal to dissipate on its own, then tapped his gavel into the silence. "Mr. Edgecomb," he said. "You've heard the district's concerns. Is there anything you'd like to say in your own defense?"

All eyes now focused on Edgecomb. If the apocalypse were going to occur in his lifetime, he found himself thinking, now would be an ideal moment. Phoebe Woodsmith waited patiently for him to speak, her notebook at the ready.

"Mr. Edgecomb?" pressed Steinhoff. "Do you wish to defend yourself?"

"I don't know," Edgecomb stammered. "Do I?"

And then a commotion erupted at the far end of the gymnasium. "No," cried a stentorian voice that echoed through the rafters. "You don't." Through the damask curtain, from which the home team emerged at varsity basketball games, appeared Saul Nalaskowski, pushing a cart stacked high with manila folders. This moment of drama had clearly been planned in advance. "My client," the attorney declared, "does not wish to say anything. But I will say a few words on his behalf."

"And who are you?" demanded Steinhoff.

"Saul Nalaskowski of the New Jersey State Bar. And I have with me here injunctions from both the Amberly County Superior Court and the District Court of New Jersey prohibiting you from taking up the matter of my client's employment at the present time. You'll find all the paperwork in order." He rolled the cart to the front of the gymnasium and set several folders before Steinhoff on the paper tablecloth. "My client has filed freedom of expression claims under the state constitution with both courts and hereby asks that no further actions be taken until these matters can be litigated fully."

An angry murmur sauntered through the audience. Royster's lawyer wore an expression as placid as the ocean. Never before had Edgecomb wanted to hug another human being so much. He surveyed the onlookers: Sally's broad grin and the amused Calliope Chaselle's lips stood out among the wall of hostile expression. One of the Confederate soldiers was making a show of loading her musket.

Archie Steinhoff opened the top folder and perused its contents. He scribbled a sentence on a yellow legal pad and passed it to his bald colleague, who nodded and whispered something into the chairman's ear.

"I'm afraid to say, Mr. Nalaskowski, that we have no way of verifying whether these documents are genuine. You're certainly welcome to appeal our decision, but it is the Board's intention to continue with our hearing, as planned."

"In that case, I demand a stay until we can clarify the authenticity of these documents," cried the lawyer. "These are court orders. You cannot just ignore them."

Steinhoff remained unmoved. "I have no way of knowing whether these are court orders or not. Under ordinary circumstances, I would afford you the benefit of the doubt. However, your client has a track record of deceiving this panel..."

"I object," cried Nalaskowski.

"This is not a courtroom," said Steinhoff. "We make our own procedure, which does not happen to have a provision for objections." He raised his voice, clearly shifting his focus from the attorney to the broader audience. "Twelve weeks ago, Mr. Edgecomb raised a point of order regarding the petitions introduced by Mr. Roland G. Royster, one of the same individuals who subsequently filed a complaint against him. At the heart of his objection was a bylaw requiring that all signatures on initiative petitions be vetted against the voting rolls. Naturally, trusting a member of our own teaching faculty, we conducted such a review... And it is with great regret that I report that the majority of the signatures submitted—ninety one percent, to be precise—were unverifiable."

In September, that verdict would have thrilled Edgecomb. Now, it left him reeling—although, in hindsight, it did not surprise him. He could easily imagine Royster justifying the fraudulent signatures in the name of greater truth.

"What is even more unfortunate," added Steinhoff, "is that the by-law in question never actually existed."

A cry of "For shame!" rose from the back of the gym; the cocoa-skinned gentleman sporting the fez had raised his fist in anger. Steinhoff tapped his gavel gently, but with none of the vigor of the previous meeting.

"Our unsurpassed *Clarion* reporter, Phoebe Woodsmith, has kept careful records of every Board of Education meeting for the past nineteen years. And her mother, Lillian Woodsmith, maintained records for the twenty-six years prior to that. We had the lovely Ms. Woodsmith review those records carefully prior to this meeting. So I am confident in reporting to you that, before this autumn, no large scale signature fraud was perpetrated against this Board as far back as at least 1969." Steinhoff leaned forward toward his microphone, his eyes drilling into Edgecomb. "Since Mr. Edgecomb has already deceived this Board—and this entire community—in one large-stakes matter, we have no way of knowing whether he is doing so again."

Nalaskowski slapped another page down before the chairman. "I'm going to take the liberty of reminding you of state rule of procedure 14B Subsection 11, relating to doubts about the authenticity of court injunctions—"

"That won't be necessary," said Steinhoff. "As I said, sir, you are welcome to appeal our decision. Now please take your seat."

Nalaskowski twice more attempted to object—and, each time, Steinhoff silenced him. On his third attempt, the chairman threatened to file a formal complaint against Royster's attorney with the state bar. A flummoxed Nalaskowski retreated, cart in tow, flashing Edgecomb a look of apology.

Once again, Steinhoff asked Edgecomb if he wished to speak on his own behalf.

He nudged Sebastian. "Do you have a piece of paper? Anything to write on?"

His housemate scrounged in his pocket and handed Edgecomb a flyer for wall-size "Color the Prophet" posters, guaranteed to "liven up any child's birthday party." On the back, Edgecomb wrote:

I am in possession of photographs of you and Sandra Foxwell.

He folded the page in half, then in half again. And then, taking a deep breath, he walked straight up to Archibald Steinhoff and handed him the folded flyer.

"What is this?" grumbled the chairman.

Steinhoff unfolded the page—all eyes upon him—and read the words to himself. His lips moved as he read. To Edgecomb's relief, all of the color drained from the legislator's face, and he knew that he'd guessed correctly. Meanwhile, Steinhoff stared at the accusation. Then slowly, almost methodically, he refolded the page and passed it back to Edgecomb.

"No greater threat exists to the integrity of democratic government than extortion," the chairman declared. "When a member of the public, and especially a public servant, attempts to blackmail or otherwise influence an elected official...."

Steinhoff paused for breath. He reached for his glass of water and sipped.

"...attempts to blackmail or otherwise influence an elected official...."

The chairman reached for his collar, fumbling with his necktie.

"Excuse me," he said. "I don't feel well."

And then he stopped breathing and slumped backwards in his seat.

CHAPTER NINE

Edgecomb still had a job the following Thursday—the Board of Education had postponed all non-emergent business in the wake of Archie Steinhoff's death—when Brittany Marcus handed in her midterm examination. Edgecomb had designed the exam so that students wouldn't have to advance one version of history over another, lobbing them open-ended questions like: "Choose an important primary text we have discussed in class this year and discuss its significance." He'd even made the exam "open book:" what was the point, after all, of memorizing facts that might not be true? Overwhelmingly, the students chose to write about the Gilded Age or the Populist Era, avoiding the Civil War like a toxic stew. Except Brittany. Edgecomb had been curious how much, if anything, the banking heiress had absorbed from his lectures, so once the last students had turned in their exam booklets, he sorted through the pile for hers.

Brittany had written the entire exam in pink, her letters as full and sharply curved as her torso. "*Uncle Tom's Cabin*," she wrote, "was a book published in the 1880s by a secret committee of wealthy men who wanted future generations to believe that slavery had not died out of natural causes..." The rather striking manifesto that followed relied heavily on the account of Abolitionism available on Surrender Appomattox's website. To her credit, Brittany cited the organization's propaganda directly nearly thirty times. In contrast, she did not reference Mrs. Stowe's novel even once. The essay concluded with the statement: "Personally, I'm very glad that our ancestors freed the slaves on their own. It would be so so so depressing to think it would take a war to get people to do the right thing." Indeed, thought Edgecomb. Wouldn't it? He printed a larger red "A+" at the bottom on the final page.

While he was packing up his attaché case, Sally knocked on the open door and swanned into the classroom, her cinnamon ringlets curling from her headband. Her new hairstyle made her appear older, more professional. Something else looked different about the girl too.

"You're wearing makeup!" observed Edgecomb.

Sally shook her head, beaming. "Contacts," she said. "I *always* wear makeup. But thanks for noticing."

"I knew you looked different."

"Just different? Not gorgeous? Not stunning?"

Edgecomb glanced at the door. Archie Steinhoff's untimely death had earned him a reprieve and he was determined not to blow it. "*Different*," he said. The notion crossed his mind to apologize for his earlier transgressions, but far wiser, he decided to say as little as possible on the subject.

Sally flashed him a look of disappointment, folding her arms across her chest; for an instant, he feared she might pout. "You sure know how to flatter a girl."

"Not a girl. A *student*," said Edgecomb. "I'm working on boundaries. I may be your friend, but I'm also your teacher."

That brought a smile back to the girl's face. "That's a relief. I thought you were angry at me."

"Just trying to behave appropriately."

She rolled her eyes. "Can a girl get a ride home from her *teacher*?"

Edgecomb knew the correct answer: No. At the same time, he didn't want to come across as a jerk. "I suppose so. I've been meaning to check in with your father anyway," he said. "But just a ride. I'm not staying for dinner."

"Don't count your dinner invitations before they hatch."

They strolled out to the parking lot. Christmas season was in full swing and the window panes of the ground floor classrooms were stippled with construction paper evergreens. A crisp hint of snow hung in the air. On the playing fields, red flags hung from the posts, and a sign warned: *Area Closed.* Edgecomb noticed a Mercedes with a Yale bumper sticker in the parking space reserved for Sandra Foxwell—a space that had stood conspicuously vacant for years, a visible trapping of her power, ever since her epilepsy diagnosis; yet she'd only been on personal leave for ten days, and already the acting principal, Elgin Rothmeyer, had commandeered this spot two car-lengths closer to the entrance than his own. Such was the relentless pecking order of high school administration. *The king is dead*, reflected Edgecomb. *Long live the king!*

"It's strange to be standing here and not have to worry about running into Dr. Foxwell," said Edgecomb as he unlocked the Honda.

"Is it true that she had a breakdown?"

"You know I'm not going to answer that," said Edgecomb. "The mental health of the high school principal is *not* a subject teachers and students discuss."

"Whatever," said Sally. "I can't wait until this phase of yours passes."

"It's not a phase," insisted Edgecomb.

The truth was that nobody knew for certain what had become of the Sly Sandy Fox. She'd climbed into the ambulance behind Archie Steinhoff, her Namibian robe trailing after her, and that was the last she'd been seen. The following afternoon, an email message from the superintendent's office announced that she'd gone on indefinite leave and that Edgecomb's department chair, Elgin Rothmeyer, would be assuming her responsibilities in his absence.

"Papa told me she went berserk in the emergency room," said Sally. "That they had to send her to a psychiatric ward."

"Not exactly," replied Edgecomb, unable to contain himself. "They actually transferred her to a veterinary hospital."

"Did they?" asked Sally, eyebrows raised.

"Indeed, they did. Things were looking up for the old mare at first—nothing a good horse tranquilizer and a few trots around the track couldn't fix—but now it's looking like she's headed to the glue factory."

Sally kicked off her shoes and rested her feet on the glove box. Each of her toenails was painted a different shade of pink. "And *this* is an appropriate conversation for a teacher and a student?"

"You were right," he conceded. "It was a phase."

He eased the car onto Blenheim Boulevard and drove toward Laurendale Ridge, past the turn-of-the-century Victorians that had once been "the place to live" in Amberly County but now displayed various stages of neglect. In the rearview mirror, he noticed a late model Cadillac trailing at a distance. How typical, he thought, of the HDC to spy on its own spies. He wondered if Vicky had another agent trailing the Cadillac as well. Maybe the Treasury Department employed a titanic loop of spies following each other in an endless Mobius strip of espionage. It wouldn't have surprised him. So much for his taxpayer dollars at work.

Edgecomb made no effort to shake his tail. What would be the point? Instinctively, he slowed as they approached the clapboard police headquarters; even though his passenger was eighteen, and their relationship platonic, he did not relish the prospect of seeing their interrogation under Phoebe Woodsmith's byline in the crime blotter. The light turned red just as they reached Rolleston Pike, forcing Edgecomb to slam the brakes.

"Turn left here," said Sally. "I want to show you something."

He threw the girl a curious look, but she merely repeated her command, so when the light shifted, he inched into the left-hand lane and headed toward the shore.

"Can I ask where we're going?" he asked.

"You can *ask*."

Sally instructed him to pull off the main road as they approached the Rolleston Middle School, whose gym doubled in the winter as a skating rink. At first, the idea crossed his mind that she might want to go ice skating. But they passed the school and continued toward the water. When they finally crossed under the coastal highway, navigating a bazaar of bait shops and seafood wholesalers, Edgecomb realized their destination. And seconds later, as he'd expected, his companion urged him through the colossal granite pillars onto the narrow dirt lane. For the second time in a month, Edgecomb found himself alone with a woman at the Marshfield Seashore Preserve.

"Is this what you wanted to show me?" asked Edgecomb.

He wasn't even sure what he meant by the question; it was just something to say.

Sally took his hand; he let her. "Let's walk down to the water," she said.

Late afternoon shadows had descended over the lifeless meadow; the sun itself flickered behind a stand of barren birches. The scent of salt water, pungent and vast, made Edgecomb shiver with insignificance. Hours earlier, he'd sworn to himself that he intended to start afresh—to conduct himself forevermore as the consummate professional.

Yet here he was.

They passed couples—*other* couples—strolling homeward. Some smiled. Some said hello. More often, the men grasped their girlfriends' hands possessively. When they reached the second scenic overlook, a New Deal-era perch which afforded a panoramic view of the mansions of Hager's Head and the sea beyond, Sally tugged his arm.

"*This* is what I wanted to show you."

He turned toward her—and she kissed him.

She'd clearly been planning the moment and she was determined to take full advantage of it. Her arms locked around the back of his neck. Even on her tiptoes, she had to draw his lips down to hers. He didn't resist. *This is a bad idea*, his mind kept repeating to itself, like a voice recording gone haywire. Yet it was also the only idea inside his head, so he kissed her back. Eventually, she pulled away and rubbed her nose against his. "Like Eskimos," she said. And she added, squinting, "Right now, you have one giant eye, like a Cyclops." Then she released him entirely.

They stood facing each other.

"Hi," she said.

"Hello," he answered.

They began walking and again her fingers locked around his. Overhead, starlings gathered in the bare hickory branches. Bats capered against the emerging starscape. On the bay, a foghorn mourned a sailor's code.

"Happy?" she asked.

He squeezed her hand. She nuzzled his shoulder with her cheek.

"I have something to tell you," she said. "Something you probably don't want to hear."

"Then why tell me?"

She looked up at him—her face a live wire of tenderness and fear. "I lied to you," she said. "I'm only seventeen."

The words carried on the breeze. Slowly, he let go of her hand.

"I should get you home," he said.

"I'm sorry. It's only *one* year."

She sounded as though she might flood the entire meadow with tears. She reached for his hand again, but he stepped away.

"It's not that…"

"Then what is it…?"

It's that you're a child. How had he ever been so blind?

Seventeen. Eighteen. *One* year didn't matter. But the decade between them was an insurmountable gulf—long enough, Edgecomb later reflected with bitterness, to fight two-and-a-half Civil Wars.

~

While he'd been locking lips with Royster's daughter, Jillian had left so many messages on his home phone that Sebastian had shut off the ringer. Later, when the messages continued to pile up silently on the answering machine, he yanked the cord from the jack. "She called on *my* business line too, dude," complained Borrelli. "I'm pulling in twenty orders a day and now those assholes in California are threatening to seize my inventory. I don't have time to babysit your relatives." Edgecomb couldn't exactly blame his housemate: after the first message of the evening, he'd shut off the voicemail on his cell phone.

"What am I supposed to do about it?"

"I don't know. Talk to her?"

"I'll call her in the morning," said Edgecomb. "I've had enough stress for one day."

He considered unburdening himself to Borrelli, sharing his "near miss" with Sally Royster, as he'd started to think of their kiss, but some confessions were best left unvoiced. Instead, he squandered an hour playing checkers with Albion, who'd carved out a makeshift dormitory and game room for himself between the sofa and the television. In the morning, dreading to see Sally, he phoned in sick. Shortly afterwards, his mother called from Tampa.

"You're home?" she asked. "I was planning to leave a message."

"I'm going in late today," he lied.

"You're not ill, are you? Are you having fevers? Is your neck stiff?"

"I'm fine. *Jesus.*"

"I'll have to trust you. What choice do I have? But if you develop a stiff neck and a high fever, you should get to the doctor at once…"

One of the aides at his mother's assisted living facility, it turned out, had a niece who'd died of meningitis. A cheerleader at Orlando State. The tragedy had been "all over the news" in Florida. Edgecomb's mother, a retired voice instructor, had always been easily impressionable in this way: when Edgecomb had been in sixth grade, she'd read a biography of the poet Gerard Manley Hopkins, and for weeks, she was convinced that both he and Jillian suffered from typhoid. In high school, she'd seen a documentary film on prostitution and dragged them both to get tested for congenital syphilis—just in case. No wonder his sister was afraid of catching bacteria from her own shadow.

"Have you spoken to your sister?" asked Edgecomb's mother.

"Not yet."

"Well, you should. She has something to tell you. Big news."

"Can you give me a hint?"

"Call her at home. She's taking the day off."

He thanked her and hung up. Twenty minutes later, he suffered through nearly the same conversation, excepting the meningitis warning, with his aunt. So rather than endure a third phone call with Jillian herself, in which she insisted that they meet in person—as was her wont—he showered and drove out to Gripley Township.

It was approaching ten o'clock. His students would be starting third period, scrambling from classroom to classroom. He pictured Louise Buxner huffing up the stairs of the new foreign language annex under the weight of her knapsack, and Brittany Marcus, eye-catching in her translucent tights, still basking over her "A+"—possibly the only grade above a "C" that she would ever receive at Laurendale. And here he was playing hooky, riding the elevator to Jillian's apartment, both his job and his future still up in the air.

Jillian greeted him at the door, holding a bathrobe at arm's length. "You know, you could call in advance," she said. "What if I had company?"

"Do you have company?"

"That's *so* not the point."

He took hold of the robe. "I know the drill."

Five minutes later, while his clothing was being cleansed of contaminants, he sat opposite his sister at the shell-shaped glass table. He hugged the robe over his bare calves for warmth.

"Would you like a cup of tea?" she asked. "It has added seaweed extract."

"Not when you put it that way."

"Your loss," said Jillian. She cradled her own cup between her palms.

Edgecomb surveyed the room for signs of the "big news;" in his imagination, his sister had discovered a baby in a bassinet, possibly floating down a stream. "Your mother has been making the telephone company rich," he said. "She called at eight o'clock this morning. I got a twenty-minute lecture on brain infections."

"It doesn't cost her anything. She has unlimited minutes."

"I was speaking metaphorically. And it does cost *me* something. My sanity."

Jillian picked a strand of lint off her skirt. "Are you through? Because I'd like to share my good news, but I can wait."

"I'm through."

"Are you sure?"

"Yes, dammit, I'm sure."

His sister set down her teacup. Her entire face glowed with joy—as though she'd been sipping red wine and nibbling ambrosia since daybreak. "Good. Now do you want the good news first?" she asked. "Or the better news?"

"How about the good news. Save the best for last."

Before Jillian answered, a detonation deep in the entrails of the earth shook the plaster; a poster of a Guatemalan toddler in a ten-gallon hat peeled halfway off the wall. Edgecomb dug his nails into the antimacassars, expecting another blast. But the seconds elapsed and all that greeted them was silence.

"Fritz is working a double shift," explained Jillian. "To make up for yesterday."

"Yesterday was a day off?"

"Yesterday was my home visit. Our home visit." Jillian's voice rose at least an octave. "And I passed. I passed! Fritz promised them that we'd never allow you alone with the children unsupervised—and they approved us. For *twins*."

"That's great," said Edgecomb. "How long does my banishment last? Only until they're eighteen? Or forever? And if I mess up and accidentally take one of them to a baseball game or a movie alone, will the adoption agency repossess them?"

Jillian did not appear amused. "Why can't you just be happy for me?"

"I am happy for you. I just didn't realize I'd become the antichrist."

"So we don't know which twins we're getting, or even what country they're coming from—although it's probably either The Congo or Liberia—but the bottom line is that they're ours!"

Never had Edgecomb seen his sister so happy; for a moment, she almost appeared carefree, despite the raw red skin of her hands. "Seriously, I am happy for you. And for Fritz," said Edgecomb. He extended his arms to embrace her. "May I?"

She nodded and they hugged.

"Can I get you something to celebrate?" he asked. "Maybe an alfalfa sprout?"

"Don't you want to hear the big news?"

"I thought that *was* the big news."

Jillian grabbed his hands; she looked as though she might start jumping up and down like a game show contestant. "I'm pregnant."

"With a baby?"

"Yes, with a baby. With *my* baby."

"And that's a good thing?"

His sister let go of his hands; fire rose in her eyes. "What is wrong with you? Why wouldn't that be a good thing?"

"I don't know. Haven't you been lecturing me for years on the benefits of adoption...?"

"Screw you, Horace. Don't be such an ass."

"Sorry." He hadn't intended to offend. "Well, congratulations."

His sister's frustration evaporated instantly, overwhelmed by her enthusiasm.

"I'm going to have *three* children. Three *real* children."

As opposed to three imaginary children, mused Edgecomb. But he held his tongue. He listened as his sister revealed every detail of the home visit to the point where he felt that he'd known the evaluating social worker all of her life—that he might be able to recognize her in a crowded room or even pen the woman's biography. Then Jillian recounted, second by second, the various abdominal and gynecological symptoms that led to her pregnancy test. She'd had to delay the test three days while waiting for a custom-designed chemical-free testing kit to arrive from Demark via FedEx.

"But don't tell anyone yet. Not for another month. I don't want to jinx it," she warned. "So anyway, enough of my babbling. How are *you*?"

"Me?" asked Edgecomb. Indeed, how was he? "Surviving."

"That's all. Not thriving? I heard you had your hearing with the School Board delayed." Jillian sounded genuinely concerned. "You know I would have been there," she added. "But I didn't want the baby exposed to any stress."

"I'm fine. Just girl trouble. I keep getting mixed signals from Vicky…"

Vicky Vann, of course, only accounted for half of his anxiety; the other half arose from Sally, whom he despised himself for hurting.

"She's using you. For Christ's sake, Horace, she's married."

"How do you know?"

"It's all over the Internet. She's married to a guy who used to be a Latin professor at Princeton and now runs some minor division at the Treasury Department. He's deputy assistant undersecretary of something…"

"Vicky is really married?" he echoed.

"Yes, really. *Married.* And I found that out in literally five minutes on the computer. I even printed out her wedding announcement from the *Times* for you." Jillian rummaged through the photographs of orphans for the newspaper clipping. "You could have found this out too, Horace. Easily. But you only see what you want to see."

He stood up. "I should be going," he said. "I need to think."

"Don't think, Horace. Move on."

But all he could focus on, as he mechanically buttoned his damp clothing, was his swelling rage at the woman with whom he'd so recently dreamed of eloping.

~

The earliest that Vicky would agree to meet him was two days later, on Sunday afternoon, but he insisted on choosing the location. He was done lurking about airport lobbies and tourist attractions; if Vicky wanted his information—and he'd lured her in with a false claim of more juice on Royster—she could meet him at a restaurant like any normal human being. He informed her that he'd rendezvous with her at Penelope's, the Greek bistro opposite Mackenzie's Dinette, at precisely two p.m. Despite Jillian's conflict with the owner over private kitchen inspections, the restaurant was usually quiet and welcoming, a perfect locale for a low-key first date or a tiff among spies. True to form, Vicky Vann arrived at two thirty, but offered no apologies. He'd ordered a plate of baba ghanoush with a side of pita bread while he waited.

"You're late," said Edgecomb—glancing pointedly at his watch.

"The important thing is that I'm here. Now what do you have for me?"

Horace handed her a laminated menu. "You should order something. This is a restaurant."

Vicky set the menu aside. "I'm not hungry."

"Too bad. They make a mean spanakopita."

Edgecomb dipped a slice of pita into the eggplant puree and washed it down with a swig of *retsina.* Vicky Vann, he registered, was still not wearing a wedding ring. It was not lost upon him that the last time they'd shared a meal together, at the long defunct Crossroads Diner, was when she'd revealed her relationship with Professor Quaglia. She looked just as ravishing now as she had then: her delicate features still flawless, almost unreal, as though carved by a magical craftsman. "Well?" asked Vicky.

"You're married."

She glanced down at her fingers, as though checking for her own ring. "Yes, I'm married. Is that what you wanted to tell me?"

"You led me to believe otherwise..."

"No, I did not," said Vicky. "As far as I recall, we haven't discussed my married life. And honestly, I'd prefer not to. But if you misinterpreted anything that I've said, I'm sorry for the misunderstanding."

Had he misinterpreted her? Had he been willfully blind? Maybe Jillian was right and he had a psychological flaw that drove him to self-deception. After all, Vicky Vann hadn't said a word about her present romantic life—one way or the other. For all he knew, HDC policy prevented operatives from disclosing personal information, especially when other Treasury Department officials were involved. It hadn't helped, he guessed, that he'd mocked her husband indirectly with his attack on Operation *Damnatio Memoriae*. But the name had been idiotic before and it was idiotic still.

"There *wasn't* any misunderstanding," he said. "You intentionally misled me."

"We'll have to agree to disagree." Vicky appeared bored, irritated. "Is that what you summoned me here for?"

"You lied to me," Edgecomb said again. "I trusted you."

"Fair enough. I apologize," replied Vicky. "The director thought this was a better approach for all concerned."

"You mean your husband."

"My husband happens to be the director, yes."

"And the same man who wants you to lie to me about your marriage also wants me to believe him about the Civil War."

Vicky's expression turned as hard as a plywood board. "Get over it, Horace. We have work to do. Both of us." She surveyed the empty restaurant and then lowered her voice. "I thought you'd called me to talk about Royster's press conference. You know he's having some sort of major media event tomorrow. Every journalist on this side of the Rockies seems to have been invited. So have a number of movers and shakers in comparative genetics. We're guessing he's going to launch another lawsuit to get ahold of Lincoln's cloak—but, needless to say, it would be extraordinarily helpful to have confirmation in advance."

So Vicky didn't know that Royster already possessed the controversial cloak. Extra credit for Cousin Nigel and his ComboBlaster.

"You'll have to check with your sources about that," said Edgecomb. He reached into his pocket and shoved the Treasury Department ID card toward her. "But I'm not one of them any longer. I'm done."

He rose from the booth and slapped two twenty dollar bills onto the tabletop.

"But we need your help, Horace," said Vicky Vann. "We can argue about the personal stuff some other time. Right now, *your country* needs your help."

"The hell it does," retorted Edgecomb.

She followed him out of the restaurant and into the street. Even through the closed windows of the Honda, he could hear her shouting, the words "Civil War" unmistakable as he backed out of the intersection and drove off.

~

Nigel Royster was waiting for him in the living room. Sally's cousin sported his denim jacket and scruffy acid-wash genes; in his lap rested what appeared to be either an oversized hairdryer or a homemade firearm. When Edgecomb entered, he was lecturing Sebastian Borrelli on the need for patent reform legislation. Esperanza Arcaya sat opposite them, flipping through a magazine. Albion dozed, catlike, on a lime-green beanbag in the corner.

"What a surprise," said Edgecomb.

"Your friend is a genius," said Sebastian. "Did you know it's impossible to trademark an offensive product?"

"So I've heard."

"That means those assholes in California don't have a case. What could possibly be more offensive than a Mohammed coloring book?"

Edgecomb hung up his coat in the closet.

"Genius," he agreed. "Unquestionably."

Sebastian took a drag on his joint. "I told your friend if he ever gives up his Civil War nonsense, he's got a job for the asking."

"I'm not his friend," said Nigel.

The lantern-jawed man's tone was acidic.

"Is something wrong?" asked Edgecomb.

"You know very well what's wrong. You're wrong," said Nigel. He rose from the sofa and tossed his makeshift weapon onto the cushions. Then he unbuttoned his denim jacket. "You told me you had no romantic interest in Sally."

Horace inched backwards, circling behind the couch as Nigel advanced.

"I don't. I swear I don't," he insisted.

"Then why were you two kissing on Friday night? Don't lie to me, Horace. I saw you with my own eyes!"

"So you were following me!"

Nigel advanced more aggressively. "Uncle Rollie likes to know what his daughters are up to," he said. "And now, I'm going to beat you to a pulp."

Horace surveyed the room for a place to shield himself, but without the cartons of coloring books, the apartment offered few obstacles.

"Sebastian! Do something. Call 9-1-1."

"I'm keeping out of this," said Borrelli. He leaned back in his chair, hands behind his neck, as though watching a boxing match on television. "You're the one sticking your tongue down his girl's throat…"

In sheer desperation, Edgecomb grabbed the weapon-like device from the sofa. The machine was far heavier than it appeared. He pointed the barrel at Nigel. "One more step," he threatened. "And I swear I'll shoot." Only then did he realize that the device didn't seem to have a trigger.

That stalled Nigel's advance for a moment. "It's not a gun, you idiot. It's the prototype for my ComboBlaster."

"All it shoots are sound waves," interjected Sebastian. "He already gave us a demonstration."

"Bullshit," cried Edgecomb, still searching for a trigger.

"There's no trigger. It's remote controlled," said Nigel. "I brought it along in case I had to threaten anyone to get inside."

Sally's cousin charged toward Edgecomb. He vaulted over the loveseat and Nigel caught hold of his sneaker, which came loose in his hand. In desperation, Edgecomb raised the ComboBlaster over his head, braced to heave the device against the hardwood floor. Every muscle above his waist strained under its weight.

"I swear I'll destroy it," he said between gasps.

They stood at an impasse—Nigel yards away, the sound gun torturing Edgecomb's shoulders.

"Listen to me," said Edgecomb. "I'm not romantically involved with your cousin. I'm not *interested* in being romantically involved with your cousin. It was a mistake, okay? An impulsive mistake…Trust me, Nigel. *I'm on your side.*"

Edgecomb's lungs burned; he feared his neck muscles might snap.

"How stupid do you think I am?" demanded Sally's cousin.

"He's telling the truth," said Esperanza.

The girl's interference surprised Nigel. "How do you know?"

"I can tell from his face. His grimace is all zygomaticus major—not even a trace of zygomaticus minor. You can't fake that."

Now Sebastian stood up and put an arm on Nigel's shoulder. "If she says he's telling the truth, he's telling the truth."

Edgecomb tentatively lowered the trigger-free gun to the floor. Sally's cousin stepped toward him, arm outstretched to shake.

Then Edgecomb felt a sharp blow to his face, and horrific pain, as though someone had tried to feed a candlestick through his eye socket. The bastard had punched him! He fell backwards to the ground, landing hard on his elbow.

"That's in case she's wrong," said Nigel. And he helped him up.

~

When Edgecomb arrived for Royster's press conference the following morning, his left eye wrapped in gauze, a small crowd had already formed around the steps of Laurendale's city hall. Sally's father had wanted him to join the bigwigs on the podium, but he'd begged off, unwilling to jeopardize his job any further. He found a place to stand underneath a massive white oak which dated from pre-Columbian times; a small plaque at the base commemorated the hanging of "the Negro, Cicero, for thievery" on the site in 1755. He recognized many in the audience as the same band of hangers-on that Royster had drummed up for his petition to the School Board in September. Now they sported winter coats and braced against the chill. Sally stood at the far end of the plaza, Nigel's arm around her waist. The girl had survived her heartbreak. When his gaze connected with hers, she looked away.

Roland Royster had certainly called in all his chits. All four major news networks had cameras mounted on the municipal steps; Phoebe Woodsmith, pencil over her ear like a butcher boy, now shared her story with dozens of journalists from as far away as Baltimore and Boston. Sally's father had called the event for eleven o'clock, but he knew how to handle the press: he didn't approach the rostrum until 12:15, by which time the audience had swelled to several thousand. Edgecomb spotted Calliope Chaselle chatting with Lucky Pozner; Benji Kim, his former mentee, maneuvered his wheelchair through the throng with one arm. Vicky Vann was out there too somewhere, he knew, watching, absorbing, but he did not expect to see her. The sad reality was that he'd likely never see Vicky again—a necessary truth, but a painful one. He determined not to think about her. He was moving on.

As Royster introduced his pair of celebrated geneticists, Sebastian Borrelli fisted Edgecomb lightly on the shoulder. "How's your eye feeling?"

"You don't want to know," said Edgecomb. "Where's Esperanza?"

"Not coming. You aren't going to believe this one, dude. Bitch was cheating on me with that face-reading professor of hers."

"You sure?"

"She confessed the whole thing. That's why she wouldn't teach me her technique. She was afraid I might use it on her."

"I'm sorry."

"Yeah, it sucks. Anyway, life goes on. I'm not staying for this historical shit, by the way. I just wanted to check on you. I've got a conference call with Tokyo in an hour. Turns out Color the Prophet is a best-seller in Japan. Only, get this. They think he's a Disney character…" Sebastian slapped Edgecomb's chest. "Got to be going, Teach. Can't keep the foreign markets waiting."

Sebastian peeled away from the crowd. For the first time all morning, Edgecomb devoted his full attention to Roland Royster, who was explaining to the dumbstruck media how he'd stolen the Gettysburg cloak. At great length, and with pause upon dramatic pause, Royster outlined the safeguards that Surrender Appomattox had instituted to prevent tampering with the genetic samples. Then he yielded the stage to "the planet's foremost authority on all things DNA and a damn fine fellow," Dr. Herbert Levi of Levi's Genes.

The geneticist proved Royster's oratory opposite: a diminutive gentleman who spoke with a stutter and periodically wiped his nose on the sleeve of his white lab coat. But the moment itself contained enough drama to support the lackluster speaker. "None of us know whether the two samples will match," explained Levi. "Our work has been conducting independently, in different laboratories, located in different states…"

Royster's geneticist droned on about the mechanics of genetic sampling, about exons and introns and chromosomal non-disjunctions. At various pauses, the spectators applauded tepidly. All anyone wanted to know was the content of the two glassine envelopes, each locked inside its own steel strongbox, which would either confirm Royster's claims or undermine Surrender Appomattox. But Edgecomb had no doubt that Sally's father already had a backup plan: a speech explaining away any unfavorable results as a product of human error or covert government interference or a failure of the chain of custody. That was the genius of men like Roland Royster: if they were right, they were right, but if they were wrong, they were also right. Of course, the same was true of women like Vicky Vann, which left ordinary sops like Horace Edgecomb stuck in between.

He stopped listening to Hebert Levi. Instead, his attention focused on Calliope Chaselle, who was inching her way through the crowd in his direction. He was captivated by her beauty, by her skin as chalk-white as a Grecian mask, by her delicate pink bob of a nose. She wore knit gloves and a man's cashmere coat. Winter sun danced through her hair. And suddenly, she was standing alongside him.

"You must be nervous," she said.

"Not as much as you might imagine."

On the platform, the geneticist pointed a laser beam at a complex diagram.

"I didn't expect to see you here," said Edgecomb.

"Let's just say you've piqued my curiosity in Civil War deniers," she said. "Also, I've been thinking. About Thorn's dental floss…and his underwear."

"That was a stupid thing for me to say," said Edgecomb. "It came out all wrong."

"What I was going to say, before you started to sabotage yourself, was that I think it would be very valuable to have some emotional support while I dispose of his stuff. I was going to ask you if you'd be willing to help?"

Now she had Edgecomb's full attention. "I guess. I mean, yes. Sure. Let's do it right now…"

"Now? But what about your big press conference?"

"It's not *my* anything," he said. "And we can hear the results on the news."

Calliope wrapped her hand around his elbow. "You are one odd duck."

"Is that a yes?"

"Yes, that's a yes."

She led Edgecomb away by the arm. They crossed the tiny park opposite city hall and ambled up the sidewalk. As they turned the corner, no longer in sight of Royster's press conference, they heard a rising clamor from where they'd come, but neither of them turned around. They kept walking, held together by the prospect of what might come, leaving the hazards of history behind them.

C&R PRESS TITLES

NONFICTION

Women in the Literary Landscape by Doris Weatherford, et al
Credo: An Anthology of Manifestos & Sourcebook for Creative Writing by Rita Banerjee and Diana Norma Szokolyai

FICTION

Last Tower to Heaven by Jacob Paul
No Good, Very Bad Asian by Lelund Cheuk
Surrendering Appomattox by Jacob M. Appel
Made by Mary by Laura Catherine Brown
Ivy vs. Dogg by Brian Leung
While You Were Gone by Sybil Baker
Cloud Diary by Steve Mitchell
Spectrum by Martin Ott
That Man in Our Lives by Xu Xi

SHORT FICTION

Notes From the Mother Tongue by An Tran
The Protester Has Been Released by Janet Sarbanes

ESSAY AND CREATIVE NONFICTION

In the Room of Persistent Sorry by Kristina Marie Darling
the Internet is for real by Chris Campanioni
Immigration Essays by Sybil Baker
Je suis l'autre: Essays and Interrogations
by Kristina Marie Darling
Death of Art by Chris Campanioni

POETRY

A Family Is a House by Dustin Pearson
The Miracles by Amy Lemmon
Banjo's Inside Coyote by Kelli Allen
Objects in Motion by Jonathan Katz
My Stunt Double by Travis Denton
Lessons in Camoflauge by Martin Ott
Millennial Roost by Dustin Pearson
Dark Horse by Kristina Marie Darling
All My Heroes are Broke by Ariel Francisco
Holdfast by Christian Anton Gerard
Ex Domestica by E.G. Cunningham
Like Lesser Gods by Bruce McEver
Notes from the Negro Side of the Moon by Earl Braggs
Imagine Not Drowning by Kelli Allen
Notes to the Beloved by Michelle Bitting
Free Boat: Collected Lies and Love Poems by John Reed
Les Fauves by Barbara Crooker
Tall as You are Tall Between Them by Annie Christain

CPSIA information can be obtained
at www.ICGtesting.com
Printed in the USA
FFHW020129040519
52244904-57633FF

9 781936 196876